THE LIMBERLOST REVIEW
A LITERARY JOURNAL OF THE MOUNTAIN WEST

FROM LIMBERLOST PRESS

Always Something
A New Chapbook of Poems by Jim Dodge

Limberlost Press announces publication of a new letterpress-printed, limited edition chapbook of poems by northern California poet, novelist, and pioneer bioregional advocate Jim Dodge. The poems are laced with a good dose of self-deprecating humor, poignant insight into a good long life, and a wry focus on getting older, living off the grid, and knowing one's family, community, and place.

On Destroying My Third Refrigerator in Seven Years by Defrosting It with a Filét Knife
>*True accidents are never senseless.*
>*If nothing else, the slaughter of large appliances discourages cupidity,*
>*And the brain-mushing pamper of convenience is surely deterred.*
>*The gods appreciate a smile when you accept your fate:*
>*Not every blossom becomes a peach;*
>*So few of us reach the pure state of relentless stupidity.*

Jim Dodge is a self-described "Taoist dirt pagan and practicing pantheist who may have been born enlightened but pissed it away through thousands of sweet attachments and too many random acts of sheer folly. Dwindling into decrepitude, he splits his time between an isolated ranch in the coastal wilds of the Gualala watershed and the semi-settled Eureka peninsula." He is also is a Humboldt State University Professor Emeritus and the author of three works of fiction: the hilariously brilliant tale *Fup* (City Miner Books, 1983; Simon & Schuster, 1984), the novels *Not Fade Away* (Atlantic Monthly Press, 1987) and *Stone Junction* (Grove Press, 1998), an earlier collection of poems and prose, *Rain on the River* (Grove/Canongate Books, 2002), and a number of other broadsides, chapbooks, and screeds.

Always Something was letterpress printed by Rick Ardinger in a limited edition of 400 copies in the summer of 2023, each sheet fed into the jaws of a century-old platen press, and then collated, folded, and sewn by hand into beautiful paper covers. $20.00 (Plus $5 postage) Idaho orders please add 6% state sales tax. Purchase this and other books at: www.limberlostpress.com

FROM LIMBERLOST PRESS

Burning Time

A Chapbook of Poems
By Annie Lampman

If, as poet Jerry Martien says, "the poem arises from the ground of its making," then Annie Lampman's poems rise from the intimate touch of a tree's growth rings, the harsh passage through a desert canyon, the uncertain challenges of raising sons, quiet stories of time burning away, the ways we make a living, the ways we make a life.

> Centuries, decades,
> last week. Today.
> Each one burned away—
> these stories we tell, lit and smoking,
> waiting as one after another we all ignite.

—from the title poem

ANNIE LAMPMAN is the author of the novel *Sins of the Bees* (Pegasus/Simon & Schuster, 2020). Born in a 19th century log home without running water in north central Idaho, Lampman later moved with her family to Headquarters, Idaho, a logging company town surrounded by mountains. From a young age she explored the North Fork of the Clearwater River, hiked into high mountain lakes and into Hells Canyon. She earned her MFA in writing at the University of Idaho and now teaches in Washington State University's Honors Creative Writing Program. Recipient of several major awards, her poetry, stories, and essays have appeared or are forthcoming in over 70 literary journals and anthologies. She lives in Moscow, Idaho.

Burning Time **was letterpress printed by Rick Ardinger in a limited edition of 350 copies in the summer of 2021, each sheet fed into the jaws of a century-old platen press and collated, folded, and sewn by hand into hardy paper covers. $20.00 (Plus $5 postage) Idaho orders please add 6% state sales tax.**

Purchase this and other books at: www.limberlostpress.com

LIMBERLOST LETTERPRESS

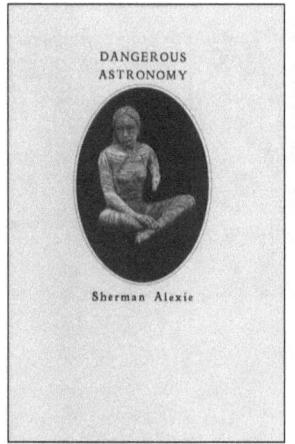

www.limberlostpress.com

THE LIMBERLOST REVIEW

No. 1, 1976

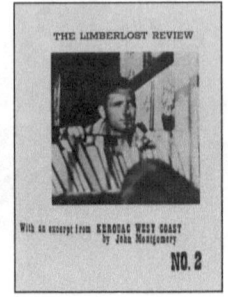
No. 2, 1977

No. 3, 1977

No. 4, 1977

No. 5, 1978

No. 6, 1979

No. 9, 1981

No. 13, 1984

THE LIMBERLOST REVIEW

2019

2020

2021

2022

2024

2025

Order your copies of The Limberlost Review at:
www.limberlostpress.com

Contact us at: editors@limberlostpress.com

The Limberlost Review

A Literary Journal
of the Mountain West

Edited by
Rick & Rosemary Ardinger

A publication of Limberlost Press
Boise, Idaho
2025

THE LIMBERLOST REVIEW
A LITERARY JOURNAL OF THE MOUNTAIN WEST

2025 Edition

Editors
Rick & Rosemary Ardinger

Contributing Editors
Chuck Guilford
Bob Bushnell

Sports and Social Media Editor
Jennifer Holley

Layout and Design
Meggan Laxalt Mackey, Studio M Publications & Design

Website Design
Erin Jensen, Golden Ratio Northwest

Cover Images
Front: "Wheel House," acrylic on board, by Randy Van Dyck

Back: Ephemeral (Owyhee Canyonlands)
Photograph by Katherine Jones

Limberlost Press
Boise, Idaho 83716
www.limberlostpress.com

THE LIMBERLOST REVIEW is published annually by Limberlost Press. This issue Copyright © 2025 by Limberlost Press, with all rights to the individual contributions returned to the authors and artists.

ISBN 979-8-218-65150-3

This journal features some of the best writing from the Mountain West and beyond, including poetry, fiction, memoir, essay, translation, commentary about books we come back to again, interviews, artwork, and more. We welcome the submission of manuscripts, but can not accept responsibility for lost items or electronic correspondence problems. For copies of THE LIMBERLOST REVIEW, please email editors@limberlostpress.com or visit our website: www.limberlostpress.com.
Printed in the United States of America.

LIMBERLOST LETTERPRESS

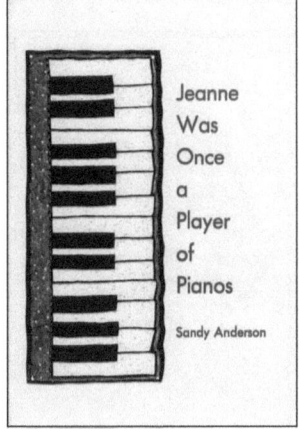

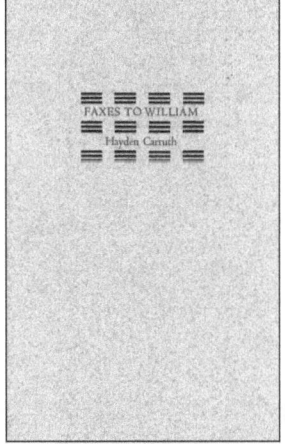

www.limberlostpress.com

LIMBERLOST LETTERPRESS

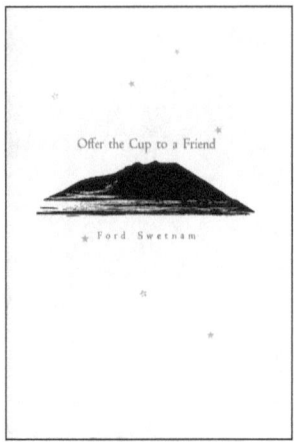

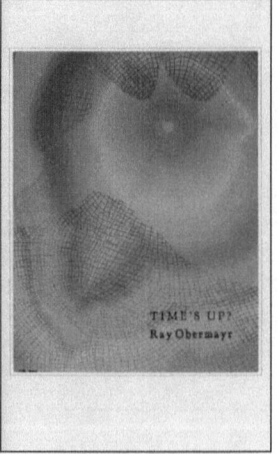

www.limberlostpress.com

TABLE OF CONTENTS

EDITOR'S NOTE
Rick Ardinger 17

POEMS & STORIES
Clifford Burke, *Four Poems* 23
Wendell Berry, *Eight Poems* 27
Bonnie Jo Campbell, *Five Poems* 37
Mitch Wieland, *The Last Days of Ferrell Swan* 43
Robert Wrigley, *Two Poems* 59
Edward Harkness, *Two Poems* 63
Tom Rea, *Hats* 67
Charlotte Mears, *The Day I Fell in Love with Julia Child* 71
Jeff Fereday, *Ruby, June 1908* 73
Howard Levy, *Two Poems* 87
Ken Rodgers, *Elegy* 89
Samuel Green, *Chopping Block* 91
Dan Armstrong, *The Open Secret* 93
Margaret Koger, *Two Poems* 99
Mark Gibbons, *Out in the Garage* 103
Georgia Tiffany, *Two Poems* 105
O. Alan Weltzien, *Through the Darkest Valley* 107
Barbara Olic-Hamilton, *The Uncounted* 111
Greg Keeler, *Five Sonnets* 119
Florence K. Blanchard, *Trip Advisor Visits Atomic City* 123
Bob Bushnell, *Six Poems* 127
Gary Gildner, *The Angel Thing* 131
Ted Kooser, *Four Poems* 143
Tim Barnes, *Two Poems* 147
Brian Olson, *Dead Horses of the Owyhee Desert* 149
Gary Short, *Two Poems* 151
Sally Green, *Two Poems* 155
Jay Johnson, *Service Call* 157
Rebecca Evans, *Over-Sized Ghazal* 171
Michael Daley, *The Restorers* 173
Gino Sky, *Three Poems* 175
Joe Wilkins, *Two Poems* 179
Sherman Alexie, *Four Poems* 181
Edward Sanders, *Hymn to Rose Pesotta* 189

INTERVIEW
Judith Freeman, *Heartland, Homestead, and Hearth:
An Interview with Montana Writer and Filmmaker Annick Smith* 195

ESSAYS, MEMOIRS, NONFICTION
Annick Smith, *Bill Kittredege: A Tribute* 211
Shaun T. Griffin, *Late November with Wendell Berry* 221
Gary Thompson, *Madeline DeFrees: Three Occcasions* 229
Howard Levy, *A Small Note on Adrienne Rich* 241
Teresa Jordan, *The Last Conversation: Remembering Terrence O'Donnell* 245
Rae Lewis, *Grover Lewis and the Shooting of Larry Flynt: An Excerpt from
 a Memoir in Progress* 263
Paul Beebe, *What Little I Know of Native Americans, Rez Dogs, and History* ... 275
Ron McFarland, *Three Days in March: Piscatorial Adventures
 in Sunny Florida* 289
Jett Whitehead, *Theodore Roethke's Roots* 293
Don Zancanella, *Becoming a Reader in the West* 301

RE-READINGS
Jim Hepworth, *'And Grace Comes by Art and Art Does Not Come Easy':
 Norman Maclean and His Critics* 317
Marc C. Johnson, *The Quintessential Columnist: Re-reading Jimmy Breslin* 337
Adam M. Sowards, *Gossamer Possibilities: Re-reading Ivan Doig's
 Winter Brothers in a New Season* 345
Kurt Caswell, *Meeting with a Sudden Shower:
 John Clare's "Journey out of Essex"* 355
Baron Wormser, *Haunted: On Re-reading a Poem by Sir Thomas Wyatt* 369
David L. Kuebeck, *Finding Redemption in Ohio: A Re-reading of
 John Clellon Holmes's* The Bowling Green Poems 375
Alan Minskoff, *Listening: The Pleasures of Fiction on AudioBooks* 387
Ted Dyer, *Wynham Lewis: Re-reading the Work of a Modernist Warrior* 393
Grove Koger, *Becoming a Whole Man: Re-reading Richard McKenna's*
 The Sand Pebbles 413
John Hoopes, *Re-reading Gino Sky's* Near the Postcard Beautiful 419
Gary Soto, *Books as Drinking Buddies* 431

GALLERY
Rod Burks 456
Bryan Chernick 178, 208, 276
Katherine Jones .... Back Cover, 16, 42, 86
Greg Keeler 102, 122, 150, 172
Glenn Oakley 118, 174, 429, 460
Riley Sophia Penaluna 130, 170, 314, 448
Betty Rodgers 447
Brad Teare 36
Randy Van Dyck .... Front Cover
Janet Wormser 126

FROM THE ARCHIVE
Remembering Bruce Embree 451

LAST WORD
Gary Snyder, *That Fellow's Razor* 459

CONTRIBUTORS 463

LIMBERLOST LETTERPRESS

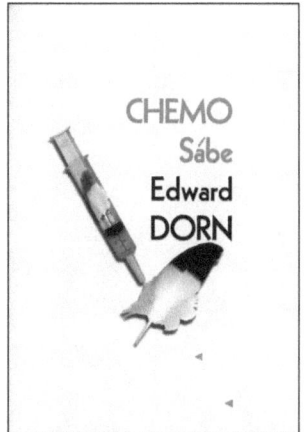

www.limberlostpress.com

In the silence left after their passing, an ancient ironwood tree keeps vigil over Hohokam petroglyphs (Ironwood National Park). Photograph by Katherine Jones.

EDITOR'S NOTE

Writing and Publishing Under the Pall of Our Self-inflicted Presidency

We begin this 2025 edition of *The Limberlost Review* several months into a new presidency that day by day dismantles our economic stability, wipes out the guardrails of health and scientific reasoning, inspires racism, demonizes our democratic institutions, destroys our long-held international alliances, makes a mockery of the rule of law, and takes a chainsaw to our cultural heritage. The arts and humanities, libraries, museums, universities, and public schools are too "woke," they say, a term that few Republicans in Congress could even define if they dared show up at a town hall meeting with their constituents. Reinstalling monuments to the Confederacy is suddenly a priority.

And so, we open this edition with Clifford Burke's "Kakistocracy" and bookend it with Gary Snyder's "That Fellow's Razor"—poems by two veteran poets of past cultural wars.

Between their voices, we have the wisdom of Wendell Berry, Gino Sky's call to beauty, Ed Sanders' drum of praise for those who led past fights against injustices, Annick Smith's belief in the landscapes of memory and identity, Sherman Alexie's humor and wary eye on history, remembrances of writers and poets who carried the light, and stories about and reflections upon the most intimate experiences and visions that make us human.

All within a hard copy anthology you now hold in your hands, a book you can take to the porch or to bed for some peace—though we hope that Congress will muster the courage to thwart privatization of the U.S. Postal Service.

Though most of the work herein was compiled prior to the 2024 election, it is under the pall of this nation's self-inflicted presidency that it appears, and it is hard to release it to the world without comment.

* * * * *

This edition appears in the spring. We recently returned from a month-long road trip from Idaho to Arizona and back, a 3,000-mile drive mostly along two-lane blacktop. We avoided major interstates as much as we could, visited Joshua Tree National Park in California, where we saw a massive, wind-torn, American flag hanging upside down from a high peak signaling national distress as similar flags are hung at other National Parks, National Monuments, National Forests and in hundreds of protests across the nation.

Signaling dire distress from Yosemite's El Capitan.

    I had with me a rough proof of this 2025 edition to read along the way, attended the annual Tucson Book Festival, had a meal again in the Wagon Wheel bar in Patagonia, Arizona, just below a photo of the late poet/novelist Jim Harrison (who frequented the Wheel while wintering there in his later years), re-reading the good work here in this *Review*, returning to Boise to get it all corrected and off to press.

    We have in this edition the work of two Pulitzer Prize winners, several current and former state Poet Laureates, several National Book Award winners and nominees, as well as a number of Pushcart Prize Award winners and nominees and recipients of many other awards.

    Not that awards are the ring-reach of the writers we feature.

    Idaho poet Bruce Embree (see "From the Archive") won no awards in his brief lifetime, yet it is always warming to see how his work still simmers among particularly younger and outsider writers looking for a voice who speaks to them, a writer who made an impactful imprint on his regional scene. Thirty years since Limberlost letterpress printed a second chapbook of poems by this little-known poet from Inkom, Idaho, we thought it worth bringing attention to Bruce's work again.

EDITOR'S NOTE

A note on the artwork in this edition: rising printing costs (along with rising postal costs) unfortunately prevent us from printing another full-color edition. Admittedly, we publish artwork herein that deserves better presentation on high-quality gloss paper—particularly photography by Glenn Oakley, Katherine Jones, and Bryan Chernick—and painters like Greg Keeler and Janet Wormser, who deserve full color. As we've noted before, their work along with the work of other artists elevates the reading of this *Review*.

* * * * *

We wanted to make note of a major transition. Meggan Laxalt Mackey, our designer extraordinaire, has moved from Boise to Vancouver, Washington. When we decided to revive *The Limberlost Review* as a literary annual journal back in 2019, Meggan was the first and only designer we talked to, not just because of her amazing talent, but because of her reputation for focus and thorough follow-through. She's never seen this *Review* as simply another project of yet another client. She jumped in and became the engine of design for a cause she believed in, and we've been full collaborators. Niece of the great Nevada writer Robert Laxalt, author of the Basque classic *Sweet Promised Land*, and educated in the art of letterpress printing at the University of Nevada's famed Black Rock Press, Meggan's talents range far more than book design. She's been a designer of major exhibits, historical interpretive signage, a writer and scholar of Basque culture, organizer of cultural events in Boise for decades, and more.

The Limberlost Review would not be what it is without her talent, energy, advice, attention to detail, patience, and unflagging devotion to the written word. She assures us, she will continue her involvement and expertise from afar, given how so much of our communication is all electronic. But we'll miss our editorial meetings over lunch and drinks, our social gatherings, and her presence and influence in southwest Idaho. Thank you, Meggan. Idaho's loss is Washington's gain.

THE LIMBERLOST REVIEW

Next Deadline:
Barring the privatization of the U.S. Postal Service and the abolishment of Media Mail rates, we're setting an October 1, 2025, deadline for submissions for *Limberlost 2026*.

As always, we make a special call for "Re-readings" of books contributors think should be re-read and why, the more personal the story the better regarding why books from the past still have a memorable resonance.

Final Note:
In May of 2025, Gary Snyder turns 95, Wendell Berry turns 91 in August, and Gino Sky turns 90 in August. All praise and best wishes to these three nonagenarians who never compromised their muse.

Meanwhile, as Ed Sanders says, "Refuse to be burnt-out!"

KEEP READING! ■

—Rick Ardinger

POEMS & STORIES

"The USA of Trump," glyph by Ed Sanders.

CLIFFORD BURKE

Kakistocracy
 14 November 2024

Old Bill Yeats taught us this,
about the worst, and the rough beast,
and we might have seen it coming
but for understandable wild optimism
that the order might be shifting
that our compatriots were true
and would not rob us of our joy.
Instead we watch that evil glee
on stupid faces as they pillage
the best ideas we've had, that all
our many beings be free and free
to thrive and have care for one another
and the one place we all live in:
that dream we've worked so hard for
won't be coming round, just yet.

Double Down
15 November 2024

We take as given the gift of the day
and the urge to make a difference
so starting out small on one day:
who knows what effects may follow
especially the next day, and the next
when the gift begins to accumulate
and the effort becomes the gift
as the days draw out in a graceful
dance in time and useful acts
for the planet for the neighbors
for the good and love in all of us
and the pleasure of letting it go

Lew Welch
Theodore Roethke

Lewie said it best:
Just step aside and the whole
crushing machine rolls right by.
What he didn't say was
how to do that, how to ignore
the noise the endless imagery
of a gross and dangerous crew
the world ending scenarios
that gloss over genuine ruin
as we all relentlessly plunge
toward the fire next time.
I know, do the work.
And another teacher said:
Be still. Wait.

Wishing
24 November 2024

Ferlinghetti were with us:
he could tell it better than I,
how the insane became normal—
it's not normal!—we who stay
alert to the news, we see the lies
our trusted sources feed us,
that these are not crazy people
the world over now in control
of deadliest devices and means
to bring down suffering on all
but their wealthiest cronies.
He said the world is awash
with fascism and fear, yeah,
and it hasn't really started yet.

WENDELL BERRY

Sabbath Poems: 2021

I

The old project hardly had re-begun
In the season of your birth. The morning sun
Had not replaced the morning fires. The singing
Of song for song had yet to come, bringing
The couples home among the leaves. Along
The cool still-shadeless creekside lanes among
The old year's fallen leaves, the wild woods flowers
Had only begun to brighten the frosted hours
Of early morning. But soon the days rose
Earlier and more kind. Thus I compose
A poem to coincidence conformed.
You came. And like that year I would be warmed.

4/30/21

II

We had the two best seats
To witness my defeats
In the battles I never won.
I forgot how they'd begun.
Seeing I had espoused
Such beauty, so aroused,
I plotted my next move,
Distractedly in love.

5/29/21

III

It puzzled me once,
that ancient call
to ceaseless prayer.
Now I know.
Help me. Help me.
If I must stay
longer at work
give me strength.

IV

MAURY, NELL, MAGGIE

I lived longer of course
as I was destined to do
and carried them one by one,
become at last still,
and laid them in the dark
and there left them alone
and forgot exactly where
I had placed them, for I gave
them back into the whole
world where they would always
be found, though we were lost
to one another. I knew
that I would pass near them
as I walked my rounds, and the sheep
in their rounds also would pass
near them. I planted no stone.
And they lived on in me
as I for my while in the world.
And it seems I remember the day
when at last in all the lost
places where we have waited
we wake, eternally spilling
back into time, and we rise
in our young unaching strength
that our old bodies remembered.
As if answering my call
that in time they did not hear,
they come. They lift their heads
under my hands. Speaking
all the same language now,
we forgive what we mistook.
They walk with me in the early

WENDELL BERRY

light across a pasture
deep in grass, where the flock
must be gathered and brought
home. "Come by!" I call
to my old companions. And so
I send them again out
into the gladness we keep
forever in our hearts.

V

APHRODITE (*Speyeria Aphrodite*)

She disappeared among the leaves
and the shadows. I looked for her
and could not see her, though she
was nearer me than I thought.
And then she opened her wings
and the light came and met her.
She shone then with beauty
of all things opened in welcome.

VI

Again I have been reading
the poem "What Are Years?"
by Marianne Moore, not
to feel spoken for,
but to feel again the honor
of being so spoken to.

VII

Coming here, he entered
his absence before he came.
He saw his country as it was,
himself not yet arrived.

He saw he had come to stay,
and he learned then to be here
by his love and work, as he
could in no other place.

Old and slow, he enters
now his absence that is
to come, the welcoming light,
the undisclosing silence.

VIII

Propelled along the creek road
in the instrument of the fire of the end
of living things, he shuts off
the shuddering, shattering sound
that so far has shut him in
and the quiet comes down, as wide
as the sun's light and older.
Way in the distance is the call
of a single bird as yet
unanswered. He hears the whole
quiet. He hears the song.

"Women Who Run with Wolves," woodcut by Brad Teare.

BONNIE JO CAMPBELL

What We Girls Did for Fun

Our whoops and howls rippled the stars
and stripes we twisted into halter tops,

held with safety pins. We stopped to light
cigarettes and check our pimples

in bicycle mirrors, to curse and stroke
our muscular thighs. Our mercury fillings

attracted radio signals from other galaxies,
but the only foreign language we knew

was French kiss—already our tongues
were wild with translation. We lost our minds

when flags twisted around flagpoles,
when murderers murdered us. Pay attention!

our teachers said. When we all screamed
at once, the night sky lit up for an instant.

When I Was an Old Man Girl

We hiked up our little skirts
above our old bony knees,
tied the kind of cross-eyed

knots we made in the old days.
There was so much to learn
that we already knew.

Way back when I was an old
man girl, we giggled
until we wet our drawers.

As the sun dappled our teacups
of cheap whiskey,
we hopscotched gap-toothed,

pigtails bouncing, turned
coughing carbuncle cartwheels
and twirled our batons

until we collapsed upon
ourselves, kissing, groping.
At night it was milk and farts

and murderous fairy tales.
Our ensuing dreams proved
the wisdom of our monstrosity.

BONNIE JO CAMPBELL

At Sixty-Three, Every Day

there will be some hard thing—
closing an account, saying a goodbye,

standing with young people atop a hill
spreading ashes that float down to a stream,

telling somebody *no*. Being this age
makes me want to put on weight

to add gravity to still being here,
if not to hurry my descent. A hill

covered with ashes can be slippery. I careened
laughing down this hill with him

whose body is now cast away. Kids,
grandkids toss stones, check phones,

kick wildflowers. My heart! A hawk
swoops, shrieks, rages, desperate, feathery.

I was Born with an Agenda

A pink jowly politician with clenched fists, demanding milk
and liberty, I was my own constituent, to hell with the rest.

I crawled down into the swamp, into skunk weed, broke out
with frogs for sessions, inked amendments on the backs

of leatherbacks. Kingfishers fished for me, leeches lobbied,
the muskrat caucus conferred. I addressed a joint session

of mallards and minnows; when we adjourned, I napped,
my sleep as sound as the principles of our Constitution.

My mother the insurrectionist hauled me back to the house,
boiled me in my tiny tub, scrubbed off my muck.

Once alone with my bottle, I vetoed her soft lullaby
lit my cigar and lay glassy-eyed in my crib dreaming

of bills, filibuster, and cloture, the turtle snap of censure.
It would be decades before I recaptured my manifesto.

BONNIE JO CAMPBELL

A Mother's Asbestos

Sure, I fed you kids PBBs.
Who am I to throw away fresh milk?
Poison filtered through four stomachs is hardly poison

Listen, child, when I was young, we chased trucks
spraying DDT, and airplanes strafed
the marsh to fight the rage of ague. We painted

lead on our walls. My milk cow stopped
eating just before cancer sprang her eye
from its socket, filled her body like pink foam.

Years later, I had cancer, too, plodded
to surgery, radiation, and I didn't complain,
just raised another glass to the gods of circumstance.

What in the hell was I supposed to do? Protect
you darlings from every goddamned thing?
I told you, don't get pregnant.

Now you buy organic apples?
What makes you long to be so pure?
What makes you love yourself so much?

In a landscape worn by water and wind, we are not the only ones who have stood in wonder (Green River, Canyonlands National Park). Photograph by Katherine Jones.

MITCH WIELAND

The Last Days of Ferrell Swan

*Heaven's wasted on the dead,
that's what your mama said.*
—"Only Children" by Jason Isbell

Alone on the sandstone bluff, Ferrell Swan waits for the sun. He stands at the edge of the outcropping, the toes of his worn hiking boots risking the drop-off, and mouths a silent prayer. He knows the dawn offers no salvation whatsoever, neither to him nor the doomed and forsaken of his kind.

The sun breaks the Owyhee range and slides into the hazy sky. Out of habit, Ferrell surveys the miles unfurling all the way to the western horizon: his sagebrush kingdom, his high-desert empire, the place his bones will surely lie. He checks on his homestead below, the metal roofs of the cabin and barn cast in pale red light. On the air rides the heady perfume of bitterroot and wild lupine, and Ferrell draws the scent far into his chest—another breath, he thinks, to keep him among the living.

With his morning ritual over and done, Ferrell turns toward home. He starts down the steep trail, careful where he places his boots in the loose shale. A half-mile distant, dust roils above the gravel road bordering his land, billowing like smoke from a wildfire. Ferrell stops and watches the speeding car, the heaviness of his dread another burden he must carry. He hasn't had a single visitor since Rilla, ex-wife and only love, lost her cancer siege in September. To Ferrell's astonishment, Rilla had wanted to spend her final months at his frontier outpost, weeks of bittersweet reconciliation and utter despair. His stepson Levon—the only other kinfolk to visit the cabin—is long gone from this earth, died a dozen summers ago when his car plowed into a tree. Now seventy-six, Ferrell considers himself a man forgotten or never known at all, it doesn't matter which. He doesn't mind being an exile from the general populace, given its steady downward trajectory. When he is feeling his most honest and forthright, Ferrell knows being alone was the plan since he could walk.

Against his wishes, the car turns off the county road, wheeling onto Ferrell's lengthy washboard drive like a bootlegger on the run. It bounces his way on bad shocks and blown springs. The beat-up Saturn needs a good washing, its cracked windshield streaked and bug-splattered, the fenders and hood coated in powdery dust. All things considered, the junker looks exactly like the one Levon killed himself in, all those years ago.

Out of breath, Ferrell reaches the bottom of the trail and hurries across the corral. He climbs the cabin steps and turns to face whatever doom is about to arrive. The Saturn pulls beneath the cottonwood and shuts down in a sudden absence of noise. Of all the possibilities Ferrell can conjure—zealots peddling religion like traveling salesmen, the Bureau of Land Management rep come to bitch, his reclusive neighbors needing another dose of company—he isn't expecting a kid to step from the car. The boy is clearly not out of his teenage years, sixteen or seventeen at best. He wears cargo shorts and a faded T-shirt with *Question Authority?* sharpied across the front. As if he has all the time in the world, the kid leans against the filthy hood, both arms crossed, and stares at him.

"So who are you?" Ferrell asks.

"Don't you recognize me?"

"Should I?"

"Probably not," the kid says. "It's been a while since I was here."

It takes Ferrell another tick of the clock to figure it out. All at once he can see nothing but his dead stepson in the boy's defiant brown eyes, a look of too many emotions all at once—challenge and need, fear and hurt, anger and sadness. Ferrell should be shocked at this surprising turn of events, but somehow isn't.

"You're Harry," he says. "You're Levon's son."

"I'm also your grandson."

Step-grandson, Ferrell almost says, but holds his tongue. "Is that a ghost car you're driving?"

"Mom found the same make and model online. Same color too."

"So you have a license?"

The boy shrugs. "Haven't got around to it."

"Don't you worry about the police?"

"A white kid in Idaho?"

Ferrell and the boy reach an impasse of sorts, run dry of words before anything of importance can be said. They stare at each other as if telepathy is actually a thing.

"Where's your mother?" Ferrell says at last, wondering how Melody could have let the kid drive all the way from Boise.

"Dead."

The word hits Ferrell hard in the chest, takes his wind like a punch thrown with cruel intent. That familiar sadness floods his insides, freezing his ribs into glittering hoops of ice. His tired heart falters against the cold.

"That can't be," Ferrell says, his voice not his own.

"I went to her funeral in Ketchum. It's pretty official."

"What did Melody die from?"

The boy spits into the gravel at his feet. "Xanax."

"What the hell is that?"

"A drug for anxiety and worry."

"And it killed her?"

"One night when I was asleep, Mom mixed her meds with a favorite Merlot. She got so relaxed she forgot to breathe."

"You want to come inside?" Ferrell asks, too stunned to think.

"I got nowhere else to go," the boy says.

* * * * *

After retiring from the crowded classrooms of Ohio, Ferrell bought 100 acres of bare scrubland, sight unseen, in southwestern Idaho. During the divorce proceedings that followed, mere days before Ferrell headed west like an aging pioneer, the judge ruled the Idaho land had no value. She said Ferrell could have his worthless acres, which drew quite a chuckle in the courtroom. Ferrell endured the laughter of Rilla's family and friends, but secretly rejoiced. When all was said and done, he got to keep what he wanted most.

Located south of Silver City, his property borders the vast holdings of the BLM, the old hideout of Butch and Sundance, a rugged stretch of outlaw territory that had once reached eastward into Wyoming and Montana, and south to Utah and Nevada. Ferrell's property is a time capsule from the Wild West, minus the train robberies and blazing guns. Surrounding his cabin these days is nothing but rocks and chaparral, pissed-off rattlers and stealthy coyotes, peregrines wheeling like winged gods across the endless blue.

*****

In those first awkward moments after his arrival, Harry stows his bulging backpack in the spare bedroom. He throws open curtains that have been shut for months. Watching the kid at the window, Ferrell is transported to another time. This is the room where his stepson used to stay during those frenzied visits, the room from which Levon snuck out at night to meet with Melody in the desert dark, back when she was the neighbor's wife and not yet mother of the boy standing before him. Down the road, Harrison Cole, Melody's despairing ex, raises Christmas trees on his irrigated acres, an inexplicable oasis, an island of bright green, among the low scrub. With a jolt that sets his knees to shaking, Ferrell realizes Cole doesn't know the fate of his former wife.

Harry strolls into the kitchen and surveys Ferrell's propane fridge and cast-iron woodstove. He nods at the pair of kerosene lanterns on the butcher-block table, their glass chimneys blackened with soot.

"I'm guessing you don't have electricity yet?"

"I'm pretty much off the grid here. When I need power, there's a gasoline generator out back."

The boy holds his cell phone in the air, searching for a signal that isn't there. "You don't even have service?"

"The nearest tower got burned up in a fire last summer. We're a dead zone now."

"What if you need help?"

"Then help won't come."

"Aren't you kind of advanced in years not to have a phone?"

"They only deliver bad news," Ferrell says. "After Rilla called about your father, I stomped my Samsung to smithereens."

"You can't hide from bad news."

"That's what Rilla used to say."

"Was Grandma right?"

"She was never wrong."

Harry glances longingly toward the woodstove. He looks as if he hasn't eaten in days. "Does that old timey thing work?"

"I got fresh eggs from the henhouse," Ferrell says. "Have a seat and I'll make you breakfast."

The boy smiles for the first time since he drove up. "Mom always said your gruff act was just for show. She said deep down you were a real teddy bear."

"Your mama was a poor judge of character."

* * * * *

After breakfast, Harry naps away the hours in the spare bedroom. Ferrell suspects the boy drove half the night, winding his way down from the higher elevations of Sun Valley, home to Melody's moneyed parents, to arrive at Ferrell's desolate land below the Owyhee range. He hopes the kid hasn't run away from home, though that must be the case. Ferrell decides it doesn't matter one bit if his grandson is on the lam.

Near sundown, the boy stumbles shirtless into the living room. He looks bleary-eyed and confused, his coal-black hair in wild revolt. His pale chest is inked with a startling rendition of Munch's "The Scream," the swirling colors sharp and vivid. The anguished face looks exactly the way Ferrell feels.

"How long did I sleep?" Harry pulls on his T-shirt and finger-combs his hair.

"Long enough," Ferrell says. "That's some tattoo."

"I got it after Mom died. It was her favorite painting."

"How'd your grandparents like it?"

"I'm here, aren't I?"

Ferrell glances out the window, his way of checking the time. "You want to feed the horse with me?"

"Chroma is still alive?" Harry says, actual elation in his voice.

"I wouldn't be feeding her if she wasn't."

Harry trails Ferrell out to the barn in the slanted light. When they step through the wide door, the chestnut mare whinnies her greeting. A shaft of late sun slices through the missing slats in the west wall, turning the flies into shooting sparks.

"Here she is," Ferrell says.

Harry lays a soothing palm on Chroma's white nose, exactly the way Rilla used to do. "She was grandma's, right?"

Ferrell nods, fresh grief rippling through him.

"Do you ride her?"

"Not anymore. I break pretty easy."

"Can I ride her?"

"She's older than you are. I don't think Chroma could tolerate a ride into the open anymore."

"I'll take it easy on her. I won't go far."

"It's a might inhospitable out there."

"Would Grandma ride alone?"

"Only time her heart felt at ease."

Harry runs his hand along Chroma's sweeping neck. "I wish I remembered Grandma better."

"You would have loved her," Ferrell says. "She sure loved you."

"So can I go?"

"How about you feed this old girl instead?"

Ferrell watches rebellion flash in the boy's eyes. For a moment that old showdown has returned, Levon and Ferrell at high noon on the streets of Dodge. But Harry just nods and walks from the barn, his head hung low. When Ferrell gets outside, the kid is heading into the sage, a small figure beneath the unbearable weight of the sky.

* * * * *

After supper, Ferrell and his grandson retire onto the porch, where they park themselves in wooden rockers. The darkness sweeps off the chaparral in a rush, washing like a flood over the barn and cabin. In the slow minutes that follow, bright star points cram the domed sky, the Milky Way a shimmering arch over their heads. Right on time, the barn owl takes wing from the tall cottonwood in the drive, wheeling across the scrubland without a sound.

"I take it you do this every night?" Harry says.

"There's nothing else to do."

"Don't you get lonely?"

"Only for the people who are gone. I don't miss folks I don't know."

"Do you know me?"

"Knowing someone takes a while."

Harry taps his fingers on Ferrell's knee, a kindly gesture he doesn't mind. "We'd better start fast-tracking, Gramps. You're not getting any younger."

"No need to remind me, son. There's not a minute I don't feel my age. Getting old is not for the weak of heart."

They enter another spell of not talking. When the quiet threatens to overwhelm them, Ferrell stands and hurries into the cabin. He grabs his prized Lagavulin off the bookshelf, then reaches down two shot glasses from the kitchen cupboard. On the porch, he sets the glasses on the rail and fills them to the brim.

"What's this?"

"Fast-tracking."

"I'm not old enough to drink."

"So now you are a law-abiding citizen?"

The boy leans forward and lifts the glass like a special prize. He holds the shot out in a toast. "To those we've lost," he says.

"And those of us left behind."

The boy downs the shot and stamps both feet on the porch boards. "Is this kerosene?"

"Single malt Scotch, from the swampy bogs of Scotland."

"I guess it's an acquired taste."

"Most things are," Ferrell says.

Over the next while, grandfather and grandson trade shots and stories. "You know," Ferrell says, waving grandly toward the sagebrush, "you were conceived on a night like this. Levon and your mama, out there in the sand."

"Mom told me."

"She did?"

"She liked to tell everyone I was a creature of the desert. She said the coyotes howled at my inception."

"Melody wasn't shy about sharing."

"Did you really call my dad a calamity magnet?"

"That's the honest truth. Levon had a special knack for finding trouble. He left a trail of destruction wherever he went."

"You think I've inherited all those calamity genes?" the boy says. "Is the blueprint for trouble encoded in my DNA?"

Ferrell thinks long and hard before he speaks. "It's nature and nurture. You might steal cars and run away from home and drive without a license, but I can tell you've got a good head on your shoulders. Your mother taught you well."

"The car's mine," Harry says and raises his shot class to his lips.

* * * * *

The next morning, the boy rises before dawn. Ferrell finds him on the porch with his bare feet on the rail, a coffee mug clasped in both hands. The empty whiskey bottle is perched on the top step, a testament to male bonding rituals of old. Ferrell's head feels like a kick drum is pounding out a steady beat.

"Your daddy used to sleep till noon when he'd visit."

"That settles it then," Harry says. "I'm officially not him."

Above the Owyhees the sun glares down as if to burn out all weakness from the world. Ferrell watches a peregrine climb the updrafts until it becomes a speck against the blue.

Harry takes his feet from the rail. He stands up and stares across the sun-blasted land. "Where did you spread my dad's ashes?"

"About a quarter mile from here."

"Like in the sand somewhere?"

"Rilla poured Levon's ashes at the coyote dens. She thought they were kindred spirits."

"Can you take me there?"

Ferrell studies the grief like a mask on the boy's face. "I've got some boots you can wear."

* * * * *

The coyote dens look abandoned when they approach, not a fresh track in the sand, no telltale signs of scattered scat. The place is absolutely quiet in the harsh afternoon sun.

"This is it," Ferrell says. "Those holes are the openings to the dens."

Years ago, the coyotes had set up shop below the bluff, digging their tunnels among the boulders and scree rained down from above. The place has always been special to Ferrell, a church without roof or walls. He thinks how he hasn't heard a group-howl in months, none of that netherworld craziness he loves, the laughter of gleeful spirits loosed upon the land. He hopes the pack moved out on its own accord, and wasn't shot dead from the air by the damn government snipers. Ferrell used to collect the coyote skulls he would find on his daily hikes, but stopped when his bookcase filled up with dozens of them, the whole crew rocking on their curved jawbones when he walked past. It gave him the chills, all those dead coyotes nodding at something he hadn't said.

"Where exactly did you put him?" Harry says.

Ferrell stares at the dark mouths of the dens, imagines yellow-gold eyes watching them without judgement or fear. "In front of each of those entrances. Rilla hoped Levon's ashes would stick to their paws. She wanted her son to run with the pack."

"Did it make her feel better?"

"For a few weeks, I suppose, but losing a loved one is like dying in degrees. Sometimes I feel I'm already dead."

"I miss my Mom every day."

"Rilla and Levon speak constantly in the confines of my skull. Your memories keep folks alive."

Harry sits down in front of one of the dens. He looks to be waiting for something to happen, though Ferrell can't imagine what that could be.

"I'm an orphan now," the boy says, as if the thought surprises him.

"I'm here."

"We're not actually related."

"I thought that when you first arrived. I don't think that now."

As if heaven has intervened, a coyote calls from somewhere atop the ridge. The boy looks at Ferrell, wide-eyed and trembling. The howl comes again and echoes off the boulders all around them. It's clearly the first time Harry has heard a coyote up close.

"You think that's my dad?"

"If it isn't," Ferrell says, "it sounds just like him."

* * * * *

After visiting Levon's final resting place, Ferrell takes the boy onto the ridge. It's Ferrell's favorite place in all his one hundred acres, the view enough to renew and restore. They cross the bluff and stand poised at the drop-off, looking at the snow-capped Owyhees rising before them.

"Does that weird underground guy still live down there?" Harry says.

"You remember Din Winters?" Ferrell points to the aluminum air vent, glinting in the sage flats below. "You see that metal catching light?"

The boy sights along Ferrell's outstretched finger. "The thing that looks like a periscope?"

"That's how Din breathes. He spends his days in three buried storage units, welded together."

Harry looks at Ferrell in wonder. "It's kind of like he lives in a submarine."

"Or a giant coffin."

"At least he's safe."

"To be honest, Din was happier when he was pretending to be a survivalist. It's not the same now."

"Nothing is," Harry says and starts down the trail.

* * * * *

That night on the porch, Ferrell and the boy are back in their spots. Ferrell has opened the last of his Lagavulin stash. It's a hundred bucks a bottle and worth every penny.

"I'm supposed to tell Harrison Cole about my mother," Harry says after the first shot. "Mom said if something happened to her, she wanted me to tell you both. She said you hermits needed to know."

"Do you want me to tell him?"

"I promised Mom I would do it." The boy stares at the stars raging above them. "How do you think he'll take it?"

"Melody broke his heart when she left him. Cole has kept up hope she might come back someday."

"He should know she can't anymore, shouldn't he?"

"I don't really know," Ferrell says and means it. "I sometimes wonder if false hope is better than no hope at all."

* * * * *

The next day, Ferrell and his grandson do chores around the place to pass the time. They feed and water Chroma, replace the missing slats in the barn, gather eggs from the henhouse. They sweep the porch and clean the kitchen, top to bottom. They eat dinner at the table as if they've been together for years.

The two strike out for Harrison Cole's in the gathering twilight. Ferrell walks beside the boy like the grandfather he wants to be. He points to the right, and they cut through the rows of fragrant conifers.

"These are all Christmas trees?"

"Mostly. Cole grows a couple acres of evergreens for the nurseries in Boise."

"You guys hang out much?"

"Not for years. When Melody ran off with Levon, Harrison let all his trees die. After too much whiskey one night, he set them all on fire."

"I bet that was something to see."

"It was like having a ringside seat to the wonders of hell."

They come out of the conifers at the edge of Cole's paved driveway. His double-wide sits in the near dark, angled against the razed husk of his Victorian home.

"Did he burn his house down too?" Harry asks.

"That came years later. A big wildfire swept through here the summer Levon died."

"Does this place always burn?"

"It renews itself that way."

Ferrell knocks on the door and steps back. He trades glances with the boy, a tinge of regret shooting through him like real pain. He's sorry to bring more bad news to the man. Before Levon came to visit, Harrison and Melody had their elegant three-story home and their shared solitude. Weeks later, when Levon left Idaho, he took Melody with him.

Cole answers the door in pressed jeans and a white button down. "Well, if you don't look snazzy," Ferrell says.

His neighbor looks over Ferrell's shoulder and grins. "Hello, Harry. You sure have grown."

Before the boy can even say a word, Cole rushes forward and hugs him close. He holds on way longer than Ferrell thinks he should, but then there's no guidelines for reunions such as this. At last Cole turns the kid loose and steps back. He turns to Ferrell and wipes his eyes.

"I saw you two walking the ridge yesterday. I knew it had to be our Harry. I was hoping you'd come visit."

Cole brings out chairs from the trailer, and the three men take up places on the cracked concrete drive. "You probably don't remember, but we used to have a wraparound porch," Cole says to Harry. "Your mother loved to sit there when the sun went down."

"I've been porch sitting with Ferrell here," Harry says. "I can see how Mom liked it."

"I loved Melody," Cole says. "I don't think I've ever stopped."

"I know," Harry says, looking nervous about the news he's come to deliver.

"How is your mother?"

Ferrell draws a breath so sudden Cole looks over.

"She's found some peace at last," Harry says.

When Ferrell glances his way, the boy lifts his shoulders in the smallest shrug.

"Does Melody ever mention me?" Cole asks.

"Let's not put Harry on the spot," Ferrell says.

Cole puts both hands over his heart. "You're right. It's just that Melody was the best five years of my life."

"She loved this place for sure," Harry says. "Boise was not the same to her."

"Where is Melody these days?"

"Ketchum."

"Does she plan on staying there?"

"She does," Harry says. "She really does."

Cole smiles at the boy. "Can you tell her hello for me?"

"I will," Harry says. "I'll tell her for sure."

* * * * *

On the way back, Harry follows Ferrell down the rows of trees. The branches reach for them like ghouls in the dark. Above their heads, meteors streak across the purple sky as if aliens have launched a surprise attack.

"Is that one of those meteor showers?"

"The Perseid," Ferrell says. "It peaks tonight."

Ferrell keeps his eyes upward, too heartsick at the sadness of the mortal world. A shooting star flares right across the Milky Way, a burst of yellow and red that melts into nothing. He thinks of all the souls roaming the heavens and not the earth.

"I couldn't do it," the boy says from behind him.

"I know," Ferrell says.

"He doesn't really need to know, does he?"

"You did the right thing," Ferrell says. "You did good."

* * * * *

When Ferrell wakes the next morning, the boy hasn't gotten out of bed. He heads to the barn by himself, previewing the pestering loneliness that will come when Harry leaves. He hates how his emotions often show up before they're needed.

Ferrell steps into the barn and says hello, but Chroma doesn't call out. He opens her stall to find the mare gone. Back in the cabin, he checks the spare bedroom to find the boy gone too. The ancient Saturn sits under the shade of the cottonwood.

"Well, damn," Ferrell says.

With his fear on the rise, Ferrell paces back and forth on the porch, his boots loud in the stillness. He scans the horizon for signs of horse and rider. When he can't take it anymore, Ferrell stalks to the barn as if he'll find the horse magically returned. He steps from the barn and sights along the ridge above, considers the dangers lurking all around. In his mind, the horse rears from a startled rattler, throwing Harry to the ground. He sees Chroma crashing down from a hidden gopher hole, trapping Harry beneath her immovable weight. That old worry returns like a forgotten foe, resurrected from the days when Levon was young and reckless, when one trouble after another came in a never-ending parade.

Ferrell is about to head into the sagebrush on foot when he spots movement to the west. The boy gallops out of the high desert like a mirage. When Harry gets close, Ferrell sees he's wearing his black Stetson from the barn. Chroma trots into the dusty drive and the boy pulls back the reins.

"I feel like Billy the Kid," Harry shouts, sweat in rivulets down his face.

"You act like him too," Ferrell says, angry and relieved at the same time. "You didn't have permission to take the horse. Something could have happened."

The boy grins down at him. "Why, Ferrell Swan, I'd swear you care about me."

"Of course I do. I care more than you could ever know."

The boy swings a leg over and steps down. "I had to visit my dad one last time. I took my mother's ashes over and spread them around."

"You brought Melody with you?" Ferrell says, surprised.

"It's a big reason I came. She made me promise that too. I had her urn in the backpack."

"Rilla is there. She wanted to be with her son."

"I figured she was."

"I'm happy they're together again," Ferrell says, pleased beyond reason at the news. "It's a true family reunion. Like the coyotes, they can roam the chaparral when the moon is full."

* * * * *

That night, Ferrell knows it's their last hours together. He wishes he had more Lagavulin, but they've drunk his stash dry. Harry goes inside and comes out with a Ziploc of weed and a small glass pipe.

"You've had that all along?"

"I have."

"And we drank all my single malt?"

"I didn't want to offend the host." Harry covers the carb and sparks the bowl, drawing in smoke. He blows out a white cloud that hangs over them, a genie with wishes to grant. Harry hands him the lighter and pipe.

"Be careful, Gramps," he says. "This stuff's a lot stronger than when you were young."

"Mary Jane's the only thing that's gotten better in my lifetime." Ferrell touches flame to bowl and draws in a hit. The hot smoke makes him sputter and cough. He stamps his boots on the porch. "Damn," he says, his thoughts blurring in his head.

"I'll leave you the weed," Harry says and pats Ferrell on the knee. "Mary Jane can keep you company at night."

"You could too, if you want," Ferrell says. "The spare bedroom could be yours."

"I know," the boy says in a genuine way.

Ferrell hands back the pipe. "I'll give your number to the lawyer handling my will. He's up in Meridian."

"You thinking about dying?"

"It's been thinking about me."

"How will I know if something happens?"

"The lawyer will call. I'll leave everything to you."

Harry gestures toward the darkness before them. "That's a lot of sagebrush."

"And tranquility." Ferrell looks over at the boy. "Can you put my ashes with the others?"

The boy rests his hand on Ferrell's arm.

* * * * *

When Ferrell steps onto the porch the next morning, the boy is packed and ready. He sits in Rilla's rocker, his sneakers perched on the rail, the untied laces hanging down. His backpack waits on the first step.

"Is this good-bye then?"

"For now." Harry pulls his feet from the rail. "I need more people around me than you have here."

"The lack of people is the point."

"Your neighbors are all misfits and outcasts."

"Why I'm here."

The boy retrieves his backpack from the steps and walks to the car. He tosses the pack through the open passenger window. When he turns around, Ferrell hands him five twenties.

"Gas money," he says.

Harry looks at the bills. "Where am I going? The beaches of Cali?"

"If you want," Ferrell says. "I got more cash if you need it."

"I'm heading back to Sun Valley," Harry says. "I need to get that driver's license. My diploma too."

Ferrell reaches out and takes the boy in his arms. He holds Harry close, presses his chest tight against him. It's the hug he never gave Levon and maybe more.

"You be careful, son. You need to take the place of us old folks."

"I plan to."

The boy gets in the Saturn and the engine rumbles to life. Ferrell watches the wreck of a car wobble down the ruts in the lane. He knows he won't see Harry again, but the time they've had together is more than he ever expected. He knows when to welcome the small miracles of the world.

The Saturn fishtails onto the county road and straightens out, headed back the way it came. The boy brings the car up to speed, his tires throwing dust like his daddy used to do, a rocket ship straight to the stars. ■

ROBERT WRIGLEY

Youth is Beauty, Beauty Youth

addressed to an infant at a sidewalk cafe

Despite elaborate and everywhere tattoos—
at least everywhere I can see—Daddy and Mommy
are very beautiful, basking in the sun and shade
of a late morning table, he of course on his phone, ear-buds in,
she nursing you, more or less uncovered.
Do you perceive the filigree of pink and blue flowers
inked down the breast that suckles you?

I am much, much older but still interested enough
to relish what I see you see, though what I hold in my hands,
as you never have, is a book: a nineteen-forty-eight edition
of the poems of John Keats, and while I wait
for death I also wait for eggs benedict and bless
the fates for these, our seating arrangements.
Should Daddy look up, I'll admire the poem's decorations.

Meaning the line drawings by one Michael Ayrton,
who "decorated" the book. Not that Daddy looks up
much at all, which makes my watching easier.
Unlike Ayrton's man and woman above the poem's title,
Daddy ran faster or Mommy slowed down,
thus here you are and you are beautiful too.
Of course you see the tattoos. Why wouldn't you?

Your parents imagine eternity hardly better than you do,
or for that matter, than I, although the time I have—
the long, long time eternity is—stares me in the face.
Your view—well, it's way better. But it will not last, baby,
nor will Daddy's, whose lightning bolts across
his deltoids will someday like a battery slacken and fade,
just as Mommy's pink and blue flowers will sag.

THE LIMBERLOST REVIEW

My brunch has arrived and still not a word
has passed between your illustrated family.
Mommy's eyes are closed; Daddy scrolls
or thumbs up more sweet music only he can hear.
Though not especially sweet, that music, I imagine.
He thinks he knows what's up, just as I did, as you will,
even as I also imagine the three of you on the urn now—
in the passage of slow time, a desolation you too will never know.

ROBERT WRIGLEY

Twerk
in camp on a mountain river

Relax. It's a hoverfly, having hovered sufficiently long
to chance a landing on the back of my hand.
It sidles some, then extends a black tongue,
or something like one, and licks or laps or kisses, all the while
bobbing its bee-like but stingerless back end.

In my seventy-fourth year, I believe I've known
the action described by the word longer
than the word itself. But it's an hour's drive on gravel
to a mountain pass and the nearest sliver of connectivity.
I can hardly believe I've used the word in a poem.

Connectivity, I mean, not what the hoverfly is
or is not doing. The mating rituals of the insect world
I also do not mostly know, along with the word's derivation.
Twerk, I mean, not connectivity, although
connectivity, in some way, might be twerking's human purpose.

If I could connect to the internet, I'd look up twerk.
I do not think the word existed when I might have
asked for or offered it. Have I ever known a man who twerked?
I hope so. I would have given it my best shot,
had it been requested, or bartered for, years ago.

But perhaps in the interests of mass data harvest
and troublesome pop-up ads, I should look up
insectile abdomen bobbing, or insectile abdomen
bobbing that resembles twerking, or the mating rituals
of hoverflies, or just plain hoverflies.

THE LIMBERLOST REVIEW

By plain, I do not mean uncolorful but typical.
The hoverfly in question, which has been lapping
or licking for several minutes now, has a graceful tapering
but stingerless abdomen, blue black with bright yellow stripes
about the head and the still bobbing pointed but unmenacing tail.

By bobbing, I don't mean to verb my diminutive name,
I do not mean to make a gerund of Bob,
although here I am, in some way, Roberting, you might say.
Just taking in what the earth in this place and time offers
and connecting it to a life I barely understand in the world anymore.

By connecting, I do not mean electronically or digitally,
and by life I mean the life I live mostly unvisited
by hoverflies, and by hoverflies I mean this brightly striped
singular harmless licking or lapping and bobbing creature,
at home, as it is, in the air, desiring nothing but a taste of skin.

EDWARD HARKNESS

Dinner with Dick Hugo at His Picnic Table Littered with Drafts of Poems

He held out a platter of cauliflower,
steamed, then chilled for an hour, salted,
peppered, shiny with olive oil,
"Try this," he said. "Simple is best."
He learned the recipe from his time
in Italy during the war,
stationed at a US Army Air Corps base.
He was twenty, put on his flak jacket,
heated suit, affixed his oxygen mask
as his B-24 lumbered to 30,000 feet
to clear the Alps for the long run
across the Adriatic's dreamy blue.
He was the plane's bombardier, his job
to read maps, flip switches, peer through
the eyepiece of the Nordeen bombsight,
pull a lever. He didn't often talk
about the war, the missions he flew
over Yugoslavia, Austria,
Germany. When he did talk, he turned comic
"I was the world's worst bombardier,"
he once joked after reading his poems
from *Good Luck in Cracked Italian*.
"Not only did I miss the rail line
at the top of the Brenner Pass,
I missed the *entire* Brenner Pass!
What you've heard is true: we won the war,
no thanks to me." He rarely spoke of the time
his bomber pancaked in a farmer's field.
See "Where We Crashed." He walked away
believing wind more than he believed in the war.
What do I believe? Unsure. Maybe the chatter
of chickadees in the rhodies, leaves

lit up from last night's rain, each leaf a gift
I don't deserve, like Hugo's cauliflower,
steamed and chilled. Like the surprise of a letter
folded in one of his books I own, mailed
to me from an undiscovered country.
The typed pages ring back his voice, that dinner
when he shared his recipe for Simple.
The words ring back the muscled music
of his poems, symphonic as Beethoven's Ninth,
memorable as the taste of cauliflower,
salted, peppered, laced with olive oil,
served chilled on a porcelain platter
the color of the Adriatic Sea.

EDWARD HARKNESS

When Should We Say Something

I don't know. Yesterday.
Elsewhere, in a school classroom,
a missile strike
erases our one future

in some far-off country
always elsewhere. I don't know
how to reach out
to touch your cheek. The cosmos

you planted nod Ah, yes.
I don't know anything as
delicate as
those silky lavender blades

radiant from gold hubs.
In the late light of summer,
the last garden
tomatoes droop like blood moons.

On a sunflower crown,
a nuthatch clicks and winces,
a sound I love,
akin to a wagon wheel

in need of oil. Elsewhere,
a tank shell finds the bedroom
window of two
sisters asleep, neither one

yet 12. Their bed explodes.
Elsewhere, two sisters pass by
on the sidewalk,
neither one yet 12, chatting

to the clack of skateboards
on the pavements grey. Dear ones,
make a new world.
I've spent my voice. It's your turn.

TOM REA

Hats

One day I come home and find you've without
comment piled all the hats and some
few gloves from the top shelf of the back closet
on the floor under the south window
between the table and the plant shelf. From the pile
I rescue my own
first: the K-mart straw,
crushed, the coarse Hee-Haw straw
one of the kids once submitted to; the decent straw
cowboy, brim quality long ago
abandoned to the lottery of other hat
closet pressures—I have not the
reverence to properly maintain
a cowboy hat; my blue-billed
white-crowned turisto-nautical
Maui cap; my maroon Natrona County
Public Library cap with its good old silver logo
of Prometheus diving down from heaven with the fire
of curiosity for a benighted world—
good guy, old P., I think,
putting it on for a moment; and oh yes
three wool stocking caps, two still wearable (one
green-patterned, one red-) and the third,
gray with two green stripes and two
moth holes you could stick your fingers through—
the hat Sue Anne Steffey knitted for me in 1972, and which I last wore
two years ago that vividly
boring day when I earned $150
pretending endlessly to be a French-speaking fur trader
out at the Seminoe Fort at Martin's Cove.

THE LIMBERLOST REVIEW

Those plus two pairs of black ski gloves
are all I rescued from an uncertain
fate and as I stacked my hats tidily
inside each other and tidily
returned them to the shelf
only then did I think beyond myself
to your hats—far more interesting than mine—
and my amazement that you might be
contemplating their final disposal.
                                                  First
among these was the little maroon velvet
pillbox you picked up with Maggie that hot
hot day in Hoboken when you both
returned in smashingly retro square-
shouldered '40s summer dresses plus
little canvas strap shoes it was as though women
by a single purchase—you two at least—
could telescope
decades one into the other
and thus merge time
into a happy stew of Syndicalist possibility   this would
have been about 1980 after that hot hot
drive across Pa. to Sandy's wedding in my mom's AC-free Dodge
with Hannah in back in the car seat squalling poor kid
from the heat and having no water
we doused her (old story)
in ginger ale.
                                                  Second
among your hats was Derb's old
gray felt short-brimmed oilman's cowboy hat
a decent
item for a Casper landman of say 1964
and if mashed down definitely recoverable—
I never could wear it, it didn't fit me but
your dad's hat I'm thinking do you really
want it no more? What can this mean?

TOM REA

                                                        And finally
The wide-brimmed, round-crown floppy black felt
there's a photo of you wearing years ago before we met
wearing your homemade
denim skirt black shirt
knowing smile and smoking
if I'm not mistaken
a cigar. You must
tell me someday the occasion but even
in the photo one is struck
not just by your wit but the hat's
versatility; with one side turned up
plus an ostrich feather
d'Artagnan would not turn it down or
with all sides down and a wide horizon
not Flint McCullough but that other guy
the wagon boss on *Wagon Train*, he'd
wear it calmly
to save the day with his competent wisdom this week
from disaster…

So I pick it up and blow
on it and off the hat a thin
cloud of closet dust puffs
into this indoor air and right
that second my dream returns

of a wrecking ball swinging easily
at the end of its cable
from the tall, tall crane
headache balls we called them as kids
the headache ball so
slowly so gracefully so inattentively
collides with the brick wall of the vanishing
biscuit factory, dismantling it wall
by fragile brick wall.

THE LIMBERLOST REVIEW

From inside
some car I hear
no sound as the walls
crumble so our bodies
will crumble soundlessly so our bodies
will fall and someone will
toss these hats toward our open
graves but away they'll blow
up against a cyclone fence somewhere
and stick there fast with the other patient trash
pinned by the wind and waiting for absolutely
nothing at all.

CHARLOTTE MEARS

The Day I Fell in Love with Julia Child

An arctic blast about to sweep the under-prepared Deep South
in a pandemic, I prepare for the loss of electricity,
turn on the ice maker for the cooler to house the frozen food,
clean and chop all the raw vegetables from the fridge,
put rice on to cook in the crockpot then
leave the kitchen, whipped, plop myself down in front of the TV
where I find Julia, Live in black & white
in a 1960s kitchen standing behind the Formica counter,
sink to her right facing me unabashed with a hint of breathlessness.

Julia begins the first of four "easy potato recipes" using
"regular utensils" though the bent fork with long flat tines is new to me
as are the brown spots on the back of her quick hands.
Using the odd fork, she remarks how handy it is,
mashing precooked sliced potatoes in a baking dish.
Moving with a little panic from counter to oven behind her,
she suddenly feels hot, "so many boiling pots going."
In close-up, I see beads of perspiration above her upper lip.
She wipes her whole face with a wad of paper towels.

Keeping up her pace, Julia turns to prepare the topping,
"Nothing like cream and butter" without using measuring cup or spoon.
Instead she grabs a drinking glass, pours the cream and stops, "It's a cup."
She adds 2 ¼ tablespoons of butter from her knife, stirs it in until smooth,
pours it over the potatoes and puts the casserole in the oven to bake,
then turns to potato pancakes already poured onto her adorned non-stick pan
and ready to flip but the flip is a flop. She picks up the debris with her hands,
puts it back in the pan speaking of "needing courage" to flip a dish and
"It's not a disaster if this happens to you. You can make it into a different dish."
She also cautions, "Potatoes are odd and can turn brown. Brown doesn't
look well, and it would be bad psychologically for the cook."

It's clear I'm in the presence of wisdom and agile improvisation, which leads
me to wonder if I will be as flexible as Julia in the face of ice and snow boxing me
inside for days. My cell phone blasts an emergency warning. It's here,
the snow and ice already inches thick, my lights flicker. I run to the TV
for the news, but instead, without resignation, there she is
pouring another round of batter, watching for the bubbles to rise:
Look how Julia flips another potato pancake a second time,
following a previous public failure on screen, perfectly, beautifully, back into the pan
coincidentally on this teachable Valentine's Day.
Voila!

JEFF FEREDAY

Ruby, June 1908

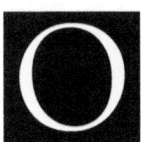Otis, the first-born, arrived early and almost didn't survive. Bowlegged and small for his age, he did not walk until he was twenty months. But his sister, Ruby, just over a year younger, had it far worse.

Ruby's legs were misshapen, with feet that dangled like dry leaves on a hackberry. Sometimes her legs moved in spasms or stiffened like drill steel, but they could not support her. Ruby's left arm was stunted, its twisted hand frozen downward. One of her eyes pointed off to the side. She could not speak, expressing herself mainly with grunts and moaning. Or unearthly shrieks. Sara and Henry, her bewildered parents, reckoned Ruby could express happiness sometimes, especially when she made cooing sounds, sort of like a mourning dove. She occasionally produced some word-like utterances, such as when she would work her mouth into a large "O" and come out with something sounding like "o-ussss!" One day Sara said to the boy, "I believe Ruby's sayin' your name, Otis. She only makes that sound when you're nearby."

The little girl could see, even with her crooked eye, and was always looking. She moved her face close to flowers that grew wild around the isolated cabin, even the tiniest ones, and would lie in the dirt with her face up real close, touching them gently with a tiny finger. Ruby could hear, and seemed to understand at least what she was not supposed to do, such as pee on the floor or throw food or knock things over.

By the time Ruby was four, she could roll around to navigate short distances, and at five, drag herself in a pitiful sort of crawl, hiked over on her right hip and using her marginally functional arm on that side. She'd rock onto her hip and produce an undulating, jerky motion, legs dragging, her little dress providing scant protection. Sara put poultices on the sores this caused, and tried to pad them with rags. Ruby seemed never to give up moving any way she could, grunting with the effort, collapsing, then lying there, then going again.

After great effort, Sara finally taught Ruby to use the outhouse, provided she was carried there and placed on the plank. At first someone had to clean her up afterward, using mullein leaves or rags or pages from the Montgomery

Ward catalogue. Even little Otis learned to help, and did not seem to mind. Eventually Ruby learned to do this herself with her good hand, at least passably, and her parents sensed the little girl took pride in this.

Otis and Ruby had three other siblings: Carl was three-and-a-half, Lester barely two, and Catherine fifteen months. As the others walked and ran and shouted and talked and sang and threw things, Ruby looked on wide-eyed, and tried in her own way to imitate. If the cabin door were left unlatched, it was a sure bet she would drag herself outside, usually smiling at her achievement and grunting softly. Otis often watched her do this, keeping an eye out as she moved toward the rose bramble or some other place she shouldn't be, grunting and dragging across the rough dirt where the chickens ran around, and the dogs. Otis would smile then, too. He once told his mother he thought Ruby was comical.

Managing the children fell mostly on Sara. Henry would be in the hayfield, or repairing the ditch diversion up in the side canyon, or working with the horses, the firewood, the garden, or the hand-cranked forge. In the fall it was hunting. Winter it was his trapline, using his webs over the snow and living on grouse and showshoe hares for maybe a week at a time. He killed the occasional cougar and turned in the ears for bounty in the spring when the game warden came down the trail.

Sara was a strong woman in only her twenty-fifth year, but she found herself muscle-sore most days, exhausted. Especially as the babies kept coming. She had enough work just nursing, changing and washing the rough cotton diapers, keeping the older ones occupied, fed, and safe from life's dangers in the remote river canyon. The toil was continuous.

Though her face already was becoming weathered, Sara was undeniably handsome, with thick, reddish-brown hair. When Sara was a girl her mother said it was chestnut. When brushing it, her mother once called it "luxurious," then piled it up and pinned it and said, "Sara, you look like one of them magazine girls." Sara thought about that comment now and then.

Now, Sara's own eldest daughter also had hair thick and reddish brown, but it often got caked with dirt, and brushing it was difficult. So she cut Ruby's hair short like a boy's and kept it that way. As the months of caring for the child wore on, and the difficulty, Sara finally cut her own hair. All the long luxuriousness she imagined, all the piled-up fashion of it, fell to the dirt outside the cabin. When she came back into the cabin the afternoon she did it,

Henry was startled, but said only, "See you cut it. Prob'ly save you some work now." Sara's eyes were red. She said nothing.

Helping Ruby with her breakfast of porridge the next morning, Sara recalled a similar beautiful summer day when she and Henry had left her parents' place just after breakfast and headed downriver on a trail that hung like a shelf hacked into the granite cliffsides, and sometimes grew faint or disappeared altogether in the sandy, slide-prone hillsides where the horses had trouble with their footing. The canyon stretched for over fifty miles and was surely nearly a mile deep. The river ran fast at the base of slopes that were all steep as far as anyone could see or imagine, except for the occasional terraced undulations, small basins, and sloping meadows that fetched up on an otherwise vertical landscape as places for game to graze in winter and for a few homesteaders to try to bust out garden plots or hayfields. A person hiking up a few hundred feet could look across the river and see peaks behind the canyon-top horizon, and going to the ridge top invariably revealed an even higher top, and more and bigger peaks beyond that.

Looking any direction from the cabin could remind Sara of the bright yellow flowers, and the purple and blue and red ones, that were everywhere on the slopes that first trip down, and the enormous yellowpine that dominated the landscape up beyond where the grassy slopes meet the mountain front, and the timber and tall shrubs and cliffs in the steep side canyons where the creeks come down from unseen places. She loved these side canyon refuges, grottos of syringa, ninebark, ferns, and mosses, all defying the summer heat, secluded and peaceful.

The sight and the feel of these things had calmed her then, even as, plodding down the trail behind the laden horses, she wondered how a person would ever find a spot flat enough to put up a cabin, much less grow gardens and raise feed for the stock. But they found this spot, and it provided enough room, even if their water had to be diverted from far up a side canyon, from a creek that cascaded into runs and pools between waterfalls. Henry had worked for almost two months digging, drilling, blasting granite, and building a wooden flume to bring the water out and around a mossy granite cliff to the "upper ditch" irrigating the top part of the pasture, then branching it into a lower ditch cutting across the slope below. The family survived on that water, and Sara appreciated seeing the irrigated pastures greening every spring.

Sara cleaned Ruby's face with a wet rag, then turned her attention to Carl, who had a runny nose. Sara administered a little whisky with honey in hot water. When anyone in the family was sick—which, mercifully, was infrequent—there was no real medical help. Shelton was a rough camp of a village, a nearly-played-out mining settlement with two saloons and miners' shacks, almost thirty miles away by trail. The one hotel had five rooms and doubled as a brothel. Its patrons were mostly men who worked hard but often were rendered unreliable by alcohol or some other demon that had pushed them into the backcountry in the first place. Sara had seen a Chinese herbalist there on a few occasions, but there was no trained doctor.

Sara could read, at least passably. Her mother had taught her at the remote ranch in another river drainage off to the southeast where Sara was born and rarely left until Henry found her and got her pregnant at sixteen. They got married on that ranch by a traveling preacher and moved into an abandoned cabin for several months before leaving that bright summer morning to come north, downriver, down into the canyon to this place where they considered themselves homesteaders though they hadn't filed for the land and which they talked about but still hadn't done, where the winters were supposed to be mild but really weren't.

She had never seen a real city, but had heard about cities and city people, picked up hints about them in catalogues, and marveled how it must be so much easier to live in those places. By 1908 she had lived in the river canyon for over seven years and had not been out, not once, not even to the county seat, which lay far to the west.

One early summer evening Sara was on her knees, cleaning up the mess Ruby had just made by grabbing the table's oilcloth and spilling a partially-mixed bowl of flour and eggs. Sara looked up as her husband came in, carrying a bucket of water. "Henry, I cain't keep up with this. I'm wore down." Two-year-old Lester was scrabbling around for some shelled peas on the floor, picking them up one by one and shoving them into his mouth. He sat down on the rough boards and held his hands out and squealed. Sara knew she was pregnant again. She had missed her monthlies a couple times and had thrown up that morning and a few days before.

Henry picked up a rag and squatted down to help his wife. "Sometimes things just go wrong," he said. "And with her, I just don't…" Sara looked over at him silently as his voice trailed off. She was thinking of it and figured

Henry was thinking it, too, what Henry had said last fall when he returned from Shelton where he'd spoken to an actual medical doctor in to hunt elk and the man had listened to his description of Ruby and told him to expect no improvement. The doctor said children with this condition, which he said likely was something having a name Henry couldn't remember and couldn't pronounce anyway, usually did not live for more than about ten years.

The silence persisted a little longer, then Henry stood up, tossing the sopping rag into a bucket. "But I think I found a pretty good gravel bar down by the Webster place, and maybe I can pan out enough to get those winter things we talked about." Sara looked at him blankly.

"And Ruby," she offered again. "It breaks my heart, but I cain't bear hearin' her wail and moan like that. And the sores she has. She's so tiny, and even almost six. With her draggin' around like that, I have to watch that she don't go over the bank. End up in the river."

Sara was watching as Henry looked sharply at her, and as his gaze went down to his boots. He sat down on a chair briefly, then stood up again, looking like he wanted to say something. His face sagged.

"It's just," she said, "I just . . . I mean I don't see how on God's earth anyone could… I cain't…" And with this she began to sob, bringing her hands to her face, her long, strong fingers spread out, the nails grimy. Henry pulled his tobacco from his shirt pocket, unwrapped some of the paper and bit off a tiny plug. He looked out into the dusk. The two ravens were just then coasting in toward the big fir at the east end of the cabin, riding the day's last up-canyon breeze and cawing as if to announce again their arrival to these humans they had adopted in some way. He put the tobacco back in his shirt pocket, turned and reached his hand toward her heaving back. He pulled it back without touching her and turned away. He went out, then muttered to himself, "I just don't…" Inside, Ruby shrieked.

Sara sat and stared out the window into the dimming sky. The yellows and blues and reds on the slopes had faded, the purple shadows turned to black. She dried her eyes with her apron. Otis came in the door with the scrap buckets he'd used to feed the dogs and the chickens. Coyotes were yipping and singing somewhere high up above the pasture. Ruby, who now was in bed in the shed-roof addition on the back of the cabin, gave out a sound.

"I got the chickens to bed, Ma, and put Minnie in the corral," said the boy. "Should I milk her?" From the back room Ruby let out with a high-pitched "o-ussss!" "I'll milk her, Otis," said his mother. "I'm glad you got them chickens put up. Now you git to bed yer own self." The boy went into the sleeping room. Sara heard him say something to the little girl, who became quiet.

The next morning, Henry was in the lower part of the pasture, well upslope from the cabin. The pasture rose above him to the base of the mountain front. He'd already harnessed the two horses and brought them up, ready to hook up to the worn, iron-riveted mowing machine. The past weeks of warm weather made this the time to get the summer's first haying done. The runoff was big, the ditches full. The two horses were tied to a shrub near the lower ditch at the downhill edge of the hayfield. The sky had faded from a dull orange-red into more intense brightness as the sun's bright line crept steadily toward him down the slopes to the west. The sun lit the outcrops, almost blindingly white and hot on the high western horizon of the narrow canyon. The high pale granite lost its definition in the glare.

Henry got the animals connected to the mower, its cutters suspended between two big steel-rimmed wheels, their spokes rust brown and rough as sandpaper. To test the rig, Henry had the animals pull a ways through the timothy and clover that grew knee-high, walking beside the machine on the high side, holding the long rawhide lines. The wheels rotated gears that slid the serrated blade of the cutter horizontally back and forth against another zag-toothed blade, fixed in place and also rusty. He had filed the serrated edges, which made them look like bright silver "w" shapes on the red-rusted parts. Holding the horses to a slow walk, the machine produced a "shuff-a-shaw" sound, uneven, the cogs and arms rattling and clanking. Henry regarded this for a few moments and then whoa'd the animals, who immediately put their heads down and resumed grazing, pulling the grass out with a twisting upward pull of their heads, their large, dark and liquid eyes seemingly peering out at nothing in the world. Stalks of forage ratcheted into their mouths, bent and disappeared.

Henry fetched an oilcan and thumbed the plunger to oil the axels and the cutting mechanism, then pulled a heavy wrench from a canvas bag tied below the seat and loosened several square nuts. This allowed him to set the blades a little lower and align them better against each other. As he tightened the last nut, he said to himself, as if giving an order to a subordinate, "Forge out a new pin for that right side," noting a place where a worn part allowed a wobble in the arm to the upper blade. Forging would have to wait. Today it should work well enough.

Replacing the wrench, Henry set the oil can on a rock just above the ditch and climbed onto the rusty seat atop a wide piece of spring steel curving up and backward above the cutter blades. The horses started moving again as Henry pulled the lines up off the animals' backs, saying, "Move!" and then, to himself, "Good team now, boys." The mower still made a racket, but the sound was more agreeable, more steady. "Shuff-shaw, shuff-shaw," with the harness hardware clinking in time with the horses' plodding. "Can get some hayin' done today." He stopped the team. The horses looked back at him, like they were surprised. Henry sat quiet a minute.

The hillside pasture sloped unevenly above the cabin, forming natural terraces—"benches," Henry called them—with each undulation, a slope followed by a flatter section, then steeper again. Looking up from the bottom, the pasture's stairstep terrain alternately revealed and then hid a person, or deer, or the horses walking up or along it. He looked down toward the cabin, whose roof ridge was barely visible over the contour below. He began mowing.

The two dogs appeared as bobbing heads barely above the cut forage downslope, coming up toward him over one of the brows. Behind the dogs Otis's head appeared, then his short body, coming through the cut grass, floating above it. The boy was carrying a stick in the crook of his arm like it was some kind of Kentucky long rifle. The dogs came up and sniffed around the horses, skittering away at the lifting of a rear hoof. Henry stopped the team.

"Pa, Mama says you should come." Henry climbed off and looked in the direction of the cabin, where there still was nothing to see but the wide canyon and the trees and brush on the opposite side. "Says she needs some help on account of Ruby, and she's tryin' to can them wild chickens you got yesterday. Ruby is screamin' pretty bad. Crapped on herself." Henry looked at him a few seconds, then looked away and said. "Okay, let's go down and see about it."

Otis looked up at him, one hand on the stick, which he now held with its small end jammed down onto the dirt like he was a little old prophet come from Galilee. The other hand stroked a dog's ear. Henry sat for a moment. He pulled his tobacco out, fingered it for several seconds and then put it back in his shirt pocket. He got Otis up on his lap and hied the horses, guiding the mower into the shade of an enormous yellowpine off the edge of the field. He tied them to the base of a shrub. "Don't want you boys runnin' off. Come on, Otis boy," he said. "Let's get you down there so you can help your ma."

On the way down they stopped at the place where the lower ditch cuts across the slope, running fast and cold, and then smoother and widening out where Henry had used pick and shovel, and the horses pulling a Fresno scraper, to scoop out a pond. He'd constructed a dirt and stone dam with a wooden gate that could close off an eight-inch cast-iron pipe set into the bottom of the dam as an outlet. The pond had been difficult to build singlehanded, which was part of his pride in it. It allowed him to pool up a lot of water and direct it into smaller ditches to water a garden and an orchard further down. There were three other homesteads on the river, but Henry's place was the only one with an actual reservoir. It kept gardens going even in late summer when some folks' ditches went dry.

Just upslope, an enormous lilac shaded the pond just above the dam, looming invitingly above a small flat spot. "Pa, this is where I can set in the shade and look around and nobody can see me," said Otis. And then, pointing at the high steep hillside across the river, "Yesterday I watched two Chinamen goin' up over Jim Crick on that trail. They never saw me one bit."

"It's a fine spot for a lookout," his father replied. "I've spent time a-sittin' there myself." Otis flopped down on his stomach and, grasping a lilac branch, slid slowly down the little grassy slope to where his lips touched the surface of the cold water. He sucked up a long drink. "Be careful thar, son. Still lots of runoff." Henry went to his knees, then also bellied down and drank, the toes of his boots holding into the slope. He pulled himself back from the edge and gazed a moment at the little whirlpool snaking down toward the outlet pipe below. Then he stood and pulled out a handkerchief and wiped his face. He looked up into the sky like he was expecting something from that direction. "Come on up outta there," the man said, leaning down to help Otis scuttle back from the water's edge. "Let's see if maybe we can help with Ruby."

At the cabin Sara sat on a stool, holding a clean dress for Ruby, who was on the floor rolling first one direction then the other, gasping and moaning. The stove fire burned away under a bucket of water and a lidded canning pot. Four grouse had been picked clean and hung against the wall, a string knotted around their feet. With the stove going it was sweating hot in the cabin. Empty canning jars sat on the window sill. Sara hardly looked up.

Henry lifted the grouse by the string, their flesh already dry and slick on the outside, and put them on a cutting board. He ran a knife across a whetstone a few times, then quickly quartered the fowl, dropping the pieces into the jars. "That might help a little," he said, unconvincingly. Otis stood in the doorway, the dogs milling behind him.

Sara nodded. "Been a hard mornin' here with her," she said, reaching for Ruby. Henry had noticed the child's soiled dress outside, crumpled in the dirt against the cabin wall like it was thrown there with some force.

"Why don't I take her up above with me today," Henry offered. "She might enjoy bein' there while the horses work." At this Sara looked up at him sharply, pulling Ruby into a sitting position while grabbing the child's good arm to thread it through the armhole in the ragged dress made from one of Henry's shirts. Ruby lolled and drooled and made a guttural sound so deep that it seemed like it was coming from somewhere beneath the floor. Sara didn't respond for a bit, then said, "Well, it's a nice day. Maybe Otis could watch over her." Henry was silent.

Sara finished with the dress and stood up, then bent down to pick up Robert, the two-year-old, who had come in from the sleeping porch with his two siblings close behind. Carl was carrying a No. 1 steel trap with a wood rat dangling from it, dripping blood. He grinned at Otis, who grinned back, saying, "Nice job, Carly. Do you want to give it to the dogs, or should I?"

"I do it!" shouted Carl gleefully, heading toward the door. Otis smiled. Spitting on a rag, Otis wiped a couple of blood spots off the floorboards.

Henry gently gathered up the mute girl, who smiled up to him, writhing and letting out a squeak. Henry hugged her a little bit, then held her like her mother did, riding on his left hip. "Or maybe just the two of you," Sara said, turning away.

"Otis," Henry said, "make sure Carl can get that trap open, and fill the kindling bucket. Help your ma here a bit." Otis looked up at his father and then at Ruby. He touched her gently on the arm, his little hand lingering for a moment and looking into her eyes like he was communicating in secret. He picked up the bucket and went out.

Otis was at the wood crib, barefoot as always in the summer, filling the bucket with the wood chips and bark that had accumulated around the splitting block, when his father strode past and angled up the hill with the little girl, now facing forward in his arms, legs dangling and swinging and her head lolling back and forth with each stride. "Otis, you help your mama with the work here this morning, and watchin' the kids. Ruby and I are going to get to the hayin'."

Otis finished filling the bucket.

Henry carried the girl upslope, walking quickly, much more rapidly than he normally would, breathing hard. He noticed he was already sweating. He reached the lower ditch, crossing it on a rough-sawn plank. Turning right, he headed upstream. The lilac came into view, and the deep wide pool with its water lazily swirling. He set the little girl down on the little flat spot in the shade below the lilac. She cooed, seemingly with pleasure, at the new surroundings. Ruby eyed the pond and made her familiar grunting noise. She looked up at her father.

"You sit still there, now," he said. "I'm gonna be just up the hill thar. You'll see me for most of the time. At least 'til we get up there a ways." It occurred to him that he had never spoken to her like this, addressing her as if she understood. But he repeated the admonition. "Sit still there." He paused, thinking. "Best you can, leastways." Then he added, "Little Ruby." He turned and walked slowly up the hill toward where he'd left the team, their heads disappearing and then rising back into view as they grazed just over the next rise in the hill. He did not look back.

Ruby sat in the bunchgrass under the lilac and swiveled her head around, taking in this place she had never been. She shifted around to look toward where her father had gone, but he had disappeared, uphill somewhere. She began to moan. This was the first time she had been truly alone, where she could not hear or see at least one member of her family. She let out a shriek, which dissipated instantly into a breeze moving upslope as the day warmed, rustling the lilac leaves and faded flower bunches and spreading what remained of the lilac scent. She turned again, using her good arm to maneuver as usual, and this put her at the edge where the grassy bank cut steeply toward the reservoir. She looked down in the direction of the cabin. "O-usss!" she called in her unearthly wail. "O-usssss!"

Otis, setting down the pail of kindling next to the cookstove, looked up at his mother. "Ma, do I need to help you with the canning, or can I go up and watch Ruby? You said I should." Sara did not look up. She was on her knees again, this time fastening a flour sack diaper on Catherine, while Lester, the two-year-old, held up a green bean, partially chewed, and offered it to his big brother. Otis took the bean, looked at it, looked at his mother. He handed it back to the toddler, who shoved it in his mouth. Finishing with Catherine, Sara finally stood and turned to regard Otis. "Well, I could use some help here for a while, but I've got the canning mostly done. Why don't you pick some service berries on those bushes by the lower garden?" She motioned with her head to the plot lying downslope from the cabin, toward the trail that made switchbacks down to the river. Pulling down a saucepan from where it hung on the wall, she said, "Put 'em in this. I think Ruby will be all right with your pa up there for a while. I can get this canning to boiling in a few minutes. When you're done you can help with the wash."

Otis took the pan and went out, called the dogs and trotted with them down to the berry bushes. He glanced up the hill occasionally, but saw nothing. As he was finishing up, he looked uphill and this time spotted the team, pulling his father across the slope on the hay mower, so far away that the sounds of it could not be heard, even if there weren't the constant sounds of the river and the breeze coming through the two big firs. The team and equipment were visible only for a few seconds as they passed over a high spot at the end of their pass. Otis looked for his sister, wondering now for the first time how his father could hold onto her and run the team at the same time. He saw no one but his father on the seat.

Otis set the pan of berries on the chopping block as he went by on his way up the hill, not looking to see if his mother was at the washtub on the far side of the cabin. The boy trotted up the path toward the hay pasture, and the ditch, the dogs behind him. He was panting as he crossed the little plank bridge.

Carl did not see his brother go up the hill, but he spotted the pan of berries. He ate a few, then picked it up and headed toward his mother. Sara was outside next to the wash table, tipping the bucket of hot water into a large washtub.

The upper branches of the lilac fretted in the breeze, the shady spot beneath it still not in view. As the boy topped the last rise where the ditch cut across, his father was just passing out of view again beyond the brow that hid the top of the field.

As the team straightened out across the slope, Henry caught sight of Otis as the boy turned and looked out along the ditch, froze for a long moment, then sprinted down out of sight. Henry stopped the team, dropped the lines, paused, then climbed off. He began walking down, leaving the team untied, their heads dropping down to eat, pulling the timothy grass out in bunches, working it into their mouths in jerky increments. The horses watched impassively as Henry, now striding fast, disappeared.

The hem of Ruby's dress floated on the pool's surface like it was perfectly arranged on purpose. Otis, out of breath, shouted when he saw her, head submerged, her one good hand near the surface and moving, but sinking down. "Pa!" Otis never learned to swim, so his instinct was to stay on the bank. He lay on the dirt and inched down as far as he dared. He grabbed a bunchgrass and stretched one arm into the water. But he could not reach his sister. Then she turned slowly, head-down in the circulation pulling toward the outlet below, moving slightly closer to him and sinking. He lunged. He lost his grip on the slippery grass. The water closed over him gently, cold and deep and quiet.

Otis grasped his sister's dress and struggled to get his own head up, but the girl's good hand gripped his shirt and weighed him down. Then they were both under and wrapped together, her holding him with her surprisingly strong functioning arm, and him with her garment in one fist, his other hand struggling vainly to separate from her. His bare foot felt the pull from the rush of water going out the pipe. Otis flailed and tried to kick his legs. His face broke the surface but then went under again. The boy's foot was in the iron pipe at the bottom of the dam, its rough edge cutting into his bare ankle. The suction held, fixing his foot there, lodged next to her lame arm. Ruby's grip on him relaxed.

Sara struggled up the hill, a tiny child on her hip and two toddlers trailing behind. She could not yet see Otis, or Henry, who was flat on his belly on the top of the dam, reaching into the water, his face turned to the side, almost submerged. Sara felt a wave of nausea and paused. She heard the dogs up above, barking frantically.

Henry strained downward. He pushed aside the girl's dress, the hem of which was moving just under the surface, and managed to grab Otis by his hair. He pulled the boy up far enough to grasp an arm, then was able to scuttle back up and yank the child free of whatever was holding him. The boy's face, blue and calm, broke the surface just above one of Ruby's tiny misshapen feet, which undulated in the swirl like a dead fish.

The little boy's face was serene. His eyes and mouth were open, unmoving. Sobbing and disoriented, Henry pulled the boy up into the little flat under the lilac, as if this were a magical place that might bring him back. He slapped the boy's face, shouting his name. The boy was not breathing. He turned the child over and struck him between the shoulder blades repeatedly, then picked him up and held him head down and hit him some more. "Otis! Oh, *please!* Otis!"

Nothing.

From somewhere, Henry heard Sara screaming. ■

Reflections on being present during a winter meditation retreat (Sawtooth Mountains, photo taken with a Holga camera). Photograph by Katherine Jones.

HOWARD LEVY

North Country

She and the Great Dane walk the January road,
the snow so thick in the woods
even the Dane prefers the plowed macadam
and whatever is humming in the frigid air
could not be loneliness or complacency
because those are contractions
and this morning multiplies
ice pendants doubling and tripling the sunlight.

Her ancestors, Scots and French,
landed near, the North Atlantic
smashing, lapping this continent's edge
as they left their boats and stood solid
on the shore, wondering how now
becomes next—
to be molded by the land's granite and tamarack
to stand tall and restrained.

Walking in this unbridled cold and snow
she wonders what stew of ambition
or rage or hope or courage,
what stew of having nothing to lose
sent them to the boats.

And strangely how that has come down to her, centuries later,
as the rectitude that illumines,
makes her in her place a daily quiet local gleam.

Had

"Had" is
a Parisian junction, a lexical Gare du Nord:
here this modulation of tense, the 15:45 that had arrived from Prague
and that delicate placement of action, the 7:30 from Hamburg
by way of Rotterdam, all the ins
and all the outs of people
who had surged over the platforms,
had dined, had slept,
had made love and conversation:
living pluperfects.

And when I follow it with "I", "had I,"
that phrase suggests I choose to register regrets,
that I have been too late in finding things,
such as real words
that turn a woman's affection into a bonfire.

Some poems *should be*
catalogues of regrets, cowardices, errors,
defeats spread out like small town stations,
but others should be kites, reorganizations
of how one can absorb the sky,
blue bisected by those kites

and the kite's tail in the wind
rippling as a flag of invitation, flying
in the belligerent beauty of the present tense,
that now of those great steel hands of the station clock.

KEN RODGERS

Elegy

I failed
Your funeral
And excused myself for work
A lie

Or something more twisted
Grown from wobbling will
And doubt

Grown out
Of a long past trapped between
The shattered windshield
Of a sixty-four Buick LeSabre
And splintered bones
Of your broken back
After I shoved you
From the cottonwood tree
In your back yard

Visions now
52 years gone
Folks on the sidewalk
In front of the Nazarene church
A place you never
Would have stepped
Your battered brogans

Gray Stetsons
Lizard skin boots
The vatos, too
You hung with smoking Acapulco Gold
Drinking Red Mountain Vin Rose

THE LIMBERLOST REVIEW

And the Basque herders
Who loved you like a brother
Their champion once
Their grand little
American man
Before needles
Took over
And meth
Mixed with coke
Mixed with smack
Heated and cooked
In your little
Flame-stained spoon

They say it was an accident
On your blue and black Harley
Headed for Tucson

The freeway pillar
The last obstacle
To stand in your way

SAMUEL GREEN

Chopping Block

> *Samuel Johnson's father had a book stall*
> *in a busy market in Uttoxeter. Once . . . he*
> *asked his teenaged son to tend the stall for him.*
> *His son refused. Many years later, Johnson confessed*
> *he'd gone to the sitet of his long dead father's shop in*
> *a bone-rinsing English rain, and stood there for many hours*
> *in penance.*

Seven cords will get us from one side
of the burning season to the other,
enough to feed the heater stove
& our plain black Amish kitchen
range. The rounds balance
on this block I bucked from a huge
madrone windfall. Tough wood
when it's dried. The face is marked
with odd hieroglyphics left
by the blade of my maul & the double-
bitted axe. We burned mostly fir
in our family house, felled & bucked
from our own five-acre wood lot
on weekends with an old yellow
McCullough—when my father
could keep it running. It was one
of my chores to split the rounds,
stack them in the shed, & fill
the woodbox next to the stone
fireplace in the house. He got home
from work after dark in the winter. All
he asked was an hour after school
at the block, but I ducked that chore
whenever I could, leaving it to him
as often as not. He tried to catch up

on his days off, seldom got more
than a week ahead. Easier to do it
himself than argue with a son
who seemed always to hide
in his books. I'd stand at the kitchen
window & watch him swing maul
in a slashing rain, lit by the porch
light, afraid he'd one day come
home to an empty house
if my mother couldn't stay warm
enough. My poor father, dead now
ten years. Well, we need to keep warm
ourselves, so there's no redemption
in slogging away at this block, except maybe
those days I make myself work in the rain,
like today, the huge drops hammering
on the fiberglass sheets of the woodshed
roof, rinsing the metal sides of the wheelbarrow
tub, tearing the carefully made web
of an orb weaver stretched between two
porch railings, wrapping the body of a termite
in silk, each bright strand trembling.

DAN ARMSTRONG

The Open Secret

Hear that? Those faint sirens in the distance? They're coming for me. Yes, as certain as dawn tomorrow, they are coming.
I know too much. That's it. The whole damn thing. I just know too much.

Not such a great quantity, mind you, just a critical fact. And I can't let go of it. I've been screaming it out my window all night. My neighbors must think me drunk or mad, shouting at passersby while others try to sleep, shouting at passing cars, shouting at dogs in the street. Someone must have called me in, complaining of my vulgar reverence in the middle of the night.

You see, something else, some larger conceiving thing, is dwelling in my mind—most likely in all minds. I'm not certain if those of the sirens are trying to hide this or if they simply don't know. One way or another, they are after me for daring to announce it—daring to scream it out loud.

And I am afraid.

The thought is so unsettling reality shifts about me like headlights in the night. I try to assess this thing within me, but it does no good. It's too big. There's nowhere to start, nowhere to end. It just pours out whenever I speak. And to anyone I might tell? I get a shaking head or a sad, suspicious look. But I can't deny what I feel so strongly. I will doubt everything else until I can reconcile with this thing within me. The starry sky seems a lie, all history a cheap novel, geometry a slick magician's inverse—compared to this knowledge, this living truth that I know. That I feel.

I'm scared and I'm confused. Scared of what I know and confused by what to do with it—other than shout it out!

But the sirens are growing louder, and I can see the whirling blue lights reflecting off the buildings several blocks away. They are coming for me. I'm not sure what they will do with me when they get here, but I don't intend to find out.

I hurry out of my apartment and take the backstairs down to the garage. My car is old but it's fast. I climb in and insert the key. The huge engine thunders to life with a rumbling that echoes off the basement walls like moving shadows. I motor out of the garage and out onto the street, where I finally give the beast the thrill it's looking for. I blast down the pavement, windows wide open. "Try to catch me now!" I scream to the wind.

* * * * *

At 120 miles an hour, an hour before dawn, riding this trafficless silver ribbon into the desert night, I try to clarify something in my mind. Some kind of conceptionary virus, *a way of seeing things*, that overwhelms me—except at speed, high speed. The sense of motion clears my brain. Ceases my doubts. Replaces my anxiety with crisp assuredness.

At a hundred and twenty miles an hour, my head conjoins with the night. I squeeze more into the pedal. The wind whips at the gray threads of my hair. I can almost stop my thoughts entirely with this speed and exhilaration. Almost . . .

* * * * *

I've been subtly, but severely mutated—and so, very probably, have you. It's taken my entire lifetime to come to this awareness and to swallow what it means. That the damage has been done. That there's no turning back.

The first serious poisoning took place almost a century ago. The real regret is that it's taken us so long to fathom its extent, its vast implications.

Hiroshima. Nagasaki. That was all it took genetically. Two severe burns and the global gene pool was irrevocably altered. Tack on another seventy-five years of experimentation in the field—Three Mile Island, Chernobyl, Fukushima—a scorch here, a sizzle there—and we have an inevitability born on the wind like radioactive confetti. Helical melt down! Musical proteins! Groping sapiens fumbling with the dice of destiny. Seven. Eleven. Snake eyes!

But far more striking than the physical deformities are the cerebral mutations that no one seems to notice. Viruses of the mind more subversive than three-eyed infants, spreading like spilled white paint on a page inked with words. Minds blown like tattered flags in the sunset. Somber purple veined with electric orange.

Imagine it. One grand cerebral virus threaded through the galaxies in breeding spirals of brilliant light. Leaving us with two choices. Deny it, as those with the sirens must have, or embrace it, as I dare to! Even more than that. I scream it to all who will listen. And thank God for this car. Unfurling my being with its gale of motion. Its speed!

Blast these inklings in my head! Rejoice in the surety of my soul! Forge into this infinite thing we share. Mutable, infinite, timeless—consciousness! But there I go again. What is it that prompts me so? What stares out from these shifting pools in my face? No dog. No harmless spider lurks in this furless catacomb. It's something grand, something eternal. Something that's taken a thousand human lifetimes to unfold. The truth told as fiction. Black seen as white. Not only are we not alone, we are not separate!

* * * * *

Picture me. Driving as fast as my car will go. For the distraction of it. Some jittery old man, frightened—and confused. My bones shake out the last tangential steps of a deep astral boogie so strong it drags the rest of me along like a cheap suit on a hanger. You got it yet? Open, unspeakable, overwhelming, ENTHRALLMENT! That's what it is. It's just too much. Too much for me anyway. So, what do I do with it? Crush it. Package it. Put it on TV?

No, I'll shout it out until they catch me.

At a hundred and thirty miles an hour, one hand upon the wheel, one upon the keys of my laptop, I struggle with all of this. Filtering through are these words you read now. Do you understand anything I'm saying? Any of it at all? Or am I just another snake-bitten lunatic groping for long forsaken visions beyond the pale? Or—or is all this that I feel simply true? Ungraspable but true.

* * * * *

Unfulfilled lifetimes rage in these re-coupled chromosomes, while what remains of a young boy's dream persists behind this steering wheel and 450-petroleum breathing horses. Years piled upon innocence. Pure light layered over and over again with ash. And now, frayed, worn, shaking, fighting bitterness, I push a single digit up through what I've been buried in to poke indignantly at these plastic keys. Daring to illuminate something inside your head—like a cryptoglyph on an irradiated screen—S-O-S. To you out there. You behind the fluid orbs—this is it! I scream to the passing landscape. SEE IT! FEEL IT! BE IT! I scream through my fingers. Take hold and fathom this thing while the opportunity avails!

* * * * *

The darkness pales away. The blazing eye of God peeks its sultry radiance over the horizon. My friend the night dwindles in piercing beams. I, the culminating moment of one man's term on earth, offer this lone memory of hope. There isn't much else I can offer, but this one memory. This one deep and puzzling memory . . .

* * * * *

I am alone, stumbling downward into a dark cavern, my domed Golgotha, with its two great windows to the stars overhead. Down I go, over charred books, tattered manuscripts, and bones, piles of bones, into some intruding passageway. The light is dim. My reason unclear. But some dark secret lures me deeper and deeper, until at last I no longer care what I find, only that I proceed (*as in this hurtling vehicle that I drive*). Grisly death takes my hand like a friend and leads this cowardly swamp fellow, this moccasin of a man that I am, deeper, eeling down this dank rat hole in search of some forgotten scribbler's wisdom.

    A bleak visage phantoms in the velvet darkness. It hovers over me, this ancient, alien face, stiff and grim. I cry out in fear. I cower. I roll onto my back. The face presses into mine. The light of a thousand generations explodes within my head, searing my cerebral cortex like the surface of the sun. And still I squint up through the glare of all prevailing truth, and dare, and dare those clear-seeing eyes, that solemn Adam, progenitor of consciousness, to illuminate me further. And it says, with soft temporal cymballing, age upon age, the words I have waited all my life to hear. "Life is eternal." So simple, so frightening—and so true!

I roll over to my knees and gather my feet beneath me. Turning, I reverse my dark descent. The passageway is blocked and narrow, choked with debris and ash. Burnt offerings from times past. Lots of ash, ash on ash. I breath it in as I fight my way up through the trash and rubble, choking, hacking, retracing the course of my life, grimly gripping this miraculous and all-sustaining piece of knowledge, The Great and Open Truth. That I will bring back for all humankind to finally know for certain. Nothing else in life matters to me now but this. It drives me upward, out of the darkness, through curtains and curtains of ash, until at long last, I see the faint silhouette of two moons, no, twin halos of starry mist, my upturned portals to Mammon's world. I have made it. I have made it back. And in this—what I have called a memory of hope—I entertain no hope of reaching those outside—*you!*

Still, with what little focus I can muster through the press of futility, I pierce one finger through the diaphanous shroud of dust and gently prod the keys, one by one, while driving at this insane terrestrial speed to slow my thoughts enough to focus and to type: *Yes, yes, there is mystic meaning to our being. Yes, yes, oh yes . . .*

The speedometer reads 135. The sky is burnt orange. Filaments of cloud trace blood red above the plain. The silhouettes of telephone poles like puppeted crucifixes string out along the black ribbon of asphalt and vanish into the distance. A haunting siren wails upon the wind. In the rearview I see the lights of another car—blue revolving lights!

I nudge the needle up to 140. The tires sizzle with the speed. The engine throbs with secondary resonances. Sweat beads across my brow. I can't outrun myself, but they will never catch me.

And yet they do.

My tank can only hold so much fuel. And they have legions of squad cars to track me from county line to county line. I am at last theirs . . . *or so they must imagine!*

It's true. I'm a sad sight for ordinary eyes—an old man. My bony legs swing to the street to confront these swaggering hulks in uniform.

"Going a little fast, old boy?"

"Just trying to clear my head," I say, turning a single sallow eye to the man who spoke, as though the impinging viruses swarming within my head are nothing.

"We clocked you at 140. That's far in excess of reckless driving in this state. Got a license, mister?"

I notice he's looking suspiciously at my laptop on the passenger seat. This makes me more uneasy than the question about my driver's license. "No license, officer."

He turns mirrored lenses to his partner. The other brute nods behind the same while admiring my flashy red rig. He turns back to me. "How about a registration?"

"No registration either, officer," I say to my reflection on the toe of his gloss black boot.

"Guess we better take you in, old timer."

"Fine," I say, standing unsteadily. "Just drive fast, my thoughts are threatening to catch up with me."

"What's that?" asks the officer, disbelieving—*this old man is offering a slack attitude to go with his total disregard for the speed limit?*

The other, sensing a quickening in the air, reaches instinctively behind his back for his handcuffs. "What did you say?"

"Nothing," I mutter, presenting him with my wrists. "Nothing at all." ∎

MARGARET KOGER

The Black Racer

And I wanted to stay beside the snake
in the road there where the clouds
rub shoulders with the bay

as it laps against the barrier isle.
I wanted to slow the slither of snake
in the road and to know why the dust

had failed to disguise the slide
of ebony scales. I wanted
an I and Thou moment, a burst
of one in one.

But the racer in the road slid quickly
into the scrub, leaving the mark
of a snake, a memory of a path

in the sand where I stood as it crossed
too rushed to raise its head,
to look about as racers do.

I could only imagine the flash of scale
as it climbed the closest tree,
but later I would see a black coil

hunger exposed beneath the salt oak
a spry detail beneath our pink balcony
on this barrier island blocking the sea

from overtaking the tranquil bay
the racer coveting a meal of nuthatch
as the flock swarmed the tree

the snake eyeing supple branches
hearing the twit and twee of
blue and gray in the dark leaves

both of us watching shiny avians
flutter in the sun and settle, claws
grasping the bark as they pecked.

Not a snake in the road now
the racer ready to twine the trunk
to snatch a blink-of-the-eye bird.

Snake and prey and I, meant
to enact this (un)remarkable tale:
a story prompted by the glimpse

of a black racer crossing that road
there where the clouds
rub shoulders with the bay.

MARGARET KOGER

A Conversation with the Poem "May Morning"

Deep into spring, winter is hanging on.
  —James Wright

Perhaps he'd truly wasted his life, or Wright
could have just loved lying in a hammock in 1961
as a chicken hawk floated over Wm. Duffy's farm

but how enchanting for him to later recall sunlight
on a Mediterranean morning as the last of Winter
grumbled in the shady recesses of his pine-clad

lairs, "bitter and skillful in his hopelessness."
Out in the Great Western Basin sixty years later
a heatwave laps at the heels of summer solstice.

May vanished and June passing into a July born
in blasts of sexless heat; for tomorrow, tomorrow
will be hot, hotter; memories of the Old Man,

his distant chill forgotten, his bitterness a shadow
on the wracked planet where wells dry and deserts
spread. How we ache for more nourishing green.

Sol, angled to singe seedlings, fracture stones
melt pavement, fever the homeless, and smite
fools who run in the sun. Sol Invictus, scalding.

Wright recalls a May morning when Winter flails,
"Angry to see the sea-pale boulder alive with lizards
as green as Judas leaves," but "he still believes."

"Poets in the Gutting Shack" by Greg Keeler. Acrylic on canvas.

MARK GIBBONS

Out in the Garage

The spinning rod in the rafters,
the broken fly pole I duct-taped
for the kids thirty years ago,
broken storm windows, a pick,
a sledge, a Pulaski, rakes and
spades, three snow shovels, scraps
of wood and sheet rock, propane
tanks, boxes of paper (mostly
old bills) and unwanted books
along with worn-out toys,
some kind of smoker/cooker
loaned to me that I've never used,
a corner cabinet filled with
outdated fluids and filters
for vehicles long gone, a roll
of screen, a short hose, the drop
light and extension cords, a stack
of tires, empty flower pots except
for some crushed beer cans, bags
of recyclables, old inner tubes,
a drop cloth, plastic buckets full
of more dusty-useless junk . . .

And I'm reminded of home,
the place I grew up, and that old
dirt-floor garage which held the same
kind of forgotten shit now cluttering
this one being challenged by armies
of ants piling earth over footers
and the fractured cement floor . . .
flashing back on that bamboo whitefish
pole, a one-foot section of Milwaukee
rail we used for an anvil on the bench

strewn with jars of rusty bolts,
washers and screws, plus those pinholes
of light shining through the tar-paper
roof. It makes me think how
temporal our lives are, how quickly
or slowly the days change in my mind
and on the ground—the dirty whirl
of it, me, one more floating speck
lingering out in the garage.

GEORGIA TIFFANY

Variations on a Theme

She stared at the oak door,
its narrow growth rings, tiny peephole,
brass knocker like a fist,
and the way he opened and closed it
for no reason, just stood there,
opening and closing.

The draft swept through the room
and up the chimney,
made the ash glow again.
A few sputters of flame
burrowed out of the coals.

She could hear the firs, now,
stirring up the chill
that had assaulted the house last night
and readied the air for snow.
She was thinking about trees,
how they can become something else—
fire, wind, earth.

On just such a day as this,
it could come down from high country,
hurl itself against the north window,
stagger any attempt to imagine
ever being warm again.
She liked snow, the honesty of it,
the thoroughness of its intimacy.

That the door was heavy, she knew,
and how loud it could slam shut.
Surely he would leave soon,
before she could think of anything
important to say.

The Cat
In Memory of Mary Ann Waters

As she sank deep into her chair
to watch *As the World Turns*
because she was dying
and because she wanted the intrigue
of someone else's life,
the cat settled on her slippered feet
and began breathing as cats do.

Its body expanded and withdrew,
its motion stroked her ankles,
sent pleasant little tremors up her legs.
The absolute absence of any moral
reason for it being there
struck her as erotic.
Nothing she had ever done
compared to now.

Outside, late afternoon sun
stopped at the porch rail.
The cat noticed,
lifted itself into an uncomplicated pause,
and abandoned her for a view from the sill.

O. ALAN WELTZIEN

Through the Darkest Valley

I

At Fort Craig National Historic Site
near the Rio Grande
eyes scan the *Jornado del Muerto,*
desperate trains of *carros y carretas*
along this northern arc
of the El Camino
that curves ninety miles east
away from the river,
too much *canon*, no water
no shelter, only isolated desert ranges
relieve the flat plain
pocked with low brush.
Night journeys of earlier centuries
searching for a spring.
No hay agua aqui.
Abandon all hope
ye who enter here.

II

Directly east
just below the *Oscura* Mountains
I picture the Trinity Site,
dark death on a scale
unimaginable to desiccated travelers
centuries gone by or ourselves.
Did Oppenheimer or Groves pause
when selecting the Site
within the *Jornada*
well before July 16, 1945,
before the 100' steel tower

and transport of The Gadget
in a coupe from Los Alamos?
Did they remember the name
when the cloud ballooned
to 38,000' in seven minutes?
Do visitors who enter
via the Stallion Gate
only two days a year,
long line,
who approach the shallow crater,
glance at jade flecks of Trinitite?
What trinity do they discover?
Do we remember the first
mushroom cloud,
grainy black-and-white,
baleful image
of childhood and beyond,
bulging bubble of deepest fears?

III

Just past the Dark Mountains
The Malpais and these names—
journey, death, Trinity, dark, badlands—
collide in irony,
nuclear chain reaction,
endless echo chamber,
their half-lives far beyond ours.
Fallout spreads in language,
rains through now.
Oppie quoted Shiva,
"I am the shatterer of worlds."

O. ALAN WELTZIEN

Though we "walk through
the darkest valley" on this journey
who walks with us,
comforts us?
I turn away
clutch hope
stumble back *ahora*.

**Jornada del Muerto* translates as "journey of death" or "journey of the dead man"; *carros* are "wagons," *carretas* are "carts"; *No hay agua aqui* means "there's no water here"; *oscura* means "dark"; *ahora* means "now."

"Stanley at Night" photo by Jim Stark.

BARBARA OLIC-HAMILTON

The Uncounted

"Forgot my book," Ray said as he opened the door of the Mountain Village Service Station.

Behind the cash register Lyudmila looked up from the book she was reading and watched him walk into his office.

Why did Raymond tell her that? She did not care why he left and returned five minutes later, and now she shivered as the 20-degree cold slipped inside with him. Two inches of snow after midnight—that is what the radio said. Not enough to worry locals. Or her. She knew snow from Ukraine. High-elevation Stanley now had 36 inches snow on the ground. No surprise. Normal for January here in Sawtooth Valley.

Ray returned carrying a book. "Looks like 14 of us at the Supper Club tonight. Not sure who's keeping the lights on in the rest of the town since the winter population is 16. With Matt cooking and Marlene waiting tables, that counts everyone in town."

Of course, he did not count her.

Ray started out the door and then paused. "You don't need to keep the lights on here. Close up early, Ludie, and go home."

Lyudmila looked up from her book. "I might do that, Raymond. What book is tonight?"

"*Lab Girl* by Hope Jahren." Ray turned to look at Ludie. "About a woman scientist who's bipolar and takes a lot of shit from the men she works with. Survives it though. She's single like you, but ten or fifteen years older unless you lied on your visa application." Ray smiled at her.

It was tease, like joke between cousins. Not a threat to turn her into authorities for lying. It was still difficult to tell with these Americans. "I am 28. See my passport."

"Sheesh. I'm just joking, Ludie. I believe you."

"Good."

Ray tapped *Lab Girl* against his thigh. "It's a pretty good book. You want my copy after tonight?"

She shrugged. "Sure. Not much to do at night in winter. Just read. I will take book."

"The book," Ray corrected. "Sheeez. Seven months in the U.S. and you still can't add 'the' before nouns."

Now Ray is language teacher. "I will take the book. Thank you, Raymond."

"Sandy's in charge tonight, so she and Mick will probably get into it again over the whole women versus men thing, you know."

Lyudmila nodded.

"Okay. Good night. Oh, and change out the calendar behind you. It's not 2018 anymore, Ludie. There's a new one from State Farm in my office."

She nodded again. "Good night, Raymond."

Lyudmila watched him walk across the plowed asphalt next to the gas pumps. Then Ray stepped into the deep footprints he made when he came from Supper Club.

Much older than her, but still strong. Sixty-three, Ray said on his birthday last month. He was stocky, a bearish man with dark hair and a full dark beard. Lumbered like a bear too. If he were taller and younger, he might frighten her when he got angry and threw newspapers at walls. But she was almost his height and much younger, so she saw him as more teddy bear than grizzly. When winter began in October, she did not have one coat warm enough for here. Ray lent her his coat and it was not so big. Just right with a second sweater. She asked to keep it and he said sure.

She was not a soft teddy bear like Ray. There was no softness on her, except her boobs, which were soft, and more than a handful. She was told this more than once. She kept her straight, amber hair long enough for one of their ponytails. Best hairstyle for mountain biking or skiing—her two favorite sports.

Lyudmila went into Ray's office. Before he left, he added another layer of cologne. Oh, Raymond. Too much good smell is too much. Even in America. She shook her head, got the new calendar and replaced the old. She flipped ahead to May. Five months and her H-2B visa expired, and she would go home to Ukraine. Her mother would be disappointed she came home with no American husband. That was her dream, not Lyudmila's.

She gave the book group 15 minutes to settle before she shut off all lights and locked up. Grabbing her backpack, she crossed Highway 21 to Mountain Village Lodge where she worked as a housekeeper. Parked behind was a 1966 International Scout shared by all visa workers. It was parked next to a small guest cabin with six bunk beds and a kitchen. Last summer all six beds were filled with H-2B workers, and they shared the old Scout. But only she stayed for winter season so both guest cabin and Scout were hers now.

She didn't mind staying alone. She liked quiet after the summer madhouse with never enough sunlight hours to finish all cleaning. Plus, she worked many nights to midnight then at the service station. In winter, hours were less at both jobs.

So was her pay.

Lyudmila started the Scout. She put on non-latex gloves stored in her backpack and covered them with mittens.

No city lights here. Not like her hometown. Here mountain sky was dark, deep dark, and stars so bright. Valley snow twinkled under a waning moon. Bright enough but not too bright.

She missed her home in Lubny more during winter. She missed laughter from her family and their snug, warm flat crowded with visiting cousins and aunts. Pierogi with butter and sour cream. Small glasses with vodka warming your soul as you sipped it, not huge glasses of cold beer these Idaho people gulped down in winter and summer.

Her name was Lyudmila.

She hated being called Ludie.

She missed being counted as one of the people.

* * * * *

Heat vents rattled and weak heat started coming. Time to decide. Michelle or Sandy? She went to Michelle's in October and Sandy's in November. January now, so enough time between visits. Sandy being in charge gave an extra twenty minutes because she would be last to leave. Plus, grandchildren visited Sandy at Christmas. Maybe all things not put back where usual?

Lyudmila put Scout in gear, drove out the parking lot, and turned right to go west out of town. First crossroad she turned left on Iron Creek Road and left again two miles later. At Obsidian she turned and bounced up rough road to the log cabin owned by Sandy Ferguson, retired pharmacist from Twin Falls. Lyudmila followed tracks left by Sandy's 2011 Chevy Suburban and parked next to her cabin's side door. She opened a wood box and felt inside until she found a key on a hook. Same as last summer when she helped Sandy move old furniture and boxes stored in an outbuilding. Lyudmila unlocked the door, took off her boots, and left them on the mat inside. After shedding her coat, hat, backpack, and mittens, she checked her watch before she took several plastic shopping bags from her backpack.

    Where to start?

    Music.

    Sandy's sound system was excellent, and she had classical music. Local radio played country or old rock and roll, not classical. Lyudmila walked stocking-footed into Sandy's living room and checked. Good. CD player already loaded with Beethoven. She adjusted her gloves, then pushed buttons and turned volume softer.

    Next?

    Freezer.

    Lyudmila looked for big multiples. She skipped two steaks, one whole chicken, one steelhead fillet, and one lamb shank. Too few each. She counted eight packages ground venison, five elk sausage, and six of chicken pieces Americans called "tenders." She took one each. Seven frozen strawberry jams, so she added one to her bag.

    Pantry next.

    She took one of everything six or more. Three types of soups, so one each. Plus, one tuna fish, macaroni and cheese, spaghetti noodles, and spaghetti sauce. She chanced taking one jar of peanut butter. It was one of four so could be noticed, but she was hungry for peanut butter, and it was so expensive in Stanley. She wanted one hamburger meal mix but thought Sandy might miss it since there were only three. One column Ritz crackers, two bags microwave popcorn, and one package graham crackers—each out of open boxes. A handful each of tea bags, sugar packets, mini-containers of half cream—all from other open boxes. One can peaches and one fruit cocktail. From Sandy's special racks for sodas, she took two Pepsi, two Mountain Dew, and two Kirkland root beers.

Refrigerators were trickier. Stanley people filled their pantries with multiples but not so much refrigerators. But this time was a gold strike! From her Christmas guests, Sandy still had many extras of cheese, salami, and butter, so Lyudmila took one each. Since Sandy stocked up for company, Lyudmila checked her liquor cabinet. Maybe extras there too. One bottle of tonic water and one red wine would go with her. Three duplicates would stay. She would buy a small gin for tonic water. Maybe a lime. There were two but taking one was easily noticed.

She looked at her almost full plastic bags. That would feed her until next book club.

Lyudmila checked her watch. There was time. She went into Sandy's bathroom. She needed toothpaste and hoped Sandy had multiples. She did. She also had an open box of condoms. Why not? Lyudmila might get lucky again with winter tourist. She tucked two into her pocket.

Beethoven was over and Lyudmila turned off Sandy's sound system. What else?

Books.

Sandy had several bookcases, but they were neatly arranged. No piles of extra books. Any missing ones would be noticed quickly. But in corner next to big chair there were two paper bags filled with books. Probably donations for library for-sale rack. Lyudmila shuffled through them and found three paperbacks with handsome men on their covers. She rearranged books and kept same ones on top. Both bags still looked full so Sandy would not miss them.

Lyudmila went back to the kitchen to start taking her filled bags outside to Scout. Then she remembered Sandy kept special snacks and treats in a cabinet above her refrigerator. Lyudmila got a stepstool from the mud room. Did getting this stepstool keep Sandy from eating too many treats? She looked like she ate plenty of them, stepstool or no.

Lyudmila took one small bag potato chips then checked cookie boxes and candy bags. Oh, her lucky night! Tucked in back were four boxes of Bahlsen cookies. Again. In November there were three boxes of Choco Leibniz Dark Chocolate cookies and Lyudmila chanced taking one. These German cookies were so good and so expensive. Now they were here again. Four boxes of her favorites! Sandy probably bought them for her grandchildren for their Christmas visit. Once last summer

Sandy bought all fourteen Mars bars Mountain Village had. She said her grandchildren were coming to visit and her grandson Bradley had sweet tooth. She always hid her expensive cookies and candy before he came so he did not eat them all. Mars bars were—what did she name them? Decoys. He ate them and left her other sweets alone. Sandy must have bought many decoys for Bradley because there were four boxes of Choco Leibniz left after his Christmas visit.

One of Lyudmila's rules was never taking first one in any row. Superstition maybe, but if first one was touched enough it had less dust than ones farther back. So, if she took first one, someone might notice dust on boxes left. She did not want to leave any tracks behind her, so she reached for the third box. When she pulled it out, she saw it had a piece of paper stuck to it with a message—

I noticed you liked these. Enjoy!

Lyudmila wobbled on stepstool. Sandy knew someone was in her cupboards. Maybe she knew who? Not many people in Stanley now. No, it would say her name if she knew. Sandy only knew other hands once touched her special treats.

Should she take cookies? Or leave them and let Sandy think no one was in her house? Maybe Sandy planted other tricks she did not notice? Her frozen meats tonight were arranged very perfect. What about soup cans? In November were they alphabetized? They were tonight. Sandy was particular. Very neat. Very precise. Maybe everything was alphabetized before but she did not see?

But her note was not angry. More an announcement. Sandy saw someone because she saw empty space. Sandy did say enjoy. Sandy did not threaten. She would take one box but leave one with note. Carefully she removed one behind box with note and readjusted spacing.

Her watch showed it was time. She took two careful trips loading her shopping in Scout without leaving puddles of melted snow inside. Kicking off her boots one last time, Lyudmila walked through Sandy's house checking to make sure she left things like they were when she got there.

She did not want her presence counted here.

Stanley was dark when Lyudmila drove into town. As she turned off Highway 21 into the hotel parking lot, she saw headlights in a side street behind her. A Chevy Suburban followed closely by a new Ford F-150. They turned onto the highway from the street in front of the Supper Club. Both headed west out of town. The F-150 was definitely Ray's and the Suburban looked like Sandy's. Odd because Ray lived the other way, in Lower Stanley.

Maybe they were going to continue their book talking at Sandy's? She thought about Sandy's bathroom with its box of condoms. Maybe they were going to play Lab Girl and Lab Boy tonight? Lyudmila smiled. That was fine with her.

She planned to open red wine and eat several Choco Leibniz cookies. Lick dark chocolate off first. Start reading book with cover picture of bare-chested, muscle man embracing woman with boobs mounded over corset top. It would soon make her warm in that special, dreamy way. And with no one else in guest cabin, she was free to do whatever brought her pleasure tonight.

Only then would the last light in Stanley be turned off. ■

*The most beautiful light is usually the most ephemeral.
A passing storm, horses on alert, and a fleeting rainbow.
Photograph by Glenn Oakley.*

GREG KEELER

Hmmm

Imagine it in terms of football.
One team follows the rules, and
the other team invents their own
rules as they go. One team obeys
the referees, and the other team
threatens them or gets new ones.
Which team would you be on, the one
that plays fair and loses gracefully
or the one that wins? Hmmm.
Now imagine it in terms of petunias
and dandelions. The petunias smell
nice, come in many colors and need help.
The dandelions smell like pretty weeds,
come in one color and grow in spite of you.

Squawk

Even in my own yard, the magpies
try to boss me around. They seem
to be mad at me for not being
able to understand them. I've
tried to do what they squawk at me.
Their main instructions seem to be
feed me, go away, or, even better,
lie down in your yard and die.
That would sort of combine
the first two. Sometimes I'll hear
them out there, bossing something
else around, usually a cat with its
ears back. Cats don't seem to
understand them any better than I do.

Just Guessing

What's the difference between having
a conversation about something and just
talking about it? I'm guessing that having
a conversation about something is
more important than just talking
about it. For example, you should
have a conversation about abortion,
but you should *just talk about* the
weather. If you had a conversation
about the weather, it might wind up
being about global warming. If you
just talked about abortion, it might wind
up being about what assholes men are.
Have a conversation about that.

Rendered

There are places you can go where people
suck the fat out of you and other places
where they will feed you the fat. There
are many more of the latter than
the former, thus the abundance of
fat people in need of rendering. You'd
think you'd have to go to church to
get rendered, but most likely your local
hospital will do it for a substantial fee.
Like the fat from your body, the money
is sucked directly out of your account
because the sucking of the fat is not insured.
The feeding of the fat is much cheaper. There are
places where they'll feed it to you in your car.

New Dog Tricks

What doesn't kill you makes you boring.
Absence makes the heart grow tranquil.
All that glitters requires a source of light.
Do unto others before they do unto you.
A fool and his money will soon be hers.
People in glass houses have good views.
A friend in need is a burden.
A rolling stone gathers speed down a hill.
A penny saved turns green after a while.
A stitch in time brings you closer to death.
The unexamined life lasts longer.
Spare the rod and save some energy.
To err is human; to forgive isn't.
He who laughs last isn't very bright.

"Interstate Blues" by Greg Keeler. Acrylic on canvas.

FLORENCE K. BLANCHARD

Trip Advisor Visits Atomic City

For a dystopian side trip
while passing through Idaho,
Atomic City fits all our criteria
for a self-guided tour of
America's Industrial Legacy.

One mile off Highway 26
No Gas, No Services.
You can't miss it.
McGhees, an abandoned bar
with broken windows
sits at the corner
amid tumbleweeds and trash
slowly collapsing
into the Snake River Plain.
Greetings from the locals:
"You Loot, We Shoot,"
sprayed across the front.

There's not much to see
in this ramshackle town:
weather-beaten trailers
broken-down houses
RVs with names like
Hideout and Jazz
stripped down cars
up on jacks
clusters of scraggly trees
a neon Bar sign
that twinkles in the dusk.

THE LIMBERLOST REVIEW

Once it was home to
a couple hundred people
with security clearance,
splitting atoms to power submarines,
dumping Plutonium into
the Snake River aquifer,
secretly experimenting
with molecular catastrophe.

On January 3, 1961,
a nuclear reactor
the size of a small grain silo
exploded in the desert.
A worker pulled a rod too far.
Some say it was over a woman.
Three employees obliterated
so radioactive that
the Atomic Energy Commission
buried them in lead coffins
sealed in concrete.

The population
dropped to 25 or 41
depending on the source,
but you no longer have to
wear a Hazmat suit.

A three-person Council
runs the town.
Crime is immaterial
although a recent feud over a
a city boundary got so heated
the mayor ordered
a second deputy
from Bingham County
to keep the peace.

FLORENCE K. BLANCHARD

For lodging
we recommend the quirky
Lost River Motel in Arco
thirty miles west:
all rooms in primary colors,
garden gnomes outside,
one wall plug per room;
for dining, Pickles Place,
home of the Atomic Burger,
Open Seven Days a Week.

"Still Life #3" by Janet Wormser. Oil on linen on board.

BOB BUSHNELL

Apart

Funny
how I miss
those things that
bothered me.

At Eighty,

I don't
ask for much—
three meals a day,
a warm bed,
and a lamp
beside me
as light fades,
and night falls.

I am
grateful for
today, and
hopeful for
tomorrow,
but tired of
talking to
myself.

What Is What

The cosmos
Keeps itself
Spread apart
And dark a lot,
And makes it hard
For us to tell
What is what
From what is not.

Curiosity

. . . Is something I
Came down with
When I was a kid
And never got over.

For a long time,
They couldn't
Figure out what
Was wrong with me,

But said it was
Going around
With a few other
Kids my age,

And should go away
As I grew older,
"But keep an eye on him,
Just in case."

BOB BUSHNELL

Cloud Bullies

A tall cumulus
blew east with his buddies,
their flat bottoms
scooting over an
invisible surface,
looking for a parade.

In the Beginning

He and His angels
argued all morning
and afternoon,
but still could not agree
on what to call
each rotation
of the world
He had just created,
until He yawned,
stretched, and said,
"It's getting late.
Let's call it a day."

"Ave Maria," linocut by Riley Sophia Penaluna.

GARY GILDNER

The Angel Thing

Mrs. Terrain and Father Boyle sat in her Jaguar in the circular driveway of her Saint Bald Mountain home. She was behind the wheel, her right hand on the priest's bare left knee. His head lay back on the headrest; his eyes were closed, hands folded in his lap. She had not yet started the car to deliver him to the rectory following his run and one of their spontaneous conferences, as she called them. Several quiet minutes had gone by before she whispered, "Francis, darling, you're scowling."

"I'm sorry."

She gave the long, lean line of his jaw a loving appraisal, resisting an urge to slide her finger up the deep dimple in the middle of his strong chin. She also resisted pinching his elegant nose—urges she would happily confess to him later. Suddenly—her tone theatrical, that of an irritated mother—"We just had a wonderful time and you have the face of a petulant, spoiled child!" She leaned over and kissed his cheek.

"Thank you," he said.

"How do you feel?"

"I was just wondering what the particular shade of red your car is called."

She looked at him and sighed. "Firenze Red, I believe."

"Thank you."

"Now tell me how you feel."

"Fine."

"No—you're feeling guilty."

"I am guilty, Arlene."

"What we do," she said, "is between us. It has nothing to do with anything or anyone else. Not the church, not Father Quinn being gone . . ."

"Dear, dear Arlene." He opened his eyes and looked at her a long moment. Then tried to give her a smile.

"Oh, Francis, you know that I am with you. That you are not alone. That everything we've promised each other is true and will remain true. That we have not in our hearts deceived—"

"I know you are trying," he stopped her.

"Yes, I am trying. As are you."

"It's only, dear Arlene, that I cannot *not* feel . . ."

She waited a moment. When he didn't go on, she whispered. "I do know, my darling."

Arlene Terrain was thirty-eight. Not quite two years ago, on the eve of her birthday, she buried Mr. Terrain. Father Boyle conducted the service. He also became the young widow's confessor; she soon began telling him—in addition to her largely venial sins—that she would be helpless without him. Francis Boyle, though he looked much older than her, was Mrs. Terrain's contemporary; where she'd had doting parents and comfort growing up, he was an orphan raised by a childless couple with little time for play or affection. He'd learned to work hard on their rocky hillside farm. Once when Arlene Terrain seized his hand saying she felt worthless, he told her she had no idea what she was talking about.

She replied, bitterly, "I know, I know, my invaluable immortal soul," and burst into such pitiful sobs, pressing his rough hand to her wet cheek, that he kept his mouth shut about what he had really meant, feeling deeply ashamed.

"I'm so sorry," she'd said, realizing how awful, how spoiled, she sounded. "But obviously the rest of me feels damn worthless—sorry again—grabbing you like that. Forgive me, Father. For my big mouth too."

Nonetheless, this tall, attractive, educated woman now giving him his hand back was worth many millions, thanks to Mr. Terrain's fierce attention to his real estate, trucking, and cattle empire. Collecting herself, she confessed that she had enjoyed the advantages and pleasures Lester Terrain's money could bring her far more than she ever enjoyed him—one of her gravest sins. Most of their decade together—"if you can call us being together"—she despised him, his money, but mainly herself. When he collapsed and died suddenly, at fifty-eight, she wept tears of gratitude—another grave sin.

"I have wasted my life, Father."

"Nonsense."

"I try to believe that helping you all out at Redemption and my other acts of charity make up a little for my deceiving Lester, but that is nonsense, Father. I am a first-class hypocrite."

"A loveless marriage is as common as—"

"—dirt?"

"Pretty much."

"Do you truly believe that?" she said.

"In a world struggling not to choke on itself, yes, I'm sorry, but I do."

"You are an unusual priest," she said, "if I may be so—"

"—you may be so."

"Then let me say something that's been on my mind a lot lately and makes me crazy every time I hear it, which is whenever another maniac with an automatic weapon commits yet another massacre we are urged to keep the victims in our thoughts and prayers. Especially when the victims are children. Thoughts and prayers do nothing—nothing—except spread more sad, hopeless, pathetic words around. What in hell *is* that, Father?"

"What you said—sad and hopeless and pathetic."

"I am so relieved I've never heard you utter such nonsense. Forgive me."

"Nothing to forgive. Thoughts and prayers will not stop bullets."

"Well, then, may I tell you, since we are moving to a new level, as it were, that I feel funny calling you Father."

"Call me Francis," he said.

"Are you sure?"

"You've been calling me that for some time. Now and then."

"I have?"

"Or my hearing, like so much else these days, is failing me."

"You must be teasing."

"As a boy," he said, "I never lived in a house with a real floor."

She only looked at him, puzzled.

"My floors were all dirt."

"I am so—"

"Then I went to seminary. I was eighteen. The church quote 'rescued me.' The only mistake it made was not throwing me to the Jesuits."

After several moments, she managed, "Still, I don't quite understand what this means regarding our—"

Urged by a soft, demanding chaos plowing his head, heart, and loins, he drew her close and kissed her.

* * * * *

The day's last light falling across their sated bodies, she was first to use the word "lovers."

"Lovers?" he repeated, a bit uncertainly, as if being brought close to such a powerful word required a credential he wasn't sure he possessed.

"Yes," she said. "And as your lover, Francis, I feel so . . . oh I don't know . . . "

"Expiated?" he said.

"Yes! Thank you."

How could a lost man not embrace this woman?

* * * * *

Father Francis Boyle was the assistant pastor of Snake River's Church of the Redemption, which had been started almost fifty years before in a former hay field by Father Leo Quinn, the pastor. It now sat on a rich green campus that included a school with grades one through eight, a convent, rectory, and a cemetery. The students came from Snake River, nearby hamlets, and from pockets in the deep outskirts, the latter areas principally inhabited by Hispanic and Native American day laborers whose children did not have transportation and were bussed in. Father Boyle had got up Redemption school's bussing operation and a tuition relief program soon after becoming Arlene Terrain's confessor.

He also introduced school uniforms, with practical assistance from Mrs. Terrain, advice from the nuns, and Father Quinn's full support: blue jumpers and maize or white blouses for the girls, khaki trousers, maize or blue polo shirts for the boys. Some parents objected, grumbling about out-of-step styling but mainly about lack of choice and socialism. Several incoherent volleys on the socialist theme—even from citizens having no connection to Redemption—were not unusual for the conservative neck of the woods in which they lived. These discharges came from self-described patriots and appeared in the Letters to the

Editor section of the Snake River *Star-Ledger*. The letter responding to such patriots from Walt Shuttleworth, the town's outspoken librarian and a published poet, inspired, as his letters usually did, the most discussion. He'd said, "Dense complaint is of course a holy right. As witness our defeated president who maintains, without a bit of proof, that he was cheated. Many Snake River folks repeat this garble; some send their issue to Redemption. These children have a fair shot to succeed like anybody else—in the classroom, in games at recess, in seeking a mate if they choose. As a devout atheist, I greatly admire the Redemption sisters, their dedication to knowledge and respect for facts, how lyrically they respond to the comedy of ignorance in an indifferent universe by calmly walking arm-in-arm down Main Street."

* * * * *

Francis and Arlene applauded Walt Shuttleworth's public letters. So did Leo Quinn who, like his assistant, had known poverty as a boy, though he long ago escaped the mean burdens of its legacy.

"Does the presence of so many comfortable parishioners bother you, Francis?"

"I try to shade my eyes from their shine," the younger priest said. "And without bitterness. But I'm not always successful."

"We can't accuse you of being a strict moralist, then, regarding the end justifying the means, I take it."

"We have work to do, as I understand it."

"Indeed," the pastor smiled.

Not aging well, Father Quinn contributed what he could to that workload, but the truth forced him to leave more and more of the heaviest lifting to Father Boyle and Sister Good Counsel, the school principal. Then he suffered his first heart attack. A large man to begin with, who enjoyed his John Jameson and his dinner, he had been warned more than once by Dr. Henry Aguirre to avoid this, avoid that—advice which Mrs. McCloud, the rectory's longtime housekeeper, repeated like a harpy. The two of them, the old priest complained to Francis, were wanting to be counted among the darkest souls on earth. They even tried—imagine it!—to convince Mrs. Kelly, his devoted cook, that the rosy-cheeked pastor's favorite foods had been declared fatty death warrants and therefore forbidden! He'd quickly pressed his palms over that particular noise, telling Mrs. McCloud *he* was still in charge, not her.

    As for a major pain in the ass, none could top Bishop Richter! Who was ignoring Father Boyle's petition to be appointed part-time visiting chaplain at Killish, the State's largest, most isolated prison a two-hour drive away. The blasted drink question! Based on a pair of measly though unfortunately back to back and noticeable enough incidents at Altar Guild and Knights of Columbus functions that the bishop got wind of. A most righteous man, Richter. "Hasn't Father Boyle," Quinn wrote his superior, "been completely sober, faithfully attending his weekly AA meetings up in Lewiston, driving more than an hour each way, going on eighteen months now?" Richter's brief response to Quinn was, he thought, vile: "Some habits call for a lifetime to change."

    Thus, Francis Boyle, for now, would stay put full-time at Redemption, saying his share of masses (Sunday and daily), hearing the bulk of Saturday confessions (because he got through them so quickly), which included forgiving the paltry offenses the nuns committed against their sisters and God (if He could bother with such sins as Sister Immaculata pilfering the Hershey's Chocolate Kiss Sister Macrina was saving for after Lent). Father Boyle also taught the eighth grade Religion class. About the latter, Sister Good Counsel nervously approached him on almost a regular basis to discuss yet another of his "somewhat unusual" questions for the youngsters—most recently, his asking wasn't the Job story less about "patience" and more about "a prideful God" not wanting to lose "a bet" with Satan? And he conducted the Monday night Devotions to Mary, plus half the funerals and weddings—most of the latter lavish enough to make his stomach ache.

* * * * *

During his long and getting longer time in that comfortable parish, his sweat-soaked dreams took him back more and more to the slums of the city where he'd previously served, to its tenderloin, its scarred and angry and often frightened bloody nobodies whose moveable church—when they were craving to have one, or barely caring, or dreamily blinking at the mention of such a concept—could be anything from a hole in the wall to an old storefront-turned-clinic where they came trembling from abuse and despair to get their dose of methadone or bowl of hot soup; and while the filth and self-pity he found in those slums mirrored his own need for the sporadic bender and repulsed him, he could not refuse the skimpy morsels of hope those horrors occasionally laid among the pieces of glass and whisky-stink within reach of his own table—a table, however, now laden with a faith in corporeal love and its glow.

* * * * *

"I prefer calling it," Arlene Terrain might say, *"being in your corner,* the double entendre very much intended. What would you call our relationship?"

"An occasion of sin?"

"And we smile talking like this."

"I don't deserve you, Arlene."

"I know you're not being sarcastic."

"I hope I'm never reduced to such cruelty."

"The Episcopalians *will* take us in if we need companionship."

"I know."

"Meanwhile?"

"Meanwhile, following our AA meeting, my fellow whiskey priest Joseph and I exchange our sins and forgive them."

"Until?"

At such moments he could only helplessly look at her, chalking up one more conversation in which he begged her forgiveness and forbearance.

"Let me be your angel, Francis."

"Yes, the angel thing."

"Because I love you."

"Dear Jesus, I do not deserve you."

She held the man and kissed the wet lashes of his eyes.

* * * * *

Then came Father Quinn's second and fatal heart attack. Bishop Richter sent his assistant, Father Kavanaugh, to represent him at the funeral. It was Father Quinn's wish that he be buried in Redemption Cemetery, that smoothly groomed, pretty knoll, specifically between the two stately oak trees he'd planted to shade his final resting site, when all those years ago he found his grand hay field. "I actually prefer this ground to heaven," he'd said more than once, standing beside Francis Boyle but looking into the branches overhead. "I like the idea of birds sending their songs down to me, and raising their young to do the same." In his will he requested that Father Boyle conduct the service, adding, in his own hand—with Mrs. Kelly and Mrs. McCloud witnessing—that he hoped the bishop could bring himself to understand that Father Boyle was the proper choice to succeed him as pastor of Redemption.

* * * * *

Arlene Terrain might open her front door to find him in shorts and sweatshirt; she knew he had just made another long run to clear his head for a little while of the demons that would not leave him be.
    She held him.
    They held each other.
    He had no thoughts.
    Or he traced the sun spots in her hair. Was made glad.

* * * * *

Eternities or moments later, he would wake, get out of bed, and study the sky. He would remember it was morning. He'd remember time and be grateful for how it helped organize our thoughts and duties. Our promises. He'd say Mass for the assembled student body, drink coffee afterwards in the cafeteria with the women who were gathered to prepare the day's school lunch. He met the Religion class. He asked for a show of hands: "Who believes that a loveless marriage is not a big deal?" The students were used to Father Boyle's far-out questions; they gave this one serious consideration, judging from the bowed heads and eyes closed in thought. Finally, no hand was raised.
    "Good," he said. "Very good."

* * * * *

Father Kavanaugh phoned to tell him that Bishop Richter was appointing a Father Helmut Kruger as Redemption's new pastor, with Father Boyle as his assistant.

"What is a Father Helmut Kruger?" he said to Kavanaugh.

"Pardon me?"

"It sounds war-like. Kruger even rhymes with Luger."

"Are you feeling all right?"

"Skip it," Father Boyle said.

* * * * *

He met with Mitt Kowalczyk, who had charge of Redemption's physical plant and was thinking maybe they should get a new furnace for the elementary school wing. But it would be expensive.

"We *could* get by another year or two with a repair job," Kowalczyk said.

"Do I see a scowl?" said the priest.

"A scowl?"

"What's your view of the matter?"

"Well, a repair job is cheaper, but—"

"Put a new one in," the priest said. "By the way, Mitt, did you know that Episcopalians call someone like you a sexton?"

"I'm an engineer," Mitt Kowalczyk said, "not a bell-ringer."

"I'm counting on you to install the best furnace there is," Frances Boyle said.

* * * * *

He told Mrs. Kelly he was having his dinner out and that she was free for the evening.

"If you'll excuse me, Father, but are you losing weight?"

"Losing weight?"

"You look so thin."

"I feel just the opposite, Mrs. Kelly."

"All those bare meals you take in your room," she said, shaking her head.

"Are you praying for me, Mrs. Kelly?"

"I am, Father. Every morning."

"Only in the morning?"

He took the woman's hands, which were pressed together. Turning them over twice, he kissed their red knuckles. Her mouth fell open. He slowly wagged a finger from left to right.

"Words," he whispered, "will only spoil things."

He kissed her forehead, nose, and lips, winked, then left.

* * * * *

He put on shorts and a sweatshirt and splashed cold water over his face. Down in Leo Quinn's office, he sat for a while at that happy man's large walnut desk—a formidable piece given to the priest by an old banker—and took up Leo's ink pen. On a sheet of Redemption stationery he wrote, "Thank you," and signed his name.

Standing, he took his time stretching, pausing now and then to salute a sequence of framed photos he admired—of Leo as a round boy in Illinois kneeling with his dog, capped and gowned graduating from high school, beaming between his beaming parents as a brand new priest, standing in his hay field with a shovel.

"Lucky fellow," Frances Boyle said.

* * * * *

He ran along the base of Saint Bald Mountain. A scent of old leaves and his own stink enriched the air, perfect for picking morels. But not now. Heading back to the rectory, he was feeling pretty good.

In Leo's office again, he went to the man's private cupboard—off-limits to Mrs. McCloud—and found a nearly full bottle of Jameson. He took it outside and sat on the ground among Mrs. Kelly's robust pots of rosemary and mint and rows of tomatoes and onions. The sky was clear and filling with stars, plus here came a nice round moon. Or round enough. Both of his hands gripped the neck of the bottle between his bare knees. Francis Boyle, a man who read the humane essays of Montaigne, the lyrical yearnings of W.B. Yeats, sat almost perfectly still and said, "I can have one drink if I feel like it."

He unscrewed the cap and smelled the sweet forbidden where his mouth would go. An image of Arlene came to him . . . approaching on her hands and knees like a cat . . . like the orange tabby that lived in the barn of his boyhood and would play with him, jump on his chest, roll over, bring him a mouse she had caught. She came forward from the foot of the bed as he lay on his back with his knees bent and his feet flat on her cream-colored sheets, taking in shorter and shorter breaths.

"Open that gate wide, monsieur. *S'il vous plait?*"

She had been to France many times, loved strolling beside the Seine in the fall when the linden trees turned gold. Ah yes, she said, there was a lean young secretary from the Spanish embassy—"though not as thin as you, darling"—whom she'd met on one of the bridges and was bringing up only because Francis had teased her once too often, saying her sins were a child's sins, a nun's sins, except, yes, for marrying Lester Terrain. The young Spanish diplomat, a poet actually, simply smiled and tipped his hat. That was all it took, she said, less than a year after making those marital vows. Now might he raise the status of her sins?

* * * * *

In Mrs. Kelly's garden, Francis Boyle felt his face go hot with shame, jealousy, and sexual pain—a vicious stew of memory and desire. But she had forgiven him all his questions and regrets about their passion.

"And," she said, "to prove I love you, I could promise to try very hard to be only clever and useful and behave strictly as your occasional night out cook. If that kind of crazy promise makes any sense, and a cook is all you need now and then—for nourishment—and to be encouraged. In a world designed, as you've often reminded me, for growth, work, decay, and death. Nothing else that matters much.

"Say the word," she told him, "and in return for your pessimism and scorn, I will serve a meal of sacrificial lamb chops and sear them with rosemary, a small luxury, that earthy herb, which I believe you are quite fond of."

A pot of Mrs. Kelly's rosemary on one side of him, a pot of mint on the other, he saw that beautiful woman grieving in her own way, telling him no, the modest Irish meal he'd requested of only boiled potatoes seasoned perhaps with rosemary was *too* modest.

"For our transgressions, we must have more. Including crushed mint in our ice tea."

"Dear lady, please forgive me," he murmured, coming back to where he was.

He spotted a nicely ripened tomato within reach. He tightened the cap on the Jameson, laid the bottle down, and twisted the fruit loose. He took a ravenous, greedy bite, and another, finishing it, feeling the slightly sharp juices sweeten his mouth—but more, feeling lucky and brave and oddly free, like a happy thief. He saw himself and Arlene looking over the lamb chops in their water bath.

"*Sous vide,*" she said, "started hours ago. Thinking of how I might fatten you up, darling."

In a swift, practiced hand he plucked up the Jameson and removed the cap again. Yes, he could have one drink, if he felt like it. Just one. In celebration! Raising the bottle at the beaming moon, he said, expansively, "To you, sir!"

He held this gesture for a thrilling moment, and another, then carefully brought the bottle down to his lap and replaced the cap.

"But not right now," he said.

He still had too much energy to burn off and could use another run. ■

TED KOOSER

With Li Bai

The water followed Li Bai down the river,
sometimes running ahead, then waiting for him,
at other times falling behind to roll in an eddy
or paw at the roots of a tree. From time to time
the master would reach up, pick a willow leaf,
and bending, propped on his stick, slip the leaf
in the water's lips, then lick his fingers to taste
what the water had tasted. The water was happy
to be with Li Bai, his blanket and stone bottle,
as the two of them made their way downstream
through centuries, past crude dooryard gates
and fine temples, and at times, when the water
had fallen behind it would, late in the evening,
come running up with a moon for Li Bai.

Vigil

At a cold window, waiting for dawn,
I held myself out like a hand

and after a few minutes, the light
glided in on soundless gray wings,

and settled on me, and started to
pick bits of dark from its feathers,

indifferent to me, and there I was,
trembling, eye-to-eye with a day.

The Flash

Somebody's car passes your house,
nobody you know, an ordinary four-door
gliding between you and the sunset,

and the sudden flash from its windshield
touches the glass in all of your windows,
in sequence, one after another, the way

a stranger, walking past, lost in thought,
might reach out and brush his fingertips
along the pickets of your fence, with easy

familiarity, knowing nothing of you,
the light from that windshield touching
light flashing back from your windows.

Spring Grasses

They seem so eager, and are such
a bright green. Nothing has teased them

or bullied them, holding them down,
and the breezes are no more than fingers

smoothing their hair. In the classroom
of sunlight, the teacher has just asked

her first question, and all of the children
have held up their hands.

TIM BARNES

Utilitarian Poetics

With Thanks to Portland Community College

He was large and rather unlovely
with a bulging forehead and
tattoos tendriling out of his clothes,
tongue, ear, and nose rings,
jeans slung on a silver chain.

He would come into my office
and ask me to help him understand
the poems we were reading. They
confused him with metaphor and
and other intricate measures. But

he wanted to know because
he sensed "something about
this poetry thing." He leaned
his guitar case against the wall
and talked of bands and practice

and rock and roll. Talking wasn't easy.
He was living, it seemed, almost
on the street and couldn't see
what T.S. Eliot meant with those
women coming and going

with Michelangelo? But he felt
something about poetry and wanted
to understand. "I think I can
use it," he said, furrowing his brow,
"to defend my heart."

Squirrels in the Attic

The squirrels are looking for the trees
they lost, the scaffolding of their kingdom,
cut clear out from beneath them
and moved to the cities.

When you hear them scurrying in your attic,
they're home again among the missing rafters
of their empires. When they chew the books
to tatters, they're just recomposing an
old story.

Ask the squirrels about the body
of their myths, where it went,
how the stick people talked,
their chatter.

The speech of squirrels
can be translated by medicine men
so old their veins are underground streams
that wake up in your basement and scrawl
little maps in rivulets.

Maybe the squirrels chatter about that old country
while munching on the new literature
and its transcriptions.

BRIAN OLSON

Dead Horses of the Owyhee Desert

Miles in the desert walking
so far, I think I might run into Jesus
so far, my feet turn into dust.
Turns out this is where the west
melts into the sky in a spread
of buttered light. Hope evaporates in bone-
dry troughs, leaving horses for dead
handing over their shallow bodies
to the stalking of slender coyotes.
You can lead a horse to water but . . .

My feet plop down drought-plagued
trails. I ponder what it takes to conquer
the cancer of growth and rise above
the checker-board pattern of
houses, subdivided by veins of canals
who have long held the reins
of progress. I sweat to forget
that I am both villain and hero. I sit split
like a rock, taking shade under a large sage
trying to silence the ghostly breath
of wandering horses and their last
short staggering steps of thirst.

"Semi Sunset" by Greg Keeler. Acrylic on canvas.

GARY SHORT

Memory, Nevada

I've been here before. Somewhere
between Tonopah & Goldfield. Strange
what the past can do when it catches up to you.
I drove this road as a young tumbleweed.
I didn't know where I was going,
but I was in a hurry
to get there. To get here.
What was your rush, Boomer, afraid
you'd miss out on something? You did,
but you don't know what it is.
I thought then there was only one horizon,
the one in front of me. Now I see
there are horizons all around.
I remember driving fast—there was no speed limit then—
playing music loud, shouting out the songs,
most likely an anthem of running or rocking, until
the bulky eight-track cartridge, that flawed invention,
warped & tangled. I ripped it
from the tape deck & tossed it out the window.
The ribbon caught, unspooled
& festooned the spikes of a sagebrush,
where in the glittering sun & wind
it must have shined like tinsel.
On this long ago road, I stopped once
to help a woman stranded with a blown tire.
She was sobbing. And I knew
this wasn't about the flat, although
it was the saddest flat tire ever seen
on Highway 95 between Reno & Las Vegas.
In the side-view mirror, what is behind you
can be out of sight, or at an angle, or
even closer than it appears.
And that woman sobbing on the shoulder
of the highway? I wonder

where she was trying to get to, where
in the wide world she went.
What'll I do, she cried, What'll I do?
I lifted the spare from her trunk.
Her hands held her head.
I'd recently been reading Rilke.
You must change your tire, I said.

Shiver

The 32-year-old climber locked in ice
for four decades in Nepal,

found & bundled, brought down
the mountain to be met
& identified by his fifty-year-old son—

that's how I see my older brother
this late afternoon, his face frozen in time
& younger than mine.

Although I love this tree I'm under,
the shadow it throws on my shadow,
the pine tree & its birds

or the birds & their pine tree do not know
my brother has been dead
forty years & has only visited me
once, maybe twice, since his death,
& both times he was silent.

How to recall the lost ones,
their faces glazed with ice.

I sit beneath the pine & watch the cat
meditate on the warbler's absent song.
The cat doesn't comprehend the bell
I've attached to his collar. The jangle. Why

he can't get close. And so he stares
& stares, his gaze fixed on the branch
& the shiver in the air
where the fly-away had been.

THE LIMBERLOST REVIEW

The summer after my brother died,
I wore his blue work shirt every day,
except for the days I would gently hand wash
& hang it on the line to dry.

The breeze would slip inside the shirt
& fill the vacant space, the long sleeves
animated by wind, waving. A brother of air.

SALLY GREEN

Pacific Tree Frog

for Anne McCracken

Not much bigger than a peach pit, so light
a small leaf could hold their weight, they take
on the safe colors of whatever is nearest
in yard, garden, or woods. Once,

one that matched the bright lime green
of my watering can shot through
the spout and landed in a flower pot
with the sound of a small stone
dropped into a puddle. Another I spooked
with the gray-striped snake of a hose. It hopped
out of the lily-pad-shaped leaves
of a nasturtium's bell-like blossoms
cloaked in a smatter of brown, green,
bronze, and rust.

Then there was the black one
hidden in the dark mats of germander under
the Gravenstein where I was hunting
for windfalls. Whatever made
another turn copper, green and turquoise,
I've forgotten; but it was that fleck of sky-color
that jumped out at me, taught me to look
closer. The old ones say that frogs are spirit

creatures, who move between worlds as easily
as land and water. Bearing wisdom and healing,
they stand for stability. No wonder carvers place them
at the bottom of totem poles and the corner posts
of longhouses. No wonder I wear a pewter pin
of a frog on a leaf for luck, or that a friend rubs
the head of a fieldstone frog resting
on a shelf like a Buddha.

It's the male that booms out his hunger,
casting need and hope like a net
into the uncertain spring nights; but it's the female
who always chooses, approaching a pond
glittering with shards of starlight or dense
as obsidian, welcome as joy, startling as grief.

Provender

> "Now, take the birds. The world seems to be letting loose
> of them fast as a horse summer-sheds its hair. Memorize
> their songs. Believe they'll come back. When they do,
> you'll recognize them, that craving."
>
> —Aunt Mabel

I wake hungry, lie in bed listening,
listening harder for bird songs
at first light. Then, close to the house, a trill,
a churr from a stand of alders in the back
yard, a whit from maples just outside
my window—thrush, junco, vireo, warbler,
wren, sparrow, finch, towhee—all warming up,
a breakfast banquet better than fried eggs, toast
and coffee. But there are fewer voices spring

by spring. All day I snack on the flare
of a Western Tanager's scarlet and buttercup-
yellow feathers in fir trees, a dozen Red
Crossbills drinking wing to wing
from the birdbath in cedar-bough-shadow,
the unmistakable whir and zoom
of a hummer's mating dive for the female
who does her judging from inside a wild tangle
of cherry. At day's end? The hurried taste
of one more call, one more snatch of song
as darkness molds itself around the house.

Lights out, small window opened next to the bed,
still hungry, still listening. For years it's mostly been
the Barred Owls' raucous call, but now, faintly,
from down toward Adams' barn, a Great Horned Owl
hoots, then another at the edge of Glenda's clearing,
one more from Judie's orchard. Closer still, a female
answers, whetting the appetite.

JAY JOHNSON

Service Call

It was snowing, and she had a bad leak under her sink. She could see water flowing in through the valve stem, and the valve was stuck open. At least, she couldn't budge it.

Jasmine Moncrief had moved to Sugar Maple Island after the death of her husband, and while cathartic in a certain sense, and worthwhile in that it distracted her from the capriciousness of Fate, it was a physically demanding existence that she had not bargained for. It was what she had.

There were no sugar maples there. Most maples were brought in by some Norwegian immigrants, bringing a bit of home. It was Canada, and early on, some children had suggested the name to their genial grandfather the mayor, and he changed the name accordingly, even though it could be thought of as somewhat fraudulent. No matter, no one was defrauded. The Norway maples thrived, became fine furniture and excellent firewood.

Her children, grown enough but without the wherewithal to offer help, did not move there, did not send money, and rarely visited. She had moved up two years previously. Danny was going to college in San Bruno while working half-time in a British car dealership. Len was an apprentice sheet-rock taper in Redding but his hours weren't steady enough yet to get a good financial footing. "You can work hard in another trade, people will appreciate your other talents," she had told him. He discounted his other talents. His father had been the same, and obviously that had not worked out well for him. He died of, well, there were medical reasons, but he was physically worn out at age fifty. Heart attack, and he should have been in good physical condition, having worked hard since he was fourteen. Cigarettes, marijuana, whiskey, mushrooms. Soul of an artist, discipline of a child. Financial fortitude of an addict. They'd had a loving marriage, and she was lucky he never mortgaged the last bit of a small inheritance, a cabin on a plot of land up in the Southern Gulf Islands, British Columbia. She inherited it free and clear in a handwritten will. It was probated at some considerable expense in California and recognized in Canada, and there she was.

She grew vegetables, she had few expenses, and she wasn't going anywhere. She was forty-two, widowed, and far away from her kids.

The snowstorm was unpredicted, and hard. In her two previous winters, it had snowed a bit, temperature dropping into freezing often enough, but the shelter of the mountains, on the big island to her west, broke up the clouds and caught the moisture. Cold, frost, a little snow, and a fair amount of rain made up her winter. But the rain and snow would be a lot worse if not for the mountains to the west.

It hadn't started snowing yet when she discovered the pooling water under her kitchen sink, shrouded by the cabinetry. It was a steady drip of water from what appeared to be the main valve for the cabin. She grabbed the knob and tried to close it, thinking it would shut off the flow, even though it would shut off all water to her home. It wouldn't turn in her grip. Water wicked up her jeans, cold. She cleaned up the spill and changed into a shift and leggings.

She went outside in the grey mist, colder now, and quickly tracked the route of the piping to the earth below her cabin. It was a single pipe, the supply for the house, and she could flash a light under the skirting of the cabin; there the pipe appeared to head nearly due north, in the direction of the jet pump, underground and insulated with that pink cotton-candy looking stuff. If she shut down the pump, that itself would be a project, maybe require getting it primed again — she didn't know if that was necessary.

It pained her, but she phoned the village handyman, Bayliss Vieuxhall. His name was on a business card magneted to her refrigerator, a vestige of the prior occupants. They had been old-school hippies, not that unlike her. They were upset when told they needed to leave, but she needed the home for herself. Their clean-up had been sufficient, albeit somewhat lacking in removing the smell of harvested marijuana in the home. But they left without any hassle or legal cost, which she could not afford.

She found the number and called Bayliss. He answered directly. He agreed to be there ASAP, but it would be slow, since he traveled by horse instead of motorized vehicle. He assured her he would bring what was necessary, and he was familiar with the problem.

"Put a bucket under it for now," he advised. She had already done so. The bucket had overflowed before she caught it.

He arrived almost an hour later with a buckboard, a well-muscled draft horse and a covered wooden box in the buckboard. It was two full buckets later, but no more extensive cleanups. He knocked, she answered, and he shed his Danner boots as he entered. He carried wool shearling slippers as he approached the house. He nodded to her, and she pointed to the faulty valve.

"I know where it is," he said.

"Can you tell me what you will charge for this?" she asked. "I'm not exactly wealthy."

"No," he said. "I can't."

"Huh," she said. "Well, just so you know I'm not wealthy."

She looked outside, and snowflakes were big and wet, accumulating fast.

"I know who is wealthy here," Bayliss replied.

He was dressed in bib overalls, checked wool overshirt, Carhartt jacket left unbuttoned for now. He discarded it, draping it over a chair at the kitchen table. He glanced at the wood stove, the fuel beside it in a small tidy pile, and saw the cookstove was ancient, wood-fueled.

She measured him. He was early fifties, solid in the shoulders and powerfully built thighs and buttocks. Wiry-haired, square-jawed, clean shaven. He was solid, more solid than her late Tommy.

How do you heat your water?" he asked bluntly. "Heat that with wood also?"

"Yeah, an old Sears heater. I think it's an antique."

"Yeah. Antique. Maybe you could get some real money for it on *Antiques Road Show*."

"I'm afraid I don't know what that is. TV?"

"Should have seen it before you left California."

"We didn't have TV there, either."

"Huh. Thought everywhere in California had TV."

She paused. "We didn't have a TV. That's all I know."

The snow had increased greatly, the flakes appreciably smaller. He looked out the window. "I'm going to water my horse," he said. "Should have done it right away. He'll be mad."

"Well, guess you'd better do it before you shut the pump off, huh?" she said. "The ag spigot is that way, toward the little shed. You can put him in there, if you want, by the way. What's his name?"

"Charlie."

He left without saying anything more, shedding his slippers for his boots, unhitched the buckboard, and led the horse to an old corral. He returned and wrested a large bucket from the buckboard and filled it in at the spigot. He closed the gate, formerly open. Then he walked back to the north side of the house, pausing at the power panel mounted there. The snow seemed to pour now, barely slowing for the big cedars which shed their load with little regard for those below, dropping snow-sheaves from the trees.

He checked at the pump and panel, and didn't find a switch or a breaker. The power to the house would have to be cut off. He went back in.

"Too late to get an electrician here, for this particular emergency," she said.

"I'm an electrician. I didn't come equipped for re-wiring a panel."

He glanced again at the pile of wood, and at the cookstove. He hadn't seen the calf-high pile there, small pieces cut for that appliance.

"Gonna get cold tonight," he said.

"Cold?"

"Under freezing. A few degrees under. Likely warm up tomorrow. Okay if I kill your power to the house? Can't believe it's wired like that."

"How long will it be off?"

"Hour. Two hours. Not too long."

"Are you going to have to prime it when you're done? Do you know?" She looked at him quizzically.

"I am highly confident. That's a self-priming unit, and besides, it'll only be off a little while. Holds its prime."

She agreed, and threw some of the cookstove wood into the Jotul heat stove, then she put a pot on to boil, while she still had water. Evening was upon them, and she lit a Coleman lantern, and Bayliss had a couple of powerful battery-powered lanterns.

"That Coleman might throw a bit of carbon monoxide. Best used outdoors, thanks," he said. She killed the Coleman.

He dumped the pressure in the system, and started to attack the faulty valve. Then he stopped, retrieved a yellow paper pad from his toolbox and then measured and sketched it out. He muttered and groused and swore, she was sure. But he was quiet, and she never made out what he was saying. She kept her distance, observing in the lanternlight. He perched in a crouch sometimes, and flipped onto his back for better access, she presumed. Occasionally he hoisted himself up and retrieved different tools. Pipe wrenches, propane torch, pipe cutters, pipe die. Fittings. Brass, copper, solder, iron. Pipe dope.

She stoked the cookstove with small fuel, awakening the embers and in a few minutes put in a few chunks of substantial fuel. She reached into the refrigerator, quiet for now, and withdrew chicken broth and onion, carrot, and potatoes. Cooking by flashlight was not optimal, browning onion and boiling carrot and potato. The smell overtook the industrial smells of plumbing.

He was into it well over an hour when he hoisted himself up again. "People who installed this should be shot," he announced. "Never should do an install like this. Even back when they did this. They should have known better."

"Like, what should have been done differently?"

"Valve shouldn't be iron. Should have used sweated fittings. If they were going to use iron pipe, at least put a union in there. Should have used a ball valve. Should have used bigger pipe."

"Is that all?"

"Want me to go on?" He smiled sheepishly at her. "That's a Gates valve. Should be a ball valve—better flow, less chance of failure." He paused again. " 'Course it was a million years ago. Might not have had ball valves then, don't know. I'm about all out of criticisms."

"Does that mean you're about done?"

"In theory, yes. I've got it all torn apart." He glanced outside, piercing the night with his heavy flashlight. The snowstorm was now ferocious, with wind kicked up and blustering, the snow in fine flakes but tremendous volume.

"Aren't you concerned about your horse?"

"He's supposed to be smart. I'll go talk to him in a few minutes, but he's on the lee side of that building right now, probably up tight to it."

"So you aren't worried about him?"

He didn't answer but lowered himself back down, crouching with the propane torch. He had already installed a union into the iron pipe, having threaded the pipe in place, working in tight quarters, and was almost to the point of installing a brass ball valve, replacing the guilty ancient iron one. Flexible braided hose to the remainder of the pipe, coiled to take up the extra length, and he would be done. He clambered up from his cramped posture. "Got it," he said.

It had snowed boot-high. He peered out again.

"Do you have a blanket for that horse?" she asked.

"Yes."

He started to leave the building, then halted. "Have a stockpile of firewood that isn't obvious?"

"Of course."

He looked back at her. Expectant. But she didn't answer further.

"I'm flipping the power back on," he said. He left, found the breaker box with his flashlight, and then the two interior lights came on. Bayliss checked on Charlie. The snow had reached a good twenty centimeters.

He re-entered the house and started gathering tools.

"I strongly suggest that you not go out into that storm to get home tonight," she said.

He kept gathering up tools, setting them carefully in place in his home-made tool chest.

"Because it took you almost an hour to get here before it really hit."

"I'd take a bowl of that soup and a glass of milk, if you were offering," he said.

"Your food's ready. And now you can wash up. Thank you for repairing my problem, and for coming out on such an awful night."

"I didn't realize it was going to be this rough," he said. "I would have let you empty the bucket all night if I had known we would have this much storm."

"I wasn't so sure I'd be able to wash up, with all that leaking."

"Yeah. That would be inconvenient," he said, and he looked at her.

"I have a guest bed. My sons use it when they visit."

"Good. Do they visit at the same time?"

"No, they haven't. If they did, one would have to sleep with me, I'm afraid."

"You could probably use the guest bed, and give up yours."

"You're a thinker. I can tell." She raised her eyebrows at him. He nodded back at her, and hid his smile.

She served soup and bread and salad for each of them, offered him milk since he had asked, and poured herself a Carlings Black Label. He stared at it.

"I'll swap you, if you would like the beer more," she offered.

"That would be swell, but then you might not have any beer," he replied.

"I have other beer, but I'm not going to waste the milk," she said. "Go on, drink up. Here's to . . . craftsmanship. Thank you again." She swapped their glasses.

He tipped his toward her, then gently sipped, and exhaled.

"Well, perhaps I should have suggested this before, but if you were to overhaul all the plumbing in here, I'd go with PEX and do the whole place right. Last a long time, fewer service calls on stormy nights. Not really my thing, I'm kinda old for that plastic plumbing, but the industry is all gone that way. Even when taking care of vintage cabins. Like this one."

"'Vintage.' I like it" she said. "Someone train you to be a salesman, or are you a natural charmer?"

"Yes."

She smiled at that. "Sophomoric, but effective. I like that, too. No use putting on airs when you don't need to."

"I agree. No need. I'm a handyman, and I'm good at it."

They ate in silence for another ten minutes. He was hungry, but ate like a schooled gentleman. He finished his serving, looked up and thanked her.

"I was glad for the dinner company, to tell you the truth."

"Yeah, well, this island is kind of limited. My timing was pretty good to be collecting a dinner."

"Perhaps I'll get a credit on the bill."

"I wouldn't take that to the bank, since you invited me for dinner."

"Sort of. You wanted some soup, as I recall."

"I did. And I'm not shy. But ultimately, you invited."

"Okay, technically, I invited. But I don't think we should argue about it."

"Or about the bill."

"Deal." She looked at him steadily. "I can't offer you anything for dessert. But I do think you should stay in the guest bed tonight. For your horse's benefit, if not for you."

He got up and looked outside, where the snow continued. "I'd like to take you up on that," he said. "I'm going to see to Charlie." He put on his Carhartt and stuffed a muffler around his neck, wool stocking cap, and plunged into the storm. Five minutes later he returned. "He's got a feedbag, shelter as good as it will get, and a blanket. He's fine. But I wish I brought a sled instead."

"That's good that he's all right." She pointed at the guest-room door. "I put out my late husband's night shirt. Towel and cloth in the drawer by the sink. New toothbrush, probably in the same drawer. If you care for a glass of scotch, I'll share that company, too. But just a short one, nothing more."

"Never turn down a drink from a lady, I say. Doesn't happen every day."

"I expect in your case, it might happen every day."

He grinned. "Well, every once in a while." She smiled back, and brought down a bottle of Glenlivet twelve-year-old whiskey. "I'll clean up first," he said.

He went to the spare room, and then the bathroom. She turned to dinner clean-up, quietly. She listened as he clanked against the commode and splashed in the sink, rummaged for a towel, and he emerged dressed down to his tank-top undershirt. He furtively looked at her, the silhouette of her in a cotton shift and apron. Strong back, slight of breast, spare. Hair in a bun, and drawn back. Practical. She turned and caught him for an instant, saw a glint of gold on his left hand. He pointedly twisted his neck to shake water from an ear. "I'll just be a minute," he said, and ducked into the guest room.

He emerged wearing his same work shirt. He eased to the small dinner table and eyed the bottle of scotch.

"Left over from my days on the mainland," she said. "I save it for guests." He nodded, as she poured two short ones.

* * * * *

JAY JOHNSON

There was skittering in the night, in the guest room. Above and beyond the wind in the branches, not muffled by the occasional soft drop of a clump of heavy snow outside the single-pane window. Then he heard what sounded like a creaky door hinge, ever so slight. Then a rustle, and the quietest chirp. The skitter was intermittent, just enough to alert him, without enough of a lapse to let him drift off. He reached over and quietly pulled the switch-cord on the bedside lamp, then he saw the tail of a tiny rodent, then the body and head, frozen to avoid detection.

"Hummph," he said. *Nothing going to scare that thing out of here, however he got in.* He turned off the light and the noise resumed. Another chirp, so quiet. His clump of clothing seemed to have intrigued the other guest, and he knew his sweat and the smell of Charlie's feed would bring the creature out, no matter what. There was a scurry, as if a foraging trip was completed. Within a minute the intruder returned.

Bayliss quietly gathered up the clean night-shirt, swung his legs out of the bed and calculated the distance to the other side of his clothes and tool chest, which he had moved into the guest room. A meter plus, and the nearest refuge for the rodent was another couple meters. He softly bounded to the far side of his clothing on the floor. He used the night shirt as a net, throwing it down in the dark. A miss, a faint chirp, and the animal escaped to his crevice. Bayliss reassessed. He moved to his tool chest, emptied a plastic tub containing solder and flux and plumber's tape and pipe dope, setting them singly in the chest. And he waited in the dark. Naked.

It was thirty-five minutes before the skittering returned. Same spot, next to his clothing. He remembered that he had stuffed a foil of cheese and bread and apple in a vest pocket, probably two days earlier on a service call preparation. No more mystery there. He was crouched, cat-like, and the rodent moved again, nearly silent but not quite. Bayliss covered him in the tub, in the dark, and the rodent moved frantically within.

"Well, not sure that is progress," he said aloud. "Now what." He weighted the tub with his iron pipe-wrench and the tiny shriek pealed again. "Wait until morning, little fellow," he said. "Now please settle down." He took a box-cutter knife from his chest and pierced

the plastic tub, cutting triangular holes in a few places. He fished out a bit of cheese and mashed down a corner of a piece of bread, and stuffed them through and into the trap. "Should have used bait,"
he said. "Probably been a little quicker."

After the bit of food was consumed and circling ended, the animal ran within the plastic tub and gave the barest of perceptible plaintive chirps. There was the sound of soft landing as the creature leapt up to the holes sliced into the tub where food went through. Then that ceased. Then the tiniest of gnawing, at the smooth side of the plastic, but it couldn't get a purchase on the prison wall.

Bayliss heard this all, listening intently out of a sense of protection for his stuff, socks and soft shoes and remembered that he had more grimy bits of edibles in his clothing, enough to attract a rodent through his clothes. And he listened to the animal's tiniest chirp to escape, chirp to find food, an almost-whine to find his cohort. The grizzled handyman had no plan for releasing the varmint, and so was somewhat trapped himself. His effort to capture the little beast had been instinct, without malice, just to see. He would not harm it. And he did not sleep any more that night, listening to the futile gnawing and scratching as the night wore on.

* * * * *

In the morning he rose and clothed himself, then saw his redemption—his pad of paper for sketching a layout, with its cardboard backing. The backing would slip under the edge of the tub, giving him complete control—a contained rodent. It was simple, and quick. He brought the entirety out. Jasmine had started breakfast—eggs and pancakes, orange sections.

"What have you got there?" she asked.

"You might never guess," he said. "Good morning."

"Yeah, you bet. No leakage, so that's a good morning. Thank you. Now what have you got?"

He held up the package, admiring his work. "Little guy, a rodent. I'm guessing a vole, can't really see it well, except looking through these peep-holes. Except they usually stick to fields, wreak havoc in gardens."

"Is what you call a vole what we call a mouse?"

"Not exactly. About the same size. Well, some folks call these field mice. Surprised your cats didn't get this one, anyway."

"Yeah, I probably feed them too well. And I'll bet this guy and his family are what was trashing my garden. I figured gophers, but the burrow-trails were really little."

"Well, very likely. I'm going to set it loose. Was thinking of the barn where Charlie is."

She came over to examine it. He lowered it, and she peered through the hole in the top, and the creature leapt up at her. "Brave little guy. Brave to the point of crazy," she said. "Not much of a tail on it."

"That would be a vole, then. Nocturnal, stubby little furry tail. Their survival is based on going forth and multiplying."

She looked up at him. "I got a little story for you," she said. "Now go turn that thing loose, if you insist on starving my cats."

He raised his eyebrow at the suggestion he could care about her cats' diet or usefulness. He struggled with his boots while holding the trap, got them on and exited. He returned in a long minute. She gestured to the sink, telling him to wash his hands.

"My boy Danny, he's kind of a sensitive sort," she started. "Gearhead and all that, but a really sweet young man. About to get married, making enough money to make ends meet now, even considering he's young and living in San Bruno. California, for goodness sakes."

"Yeah, I'm sure that speaks well for him."

"You bet. So, earlier on, he picks up work in a brand-new place, build on brand-new ground, Land Rover dealer carved out of that dry place. New concrete, just right for car work, expensive construction."

He looked at her sidelong.

"So he's working with other young guys, you know, not bad kids, just kind of young. And kids can be cruel, in dumb ways." He shrugged and nodded. "So what do they do? They're in this new building that was a field a year previously, back up to the hills of the coast range, the way he explained it. They're on break, and this little mouse comes scurrying across the floor, just, you know, darting in and out of the new shop rags and in and out of the break room, and the little turd gets cornered in the break room. So what do these geniuses do? They take a can of starting fluid—you know, like ninety-eight percent ether—and spray it at the mouse, got him terrified and cornered, and load it on him, and of course, being ether, it knocks him out."

Bayliss nodded.

"Didn't kill him, and they had enough sense somehow not to handle him, or get bit. He's out, out cold. So sensitive Danny, he's looking at this mouse, didn't do anybody any harm, looking at the darn thing, and he takes it on himself to grab the oxyacetylene torch."

Bayliss grinned, crow's feet crinkling.

"And goes to the mouse, grabs a shop rag, picks up the mouse in the shop rag, the poor little thing was limp in the rag, warm but really, you know, messed right up, and he picks up the torch, what he calls the mixing handle." Bayliss was smiling broadly. "And he cracks the oxygen valve a little bit, get a little pure oxygen flowing out the tip. Slow, like, and he somehow knew that straight pure oxygen would kill the little mouse, so, he's gently waving it back and forth in front of the mouse's face." Bayliss shook her head slightly. "So about then a delivery truck driver pops his head in, and there's this big kid, nursing a mouse with a torch. Driver just stares, shakes his head, and turns away, like he's never seen a kind person before." She was practically glowing with pride for her son. "The damn goof. He describes this little mouse, who starts coming to, shaking, and quivering, poor little squirt, and then you don't know where a damn mouse has been, whether it's spreading hanta or rabies or whatever, and Danny sets the guy in a cardboard box, and flows a little more oxygen in the box, and the mouse is coming around."

"And," Bayliss said, "they lived happily ever after?"

"Well, the guys who blasted the little mouse were feeling a little bad about what they had done, I guess, and the foreman told Danny to get back to work, and he set the box near his bay, under the bench for a little while. Watching to see the mouse. Mouse got pretty animated, I guess you'd say. So, mouse seemed to have pulled out of the anesthesia, so to speak, survived the Recovery Room, you know, and Danny took him outside, looked around for dogs and cats, and turned it loose."

"Well. Poor little guy, if he lasted a day or two, he was constipated for a week. Anesthesia and all that," Bayliss said.

She laughed. "Never worried about the mouse's reaction to ether. Probably not all that different, except they go through a lot of roughage, I suspect."

He chuckled. "My kind of guy," he said.

"Yeah, I thought you might think so. He'd be a good guy for you to meet. Mechanical, and so on." He looked at her, appreciatively. "Now, go on and eat up, you best be on your way with your chores."

"Yes, that's right," he concurred. He politely finished without saying more. He moved back, got up, cleared his place, and went to the guest room and cleared out his gear. She set the kitchen in order, and poured another coffee into a paper cup for him. He moved to the door with his tool box. Icicles dripped in the sunlight, an unusual sunny morning.

"Your wife would seem to be a pretty lucky woman," she said.

"I like to think so," he replied. She frowned slightly and shook her head. "But I'm luckier. She treats me right, and I try to deserve it."

"You keep trying, you've done all right," she said. "I'll send Danny by to meet you when he's up for a visit. In the meantime, you have your wife give me a call." She smiled. "I think we'd be friends."

"I'll do that." He handed her a sheet of yellow paper—a list of parts, itemized labor, all with prices, totaled up. "No extra charge for the emergency call." He turned and headed to the corral, and she heard him quietly cursing the deep wet snow. ■

"Healer," linocut by Riley Sophia Penaluna.

REBECCA EVANS

Over-sized Ghazal

We ungendered fashion—athleisure wear, sunglasses and tees over-sized
& Billie Eilish-styled, un-form-fitting ourselves, bigger, baggier, over-sized.

Opinions drop. Our reasons for body-hate, body-shame lost in the double X
sweats. Comfy fit be the rage, our bodies no longer caged, we soar as we oversize.

Even our sunglasses cover most of our faces, we disappear, begging others
to unnotice. Who can't resist the temptation to hide, to mask, to over-size?

We lug our handbags, larger than luggage, larger than life. We lug ourselves
as we over-fill with door-dash, our orders super-sized, over-sized.

Even our cell phones, once pocket-size, now thrice-their-size, and oh!
the cost. The high price of loss within our disconnect, technology over-sized.

Yet our thoughts—under-sized—language reduced to one-moment
memes and one-minute TikTok, while book-banning takes over sides.

I, Rebecca, reinstate the long read, the slow walk, the tee shirt that fits
and holds reason for words and declare that love be the one thing over-sized.

"Rises" by Greg Keeler. Acrylic on canvas.

MICHAEL DALEY

The Restorers

    When his neighbors on this stretch of creek
unclogged the stream,
winched boulders and lay flat rocks in place,
let their schoolkids take a day to plant the bank
in alder and doug fir seedlings a flycaster picked up
at the Natural Resources department's yard sale,
and the resolute back country bicycle club
monitored smolt at the weir,
he shamed the County into action,
put a stop to
silt erosion overloads of gravel spawning beds
and restored eternity to this one stream—

    Salmon flocking, a thick bolt of thousands, sunlit,
blood-brown across a cow field's once shallow floodplain,
rush over one another,
fall off the margins of current,
flutter the grass, unable many of them
to reach the gravel bed
where fish by the hundreds flash over carcasses,
piles of bruised flesh flap along the shifting banks,
climb uphill to the trickle at the pools,
each to deposit a payload of thousands of eggs
nested in the clean gravel he gave them—

    Attentive to the spiral of need,
and too arthritic to bend
or anchor a tree on the streambank,
he hobbled home for supper, laughed with his wife,
puzzled over grandkids' handwriting,
made some money, watched the News, but one day
he rambled with a whiskey flask to salute the leapers—
before memory was a memory—
cocked his sunburnt squint upstream and said, "I did that."

The meadow grasses were frosted white when this bull elk emerged from the fog, bugling his challenge. Photograph by Glenn Oakley.

GINO SKY

Our Daily Bread

Missing you
when we gathered at the Swig & Toke
for those righteous
ensembles
called
Civil Rights
Vietnam
Women's Liberation
Grape Pickers
Draft Card and Bra Burnings
and Christmas
became Buddhamas

to have forgotten
how unliberated we have become
with diamonds
left in our socks & stocks

we lost
those songs to save us
from this Second Coming of Depravity

we need those gatherings
once again
to Rap & Wrap us up
to fight once more
for what we cherish

Our Daily Constitution

Warriors of Beauty

We must all survive
to be lovers   teachers   friends
that is my wish

can we hear the quest
can we smell the truth
can we believe that we are the revolution
can we sing march dance all
at the same time

can I live inside of you
you inside of me
can we breathe the same breath

can we just be beauty

one flower at a time

GINO SKY

*Dear Earth**

I love you—passionately and sadly,
I love you
even when your sky looks like cigarette
stained fingers,
and your rivers filthy, I love you.

As a child—naively and timidly—watching
you grow brighter.
I love you bravely, and strongly
as I feel your spirit in me demanding dedication.

Every morning, I embrace your light,
Filling my body with your spirit—
always a new creation,
always the sadness at sunset.

It is you that I demand of myself as truth.
It is you that I bow to your life.
It is you that I become the catcher.
It is you—bruised and battered—still the acrobat
flying—waiting for me to catch you.

Oh Earth, how I love you.

*Written in the Grateful Dead's Deadhead Office
when Goldie Rush was working there—
above Ed's Superette, Stinson Beach, California, 1974

1932 Ford Model A 4-Door burned in the Eaton Fire in Altadena, California, photographed by Bryan Chernick, March, 2025.

JOE WILKINS

More for Me

Saturday afternoon the rain breaks so we walk to the food truck on 4th. My son's friend's father owns the truck, slaps hamburger patties & fishes pickles from an enormous glass jar in a backwards ball cap & black apron emblazoned with the intricate silver logo of a heavy-metal band. My son's friend is nearly giddy to see us, but still does his job—takes our orders, asks my daughter if she wants mustard, touches the button that means I get emailed a receipt. Later, with no one queuing at the window, my son's friend ferries out his own lunch & sits with us. We talk burger toppings, teachers, & basketball. I coached my son & his friend last year, & this year my son's friend tells me he's doing his best to stay eligible, has mostly As & Bs, except for a C in language arts—that's his favorite, but it's the hardest too. Legally, my son's friend has to be at all times either in school, at basketball practice, or with his dad. His mom is just out of court-ordered rehab. I saw her, briefly, at the boys' last game. She stood a few minutes on the sidelines, she was so skinny her wrists looked wrong. My son's friend shakes his hair out of his eyes & lifts his overflowing basket of golden, thick-cut fries. *Have some*, he insists. *There's more for me. My dad always has more for me.*

Because he will always be my child

                                            I turn the knob such that the gears
      mesh in silence & open slowly the midnight
door—
                    & indeed my son yet gathers
          while he sleeps (his a body bigger

                    than mine now, his the hands
      that will—*please, God*—
                              bury me)

the moon in the hollows of his eyes.

SHERMAN ALEXIE

The Reservation Broadcast System

That was the summer

a broken TV

served as the stand

for a smaller TV

that worked.

The Wreck, 1985

Driving on empty, telling myself
the joke that nobody can make
a car go farther on an ounce
of gas than rez Indians, I dreamed

of winning the lottery. But not
the big money. Not the millions.
It's dangerous to dream too big.
I just wanted to win a few thousand—

enough to take my parents
and siblings on a crazy-spending
weekend in the city. Get a hotel
room. Eat fancy food. Buy new

clothes. And 56 novels for me
to read. Then my car remembered
it was winter and slid on ice
toward the twenty-foot drop

on the left before running into
the shallow ditch on the right.
The car was okay. I was okay.
It was a minor crash. My car

sat in a reservation ditch so
I knew that some random truck-
driving Indian would eventually
wander by and pull me back

onto the road. And, hey, maybe
you think that I learned a safety
lesson about distracted driving—
about distracted *living*. But

SHERMAN ALEXIE

I didn't pause. You know what I did
after my cousin showed up
and got me back onto the road?
I remembered that I had no

gas so I started crooning
a powwow tune while using
the steering wheel as a drum
and my voice as my voice

and drove my emptinesses all
the way home where I shared
a sleeve of saltine crackers
and butter with my sisters,

brothers, and the five stray
dogs who, at separate times
over the years, had all strode
into our unfinished home

and declared us their humans.
We were their lottery win.
So, yeah, here's a little thing
for you to know: When

you're poor, your dogs and you
eat the same food. And if you
sing the higher notes long enough
then your dogs will howl, too.

Storyteller

While the other Indian
kids played outside,
I often sat beneath

the kitchen table
and listened
to my grandmother

telling the old stories
with five or six other
grandmothers.

They often spoke
in the tribal language
so I didn't know

exactly what
they were saying
but I could follow

the narrative
of their laughter,
curses, and mumurs

of empathy.
Sometimes, stories
are made only

of sound. Sometimes,
the most sacred
spaces are those

that exist
between words.
Sometimes,

my grandmother
would command me
to leave the kitchen

SHERMAN ALEXIE

and go outside
to play with the other
Indian kids. I think

she wanted
me to learn
that you can't tell

your own stories
if you haven't
participated

in your own life.
I think she wanted
me to learn

that you can't tell
stories about
the world if

you haven't
experienced all
of the world's

sorrows,
boredoms,
and glories.

I think, more
than anything,
that she wanted

to teach me
that stories
are meant to be

lived.

Beadwork

My grandmother's house
smelled like smoked salmon

and buckskin. If you went
barefoot, you'd step on beads

all the time. Sometimes,
you'd have to sit to remove

the five or six beads stuck
to your sole then drop them

into the glass jar sitting
on the bookshelf. One day,

for reasons I don't understand,
I ran outside with that jar,

grabbing handfuls of beads,
and flung them all over the yard.

My grandmother wasn't angry.
She knew on my first hour

in the world that I'd always be
the oddest one. She said so.

My grandmother died 44 years ago
but I assume that some

of those beads are still lying
in the dirt around her house.

SHERMAN ALEXIE

And I like to imagine that other
beads have been used

by birds and insects to build their
nests and hives. I like to imagine

that a few of those beads have grown
from seeds into trees. I like

to imagine that the pines towering
over my grandmother's home

are also her grandchildren. I like
to imagine they wrote this poem.

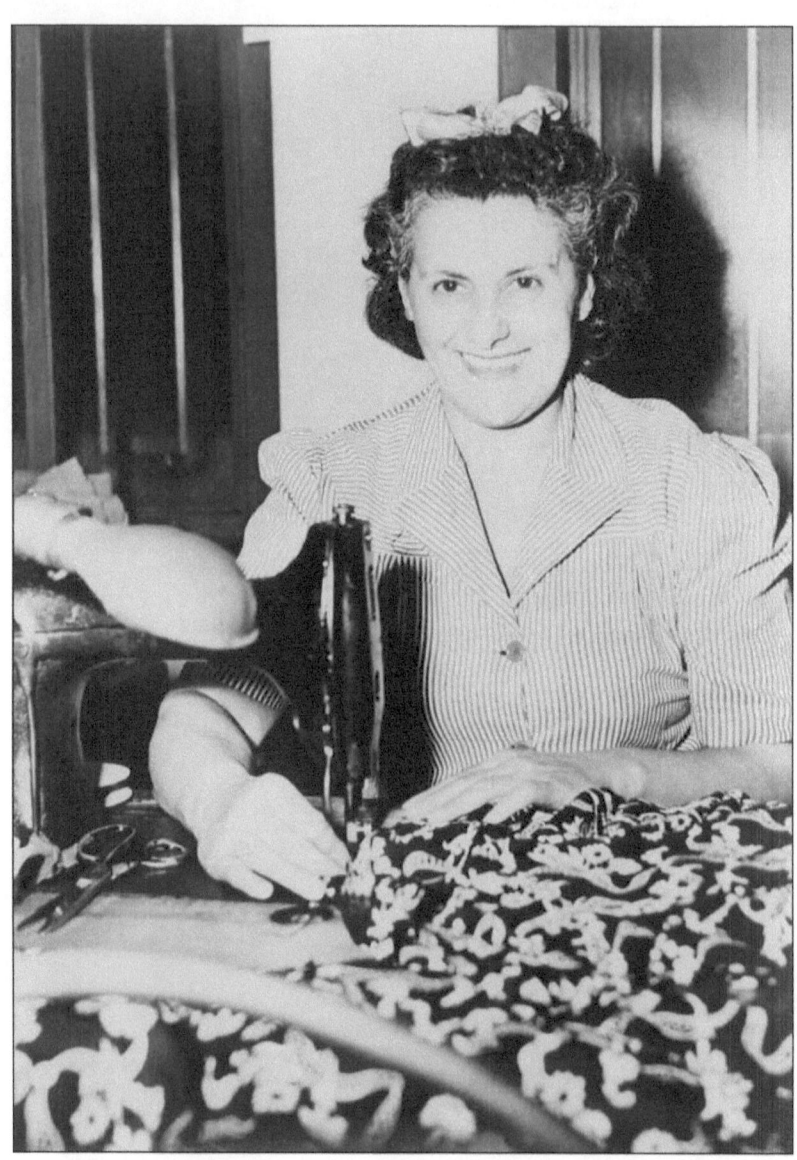
Rose Pesotta, feminist, advocate for workers' rights, 1896-1965.

EDWARD SANDERS

Hymn to Rose Pesotta
(1896-1965)

Who is Rose Pesotta
        in the time-mists?

She who had been active since 1920
as a leader among women workers
in the clothing trade/industry

in a letter to Emma Goldman on April 15, 1935
wanted to discuss the failure of Socialism in the USA:

"What I cannot understand it this," she wrote.
"40 years of propaganda and enlightenment
                      meant nothing to these people?

If you could see the literature, hear the radio speeches &
the arguments advanced against us you would think
that they were a hundred years behind the times."

Yet on she marched.

Rose Pesotta the spring o' '36 helped organize
the first big strike
        at the Goodyear tire factory in Akron

She'd been loaned
        by the International Ladies' Garment Workers Union
        to the Congress of Industrial Organizations
        the rebel wing of the American Federation of Labor

Rose was an anarchist
        She wanted a society with industry a cooperative enterprise owned
            by the workers
                and not by politicians or bureaucrats

            Twenty-two years non-stop
            for a cause wrapped in gauze

THE LIMBERLOST REVIEW

The loneliness of a traveling organizer
       living in "grim lodging houses,"
       hanging out at rallies waiting to speak,
       picketing in blizzards and rain
       train trips from factory to factory
       ever facing the hubris & spit-anger of
                           the hirelings of capital
       the sneers of the press
       & the clack of the Chariot

       "Each morning I stand by the river,"
       she seemed to sing,
       "begging those who cross

       80 years on the bridge of sighs
       handing out phantom

       —stuck in their ways
       unable to change

or maybe I myself am stuck

             Please take my page
             before tears make it wet to read"

In 1942 she "retired to the factory bench as an ordinary 'operative'
(worker in charge of a machine) and two years later resigned from
       the [union] executive."

       scorched at age 45 from
       the non-stop work
             to improve work conditions & pay
             for the ungrateful masses.

Of course, no one really thanks anyone
and thanklessness
             through the ages
             goes thankless.

EDWARD SANDERS

She was unhappy over male-dominated unions
& that socialism had not driven stanchions
into the lives of the American working class

Oh Rose Pesotta, some day let us build a
monument to you beside the White House
as big as Jefferson and Lincoln

May you travel from factory to factory
in a peaceful eternity of sharing!

The issue of whether
  a planned economy
  could work
  for the sustained benefit of all
  & ban hunger & pov

  was never addressed
  in the murd-slither of Stalin
  the murd-dither of Hitler
  the post-war curse of McCarthy
  the Washington Consensus
  & wither-dither of the
      worldwide right

  Of course there's the famous American
    "Exceptionalism"

  Why didn't it happen here?
  Did not Marx
    pronounce
  that it was inescapably
  stitched in the muscles of history?

  Of course, what did Anarchía pronounce?

> Yet I think of Rose Pesotta in this regard
> who after 30 straight years
> > as an on-th'-line
> > union organizer
> > lamented how three decades of picket lines
> > > meetings, leaflets, articles, arguments & urgings
> > > > had made no mark
> > > > > on an unresponsive working class
>
> and that
> handing the people leaflets for centuries
> > on the bridge of sighs
> > might utterly fail.
>
> What did it matter?
> > what did it do?
> And what do people really want?
>
> "I know what they crave:
> > *panem et circenses*
> > & shotgun shells"
>
> > "No! No! here's what they crave:
> > *panem et circenses*
> > & NASCAR fumes!"
>
> Handing out leaflets
> > on the bridge
> > to the passing entities
>
> > > or handing them down from
> > > the bridge
> > > > to the boats beneath
>
> > hoping hoping
> > but seeing them unread
> > > or tossed into the Hokusai

INTERVIEW

Annick Smith. Photo by Tony Cesare.

Heartland, Homestead, and Hearth:
An Interview with Montana Writer and Filmmaker

ANNICK SMITH

Judith Freeman

For the last 52 years Annick Smith has lived on a ranch on a quarter-section of land near the Big Blackfoot River, outside the old sawmill town of Bonner, Montana. She and her husband David moved there in 1971, living for almost two years in a one-room cabin with their four boys, a German Shepherd, a black Lab puppy, a cat and no plumbing or heating except for a wood stove, while they built the recycled hand-hewn-log house where Annick still lives. The ranch is where David died in 1974, collapsing in the kitchen from a pre-existing fatal heart condition. Annick was 38 at the time. One of the first people she called was the poet Richard Hugo.

A few years earlier Hugo had persuaded David to move from Seattle and accept a job in the English department at the University of Montana where Hugo taught poetry. Hugo was at the center of a vibrant writing community in Missoula, and he became a close friend to Annick and David. In his collection of poems *31 Letters and 13 Dreams* Hugo's "Letter to Annick from Boulder," published after David's death, begins with this poignant line:

> *Dear An: This will be your first widow Christmas.*

It continues several lines later:

> . . . *I can't lose your pain, the sound*
> *of your sobbing over the phone, the disbelief that this, this is done.*
> *It is done, dear An. It is lousy and never over, but done*
> *and you're in Spokane, making the movies he would have loved*
> *about Indians, the tribes in decay and the tribes triumphant* . . .

The poem says so much about the moment in Annick Smith's life when everything changed. Not long before David's death, they had returned to Montana after spending a winter in Los Angeles where they had gone to pursue a dream of writing screenplays, a riotous experiment she writes about in her essay collection *Homestead* (Milkweed Editions, 1995) that found them living with their boys in a cheap two-room apartment off Hollywood Boulevard. Things had not gone as hoped in California. They had returned after that hard winter in L.A., not so much disillusioned as sobered by the reality of trying to break into the film business. But David was still committed to writing movies and had hoped to produce a documentary series on Native Americans of the Northwest. Annick found herself in Spokane, producing movies that her husband would have loved, stepping forth in the midst of her grief to begin making a place for herself in the world of film and literature as a true voice of the American West. That voice has only gotten stronger over the years, in the books she's written and edited, and in the movies she's produced, including the remarkable film *Heartland* (1979) set in 1910 Montana and starring the brilliant Rip Torn and Conchata Farrell. *Heartland* remains one of the most authentic portrayals of Western white settlement.

At 88 years of age, Annick is still a very handsome woman. Her long white hair forms a penumbra of silvery light around her face and at times, in the right light, seems to be made of glowing filament. She has a ready laugh and sense of humor and in spite of a recent hip replacement she sets a lively pace on a walk.

I've known Annick for years, and my husband Tony and I often make a driving trip from Idaho to spend a few days with her on her ranch

AN INTERVIEW WITH ANNICK SMITH

in the summer. During our last visit I asked if I might interview her, and she agreed, although not too enthusiastically. One senses she's reluctant to talk too much about herself, not out of any shyness or false modesty but rather a kind of deep-seated reserve that I think of as part of her innate authenticity. It's a good word to describe Annick: she's authentic—deeply authentic, as was the man she became partners with after David's death, her long-time companion William Kittredge.

* * * * *

The night we arrived, Annick had made pasta puttanesca and we poured gin and tonics and sat outside on the deck in the evening light with a view of the woods and wide undulating meadows that surround her house, her dog Betsie nearby. Annick is never without a dog, including the chocolate lab who was featured in her book *Crossing the Plains with Bruno* (Trinity University Press, 2015). I commented on her great love of dogs, and she replied, "Well not all dogs. They're like humans. I like some more than others. Dogs allow you to enter different worlds if you pay attention. They're much less troublesome companions than human beings."

In other words, to be an Annick dog, you'd better be a good dog.

Betty Boop and Rasta, photo courtesy Annick Smith.

Over the next few days, we took walks together up Bear Creek ("Do you see many bears?" I asked her on one of our walks, and she replied nonchalantly, "Not really, we've only seen three since spring"). We made meals together, fixed drinks in the evening, wandered her two-story log house looking at the many photographs of friends and family that cover table tops and walls, including photos of her three granddaughters and her four sons, Eric and Steve and the twins, Alex and Andrew: the latter are filmmakers who followed in their parents' footsteps (among their projects, they adapted their great friend James Welch's novel *Winter in the Blood* into a beautiful film). She pointed out the sculptures made by her father, Stephen Deutch, and the book of his photographs published in conjunction with an exhibition of his work. One afternoon we took a picnic to Red Rocks, her favorite spot on the nearby Big Blackfoot River, and sat on the beach until a lovely refreshing August rain sent us back to the ranch. But mostly we just sat around her dining room table and talked about our lives and her long career as a writer and filmmaker.

* * * * *

I learned more about her rather extraordinary background, as the daughter of Hungarian Jews. Her father was born in Pest, Hungary, her mother in Transylvania. Both her parents were artists, her father a sculptor, her mother a photographer who taught her husband how to use a camera. They met in Paris in the 1930s, where after their marriage they ran a photography studio in Montparnasse. Annick was born in Paris in 1936, though the family moved to Chicago when she was young. In that most American city her parents established a successful commercial photography business, Deutch Studio: one of their main clients was the department store Marshall Fields. Models, clothes, styling, glamour were all an early part of her life, as were vacations at a summer cabin on the shores of Lake Michigan.

She and her two sisters, Kathy and Carole grew up surrounded by artists and writers. Novelist Nelson Algren was a close family friend, as was Studs Terkel. It was a fertile environment for a girl who spent hours listening to adult conversations centered around art and writing

AN INTERVIEW WITH ANNICK SMITH

and politics. Her father had been communist who longed to go to Spain to fight in the civil war—until her mother nixed that idea by reminding him he had a young daughter. Of that time, she has written:

> In the rambling apartment where I grew up, three stories above Lakeside Street on Chicago's North Side, I would lie on my parents' bed and study photograph albums. The bed was strange and illicit, charged with sexual energies, the perfumes of my parents' bodies. The pictures in the albums were even stranger. There was a skeletal great-grandmother in a babushka, her old man holding his black hat. I felt no connection to those country people—peasants really . . . I heard whispers that gypsy genes had darkened my Grandma Deutch's bloodline. That was swell by me . . . when I asked Grandma, "Are we part gypsy?" her answer was emphatically no. If poor country Jews were on the low end of the Hungarian social ladder, gypsies were the bottom rung. Being gypsy, however, like being French, was a story I needed to believe in. I was creating the romance of myself, and to this day I ascribe my nomadic ways, longing for wildness, and disdain of material belongings to blood that is partways gypsy.

Annick attended the Francis Parker School, a private Deweyite progressive school, an experience she credits with changing her life. She had a wonderful teacher who introduced her students to Greek myths, the Bible and the *Odyssey* while they were still in 4th grade. The school was only two blocks from Lincoln Park Zoo, and she often went to the zoo before catching the bus home. She was especially attracted to the great ape house where there was a gorilla she would closely observe day after day. It was clear as she spoke about this time that both the experience of the animals in the zoo, and the wonderful teacher, formed early and deep responses to the world.

* * * * *

When I finally sat down with Annick on our last day together I had a list of questions and began by asking her about her first book of essays, *Homestead*, published in 1995. How much influence, I wanted to know, did writer Bill Kittredge have on encouraging her to publish that first collection?

Smith: I was 38 when David died and 44 when I made the film *Heartland*. In between I had met Bill. I thought I might be a filmmaker at that point. I thought I might go to L.A. and seriously pursue a career in film, but Bill convinced me I should become a writer. Before then, I never felt secure in that identity. I couldn't call writing a vocation until I started doing it. I'm not a self-starter. It's easier if I have an assignment. *Homestead* was put together almost exclusively from pieces I'd already published in magazines, with a few new ones.

Freeman: *Was Richard Hugo also a mentor to you?*

Smith: Dick is interesting. Early on I wrote some poems, rather secretly, and Dick said, *these are good, you're a poet*. But I was a widow with three kids at home, and I knew I'd have to go back to school if I wanted to be a poet. I'd have to study, and I couldn't do it. Bill was definitely the one who pushed me to become a writer. *Why not write a piece about your place?* he said. All along he read my stuff and helped me. But I never took any classes.

Freeman: *How did the Montana anthology* The Last Best Place *come about? Did you know that title would become so iconic, sort of the motto for Montana from that time on?*

Smith: No, we didn't. Bill thought of that title. We came up with the idea together. We knew we had something special. We put together an amazing team: Jim Welch on Native American stories and myths; William Lang on journals of exploration; Mary Clearman Blew on

THE LAST BEST PLACE
EDITED BY WILLIAM KITTREDGE AND ANNICK SMITH
A Montana Anthology

AN INTERVIEW WITH ANNICK SMITH

literature of modern Montana; Richard Roeder on homestead literature; Bill Bevis on contemporary poetry. Bill [Kittredge] edited the contemporary fiction, and I did the editing for cowboys and Indians. Ivan Doig was part of the group, our kibitzer in chief. We just had a great time working together for four years. The book was a surprising bestseller and has become a model for regional cultural/literary anthologies.

Freeman: *Would you talk a bit about* Heartland *and how that film came to be?*

Smith: In Spokane, I had met Beth Ferris, a young filmmaker. She was my partner in shooting, writing, and editing a documentary about Dick Hugo, *Kicking the Loose Gravel Home,* in 1976, and after that we decided we wanted to make a "women in the wilderness" film, so we formed a corporation and gathered with a couple of other women to try to find stories about women who came West in the handcart companies, for instance, or Calamity Jane, and then Beth found *Letters of a Woman Homesteader*
by Elinore Stewart in the library. It seemed like the perfect story because it was basic, and simple. Beth wrote a script, and I was producing. We saw a film the director Richard Pearce made called *The Gardener's Son*—with a script by Cormac McCarthy—and we loved it! We said let's go see Dick Pearce. We wrote him a letter. He was living in New York City. We went to see him and gave him the script. He showed it to the producer Mike Hausman, and they said, yes, we're interested. Putting together Dick and Mike gave the project legitimacy. But Dick said, we need another eye, and we gave it to Bill [Kittredge] for a rewrite. We got money from the National Endowment for the Humanities and borrowed the rest. We tried hard to make it come out true to the actual West, and it did. Initially we wanted Ben Johnson for the lead, but he asked for too much money. Dick sent it to Rip Torn and he agreed to do it. But Rip wanted to play

the part with a Scottish accent, and Dick had to tell him he didn't want him to do that. But Rip came to the set with a terrible Scottish accent and when we started shooting it just came out of his mouth, and we had to go with it.

So, he became a Scottish emigrant! Rip was so into it. He comes from a Texas ranch family—his cousin is Sissy Spacek. He spent his time lassoing fence posts and drinking bourbon. Bill was on set, and Rip recognized Bill as being so authentic. Rip said to him after he'd arrived, "I drove through all these little towns in Montana and I wanted to stop at all the bars and pick a fight," and Bill simply said, "Good thing you didn't."

Freeman: *At what point did you decide you wanted to be a writer and stopped making films?*

Smith: I wanted to be a writer when I was a kid. Then by the time I was a teenager I thought, okay you're not a creative person. I never had the confidence until Bill encouraged me to write, and he did it for selfish reasons. When I thought of going to L.A. to seriously pursue film, Bill said he didn't want me to go. He wanted me to stay in Montana. And that's when we began working on *The Last Best Place* for the Montana centennial.

Freeman: *How did you get together with Bill?*

Smith: I knew Bill before we got together. David was in the same department with him. We admired Bill's writing very much. Bill had given a party for Ray Carver. David and I had just come back from L.A., and we went to the party. Everyone was drinking, getting drunk, as people did in those days. I sat next to Bill. He began telling me how he had a son and daughter he hadn't seen for ten years. He was weeping. That really touched me, and that was our first connection.

Then a couple of years after David died, I was working on the Native American documentaries in Spokane and I would come back to Missoula on the weekends and stop in the East Gate Bar for a drink— that was where Bill hung out and held forth with students, along with

AN INTERVIEW WITH ANNICK SMITH

Jim Crumley and Jim Welch. He asked me for a date. We went to the movies. He was sober. But when we came out, a guy ran into us, just a fender bender, but I remember thinking, *Oh this is the beginning of a real car wreck!* And it was. We didn't live together, by choice. He called me his traveling companion. We finally got married on January 2, 2020, less than a year before Bill's death on December 4th.

Freeman: *I remember when Bill accepted the* Los Angeles Times *Book Prizes' Robert Kirsch Award in 2005, given to honor a writer whose work has made a significant contribution to Western literature. I thought it was one of the most authentic acceptance speeches I'd ever heard, and it made me realize what a genuine person Bill was. Was Bill the last no-bullshit writer?*

Smith: (Laughing) Oh I hope not! Bill used to say that the era we were living in wasn't the golden age of literature, it was the bronze age. I think it may be getting worse.

* * * * *

We discussed the work of writer Alice Munro, as I agreed to join Annick at her book club meeting where they'd be discussing one of Munro's stories. I quoted to Annick a passage from Munro's story: "I pondered the possibility I needed a male presence behind me to affirm my talent and my right to use it." I asked Annick if that was what Bill had done for her—and maybe David: Had they affirmed her talent, and her right to use it?

Smith: Bill was a great teacher, and so was Hugo. They both inspired so many students and made the University of Montana a center for writing. David was also a very important presence. He did affirm my intelligence and talent, and we tried to do projects together. He was a strong person. I spent a lot of my life trying to please him. After David died, I became liberated. I started to do stuff on my own, including producing the ten-part series on Indians of the Northwest, called *The Real People*. There I was, a 38-year-old widowed Jewish woman from Chicago!

And this was the mid-seventies, the era of AIM [American Indian Movement] and Indian activism. I was working with and against the tide. I was in charge, and I was challenged. I had to spend time apart from my family. I commuted to Spokane from Missoula. I had to earn the respect of the Indians I was working with. It was a very turbulent time—but liberating. I was older when I came to women's lib. I was a 1950s woman, and a rebel—but a very nice one! (Laughter)

Freeman: *In one of your essays, you mention having affairs with younger men at this time.*

Smith: Yes, for a short time, but I became bored. It didn't last. After that came Bill, who was a very troubled and troubling man, but he really did stand behind me and affirm me. Any man I was ever serious about shared my sensibility about what matters. A shared intellectual curiosity had to be there as well as the physical attraction. I did get attracted to powerful and charismatic men.

Freeman: *How did Montana become such a center for writers and great Western literature? Why here, and not Utah, or Idaho, or Nevada?*

Smith: I think in *The Last Best Place* we addressed that. Montana has a long tradition of storytelling, from the Native stories through the cowboy and homestead period, and the novels of A. B. Guthrie, Dorothy Johnson, Wallace Stegner, and others. Early on, the University of Montana became a center for writing. In the 1960s they brought in Hugo and he was such a great teacher. People came to study with him. Then Bill began to attract fiction writers. It was one of those lovely conjunctions, bringing people together, and it wasn't nasty or competitive.

Freeman: *Western writers have often gotten short shrift, been treated as lesser somehow. I'm thinking how even the* New York Times, *in their obituary of Wallace Stegner, called him William Stegner.*

Smith: That would not have happened with Philip Roth!

AN INTERVIEW WITH ANNICK SMITH

Freeman: *Have you ever felt that sense of a "Western slight?"*

Smith: I think Bill felt that more than I did because he was from the West. I didn't care as much. And now I'm much more divorced from all that because of my age and my current lack of production! (laughter)

Freeman: *I think of you as a writer who in your work has paid very close attention to the natural world, whether in an essay on whales, or the grasses of the great prairie. Do you think of yourself as a nature writer?*

Smith: I don't want to give labels. I'm sort of a memoir writer, connected to place. Maybe my epitaph could read "She was a decent writer."

Freeman: *Barry Lopez, a writer you were close to and who consulted on your last book* Hearth, *quoted Aldo Leopold in his introduction: "One of the penalties of an ecological education is that one lives alone in a world of wounds." Do you feel that as well, given the climate crisis and the grief we're all feeling?*

Smith: That's not me. I actually don't believe anyone lives alone. You look out the window and there's life. Whether it's a city street, or nature, or a dog is in the room with you.

Freeman: *Was Richard Hugo funny? I find certain lines in his poems to be so funny.*

Smith: He was hilarious! I found a letter from him, and it was so funny. Jim Welch also had a very dry sense of humor. Hugo had a wonderful laugh. And so did Bill.

Freeman: *Do you have any favorite stories or memories of Hugo? Or Bill, and Jim Welch, and Richard Ford and Crumley, or Jim Harrison and Tom McGuane, all friends of yours over the years?*

Smith: (Laughing raucously). Yes, I do . . . I have some favorite memories, but I don't want to talk about them!

Freeman: *The last book you published was an anthology of essays by different writers called* Hearth: A Global Conversation on Identity, Community, and Place *(Milkweed Editions, 2019), which you edited along with Susan O'Connor who you have collaborated with on other projects, most notably the beautiful anthology on the prairie,* The Wide Open *(University of Nebraska Press, 2008) with photographs by Lee Friedlander, Lois Connor, and Geoffrey James. I see a strong theme in your work, notably in the titles you've chosen—* Homestead, Heartland, *and* Hearth—*all revolving around home, family, place. Is this at the center of your work?*

Smith: That's for other people to say. This hearth, this home, has always been here for my children and family and friends. The ranch has always been a gathering place, and hopefully it can remain intact after I'm gone and continue to be the hearth for them. But you never know.

* * * * *

I felt like maybe that was a good place to end, but Annick surprised me by saying, "You didn't ask me anything about being old," and we laugh.

"What can you say about being old?" I reply.

She made me think of a line in the opening paragraph of the first essay in *Homestead*, a scene where she looks down on the old log house on the ranch that she and David are thinking of buying: "If I lived here, she wrote, who would I be? I imagined a sturdy woman with skin lined and cracked as hewn logs."

Now she has become that woman, living in a log house they took apart 52 years ago and put back together on this ranch. Her tanned and lined face, with its strong profile, gives her an almost Native look, the kind of beauty working ranch wives and Navajo grandmothers possess, a very Western kind of beauty, in other words.

AN INTERVIEW WITH ANNICK SMITH

"It's hard," she says about aging. "But I accept it. I accept physical limitations. I feel much less competitive and less anxious. This reconciliation with aging? It happens outside of consciousness. It's not really a decision you make. You find yourself spending a lot more time looking out a window. It takes more time and energy to connect with people and socialize . . . and then come back and recuperate," she adds a bit wistfully, but in her voice there's a great sense of peace and gratitude, the kind of feeling she imparts at the end of the first essay in *Homestead*, when she recounts a dream she had of David not long after he died. In this dream she knows he is happy. He's smiling at her:

> *I awoke feeling comforted. I heard the odd, creaking talk of swallows building their mud-dauber nests under the peaked eaves of our roof. Early morning sun slid into open windows. I was at home, and not alone. Out by the stone pile a long-eared coyote cried the day alive. We can never be abandoned. The love you have had will never abandon you.* ∎

Annick Smith and William Kittredge. Photo by Carol Deutch.

1932 Ford Pickup truck burned in the Eaton Fire in Altadena, California, photographed by Bryan Chernick, March, 2025.

ESSAYS, MEMOIRS, NONFICTION

*William Kittredge and Annick Smith, early days.
Photo by Tom Bollinger, courtesy Annick Smith.*

ANNICK SMITH

Bill Kittredge: A Tribute

> *Death steals everything but our stories.*
> —Jim Harrison

After being Bill Kittredge's partner for over 40 years, it seems odd to be writing a tribute to him and his work. I know too much. There are too many roads we traveled. Too many stories. And at least a few secrets. So, the best I can do is say a few words about the authenticity of the man, his insights and knowledge of a real West, his original and unmistakable voice, and his genius as a teacher.

Bill was a big guy with a big laugh, an even bigger prophetic voice, a huge appetite for knowledge, and a craftsman's quest to perfect his art. He loved the fellowship of writers—especially but not exclusively Western writers—and took satisfaction in sharing his knowledge and craft with students of all backgrounds, sexes, colors, and ages, as long as they were intent on doing the best that they could do. He was a man who hated pretension and loved excess. As anyone who knew him will tell you, Bill Kittredge reveled in excess, deplored excess, regretted excess, and had an unquenchable thirst for ways to transcend his own bad behaviors. This made him a good judge of the West's bad behaviors, and of human weakness in general—all of which he knew too well.

Often called "The Buffalo" for his great dark curly-haired head, hunched shoulders, short legs and general resemblance to that iconic roamer of the Plains, Bill was a shaggy beast of a man. He grew up horseback on a huge, isolated cattle ranch in the high deserts of southeastern Oregon. From childhood on, he worked with cowhands and laborers and cooks and hard scrabble ranch men and women— and these were his models, heroes, and the people he wrote about, even as he left their world and became a writer and an intellectual and a university professor in faraway green and bourgeois Missoula, Montana.

But he was also born into privilege—an owner as well as a ranch hand. His people were not rich folk from the East, but scab-handed pioneers who had worked and plotted and lucked their way to owning the largest ranchlands west of Texas. Bill's grandfather patriarch—the first Bill Kittredge—created the MC Ranch. He was a shrewd cowboy with an unforgiving work ethic—cold-hearted, smart, controlling and ambitious—who earned his place in the Cowboy Hall of Fame. Bill's parents, Oscar and Josephine, were even smarter, but self-indulgent and upwardly mobile. They hobnobbed with bankers and governors and people of power that Bill deplored. He loved his family but came to despise its heedless destruction of the natural environment that gave them sustenance and profit.

The double life of Bill's formative years was his inheritance and his nemesis. Power and guilt. Powerlessness and rage. Empathy and tenderness. He was attached to his land, yet complicit in its agribusiness deconstruction. He loved his wife and children, yet left them to inhabit a new life. Situated in the almost abstract isolations and splendors of the interior West, these emotions and contradictions were at the heart of his creative work. The MC is where Bill Kittredge's imagination lived. Where his ashes are scattered. He never escaped the homeland.

* * * * *

A young Bill Kittredge at work on the MC Ranch, and with the day's catch. Photos by Josephine Kittredge.

ANNICK SMITH

Here is one of Bill's homeland stories from the opening of *Owning It All*, his first book of essays about the West and its mythologies:

> In the long-ago land of my childhood, we clearly understood the high desert country of southeastern Oregon as the actual world. The rest of creation was distant as news on the radio.
>
> In 1945, the summer I turned 13, my grandfather sentenced his chuckwagon cow outfit to a month of haying on the IXL, a little ranch he had leased from the Sheldon Antelope Refuge in Nevada. Along in August we came to lunch one noontime, and found the cook, a woman named Hannah, flabbergasted by news that some bomb had just blown up a whole city in Japan. Everyone figured she had been into the vanilla extract, a frailty of cooks in those days. As we know, it was no joke. Nagasaki and then VJ Day. We all listened to that radio.
> Great changes and possibilities floated and cut in the air. But such far-off strange events remained the concern of people who lived in cities. We might get drunk and celebrate, but we knew such news really had nothing to do with us. Not in the far outback of southeastern Oregon.
>
> When I came back from the Air Force in 1958, I found our backland country rich with television from the Great World. But that old attitude from my childhood, the notion that my people live in a separate kingdom where they own it all, secure from the world, is still powerful and troublesome . . .

* * * * *

Believing you own it all in security and perpetuity is a recipe for disappointment, a sure road to rage when things don't work out as planned. "Redneck Secrets" was Bill's first, and perhaps most memorable, essay. Written in 1979, I find it prophetic—illustrating with humor and precision the anger, pride, and fear of change that underlies our country's current deep divisions.

To Bill, Redneck was a descriptive word. He knew he was Redneck, as were many of his closest friends: Ray Carver, Jim Crumley, Richard Hugo, Max Crawford, Robert Stubblefield, and yes—Jim Welch—to name just a few. These were men from the outback—working class Americans, hard drinking, brilliant, blue-collar guys who wrote from the insides of their worlds, as well as from the outside.

In Bill's universe there were good Rednecks and bad Rednecks. Good ones yearned for community and had dreams of recreating a lost paradise—which, of course, never existed. Theirs was the white American's pastoral myth of conquest, settlement, ownership, and freedom. Good Rednecks revered their land and nurtured their families. We are all, in a way, good Rednecks.

"Bad Rednecks," he wrote, "originate out of hurt and a sense of having been discarded and ignored by the Great World . . . . Bad Rednecks lose faith and ride away into foolishness, striking back . . . Why bad?" he asks, "Because they are betraying themselves . . . "Not long ago in the American West," Bill continues, "it was easy to think we were living in harmony with an inexhaustible paradise . . . But aspects of our paradise have been worked to death." And now, says Bill, "A wave of newcomers is moving in . . . we are overrun with tourists, computer companies and good Thai restaurants . . . But these new settlers are not just well-to-do citizens making a getaway . . . but also refugees out of Mexico and Southeast Asia bringing the enormous energies of the dispossessed."

Remember, Bill wrote this essay in 1979, but he could have written it yesterday. He goes on:

> Again our culture in the West is remixing and reinventing itself. It's a process many locals . . . have come to hate . . . Some have grown deeply paranoid, and band together; the weakest pity themselves; some like to think they are warriors, defending their society; others are insane in their anger . . . Out-of-power groups keep fighting each other instead of what they really resent: power itself.

Ending his Redneck musings, Bill asks, "What to do besides brood on the ultimate unfairness of things?" But his is no country and western song of self-pity. "Despair," he concludes, "is a useless way of connecting to the world. Slow down . . . and love what there is . . . all of us have no choice but to reimagine and embrace the future."

* * * * *

The future, for Bill, resided in creating vivid stories of authentic American life and helping to fashion a myth of renewal to replace the worn-out old myth of conquest and supremacy. "Most of the species [he meant Westerners] we are talking about," he writes in *Owning It All*, "live in a racist, sexist, imperialist ideological framework of mythology as old as settlements and invading armies. It is important to understand that the mythology of the American West is also the primary mythology of our nation and part of a much older world mythology, that of lawbringing. In America," he concludes, "this secular vision went most public in a story called the Western."

If he were talking to you today, Bill might point out that charismatic leaders, social media, Fox News, the Christian right, gun lobbies, and disaffected populists have taken the violent messages of yesteryear's Westerns into heartland politics—onto tee shirts, flags, and red hats proclaiming MAGA. Make America Great Again. Again? Today's old ruling class, and its disappointed white folk want to return to a mythical past that exists only in imagination. As if America wasn't great right now. But where is the competing myth? And how would anyone proclaim it?

It is no accident that Bill's best friends, and often his drinking companions, were ground-breaking, myth shattering writers such as Raymond Carver, Annie Dillard, William Merwin, Jim Crumley, Rick Bass, Gretel Ehrlich, James Welch, Richard Hugo, Debra Earling, Richard Ford, Barry Lopez, Bill McKibben, David Duncan, Terry Tempest Williams, Doug Peacock, Max Crawford, David Quammen, Pico Iyer, and many more. The stories they tell are authentic, particular, and complex. Literature, not propaganda. And, therefore, no fodder for slogans or politics.

Speaking of complexity, Rebecca Solnit said in a tribute on hearing of Bill's death: "No one ever modeled more elegantly than Bill Kittredge how you could recognize your own complicity and celebrate your deep love of place . . ." Gary Nabhan wrote: ". . . he challenged us to think beyond the horizon of our own messy lives to forge a West that would be more inclusive, reflective and refreshing. The twinkle in his merry eyes will never die, but will circle around us like a meteor of hope." Alison Deming adds: "Kittredge was one of the great spirits of American literature . . . a man who cared deeply about the fate of the American West . . . He led me to see the region as a crucible for transforming our pathological way of life into something more just, more generous, more in keeping with the land's beauty and the dream of a moral life."

And then there are the voices of younger writers who came to study with Bill at the University of Montana's Creative Writing Program, where he taught for almost thirty years. Scores of students learned their craft from him—and many of them are respected authors and lifelong friends. Such friends and students include Andrew Sean Greer. Andy says, "It is hard to describe what it meant to me for a nearly retired rancher [and teacher] to see, in a gay man telling gay stories at that awful time [1994], something worth finding the energy to pursue, to support, all the way to ensuring my publication for the first time."

Janisse Ray came to Bill's class in 1995, his last year of teaching. She says, "I am forever grateful that he read my feeble attempt at a first book and handed it back to me, staggeringly crippled as it was, with hope in his voice. As he did with so many writers, he found something to praise. The debt I owe is immeasurable."

Forgive me for not naming the long list—you know who you are—but here are a few more of his horde of students who have become acclaimed writers: Sharman Apt Russell, Neil McMahon, Ralph Beer, Judy Blunt, Robert Stubblefield, Deirdre McNamer, Bryan DiSalvatore, Teresa Jordan, William Finnegan, Kim Barnes, Robert Reid, Florence Williams, Kevin Canty, Amanda Ward, and Richard Manning—who says of Bill, "I look up to few people on this earth but knowing Bill allows me to say I at least know one truly great man."

* * * * *

I'll end my tribute with more words
from Bill. Words for which he is justly
famous. This is from the ending of
Hole in the Sky, Bill's most popular
book—a memoir about family and
life on the ranch: its beauties and
terrors; its history and nature;
its truth and consequences.

> We are animals evolved
> to live in the interpenetrating
> energies of all the life there is,
> so far as we know, which coats
> the rock of earth like moss.
> We cannot live, I think, without
> connection both psychic and
> physical, and we begin to die of pointlessness when we are
> isolated, even if some of us can hang on for a long while
> connected to nothing beyond our imaginations.
>   We must define a story which encourages us to make
> use of the place where we live without killing it, and we
> must understand that the living world cannot be replicated.
> There will never be another setup like the one in which we
> have thrived. Ruin it and we will have lost ourselves, and
> that is craziness . . . .
>   I want to think that all creatures, even us, are in love
> with the makeup of their actualities like bats at the throat
> of some desert flowers while no one is watching, spreading
> pollen in ways the flower would love if flowers did such
> things. And maybe they do.

* * * * *

Bill died on December 4, 2020, of a massive brain hemorrhage and stroke. He was 88 years old, having outlived his parents, his two past wives, his brother and sister, and most of his dearest pals. He was a grandfather to his daughter's four sons, a great grandfather to their children, and an inspiration and thorn to my boys as they grew into men. He had lived to be much older than anyone believed he could, given his habits and history. His daughter Karen and son Brad were at his bedside, as was Sandy, his friend and housekeeper, his devoted caretaker Libby, and me—finally his lawful wife after forty-three tumultuous years of living separately and together. Bill liked to call me his "Traveling Companion" and that's what we were—travelers and companions to the end of his journey, if not yet to mine.

During all the years we were together, hungover or sober, grumpy or smiling, winter or summer, in his Missoula condo or a Paris hotel, in a Santa Barbara beach house or up at my place in the Blackfoot Valley, Bill wrote every morning and every spare hour. That was who he was. A writer. He wrote every day during his last year, until the morning he couldn't lift his hand, intent on finishing the 4th draft of an updated autobiography called *Another Summer to Run*. Here is the ending of that unfinished work—his last written words:

> *The danger is our inclinations. This earth is our chance . . . Hoping it's possible to find cures, I'm living in a deer park up Rattlesnake Creek, near a wilderness where Annick walks with her dogs. Daylight is a reason to continue. On that note, adios. See you in some other seaport.* ■

ANNICK SMITH

William Kittredge and Annick Smith. Photo by Eric Smith.

*Shaun Griffin with Wendell and Tanya Berry.
Photo by Deborah Loesch-Griffin.*

SHAUN T. GRIFFIN

Late November with Wendell Berry

Long before I drove up to Lanes Landing Farm, several things endeared me to Wendell Berry: his unabashed love of the poetry of Hayden Carruth, his stubborn insistence on living without the confines of the technical world, and the breadth of his heart and mind that imbue so much of his writing about subjects that "matter to me: peace, economic justice, ecological health, political honesty, family and community stability, good work."

I

Out of Hayden Carruth's and Wendell Berry's mutual desire to meet and I suspect, a reverence for one another's work, in the summer of 1973 Carruth drove his family from Vermont to Berry's Kentucky farm. Carruth missed the house on the first pass and backed his AMC Gremlin up because there was a man standing nearby. Carruth asked, "Is that you Wendell?" and the conversation went on for the next four days. Carruth's son Bo, remembers Berry directing his prized work horses with his voice as they pulled the wagon. No doubt this moment has been properly embellished but the truth of it has also been affirmed: mutual respect. By then Carruth was making a name for himself as a poet, critic, and essayist, and Berry was the eloquent spokesman for rural farming, living with the land, and making books grounded in a belief in people and community. The two couldn't be more different. Carruth was a firm non-believer and lived accordingly. Berry lives in relationship with family and work, and the growing awareness of these touchstones in agrarian life. They were different in temperament, and yet completely absorbed with the creation of their poetry and prose and this passion for their craft further united them.

II

In the early 2000s, I was in New Hampshire for the first meeting of thirty-four state poets laureate (I represented Nevada Arts Council as the state did not yet have a laureate). It was an auspicious gathering—

Tree Swenson, then director of the Academy of American Poets and co-founder of Copper Canyon Press, was the keynote speaker. I felt strangely out of place, but Baron Wormser, Maine's poet laureate at the time, kept me smiling. I began to talk with a novelist from the Midwest when I discovered we had an interest in Wendell Berry. He had invited Berry to speak at a sustainable agriculture conference, which was the subject that brought both men together. I tried to convey my desire to understand how Berry leapt across the page in so many domains. The novelist smiled. "He is one of the few writers, I believe." Weeks later the novelist sent a picture of Berry raising a glass of wine to their shared vision of the land, of reckoning with its dissonant keepers.

III

About seven years after the conference, I was compiling and editing a collection of essays about Hayden Carruth and his work. I was at home on a hot day at the kitchen table when the phone rang. "Hello Shaun, this is Wendell Berry. Are you still working on that book about Hayden? I'd like to send you something if it's not too late."

Berry wrote a beautiful essay for the book entitled "My Friend Hayden." While working from different geographies, he and Carruth were alike in central ways: literary labor born of necessity, and bedrock values that informed that labor. It's safe to say they distrusted the largesse of American plunder or at the very least, chose not to avail themselves of its immediate privilege and access. Berry resisted what the computer stood for—the mechanization of tools that worked fine—a pencil and a mind. No amount of progress would justify this indulgence. Carruth similarly resisted the corporate swallowing of small farms in northern Vermont. Witness his long poem to Marshall Washer. These seem like different actions, but at root they are grounded in the resolve of two writers whose conviction is foremost in their work.

SHAUN T. GRIFFIN

IV

Because my book on Carruth took years to complete many people helped me to find a publisher, not least of whom was Berry (*From Sorrow's Well: The Poetry of Hayden Carruth*; Univ. of Michigan Press, 2013). Like most of the authors in the book, Berry regarded Carruth as unique among twentieth century American poets, just as Carruth believed Berry's voice to be unique. It was then I returned to Berry's poems, books, essays. One essay, I copied and keep with me whenever I leave the house to teach: "The Way of Ignorance," which closes with this paragraph:

> Of course, the way of ignorance is the way of faith. If enough of us will accept "the wisdom of humility," giving due honor to the ever-renewing pattern, accepting each moment's "new and shocking / Valuation of all we have been," then the corporate mind as we now have it will be shaken, and it will cease to exist, as its members dissent and withdraw from it.

This, it seems to me, is a clarion call for our time. So much of our political invective is cover for the absence of knowledge, and certainly the absence of humility. The essay is close to the Buddhist perspective that one must live intentionally and only then can they understand humility. Of course, this and so much of what is in the essay—and Berry writ large—is antithetical to modern culture which is why we need him. Both he and Carruth have fought the dogma that has accrued in their time—that we are special beings who require much of the earth to keep up, with whom I'm not sure. And this has made them suspect—although Berry has clearly become a pillar of American thought and humanity. Still, when I read their words, I read their isolation at having written what they believe. Then I return to these lines from Berry's essay on Mark Twain in *What Are People For?* because they so eloquently aspire to the world we have yet to live in.

> He was finally incapable of that magnanimity that is the most difficult and the most necessary: forgiveness of human nature and human circumstance. Given human nature and human circumstance, our only relief is in this forgiveness, which then restores us to community and its ancient cycle of loss and grief, hope and joy.

V

It is only after years in a place that one becomes part of it—owns it—like you might the suffering or the joy of its people and land. This is the substance that Berry has turned over and over to craft a narrative of rural Kentucky that is close and personal—steward of the soil beneath him, a life lived in community, and trusting someone enough to belong to that locale. A worthy endeavor matched only by his determination to abrade the consciousness of corporate ag and the loss of work and family of that land. So much of what he believes is grounded in the history of his beloved home. This was echoed by Gary Snyder, who after a reading in Reno, shared Berry's belief in the restorative purpose of small farming economies, his early and persistent criticism of environmental threats, and his willingness to stand in the debate on the extremes of climate change. Snyder and Berry's correspondence, gathered in *Distant Neighbors* (Counterpoint, 2014), is a tool for addressing the refuge of writing against the grain as Jack Shoemaker, their mutual publisher and champion, can attest.

VI

Still more years passed and I wrote Berry to ask if I might visit. He was busy but promised to find time. He sent a hand-written map so I would not get lost when driving from Louisville. I too, drove by his house and turned around to walk up the drive and knock. His wife Tanya answered the door. "We've been expecting you." She seated my wife, Debby, and me at the kitchen table, the room plied with books from floor to ceiling. "Wendell's outside. He'll be in soon," and we sipped tea and talked about Kentucky and why we had come from the West to meet them.

SHAUN T. GRIFFIN

Wendell came in through the back door in work clothes. He sat down at the table and asked us about our journey. Both Debby and I felt like we were sitting in the room of something intangible: the wellspring of Wendell and Tanya's sincerity. He, too, wanted to know if we had come for other business in Kentucky? "No," I said, "we came to visit you." About that time, we got lost in conversation. I remember him asking about the prison poetry workshop I taught and his intimation that it was something to be valued. When Debby and I looked up it was getting dark, long past when we were supposed to have left. We stood and hugged, and I tried in vain to thank him for one more intrusion on his time. We got in the car and turned back to the highway. Berry was across the street, near the barn leaning against his old pickup—he had gone to feed the sheep. Fitting for the man who could not tell me all that I came to ask but told me so much more of what it meant to be a person of that place.

When we returned home Berry sent a letterpressed book, *The Great Interruption: The Story of a Famous Story of Old Port William and How It Ceased to Be Told (1935-1978),* with wood engravings by Joanne Price. The book was printed by Larkspur Press in Monterey, Kentucky. There was a note inside dated 11/24/19: "We meant to give you this yesterday but were too distracted by conversation."

VII

I write letters to Berry as he is one of the last true correspondents. Most writers don't do that—they email or text but don't write in pencil as Berry does. I try not to further intrude. At ninety he doesn't need any more distractions. His family and work and writing are more than enough to keep him occupied. Every word he writes is considered. He is equally careful to cultivate a caution that merits what we seem so willing to lose—the fragile ecosystem of this planet and the further complication of not knowing if words will be enough to avert its loss.

When I read the profiles of Berry they often infer something that cannot be articulated—close to Donald Hall's "unsayable said." Like the current in the Kentucky River out his door, Berry layers complexity in book upon book that accrues to an imagined place we learn is possible—

even as it belies description. A paradox that is fitting of the Wendell Berry I know. When I ask questions, he defers. Let the words do the talking. Surely there will be adequate stories and just as surely, I will not name them.

VIII

And then I wrote him a poem. I told him he didn't need to write back, but he did, to thank me.

Raveled

Your letter came—the postmark
derivative of another time—
the one you straddle
with pencil and paper, the anti-electric
years spent at your desk, burning
words to page, pages to books—
so many I cannot count them,
between the lives of a man
sitting at the river's edge,
the brown water pushing down
to the eddies under the maple
and rosebud—a man letting go
of this time, this place without
a way to step in or across—
what the future does to its
followers, and you abide the current,
the shadows float by, unattended—
winnowing farms and fealty,
the bones beneath the land—
this time you set loose, downstream,
without so much as a cutbank
in the rivered shallows below. ■

SHAUN T. GRIFFIN

Madeline DeFrees at her 90th birthday reading.
Photo courtesy Gary Thompson.

GARY THOMPSON

Madeline DeFrees: Three Occasions

I
Madeline at Eighty & Double Dutch, *Hugo House, September 4, 1999*

Madeline at eighty is like Madeline at fifty, only better. In any given room of poets, she is still likely to be the most knowledgeable and insightful, traits she brings to the classroom, most recently at Richard Hugo House, and to any room she enters. She is still a warm and loyal friend, but perhaps because I'm that much older too, the friendship seems deeper and more important. Her mischievous eyes crinkle with joy. And she is still writing poems, many among the best she has ever written.

I mention all this not so much because this chapbook, *Double Dutch*, is published on the occasion of Madeline's eightieth birthday, but because the idea for this series of poems originated back in the mid-1970s. The lead poem, "Burning Questions," which presents the main concern of this little collection (the mother turned the father "French overnight, beat the Dutch/out of his name . . .") was one of the earliest poems in her *Imaginary Ancestors* series written during the 1970s and 1980s and published as a full-length collection in 1991. At some point in the past few years, Madeline must have realized that she never really took up the "Dutch question" posed in that 1991 book; these poems, then, return to a theme she glimpsed years earlier.

* * * * *

I first met Madeline in the high-August days of a Montana summer, 1972. I was supposed to be apartment hunting in preparation for moving my young family to Missoula where I would begin graduate school in the autumn. In reality, I was carousing with old and new friends, mostly writers and poets, and living some of the fastest and most exciting days of my life. One afternoon, Bill Kittredge, Ray Carver, and I were lazily sipping drinks at the Eastgate Bar when I mentioned that I had recently read *From the Darkroom* by Madeline DeFrees (formerly Sister Mary Gilbert), and I was looking forward to taking a class from the poet. Bill, always the gracious—even gregarious—host, made a phone call and somehow arranged for the three of us to visit Madeline, and off we drove to her place near the University. She was living in a small apartment, perhaps a former maid's quarters, on the top floor of a rather stately home. The place was tiny, made tinier by the massive presence of Bill and Ray, but somehow we squeezed into the living room, sipped the beers that Madeline served in iced-tea glasses, and talked poetry and the writing life. Madeline, small and quiet as she was, managed to hold her own alongside two of the West's top yarn-spinners. She dazzled me with her humor, vitality, and intelligence. It was in that tiny living room that summer afternoon that I first encountered the name of Gaston Bachelard and his *The Poetics of Space*, a book she was excited about and planned to assign in a fall quarter class. As it turned out, that book would occupy much of my intellectual life for months to come.

That first class from Madeline, a seminar in poetic theory, quickly doused any notion that getting an MFA degree from the University of Montana was going to be a cinch. The featured poets were Maxine Kumin (*The Nightmare Factory*) and Weldon Kees (*Collected Poems*, out of print, but typed and duplicated by Madeline for the class), but mostly it was daily doses of Bachelard, with several outside essays by the likes of Valéry and Eliot, which challenged us most. Each morning, or so it seems in retrospect, Madeline would begin class by saying something like, "You know, I just can't get Bachelard's idea of nests out of my mind…" and off we would go, perhaps applying the idea to love nest imagery in Kumin's poems or others she handed out or recited from memory. She insisted that we apply the theories to actual poems, and she assumed we had experienced a wide range of poems and had them available for instant recall, as she most certainly did.

We disappointed her at times. One day, the discussion sputtered to an embarrassing halt when we failed to identify, after much prodding, an allusion to a famous line of Wordsworth's. She was stunned, I think, and probably hurt in that way a good teacher hurts when her students fail, especially at something so basic. Most of us were chagrined, ashamed at our sophomoric ignorance, but Madeline began the next class session with her usual enthusiasm, curiosity, and humor—a testament to her resilience as a teacher. I have told a version of this story to my own students dozens of times over the years, and I always end the story with this observation: Madeline DeFrees is the smartest and best-read poetry teacher I have ever encountered. She encouraged her students to respect, yet also to challenge, our literary traditions and conventions, and she showed us how to do that with thoughtfulness and grace. She was a pivotal teacher for me, and I would guess she inspired hundreds of others over the years and across the country.

* * * * *

"I do have other models, however. For sheer staying power (an important quality for us turtles) I turn to those who have retained creative vigor into advanced years: people like Picasso, Casals, Robert Penn Warren," Madeline said in a 1980 interview. While these seven poems in *Double Dutch* reveal Madeline's nearly thirty-year exploration of real and imagined ancestry, they also exemplify the on-going vitality of her creative vision and craft. Newer poems such as "Vermeer's 'A Woman Holding a Balance,'" "Still Life," and "Double Dutch" are outstanding, certainly among the best she has ever written. And so, Madeline at eighty, like Madeline at fifty, is singing wonderfully, still teaching the rest of us a little something about the beauty and power of poetry.

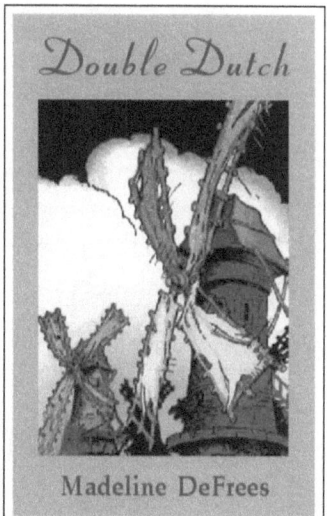

Double Dutch

> *[The Amish]...serenely devout people: men who begin
> milking the cows in darkness and hard-working women...
> like figures out of...Vermeer.*
> —David Remnick

Dutch on both sides of his family tree—now I can
say it—this was my father's history.
The Mennonite blood of his grandparents, a peaceful
tide in his veins, kept my bookkeeper father
a farmer at heart like men
in the ancestral lines.

              Mother adopted the Irish,
knowing less of Vermeer than she knew of her own
flesh and blood. He would have painted her
Dutch, and that was Mother's *bête noire*. A phrase
to please her because it comes from France.
Against the odds, she Frenchified Dad, denied his
inheritance.

              Confused and out of touch, I lived that
double lie, an alien among the Dutch, shadowed
on either side by French illusion, Irish myth.
The legacy I traveled with
extended to the playground. North and south,
eggbeater ropes coming at me. Trapped between, I
swallowed the heart in my mouth—Irish—and bounced
like a Mexican bean.

If I beat the Dutch out of my
classmates, tied everyone in French knots, it was
only a game. In a children's book, I
discovered the Scots renamed Double Dutch
Double French. They were a match for Mother. And
Dad? Forty years underground, he deserves
this retraction: Dear Dad, I admit,
the French and Irish were fiction. I'm on your side.
I'm Dutch.

II

"The Odd Woman," AWP Conference, Vancouver, B.C., March 31, 2005

Madeline was busy selecting and arranging the poems for her book *Blue Dusk* around the time I settled in the Northwest and became a neighbor of sorts, though a neighbor who had to cross a dozen miles of Puget Sound just to drop by for lunch. As she narrowed her selection, she asked my opinion a time or two, though she received more extensive advice from other friends like Tom Aslin, Pat Solon, and Joan Swift, and I presume she received some guidance from Copper Canyon editors. However, I strongly suspect that the remarkable cohesion, balance, and order of *Blue Dusk* is almost completely Madeline's doing, and I further suspect, knowing Madeline, that she could tell you exactly *why* each poem was chosen and *why* it was placed where it was.

    I've seen her do this kind of work before. When I was struggling to pull together a collection of poems that would satisfy my MFA committee, Madeline was my director. She probably got fed up with my hemming and hawing, so she agreed to help. She took a stack of my poems home for the weekend, then called me on Monday and asked me to stop by. When I got there, I was surprised to find my poems spread across her living room floor; they were arranged in four rows, with each row representing a section of the book, she told me. In addition, she had glued together two sheets of graph paper to form a 16 x 11 inch flow chart with a red-outlined box for each poem. Each box contained key phrases and images from the poem written in pencil; then common motifs were noted in green ink, with certain connections made obvious by red arrows; and finally, the overall theme of the collection was written along a slashed black line that cut diagonally through all four rows and linked the first poem with the last. That's how you organize a book of poems, Madeline-style!

I recently re-discovered that flow chart, and I'm even more amazed by it now than I was back in her living room, staring at my poems arranged across the floor. In fact, I just might have it framed. I'm guessing Madeline had her own poems spread across her office floor while she was putting together *Blue Dusk*, and I'll bet there's some kind of flow chart tucked away in her papers that should be framed in gold one day. That's because *Blue Dusk* is a rare accomplishment: a careful selection of old poems in an equally careful and subtle re-arrangement, along with a generous selection of new poems that includes several of the very best she's ever written. The book deserves all the awards and accolades it has garnered.

"The Odd Woman" is one of thirteen poems chosen from her second book—her first published under her given name—*When Sky Lets Go*, which was published by Braziller in 1978. It too is a remarkable book, though probably not as well wrought nor as consistently accomplished as *Blue Dusk*. The poems were written during a rich and vibrant period of Madeline's life, approximately 1964 through 1977. The earliest were written as a nun, Sister Mary Gilbert, while teaching at Holy Names College in Spokane, where she had been cloistered

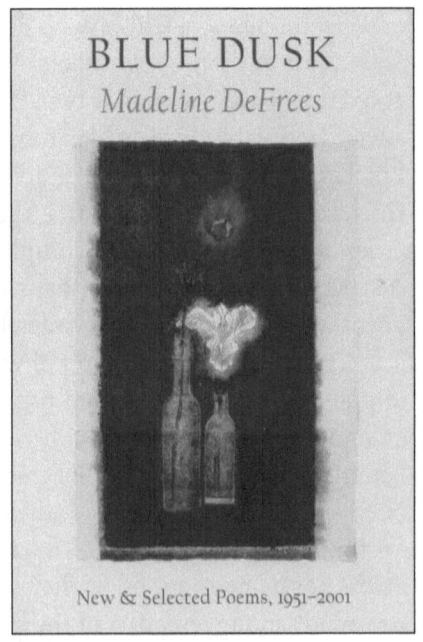

New & Selected Poems, 1951–2001

since 1950. Then, in 1967, she was hired by the University of Montana, and of course her world changed quickly and profoundly as she confronted life outside the structures of the convent. She had to literally reinvent herself during this period, and in these poems we find the jumble of emotions, sensations, and ideas that comes with this almost-mythological task—the sky that lets go in this book is sometimes dark, sometimes wonderfully bright.

I knew Madeline during this time, from 1972 on, to be precise. In fact, "The Odd Woman" was occasioned by an English Department faculty party at the Chairman's house that we both attended, or so we believe after talking about it over an outdoor lunch in early spring, 2005. However, as a grad student surprised to find himself sipping drinks with faculty members other than creative writing teachers, I certainly remember the evening differently than Madeline does. For instance, I had no idea the "guest of honor" was a medievalist from the East coast and a candidate for a position I didn't even know existed. Also, being a newcomer to Montana and not much blessed with hunting skills, I paid little attention to the hunters as they regaled the guest from the East about how you go about dressing a pig for an old-fashioned pig roast, a subject the guest had apparently brought up herself. And finally, I did not realize how uncomfortable, how odd, Madeline felt at the gathering. Like the other grad students present, I was simply happy sipping the Chairman's bourbon and gaining a glimpse of academic life outside the structures of the classroom.

If you made a flow chart for *When Sky Lets Go*, there would be a number of reoccurring images, strategies, and motifs, several of which would be jotted down inside the red box for "The Odd Woman." Even a cursory reading points us toward one of the motifs: driving. Madeline learned to drive after she left the convent, so it's easy to understand her fascination with this normally routine part of modern life, with its sense of independence, exhilaration, and freedom, as well as the obvious dangers and fear of losing control. In addition, her early driving experiences were in Montana, where it seems to be an obligation of every Montanan who has survived even a single winter to worry newcomers with tales about the horrors of black ice and the dangers of mountain driving. So driving is a charged subject in this book, as well as several offshoots, including the deer in the headlights syndrome. We find lots of river imagery, usually dangerous and somewhat ominous, though that is a bit oversimplified I suppose, but we ought to note it on our chart in green ink. And while I'm oversimplifying, I'll point out that many of the people in these poems have an "odd" quality, maybe even surreal, with a Fellini-like aura that makes them memorable, and we'll meet a couple of them in this poem. Finally, we might add to our flow chart a few examples of the word play and punning that Madeline uses more productively than any poet I can think of. And that's how this wonderful poem begins.

The Odd Woman

At parties I want to get even,
my pocket calculator rounds everything off,
taught to remember. I'm not so good
at numbers, feel awkward
as an upper plate without a partner.
Matched pairs float from the drawing board
into the drawing room, ears touched
with the right scent,
teeth and mouth perfect.

The cougar jaw yawns on the sofa back,
his molars an art-object.
The old and strange collect around me,
names I refuse pitched at my head
like haloes. This one is a dead ringer.
It rings dead. I pat the head of the beagle
nosing in my crotch and try to appear
grateful. A witch
would mount the nearest broom

and leave by the chimney. At ten I plot
my exit: gradual shift to the left,
a lunge toward the bourbon. The expert hunters
are gutting a deer
for the guest of honor. Soft eyes
accuse my headlights. I mention
morning rituals. A colleague
offers to show me the door I've watched
for the last hour.

We come to my coat laid out
in the master bedroom, warm hands curled
in the pocket. I know
how a woman who leaves her purse behind
wants to be seduced. I hang mine
from the shoulder I cry on.
Say good night to the Burmese buddha,
hunters in the snow,
and leave for the long river drive to town.

III

Celebration of Madeline's Life,
Elliott Bay Books, January 9, 2016

    In the summer of 1999, Madeline had not published a new book since 1991 when *Possible Sybils* came out from Lynx House Press, and she seemed a little anxious about that, especially since she had been writing prolifically and what-she-considered *well* throughout the decade. She would turn eighty at the end of the year.
    Enter our friend, Quinton Duval, who, like me, had been a student of Madeline's at Montana in the early 1970s. Quinton had recently founded Red Wing Press, which specialized in publishing elegant, simple, and carefully-edited chapbooks that focused on six to ten poems, and he wondered if Madeline would like to publish

a little book to commemorate her eightieth birthday. She quickly said yes, and the project began. She and Quinton selected seven poems (three of them quite new, including "Still Life,") and I was recruited to write an introduction. We were working against a tight deadline because for some reason the celebration of her eightieth birthday was already set for September 4th at the newly-established Richard Hugo House, not closer to her actual November 18th birth date.

Needless to say, we met that deadline and the result was *Double Dutch*. The three of us were quite pleased with the way that little book turned out, and as part of the celebration, Madeline read "Still Life" and one or two other poems from it. Those poems were the hit of her Hugo House birthday party and *Double Dutch* went on to find its way in the world, going through two or three printings.

Our renewed friendship deepened over the next few years. Sometimes I would drive her to her own reading events throughout the state, but more typically, I would ride the ferry over, pick her up at her place on 11th Avenue, and we would go to lunch and on to a poetry reading at Elliott Bay Bookstore or Open Books or elsewhere. In the process, she took it upon herself to show me around town and to introduce me to the ways of Seattle, though you must remember that Madeline had virtually no sense of direction and no internal compass, at least when it came to her physical location. One afternoon, we were hiking down from an event at The Frye Museum toward 1st Avenue (picture Madeline in her sneakers bouncing along—over 80 years old!). When we turned onto 1st, she suddenly blurted out, "All you need to know about this place is: *Jesus Christ Made Seattle Under Protest!*" I had no idea what she was talking about! Were we talking about religion? Seattle? Poetry? But as we trooped across James Street to Columbia to Madison, past Seneca and University and on to Pine and Pike, I gradually, and very physically, got the point, and I'll never forget that afternoon that Madeline hiked me from *Jesus* to *Protest*, as I learned my lesson for the day.

In the end, I come back to this thought from my introduction to *Double Dutch*, slightly modified: "Madeline DeFrees was the smartest and best-read poetry teacher I have ever encountered. She encouraged her students to respect, yet also to challenge, our literary traditions and conventions, and she showed how to do that with thoughtfulness and grace . . ."

As long as one student of hers is in this world, Madeline will be remembered and revered, and quite possibly, for much longer than that. This is my favorite poem of hers:

Still Life

> *The question that he frames in all but words*
> *Is what to make of a diminished thing.*
>
> —Robert Frost, "The Oven Bird"

After your letter arrived I left the oven on
all night and never once
put my head in it. After your letter arrived
I let one foot follow the other
through the better part of the day. Your letter
lay on the kitchen table by the paring
knife on the stoneware plate with the apple core
like a Dutch still life restored to
its muted color.

    In the sink a spiral of lemon
peel twisted like smoke toward the past and I
think that I let it lie.
The first day of night these eyes you opened
were glassed and dry as your late martini.
The next they brimmed into morning.
It was time to rehearse the Sunday phone call,
the new role laid out for learning.
When you asked,

> *Did you get my letter?* I picked up
> the cue as if you had wired me
> roses in winter or proposed
> a pas de deux. Then partly for your sake I taught
> myself to sing the best song I could make:
> the burden of the oven bird's diminished thing. Sang
> wash of sunlight on the sill and apple core,
> sang water glass half full of emptiness. Sang body
> all in shadow that I must bathe and dress.

P.S. We gave away the last remaining copies of *Double Dutch* that afternoon, a posthumous gift from Madeline and Quinton. ∎

Madeline DeFrees with former student and publisher Quinton Duvall. Photo courtesy Gary Thompson.

HOWARD LEVY

A Small Note on Adrienne Rich

It is 1973 and Adrienne Rich has just published *Diving into the Wreck*, a book with its centerpiece poem, "The Phenomenology of Anger" which entwines the violence of Vietnam and the world's other violences with the personal violence she feels from men.

> How does a pile of rags the machinist wiped his hands on
> feel in its cupboard, hour upon hour.

And the poem ends in a very quiet manifesto:

> Every act of becoming conscious
> (it says here in this book)
> Is an unnatural act.

And that year she is also teaching in the Graduate Creative Writing program at the City University of New York.

Adrienne Rich, New York City, 1973. Photo © Nancy Crampton.

I am in the second year of that program and sign up for that semester's workshop. For my first year, I worked with Joel Oppenheimer, the bearded, funny, laconic poet, trained at Black Mountain College with Olson and Creeley and all the Projective Verse folks. So, Adrienne Rich, fresh with Diving into the Wreck, is obviously from the whole other pole, if not universe.

Of course, this is now more than fifty years ago, and some memories have flattened and some have actually remained absolutely clear. We come into class that first day in September, in memory maybe about fifteen of us, maybe a bit more men than women but close and she hands out an index card to each of us.

The first challenge from her. "I want you to write down what you want to get out of this class."

And I think to myself, this is Adrienne Rich, what is it that she can most teach me. So I write down one word. "Bravery."

Later during the semester, in a one-on-one conference, she tells me how she appreciated my answer, reinforcing that she thought that writing truthful poems, as she would often say, was a radical and political act. And she recognized how unnatural it was to pull the truth, both personal and social, out from the bottom where the "wreck" was, how the conscious act of diving into it required much in the way of bravery. It was certainly how she wrote.

And so the weeks went on, each class devoted to one person's work, until the firestorm. I don't think that any of us understood how the class was grating on her, how the commentaries on the poems and the poems themselves from one of the two groups, the men, not the women, rankled her, but they clearly did.

We were working on this one man's poems and they were rather sloppy and not terribly good. They tried to get by on brio, on the camaraderie of guys just hanging out, and there was this poem about shaving. Quietly, something about this poem triggered her, maybe that male *je ne sais quoi* and she stopped the class to muse on this question. Maybe not the exact words, but the gist: "I often wonder how a man puts a razor to his neck every day and survives." The silence, yup, was deafening, and I thought two rather contrasting thoughts. One was the obvious wish that men would/should slit their throats daily until there were none of us left and the other, the far more powerful other, that she understood that there is a real toll on men who daily face a moment of easy suicide, who see every day the absolute thinness of their continued existence.

And that dichotomy was Adrienne Rich.

But that was not the firestorm. A few minutes after that, she announced to the class that the men would have to leave, that she did not want to work with them any longer. That we had hogged the commentaries, that our presence had always constricted the women.

Needless to say, the rest of the remaining time of the class that day was spent in heated discussion. On the obvious logistics level, this would not happen. We had registered and paid for the course, she did not have the discretion to wipe away that reality. But the emotions were powerful, many of us, both men and women, diving into our own wrecks.

That night, I wrote her a five-page, single-spaced letter about trying to hear her, trying to understand how what I had heard was preconditioned by my own sense of male inferiority and female existential power, all the puerile thinking of an unsure twenty-something man, and how hard it was to listen to her without invoking the fear of the mystical, all powerful female figure. And she wrote back a very warm and encouraging letter, a very human letter as she appeared touched by my effort to hear.

While some part of her, at that time, seemed to believe that the Y chromosome was inherently criminal, her humanity recognized the self-same humanity of those Y's.

A few years later in 1979, I was teaching English in a private high school in New York and decided to honor her and her message by offering a course in Women's Literature (Austen, Gilman, Hurston, Kingston and Rich) to the Juniors and Seniors. I asked a female faculty member to team teach with me, but that did not pan out. I wrote to Adrienne and asked her if she would come read and talk to my students, but she was unable to do so. She did offer that she would have preferred team-teaching with a woman but thought that a man who had learned how to listen would be certainly better than nothing. She praised the multi-ethnic reading list and when, later that year, I won an award for my poetry, she wrote me a lovely note of congratulations.

I am not sure if I ever learned bravery from that class, probably a coin flip, but what I did learn was the eye-narrowing necessity of bravery and how I might learn when I stopped short. Bravery became the mantra of revision, the working, over and over, to find the poem that was busting out of silence, but not fully formed. I tried to and finally, I think, learned how to read the dead parts of the drafts and how it was the dead parts, the resistances, that really told me what I might be trying to get to. And so, the bravery, for me, became the work of decoding what I was not saying. I took it inside, rather than outside as Adrienne did, maybe because of the terrain of my privilege.

And maybe, I learned too the bravery of writing and writing poems that were often not read because my "success" was limited. That the work needs to be done, even if it does not accord you too many celebrations. That the radical and political act of bringing truth to the world, even a moment of purely private truth, moves the world along and that is enough quiet reward.

But I could read her bravery, of course, both in the work and in the class (just imagine saying that out loud that you were tired of the men) and I understood, because of how she touched me, that the phenomenology of her anger included a huge space for quiet human connection. And I think in her later work that human connection gained greater and greater voice, never forgetting, though, the anger beside it.

And, as she has, over time, become absolutely ratified as the iconic feminist poet of that era charging at the gates, which she certainly was, what should not be missed is that her politics were built, truly but not obviously, on the foundation of the depth of her humanity. ∎

TERESA JORDAN

The Last Conversation
Remembering Writer Terence O'Donnell

"How long does he have?" I asked. "A few weeks," she answered. "Maybe more."

"Is he awake?" I asked. "Can I talk to him?"

She put him on the phone. His voice was weaker than usual but still resonated with its customary warmth.

"Hello, dear. How are you?"

"Terry, I'd like to come see you."

"Yes," he said. "That would be nice."

I'd sensed something was wrong before I called. Terence O'Donnell and I were never daily friends. During the years I lived in Portland, Oregon, we got together every month or two. I left for a while to work on a project in Montana; when I returned, it was if I had never gone. A few years later, after I married and moved away for good, we wrote each other only two or three times a year, but whenever I visited, we picked up where we had left off.

In early 2001, however, I grew worried. A couple of months earlier, Terry had sent a copy of his new collection of short stories, *Seven Shades of Memory: Stories of Old Iran*. I immediately wrote to tell him how much I liked it but hadn't heard back. By this time we had known each other for almost thirty years and I knew he would grant a compliment the respect of acknowledgement.

The woman on the phone introduced herself as a hospice nurse. Terry had esophageal cancer and had just returned from the hospital to die.

* * * * *

The next day, on my flight to Portland from my home in Salt Lake City, I closed my eyes and let Terry come fully into view. I remembered an evening we spent together on my front porch in the hills above the Willamette River, drinking gin and tonic and watching dusk settle over the industrial district below, the blue and orange vapor lights along the water blinking on as the afternoon faded into night. It had been a typical Oregon winter, gloomy and wet, but a few days earlier the tulips and daffodils had exploded into view and today was the season's first full day of sun. We were both in a glorious mood.

This was Terry's first visit to the little bungalow I had just purchased in the Northwest Hills. The neighbors called it the Birdhouse after the Bird family who had lived in it for years, and the name fit perfectly for it was perched on a steep rise, connected to the street below by a series of switchbacks and stairs. This was my first house and I knew it wasn't practical—in addition to the difficult ascent, it was in such poor repair that my friends immediately christened it Casa Dry Rot—but I had fallen in love with its Craftsman-era charm, particularly the porch and pergola that ran the full breadth of the front and looked out over the wooded neighborhood, the Columbia River, and, on sunny days like today, Mount Hood off in the distance.

One of my first repairs had been to replace the rickety porch rail with flower boxes and earlier that evening I had been planting petunias when Terry parked on the street below. I watched as he extricated himself from his little red Fiat: first came his cane; then his short, blue-jeaned legs; and then, with a great push, the rest of him. As he got his feet under him and straightened his tweed driver's cap and rumpled jacket, I called down a hello.

"There you are!" he said as he glanced up and caught sight of me. "Look at you, a sprite among the flowers."

"And you," I replied, "you look like an Irish raconteur," which, come to think of it, he was. I remember laughing, and there is something in that laugh—perhaps in any laugh from a balcony to a dear friend down below—that rings for me now, so full of joy.

Terry started the long trek up. He had been hit by a truck as a boy, an event that relegated him to bed for a large part of his childhood and left him with one leg shorter than the other, the foot canted at an angle.

Now in his sixties, each step took effort. At the top of one switchback he stopped and turned to take in the view; at the top of the next, he leaned over and picked a yellow pansy for his buttonhole. His ascent was not slow so much as unhurried, and there was grace to it. The grace with which Terry accommodated to whatever lay before him was one of the many things that set him apart from the rest of us.

When Terry reached the top of the stairs, we embraced and kissed in the European way, on both cheeks. Then we stood at the flowerboxes and looked out, locating this landmark and that. In time I maneuvered him over to the glass-topped table where I had set out almonds and olives and now, as we enjoyed our drinks, Terry brought a gift out of his satchel, a hanging lantern. "It's from the Garden," he told me, "and I thought it would look good here." I knew that the garden he referred to was the pomegranate orchard in Iran where he had lived for many years as a young man. "Oh, Terry," I said as I ran my fingers along the ornate brass at the top and bottom and manipulated the bellows of ivory-colored oilcloth. "It's beautiful."

Terence O'Donnell. Photo by Teresa Jordan.

I found a candle and hung the lantern from the pergola above us. Now we sat under its warm light, talking about writing, the subject that had brought us together in the first place. That night we were discussing the ways in which a good writer can evoke character with a few deft strokes. "And you, Terry. If you had to describe yourself in one word, what would it be?"

He leaned back in his chair and stretched his legs out in front of him as he thought. Then he leaned forward. "*Flaneur*," he said, and when he saw my puzzlement, he continued: "a pedestrian, someone who walks around looking at things." He flicked his tongue over his lips, a tic that signaled he was feeling mischievous. "A flaneur is a bit of a loiterer, really, not good for much." He tipped back in his chair again and let fly his earthy laugh.

* * * * *

Terry was not, in the conventional sense, a handsome man. Short and round faced, myopic behind wire-rimmed glasses, he had a wide and juicy mouth, and such pure relish of language that he often licked his lips as he spoke. He loved children and they him; one child of whom he was especially fond called him her Grandpa Toad. In sartorial matters he was, shall we say, unfussy, but his manner was elegant and courtly, almost of another age.

So was his storytelling. Before I met Terry in person, I came to know him through the pages of his first book, *Garden of the Brave in War: Recollections of Iran*, titled after the name of the orchard where he had lived in the 1960s and early 1970s. The contemporary memoir is often a vision quest of sorts, a confessional search for self, but Terry's book belongs to an earlier mode. A chronicler like Chaucer, Isak Dinesan and John Steinbeck, he was outward looking rather than self-reflective. This is a highly personal book but not self-absorbed: Terry regarded himself with the same keen eye and nonjudgmental affection that he did the Persians he lived among.

Terry's greatest strength was not in asking questions but in spending enough time for the answers to offer themselves of their own accord. The term "flaneur" is often associated with the self-indulgent indolence of someone who strolls the boulevard as much to be seen as to take in the street life—hence Terry's self-deprecating laugh. But he was a flaneur in the more generous sense that Flaubert alluded to when he defined it as someone who walks the city in order to understand it. He walked the Persian countryside—and rode horseback and drove his decrepit Land Rover across it—for no greater purpose than to be a part of it.

Once, crossing the desert, his radiator overheated and he made his way to a tribal encampment to ask for water. The men who came out to greet him possessed, as Terry described it, "like so many tribesmen, that look which I have only seen before in Byzantine icons and in the faces of the Aran Islanders—a kind of stunned staring like men caught dreaming of eternity."

The tribesmen led him to the *kalantar*, the chief, who invited Terry into his tent and saw that he was fed—a skewer of kabobed liver, sheep's milk, bread.

> The *kalantar* said he had a question to ask me. Since my countrymen were rich, was it not possible for them to sit all day and think? I told him they did not. He was puzzled. Then he went on to say that he was certain that if he sat thinking for a year or two—it might take three—he would be able to conceive the construction of a radio. Having done so, he would simply go to town, buy wire and metal, and make it. He added that sometime, as a kind of experiment, he might do this.

They chatted for a while and then, at the chief's invitation, Terry retired to a hill overlooking the camp and took a nap. It was dusk when he awoke:

> The evening fires had been started; sparks were blowing in the smoke and I could see in the outline the bending figures of the women. From behind the hills, which were black and craggy now, came the rising moon. I wanted to stay but I knew I couldn't.

The *kalantar* and some of the others came up to me. The food, they said, would soon be ready, and after that I could sleep again. I looked at their faces and at the fires and again I was tempted.

But I had made certain promises. They did not say that I should break the promises, but only that I should put them off for another day. I started walking to the Land Rover. They came along with me, looking puzzled and hurt. "Why?" the *kalantar* asked. "After all there is time—time," and he motioned toward the plain, the mountains, and the sky."

Terry never saw the tribesmen again, but he became deeply entrenched in the life of the farm and nearby town. He engaged a servant, the cousin of a village friend. Mamdali—short for Mohammed Ali—came from a more remote village and brought his wife and children. Terry had never had a servant before and he anticipated a simple, practical relationship: He would explain what housekeeping and other services he needed, Mamdali would provide them, and Terry would pay a wage. Mamdali saw his duties differently. He took little notice of the house and focused instead on Terry himself, guarding his physical and spiritual well-being as well as his reputation.

He brought coffee each morning, assessing Terry's state of dress by calling out, with his knock, "Are you an Arab or an Iranian?" a reference to the old Persian view that Arabs were uncivilized and "went about unclothed and ate lizards." He interpreted Terry's dreams and instructed him in matters of hospitality, almsgiving, and ritual acts of gratitude. Terry appreciated the cultural instruction but resented other attentions, at least at first, like Mamdali's habit of adding "God willing" each time Terry stated an intention. "I did not care to be crossed in my belief that my acts were willed by me."

Then there was Terry's habit of skinny-dipping in the garden pool each morning. According to religious law, the exposure of private parts "has sin," but Terry enjoyed the morning ritual. Mamdali and his family could stay away if it offended them. The subject incited a great deal of bickering and one day Terry succumbed to the oldest cliché: "If God had not approved of one's member . . . ."

"It is not bad," Mamdali interrupted, "but if God had wanted it displayed, he would have put it on your neck."

In truth, Mamdali was mostly tolerant of Terry's lapses, even his fondness for vodka. "He disapproved of this but put up with it, for after all I was not at fault for having been born into a benighted religion that permits intoxicants." But one night Terry got very drunk. He fell in his study and the crash brought Mamdali running. He found Terry stumbling with a cut on his forehead and grabbed the decanter away from him. They fell into violent argument and Mamdali left, only to return with a rope with which he dragged Terry to bed. Then he forced Terry to drink a "dose," a mixture of opium and herbs, to calm him.

The coming dawn, Terry woke to find his constraint loosened. "Looking around," he wrote, "I saw that [Mamdali] was still there, sitting on the floor against the wall, and from the way his head was tilted back I thought he was sleeping. But as the light grew stronger, I realized that his eyes were open, though heavy lidded, and that he was watching me—Mamdali, the keeper of the Garden, and of myself."

* * * * *

As I read deeper into the book, I fell ever more under its spell. A friend had given it to me, saying she wanted to introduce me to Terry after I had read it. I had just published a book of my own—my first—about women who worked on the land and she thought we had much in common.

Someone who is learning to write reads with a particular hunger, and I devoured *Garden of the Brave in War*. For my own book, *Cowgirls: Women of the American West*, I had interviewed dozens of women

Terence O'Donnell at a book signing. Photo courtesy Oregon Historical Society.

who worked on ranches and in the rodeo. I had been inspired by the work of Studs Terkel, whose collections of oral histories, *Working* and *Hard Times*, had introduced me to the extraordinary eloquence of ordinary people when they speak of what matters to them most. I had devoted most of the book to the women's own words, but I had tried to introduce each one with a sketch that would crystallize her in the reader's imagination. I knew how hard it was to find the telling details. My work suffered by comparison with Terry's and I was shy to meet him.

When my friend brought us together over dinner, Terry told me he had read my book and liked it. This was what I dreaded most, the perfunctory pat on the back, and I instinctively dismissed it: it was the work of a beginner, full of purple prose . . .

"Purple," he said. "I didn't find it so. Give me an example."

"Well, I call pumps in an oil field, 'giant steel mosquitoes sucking crude . . . .'"

"Actually," he said, "that's quite descriptive."

He had not responded to me as an insecure young woman whose fears he needed to allay. He had responded to me as a writer with a professional concern. In a word, he cut through the bullshit.

Perhaps it's a fool's errand to try and dissect a friendship. The chemistry is different than that in romantic love, but it can be as strong and as mysterious. Some part of it lay in our shared Irish genes, our love of storytelling, and our affinity for people who worked with their hands. Certainly, as in many friendships that bridge the generations—Terry was some thirty years older than I—there was the bond between a generous mentor and a willing apprentice. But from that first moment, I felt a sense of peace and homecoming, something I could never put language to until I ran across the concept of a soul friend, the *anam ċara*, in the writing of another Irishman, poet John O'Donahue. "In everyone's life there is great need for an *anam ċara*, a soul friend. In this love you are understood as you are without mask or pretension . . . . Where you are understood, you are at home."

I was twenty-seven years old when we came into each other's lives, and I needed both a guide and a home. When my mother had died suddenly a few years earlier, the sun fell out of the sky. She had been the one person in whose presence I felt entirely embraced, and I believe she felt a similar comfort with me. In the isolated world of the Wyoming ranch where I grew up, my father's family took up much of our lives and, with the exception of one great aunt who lived a few miles away, they were a prickly lot, prone to disapproval. In their eyes, my mother and I came up short.

TERESA JORDAN

With her death, my father and I grew estranged as well. When I was a child, we had been inseparable. I was gutsy and indomitable and embraced the hard and dangerous work of the ranch with an enthusiasm my brother lacked. I suspect my father saw himself in me. I know he hoped I would become a military commander or corporate CEO, aspirations he felt had slipped out of his own grasp when he lost his hearing as a young tank commander in postwar Germany. But as I developed a mind of my own, it was clear I would not fulfill his dreams. He was a warrior who liked rules and rigidity; I leaned toward an artistic life. My mother bridged the gap between us and kept us more amused by each other than annoyed, but in her absence he took my Eastern education and bohemian pursuits as a personal betrayal; I felt similarly abandoned by his lack of benediction. In our great sorrow at her passing, we lost each other as well.

Then, in the economic turmoil of the 1970s, the ranch passed out of our family. By the time I met Terry, I was untethered and, in terms of guidance, largely alone.

Terry once told me a story from his childhood. Shortly after the accident with the truck, an infection of the bone, osteomyelitis, set in. That was in the 1930s, before antibiotics, and no one expected him to live. To everyone's surprise he survived, but he was bedridden for years and had few friends his own age. Instead, he drew close to many of the adults who visited his family's home on the Oregon coast, including a fisherman, a big Pacific Islander who was a powerful swimmer and would carry the boy on his back out to Tillamook Lighthouse to play chess with the keeper. Then, at the end of the afternoon, the fisherman would swim Terry back to shore.

Something in Terry recognized the orphaned child in me who yearned for passage to a larger world; something in me recognized Terry as the one who could carry me to the lighthouse and then deliver me safely back to dry land.

While I was searching out women who worked on the land, I ran across the memoir of Margaret Duncan Brown, a Colorado woman who continued ranching alone after her husband died suddenly in 1918. "I have spent the first half of my life explaining," she wrote at one point. "I'm going to start the second half of my life without explanation."

I included the quotation in my book, struck by its promise of maturing into an unapologetic life, and this yearning, too, drew me to Terry. I don't ever remember talking about fears or insecurities with him, nothing so direct. Instead, through our long and rambling conversations, Terry would tell a story or make an observation that cut to the core of how to live authentically. Once we were talking about the self-help movement. "We Americans assume we have not only an inalienable right to be happy," he said, "but a duty. If we aren't giddy, we feel cheated, inept. In French, the word for happiness is *bonheur*, good hour. There is a sense of savoring the perfect moments, the small happinesses. No one expects they will last forever."

Another time, Terry told me that it was easier being a cripple in a foreign country than here in the States. He liked to use words like "cripple": politically incorrect, a little shocking. "Overseas," he told me, "people will ask you outright: 'What happened to *you*?' Here, everyone pretends they don't notice."

About coming of age: "Maybe maturity is that day you wake up and realize your parents are never going to change. And they don't have to change for you to have a good life."

* * * * *

"Make sure your tray tables and seat backs are in their full upright position . . . ." The overhead voice brought me back to the present and the realization that Terry's own good life was ending. We landed and I rented a car to drive downtown to Terry's studio apartment. Cynthia, the lead hospice nurse, buzzed me in. She told me Terry had been seeing visitors all day but now he was alone. She led me into the living room where he dozed lightly in a hospital bed. He woke when I entered and seemed delighted to see me. I leaned down and we kissed. He looked at me closely. "You look so fresh," he said, "in your blue jeans. And your warm sweater. How soft it is, such a rich color." He touched my small woven purse. "So nicely made. Is it American Indian?" When I said it was Indonesian, he said, "Of course."

We talked about many things. I had not expected him to be so clear, his mind so active. We talked about his book of stories, and he said it had been wonderful to get my letter. He apologized for not writing back: that must have been almost exactly when he got sick. "The heart soars at compliments," he said, "but truly, you learn from criticism. What didn't ring true?"

His request for criticism was not politeness. I knew that his hope in coming home was to finish the last two chapters of the novel he had in progress. He was still thinking of how words work, of storytelling. We talked about his tale of two American women on holiday who quiz their Iranian waiter about the lives of women behind the veil. Terry spoke of his fatigue with the assumptions and condescension of Westerners, "and yet I liked those American women," he said. I knew it was true. There is affection on every page, just as there is an unblinking awareness of human frailty.

Terry asked if I was happy, and I told him yes. He wanted to know about Hal, my husband. He had watched me flail my way through a number of relationships, but he had warmed to Hal immediately. I told him it seemed uncomplicated, really: I loved Hal, and felt entirely loved by him in return. Terry was surprised to learn we had been married ten years. "So long," he said. "It seems as if you just left."

Watercolor by Teresa Jordan of Terence O'Donnell and Jordan's husband, Hal Canon at O'Donnell's retirement cottage on the Washington coast, "Crank's Roost" (c.1998 or 1999).

"Of course there are times that we make each other angry," I said, "Furious. But Hal is quirky and full of play. I get mad, but I never get bored."

Terry told me about seeing our mutual friend, Dorothy, a couple of years after her husband, the poet William Stafford, died. "I said to her, 'you must miss him so,'" Terry related, "and she replied, 'Oh yes, I do. He was such fun.' I thought that was wonderful, that she remarked not that he was so wise or so talented, but so *fun.*"

Bill and Dorothy's marriage was renowned for its closeness, and I remembered a story their son Kim had told me. When he was going through a divorce, he said to his father, "You and Mother have always seemed to get along so well. How do you do it?" Bill answered that it was true: 97% of their marriage was sweetness and light. "And the other 3%?" Kim asked. "Arsenic," Bill replied.

"Persian marriages are arranged," Terry told me. "They aren't for love, but in four or five years a couple, if they are lucky, can construct a sort of scaffolding around the marriage, an accommodation for each other, a way of working around the habits or traits that drive each other crazy. They find a way to wall off what might be disagreeable, and in the common space that is left, they find, over time, something that is love."

Terry told me that he had been surprised to find that one retires twice. When he was 65, he retired from his positions at the Oregon Historical Society and Portland State University and started drawing his pensions and Social Security. He built Crank's Roost, his cottage at the coast; he wrote more; his life changed in many ways. "But then there comes a second retirement," he said, "a time when you retire from the world. The world has changed and it's a whole new world. It's a world for the young, and I don't mean the twenty-year-olds. But it's not for me, I have no desire to understand it or master it."

"Terry," I said. "I hear what you are staying, and yet your curiosity seems very much intact."

He took in this observation. "Yes," he said after a moment. "I guess that's true. There is much about this new stage of life that is unexpected, and fascinating. For one thing, with hospice care, I'm suddenly inside this world of single mothers. It's a world that never intersected with mine before. I drive the nurses crazy, I ask so many questions."

He asked about my work, my home, my friends. In each case, he listened carefully and then responded with a story or observation of his own. It was the familiar and generous rhythm that I had always loved about our conversations, and it was easy to forget that he was lying in a hospice bed with only a few weeks to live. At one point he gestured toward the black and white photographs that covered the walls in the alcove where his desk stood. He told me he could see all the parts of his life since boyhood in the faces gathered there. "These will probably be the last things I see," he said with great warmth, "those faces."

"Terry," I said at one point, "I need to tell you something. When we spoke on the phone yesterday, I told you that you had no idea how much you meant to me, and you said that was probably true. Many of us who aren't close to our own families create families of intention, and in that, you are bedrock. I was thinking on the plane about that universal hunger for parental approval. But it struck me that perhaps even more important than receiving approval is being able give it, to have an elder whose model you lean on when you question how to live your own life. You are that person for me."

Just then, Cynthia brought in another visitor and the moment was over. Perhaps the interruption was timely; we had never been much for confessions of the heart.

Terry introduced me to his friend Mort, an Iranian he had known for many years. Mort had helped get Terry home from the hospitable, so I was particularly happy to meet him. They talked about Mort's work and family: the daughter who was vice-president of her college and intensely political, the son who was a fireman. "For Persians," Terry said, "their sons are the whole world. They are raised to be doctors or lawyers or gods." At first, Mort had been mystified by his son's choice of a profession, but he had come to support it. And then there was the youngest daughter, just older than a toddler, "a giant powder puff of a girl" in Terry's description, healthy and soft and incredibly loving.

I could see that Terry was tiring, and that he and his friend should have time alone, so I rose to say goodnight. I kissed Terry and hugged him for a long time. I told him I would stop in again in the morning on my way to the airport. He slept very deeply these days, he said. He might be quite sleepy in the morning, but he wanted me to come. I went to the kitchen to thank Cynthia for the wonderful care, for helping Terry be at home. Terry called me back into the living room. He had forgotten to ask after my father and brother. Once again, we said goodnight.

* * * * *

I spent the night with a friend on the far side of the Willamette River and left next morning in time to have an hour and a half with Terry before my plane. But as I drove onto the Hawthorne Bridge, bars came down and lights flashed as the center portion rose for a ship to pass—slowly, so slowly. I watched the clock and tapped out my frustration on the steering wheel. Then, after the bridge had lowered back into place, the car in front of me stalled. I told myself to breathe deeply and found myself thinking of the *kalantar* in the Iranian desert: "After all, there is time—time."

When I finally arrived, another nurse, Mercedes, came downstairs to let me in. As we walked up to Terry's apartment, I told her how much I valued him. "So many people say that," she said. "Everyone who comes here says that. Can you tell me why?" I always felt heard when I talked to Terry, I told her. He had a way of bringing people out, but it was more than that. In his presence, I listened well. Afterwards, I understood the world better. But I also felt like he got something in return, and that sort of reciprocity was rare.

She told me Terry was awake and had eaten his breakfast. When I came into the room, I saw he had the paper in bed, but he was dozing. He woke and asked me to come close so he could really look at me. "I can't see so well anymore," he said, "especially out of my right eye." I leaned close and kissed him, and he put his hands on either side of my face. "I like the look of a mature woman," he said. I told him that I liked getting older, that I liked each year of it: not the loss of the arrogant strength of youth, but the way you learned more about love, about being loved.

He asked how I slept and then told me he had dreamed wildly. "Not bad dreams, interesting dreams. I dreamt about you. You were saving this old hotel in Butte. It was tall and you were very large. You stood straddling it. You were a bulwark against its destruction."

Early in our friendship, I had moved to Butte, Montana to interview miners displaced by the demise of the Anaconda Copper Company. The project interested Terry and he loved my descriptions of the faded city, a jumble of Victorian mansions, workers' hovels, and the tall steel head frames that towered over mine shafts. I told him I liked his dream. I liked hotels: all those rooms, all those stories.

Terry was alert at first, but then, as we talked, he drifted in and out. Once, after he had dozed for a couple of minutes, he opened his eyes and said, "What do you think of the word 'zeal?'" He had used this word to describe someone in an early chapter of his novel, but it didn't ring quite true. We discussed it as an enthusiasm that steamrolled over other concerns, that swept everything else out of the way. "Yes," he said, "zeal is not right for that character. I need to go back and change it." He said he didn't know if he had the concentration to finish the book.

As he spoke, he was feeling around for something on his bed, and I asked if I could help. "My pen case," he said. I could see it on his desk, and got up to fetch it. "What a beautiful case," I said as I felt the well-worn leather.

"Yes," he said. "Totally unnecessary, really, but I've always liked it." I handed it to him, and he stroked the leather, then opened the case and took out his pen. "This is a good pen, a lifetime pen," he said of the chrome ballpoint. "I was thinking of giving this to you, but I have decided to give it to another young friend. She has been having a very hard time. She has been almost suicidal. I think she can use encouragement." I watched him finger the pen, and I felt desire, tangible as a taste in my throat, rise up in me. I wanted that pen. But even now, on his journey to the farther shore, he was ferrying another young writer to the lighthouse.

Terry closed his eyes. "There will be another contingent here soon," he said in a moment, "six of my other officers." I thought he was talking about another group of friends but then he said something about them rounding up the pens. I had the sense that he was half in dream, and he imagined the pens animated and moving about the room. As he nodded off again, he gestured with his left hand, as if calling the pens back to him. His breathing got quieter and his head fell back with his mouth open. He became more and more still and I sat holding his hand. At first I felt peaceful but then I grew scared. I called the nurse, and though she didn't hear me, Terry woke. "Oh, I drifted off. I'm sorry."

"Terry," I said, "You scared me, you were so still."

"You are taking good care of your sister, aren't you?" he said. I said that I was trying to help my brother. "Oh yes," he said, "your brother."

I sat with Terry as he dozed, and always that question: should I stay? I wasn't worried about missing my plane; I could catch another. Or should I go so he could rest, so he had energy for others? A couple more times I thought he was slipping away. When I realized that he was just drifting, resting, I decided I should go. I put my hand on his forehead. He woke. I kissed him and told him how much I loved him. I told him how good he smelled.

"Do I?"

"Yes, you always do. I always notice. Very clean, but also fragrant."

"But my breath must be bad," he said, "with all the chemicals and everything…"

"No," I said, "your breath is fresh," and it was true. He told me to travel safely, to go with God. "And you, Terry, you travel safely also." I kissed him again, and said goodbye.

I was crying when I stepped into the kitchen. "Thank you," Mercedes said, "for telling me what you did this morning. You gave me a gift." I thanked her for helping Terry be at home and left. It was mild outside, moist and green, and traffic to the airport flowed easily.

*****

In his years in Iran, there were times that Terry was, by his own description, too fond of the sauce. Once he got into a street fight and was knocked unconscious. He woke several days later to find himself in his room, surrounded by neighbors: women in *chadors* doing their mending, children playing about the bedstead, old men knitting and talking among themselves. Occasionally, one of the women would ululate but the general air was calm, lighthearted. As Terry gradually came to his senses, he wasn't sure if he were alive or dead. It was really quite wonderful, he told me, all these people present for him even as they

O'Donnell. Photo courtesy Oregon Historical Society.

went about their daily lives. What a lovely way to go, he thought, surrounded by so much life.

Terry died a few weeks after my visit, with only a nurse in attendance. He had a coughing fit and that was the end. But I don't imagine him alone; I don't imagine him feeling alone. However bad the coughing, I know he looked up and saw the photographs on the wall: so many places, so many stories, so many of us who loved him, who carry his love for us out into the world. ■

Headstone: "In Honor of Terence O'Donnell, 1924—2001. Consummate storyteller and Friend of the Persians." Photo by Teresa Jordan.

Editor and writer Grover Lewis. Photo courtesy Rae Lewis.

RAE LEWIS

Grover Lewis and the Shooting of Larry Flynt, March 6, 1978
An Excerpt from a Memoir-in-Progress

Editor's Note: *Fifty years ago, Grover Lewis (1934-1995), an innovative and inspiring practitioner of 1970s New Journalism died of lung cancer in Los Angeles. An editor and writer for such publications as* Rolling Stone, New West, The Village Voice, Playboy, Texas Monthly, *and more, Lewis's in-depth articles on such events as the horrific 1969 Altamont Music Festival, profiles of actors Robert Mitchum, Lee Marvin, Paul Newman, blues icon Lightnin' Hopkins, diva Barbara Streisand, writer Ken Kesey, and behind-the-scenes stories about the making of such films as* The Last Picture Show *(1971, in which he had a small part), and Sam Peckinpah's* The Getaway *(1972), increased Lewis's reputation and the readership of the magazines for which he wrote. He turned celebrity profile assignments into more intense explorations of the American culture of his time, and through his work, a fledgling magazine like* Rolling Stone *was elevated from a newsprint rock-n-roll tabloid to a forum for serious social, political, and cultural exposés.*

Often fueled by a creative cocktail of alcohol, amphetamine, cannabis, and a constant flow of cigarettes, his reporting in its heyday rivaled and complimented the roving journalism of his friends and fellow writers Hunter S. Thompson, Tim Cahill, Tom Wolfe, Dave Hickey, and Kenneth Turan, and his colleagues, editors, and readers praised his lucidity, accuracy, and truthful analysis of the subjects before him. As many of his contemporaries have said, Grover Lewis set the standard for many magazine writers of his day.

Thankfully, University of Texas Press preserved some of his best work in Splendor in the Short Grass: The Grover Lewis Reader, *edited by Jan Reid and W.K. Stratton (2005). The title essay, subtitled "The Making of* The Last Picture Show" *(Rolling Stone, 1971), and "Cracker Eden: Oak Cliff—a Report, a Memoir" (Texas Monthly, 1992) particularly are considered classic works of magazine journalism of his time. The volume also is peppered with a selection of his poems from* I'll Be There in the Morning, If I Live, *a 1973 collection published by Straight Arrow Books. In 1995, he had signed a publishing contract to complete a memoir but died about month later at the age of 60.*

THE LIMBERLOST REVIEW

Today, his widow, writer and artist Rae Lewis, is at work on a memoir about her life with Grover Lewis. She remembers an intellectually gifted and complex man, a sensitive Texas-born writer who, as an eight-year-old, survived the horror of his parents killing each other with the same pistol. Rae recalls his commitment to his work requiring frequent traveling, long absences, eating and drinking between cigarettes on the run, and the constant typewriter-pounding pressure of deadlines.

In the following excerpt from her memoir-in-progress, Rae Lewis recalls a particularly nerve-shattering incident in 1978 when Grover was covering for New West *magazine the First Amendment/censorship trial of* Hustler *magazine publisher Larry Flynt (1942-2021) in Lawrenceville, Georgia. After a lunch break during the trial, Grover was walking just a few feet behind Flynt outside the courthouse when Flynt and one of his lawyers were shot in an assassination attempt by serial killer Joseph Paul Franklin. Both survived, but Flynt for the rest of his life was paralyzed from the waist down. Rae Lewis recalls the trauma Grover experienced as a witness to the incident. And, of course, he had a next-day deadline to meet for* New West *magazine reporting the breaking story of the violent act he'd just been part of.*

RAE LEWIS

Nothing about the Larry Flynt story had anything to do with Grover, except, of course, the fact that it was Grover who was walking twelve paces behind Flynt, in Lawrenceville, Georgia, when shots rang out and Flynt staggered and fell to the ground with bullet wounds that would leave him crippled for the rest of his life. In the stunned seconds after the shots were fired, Grover turned on his tape recorder capturing the sound of a vehicle speeding away, but everyone's attention was focused on Flynt who was writhing in his own blood and groaning pain.

Grover, Flynt, and Flynt's two attorneys were returning from lunch to the Gwinnett County Courthouse where Flynt was on trial, defending himself against obscenity charges relating to his publication of *Hustler* magazine. Flynt had walked ahead with Gene Reeves, one of his attorneys. Grover and Flynt's other attorney, Paul Cambria, Jr., were walking behind them.

My part of the story began with a phone call. I was at my mother's house in Kanarraville, Utah. My father had died the previous December, and I had come home to be with Mom for a few days while Grover was covering the trial in Georgia and interviewing Flynt and his wife, Althea, at their home in Columbus, Ohio. The phone call was from attorney Paul Cambria who told me about the shooting. The first televised reports were saying that a writer who was with Flynt had also been shot. Grover had asked Cambria to call me because he didn't want me to hear the first report on TV news and be worried. Grover was unable to make the call himself because he was being interviewed by the Georgia police.

Moments later I received another phone call. This one from *New West* magazine editor Jon Carroll. Immediately upon hearing the news about the Flynt shooting, Jon decided to pull apart the March 27th issue which had just been "put to bed" and insert the Flynt shooting as the new cover story. He was arranging through contacts in Georgia to get Grover back to Los Angeles and he wanted me back there too. I told Jon I would leave as soon as I could get the car loaded. I kissed mother goodbye and as I was going out the door she handed me a small handful of Valium. I was on the road back to Los Angeles less than an hour after the phone calls.

Grover was waiting for me at the home of Larry Dietz and Penny Bloch when I arrived late that afternoon. Larry had, until very recently, been Executive Editor at *New West*, and Penny still was a copy editor there. Grover was a wreck. Clearly in shock, his pupils were dancing around even more vigorously than usual. He was well-oiled from a long flight that served cocktails, but clearly the alcohol had had no tranquilizing effect on him. His hands were trembling and cold. He was disheveled and frantic and wound up tight, and there was a peculiar odor emanating from his person. Not just body odor you'd expect from a smoker who had been traveling and hadn't showered in a couple of days but something funky and rank.

Larry had picked Grover up at LAX and the plan was that Grover would tell the story to Larry, and Larry would sit at his typewriter and transpose it into publishable form that would be a reasonable facsimile of the tone and voice of a Grover Lewis story. Penny and I would transcribe tapes and edit the pages as they rolled out of Larry's new IBM Memory typewriter. It was crucial that Jon Carroll have the manuscript in Beverly Hills by early the next morning, so he could meet his print deadline. Missing the print deadline was not an option.

The story came out in lumps and bumps. Lucid, informed paragraphs of reportage would pour out of Grover for a while and then he'd veer off into murky territory, paranoid fantasies filled with violence and raw fear. He believed the shooter was still out there looking for him and could show up at any moment. When he'd slip into one of these episodes, I would sit by him and talk to him, soothing and reassuring him. Penny would heat water and make him another toddy out of Dietz's high-dollar Scotch, and Larry would turn up the thermostat and find another sweater. This would settle Grover for a while, and we'd all return to the story. As the night wore on, the three of us were exhausted and impatient, and poor Grover was still amped up and wired. His wild rants were becoming ever more frequent, frightening and elaborate. He complained constantly that he was cold, and finally Larry brought out a blanket and his navy blue Brooks Brothers blazer. He helped Grover into the jacket, and I tucked the blanket around him. As I did so, I vowed to myself that I would take him to the emergency room as soon as we were released from this hellish project.

As first light appeared over the Santa Monica Mountains, we had the story in decent shape, and we all hoped to get a few of hours of sleep before Larry delivered it to Jon Carroll. As Grover and I were preparing to leave I told him he should take off Larry's Blazer and return it to him, but Grover refused, saying the jacket was warm and he needed to keep it against the early-morning chill. I persisted and told him it was only a short drive home where he had warm clothing of his own, but Grover was adamant that he would not take off the jacket. Ever the gracious host, and sensing a stalemate, Larry said it was fine. Grover should keep the jacket on, and we could return it in a day or two.

When we got home, I gave Grover one of mother's valium, hoping it would help him sleep. He wanted another hot toddy, and I made him one, skimping a little on the booze. I took a valium, too, and began preparing for bed. Grover's bed preparations involved taking off his shoes. Everything else stayed on. I was far too weary to object, and we collapsed into bed and sleep.

Sleep didn't last long. The phone began ringing around 7 a.m., waking us both. It was Jon and he told me that Larry had asked for a shared byline on the story. I handed the phone to Grover. I heard him tell Jon that, under the circumstances, he was willing to share his byline, which I thought was both generous of Grover and the right thing to do. It occurred to me that perhaps Grover's decision was aided by the fact that he was still wearing Larry's navy blue Brooks Bros. blazer which was, in fact, looking a little rumpled.

Back on the phone with me, Jon insisted that I spend the rest of the week at home with Grover, to calm and anchor him and encourage him toward re-entry. Obviously, Dietz had told him of our overnight excursions into the dark zone. But re-entry proved elusive. In the next couple of days Grover's drinking did not taper off at all. He refused to take off his clothes or attend to his personal hygiene and all my efforts to get him to a doctor—or even outdoors—failed miserably. I might as well have suggested a trip to Mars. He paced around the apartment and kept the thermostat up high. Chain-smoking cigarettes, his only "nourishment" was black coffee laced with booze.

On Friday morning, feeling defeated and dispirited, I drove into the office by myself to pick up copies of the new issue of the magazine.

Grover was just getting up as I arrived back home. Having the magazine in his hands improved his outlook at once. The cover was red, of course, and had a reasonably accurate drawing of Flynt and Grover done by Julian Allen. The cover line read: "The Shooting of Larry Flynt, An Eyewitness Account, By Grover Lewis." We took our coffee into the living room and settled in to read the story. Larry did get his share of the byline, and we were relieved to discover that it all held together rather nicely.

Encouraged by the improvement in his mood, I persuaded Grover that it really was time to take off his by-now-rather-fragrant collection of clothing—he had lately added a Pendleton Black Watch scarf to his ensemble—and take a good hot shower. While he was in the bathroom I snagged Larry's jacket, emptied the pockets and hustled it out to the car so I could get it to the cleaners as soon as possible.

Freshly showered and shaved and in clean (warm) clothes of his own, Grover looked wonderful. My spirits surged and I felt like smiling for the first time in days. Here was my knight-errant, home again. Mine, again.

Over the weekend things continued to improve. Grover did not reflexively reach for the Wild Turkey to juice up his coffee. He ate a couple of donuts. We ventured outdoors and walked to Palisades Park to look at the ocean and the sunset. On Sunday morning we went to our local deli, and he actually ate breakfast: sausage, eggs, grits, biscuits and gravy. It was the first meal he'd had since the shooting. On Monday we went into the office together.

We were welcomed enthusiastically by Jon Carroll and the editorial and art staffs, and as word circulated that Grover was in the office, staff members from all the other departments drifted by to say hello. There was genuine concern for Grover, and he was visibly delighted by the responses to him and to the story. Joe Armstrong, the new Publisher of both *New West* and *New York*, was in town and with some fanfare he presented Grover with a bonus check for $1,200. Hazard duty pay, I supposed. The story was something of a coup for the magazine. Except for television and daily newspaper coverage, ours was the first periodical on the newsstands anywhere in the country with a story about Flynt and the trial and the shooting.

 Grover got a lot of attention that week; not all of it pleasant. Two FBI agents came into the office and talked briefly to Jon and to Grover. They wanted to "borrow" the cassette tapes he had of the Flynt interviews and the aftermath of the shooting. They said they would make dupes of the cassettes and return them in a few days. We handed them over pronto. True to their word, the same agents returned them a few days later. More disturbing, there were several threatening phone calls, both to the *New West* office, and to our home. One woman called twice. Both times at 3 a.m., and when I answered she spat out one word: "Pig!" Later in the week, Dick Adler wrote in his gossip column for the *Herald Examiner*, "How could Grover Lewis be an eyewitness to anything? Everybody knows he's blind." The solution to the threatening phone calls was obvious: get an unlisted number, which I did, immediately. The *Herald Examiner* swipe was old news by the next morning when another edition of the paper hit the newsstands.

 Grover was coming into the office every day now and we'd have lunch together or with other staff members or writers. With the infusion of bonus cash fattening our budget, Grover wanted to go shopping. Specifically, he wanted to go to Brooks Bros., which was conveniently located right across the street on Wilshire Blvd. And, to be precise, he wanted a navy blue blazer, just like Larry's that he'd worn for four days straight. It would be the first of several he would own over the years. I went shopping too, but I went to Neiman-Marcus for new shoes and perfume.

 New West was a bi-weekly publication and the high point of the issue's run on the stands was Grover's appearance on Tom Snyder's late-night talk show on NBC. This felt like the big time for sure and we both dressed up. Grover, of course, wore his new blazer. A stretch limo showed up at our apartment to pick us up and drive us to the Burbank studios. "I could really get used to this," I said to Grover as he handed me into the back seat. Sidney Sheldon was Snyder's other guest that night and it was jarring to be in the same pre-show hospitality suite with those two very different writers. Sheldon, so very smooth and polished, phony as a three-dollar bill, and Grover, hyper-articulate, but still bristling and as serious as a heart attack. Sheldon clearly had no idea who Grover was (he scarcely knew who Flynt was, or so he claimed). But Grover, demonstrating that he could be rational and poised when the situation required, reined in the adrenalin, and was gracious and charming. I was on pins and needles the whole time; grateful when the show-attendant walked each of them to Snyder's desk, so I only had to deal with one of them at a time. Sheldon was there to promote his new book, which sounded, to me, depressingly like all his other books, the ones whose sales had made him a very rich man. I don't remember that much about Grover's interview, except that both Snyder and Grover were focused and intense and Grover's comments seemed to carry a subtext: Something corrosive and dangerous had been set loose upon the land.

 Grover was so buoyed up by the attention and the bonus money (not to mention the cross-town travel-by-limo), that I began to think perhaps we were out of the woods, but my optimism was premature. By the time the next issue of the magazine came out, the spotlight had moved on to other players and while I was at the office every day, Grover was home with no one to talk to and nothing much to do.

 As the coming weeks unfolded, I began to understand that, for Grover, being in such close proximity to gunfire and seeing Flynt fall bleeding to the ground, had been a mind-shattering event. It had thrust him back into the violence of his childhood, and the deaths of his parents; the mysteries surrounding their double homicides, and the disastrous impact their deaths had had on his life. In no time he had slipped into the haunted precincts of his past and from there it was an easy slide into depression. A professional, if I'd been able to get him to one, would have diagnosed his condition as PTSD.

 Lacking the concentration to read, Grover played music and watched old movies on TV, but he called me at work two or three times a day, just to talk and to ask when I'd be coming home. One afternoon he called to say there were FBI agents on the porch and they kept ringing the doorbell. "Did they show you identification?" I asked. Grover said, "I didn't answer the door." I said, "I think you should answer the door and ask to see their identification and if they are really from the FBI you should let them in and talk to them." I told him I'd call again in a few minutes to check on the situation and make sure he was okay. That seemed to satisfy him and when I called a few minutes later, he said he "was fine. When are you coming home?" He made no mention of any FBI agents out on the porch, or elsewhere.

* * * * *

Eventually, our lives did begin to resume their familiar contours. Grover had eased way back on the hard liquor. He regularly was taking walks. He began going to the neighborhood library to catch up on new books and magazines. He visited his local barber and got a haircut. These were positive and encouraging developments.

One Saturday morning in early May, I was puttering around the apartment enjoying the prospect of the weekend and spending some time outdoors in the heavenly southern California weather. I was in the bedroom and Grover came in and said, "Come into the kitchen and have some more coffee, I need to talk to you about something important." He held out his hand to me. His tone was somber and left no room for argument. I had a pretty good idea about what would be coming next.

Seated in the breakfast nook with our coffee, he took my hands, (both of them this time) and said "There is something I haven't told you. I deeply regret it, but it is something you need to know. I have two children, Shannon and Clay, and I have been estranged from them for many years." We continued holding hands and I looked at him as sweetly as I knew how and said "Well, honey, I already knew that."

Letting go of my hands, Grover immediately became defensive, as if I was the one guilty of betrayal, and in a sharp voice he said, "How could you have known about it." I ignored his sharp tone and, again, as sweetly as possible, I said our friend Knox told me about the kids when he visited us in San Francisco four years ago. He looked stunned, and for perhaps the only time in our lives together, he appeared to be speechless, so I continued. "That's all I know. That you have two children."

"Why didn't you say something to me about it?" he asked. This, too, in a sharp tone.

"What was I going to say?" I said. Me, still being sweet. "Obviously I spent a lot of time thinking about it. But just as obviously I knew I wasn't going to be going anywhere, even if you did have kids. I guess I figured that if you could keep a secret about the children, then I could keep a secret about them, too." Then I said, "Now that our secrets are out, why don't you tell me about the kids."

It was a tearful, sometimes wrenching story and we sat at the table the rest of the morning while it unfolded. He got out pictures of them and, of course, they were beautiful children. He told me they had been adopted by his ex-wife's second husband and that he had had no contact with them for many years. He deeply regretted that fact, but he had no idea how to address it. At present he didn't even know where they were living. At the end of our conversation that morning I had a much clearer understanding of the man I was married to; some of his history, a few of his fears and at least one of his failures. I also had a clearer understanding of the depth and configuration of the emotional scars he still carried from his own ghastly childhood of neglect and abuse.

My reluctance to confront Grover about the children after I had learned of them was centered in my belief that his health was in perilous condition. I understood that if trust was ever to grow between us, we first had to survive or, more precisely, Grover had to survive. Since Grover had never once thus far demonstrated the slightest interest in survival, I was obviously the one who had to come up with a plan.

Mine was the easy part of the puzzle. My personality is not a complicated one. I am not an angry person. So, when Knox, in his own blundering way, informed me that I had step-children, it was relatively easy for me to regard it as just another piece of unmoored information.

Grover's part was more problematic. His was a complex personality. He had a formidable intellect and was obviously tough-minded. He possessed a steel-jacketed logic that was difficult to argue with. For a man whose life had dealt him a dark hand full of bum cards, he had a keen wit and his delight in wielding the English language in colorful usage was palpable. There was a musical quality to his voice and in conversation his precisely articulated words came out as if each had first been struck by a tuning fork.

Nevertheless, his physical package was visibly fragile, the embodiment of years of neglect and excess and faulty nutrition. He no longer used amphetamines, but he still, not infrequently, drank as though death was his object, not mere diversion.

Compared to the complex workings of Grover's mind, and my own daily encounters with his brilliant and inventive conversation, his dissembling about the kids was a minor transgression and some part of me feared he might not survive a confrontation. Specifically, I feared he was not long for this world. But every day he made me laugh. Every day he brought music into my life. In my mind, in those years, finding out the "truth" about his kids was simply not worth the risk.

After that May-Saturday confessional, our relationship finally acquired the element of trust that had been missing for four years. Without the necessity of keeping secrets our marriage blossomed, and we relaxed into domesticity and true intimacy.

I think for the first time Grover realized that my interest in him was not superficial, that my commitment to him was genuine. I think he realized something else, too, something I had known from the beginning: He needed a lot of love, and I had a lot of love to give him. ■

Xeroxed photo of Rae and Grover Lewis and New West editor Joe Armstrong. Image courtesy Rae Lewis.

"*Rez Dogs vs Bull Snake*" *photographed on the Navajo Nation in Navajo, New Mexico, by Bryan Chernick.*

PAUL BEEBE

What Little I Know of Native Americans, Rez Dogs, and History

All these years later, I can still see him. Gilbert Teton is at the other end of the bar, brooding, by himself, on a stool, bent over a drink, with no one to his left or right to bother him. His head is cocked to one side, as if he is listening to something. Maybe Gilbert is replaying a debate on some issue before the Shoshone-Bannock Tribal Council, which governs the Fort Hall Reservation near Pocatello, Idaho; Gilbert was the powerful Council Chairman in the mid-1970s. Or maybe he is miles away, hearing in his head the melody and words of "Indian Sunset," a haunting song that deplores the vanished Indigenous way of life. Gilbert found meaning in the Elton John/Bernie Taupin song. He played it every week on his radio show.

> *. . . Now there seems no reason why*
> *I should carry on*
> *In this land that once was my land*
> *I can't find a home.*
> *It's lonely and it's quiet*
> *And the horse soldiers are coming*
> *And I think it's time I strung my bow*
> *And cease my senseless running*
> *For soon I'll find the yellow moon*
> *Along with my loved ones*
> *Where the buffaloes graze in clover fields*
> *Without the sound of guns . . .*

For forty years, I had not thought of Gilbert Teton, until one day recently. I was in a coffee shop, reading a book. Unexpectedly, above the sounds of voices and coffee-making, I heard the words and piano chords of "Indian Sunset." And there, in my mind's eye, was Gilbert, at the far end of the bar.

Gilbert Teton was born in 1941, at the old Indian hospital at the Fort Hall Indian Agency. He was a track star in high school. After practice, instead of catching a ride, Gilbert would run home to his mother's log cabin in a remote part of the reservation. He was known for his unfailing optimism. After two years in the Navy, he studied history at Fort Lewis College in Colorado. In 1975, he won a seat on the Fort Hall Tribal Council and served two terms as chairman.

I knew Gilbert not as a politician, but as host of his radio show. It was by listening to the show that I was exposed to "Indian Sunset." I had never heard it before. The song is emotive. Elton John has described it as a six-minute movie. It is one of his favorite pieces to play during a concert. Critics have pointed out some historical inaccuracies. A soldier did not shoot Geronimo. He died of pneumonia. But that didn't matter to Gilbert. The song felt true. He played it often, and as I absorbed the words, I began to wonder what feelings the song stirred inside him. Sadness? Loss? Anger? I never asked, though I badly wanted to know. Gilbert is gone now, so his thinking lies buried with him in a cemetery, close to the log home where he grew up. There is a hint, though, of what he believed. Gilbert married Colleen Alvarez in 1994. She died in 2022, twelve years after Gilbert passed. In her obituary is a telling line set apart in its own paragraph: "She had traditional beliefs." Gilbert did, too.

I never met a Native American when I was growing up. Their world had vanished from Vermont, long before I was born. The closest I came to visible evidence that Indians once inhabited the lands of the Northeast was an ancient path worn into the hills beside the West Branch of the Susquehanna River in Pennsylvania. Members of the Indigenous tribes of northern Pennsylvania walked the path to reach the Great Island, a rendezvous site in the middle of the river, near present-day Lock Haven. If Native Americans still lived in Pennsylvania, their numbers were small. There are no federally recognized tribes in the state. All that remains of their presence is a handful of place names: the Allegheny Mountains, the Juniata River, the towns of Punxsutawney and Conshohocken. Otherwise, the Indigenous people of Pennsylvania have passed into history.

Years later, I moved from Pennsylvania to Pocatello, Idaho, where I landed my first professional job as a journalist. Other than Sun Valley and potatoes, I knew nothing about Idaho. But when I saw its rugged beauty and vast regions of wild land, I was spellbound. Idaho was the antipode to any place I had lived. A hitchhiker I gave a ride to said if you could flatten out Idaho it would be three times the size of Texas. I didn't know if that was true, but I knew I was in an exceptional place, with remarkable people, including thousands of Shoshone-Bannock Indians who lived on the sprawling Fort Hall Reservation near Pocatello.

One day, I drove into the hills south of town. The road climbed and curved through a canyon to a divide, where, in the distance, a broad valley lay between rounded mountains. The road descended into the valley, which had been sectioned into enormous fields of dryland wheat that had been harvested recently. A few weathered farm buildings stood dark against the sky. There were no houses. The valley seemed deserted.

I came to an intersection, where my road met what I presumed was the main road through the valley. Turning to the right made sense since I had come from that general direction. Maybe it would return me to Pocatello. To my surprise, I soon came upon a small building. On it was a hand-lettered sign. It read: BAR. No other buildings were in sight. The bar was surrounded by sagebrush. A truck was in the parking lot. The bar was open. I decided to stop.

Inside the bar were two stools and a countertop. On one stool sat a man about my age. He was solidly built, with a face dark from the sun. He looked at me, then waved a hand at the empty stool. "Have a seat," he said.

I ordered a beer and introduced myself. He said his name. We exchanged a few pleasantries that I don't remember. Then he asked me about the deerskin shirt I was wearing. It was a gift from my wife. She had purchased it for me a few years earlier at a flea market in Pennsylvania. With rawhide fringes across the chest and at the cuffs, it was stunning, and I was proud of it. I was especially happy to be wearing it that day, for I was out West, where in my imagination the land was wild and open and men still wore leather. I admitted to my new friend that I had not hunted the deer or made the shirt. But instead of admiring it or complimenting me he took offense.

"So, you bought it," he sneered.

I felt like a drugstore cowboy. All hat and no cattle, as the expression goes. I didn't know what to say. He had exposed me. I was a poser.

Things got worse. I tried to turn the conversation to him. He had a ruddy face and high cheekbones. His hair was cut short. He wore a work shirt, denim jeans and boots. A cowboy hat sat on the bar beside his beer bottle. I didn't know who he was, only that he wasn't white.

"Are you Mexican or an Indian," I asked.

I have said some stupid things in my life, but this was totally unacceptable. The man stared at me in disbelief. He said nothing. The seconds dragged on. He drained his beer, clapped his hat to his head, and stood up.

"See you later, Kemosabe," he said, and walked out.

There it was: my first encounter with an Indian. It hardly could have gone worse. I had met a fool, and it was me. If any good came of it, I quicky learned to distinguish between Mexicans and Native Americans. Despite what people say, there are stupid questions.

* * * * *

There would be better encounters. One day, I watched a roundup of buffalo on the Fort Hall reservation. In 1963, the reservation acquired a small herd. The buffalo would be a living connection to a bygone past. The herd grazed on bottomland near the Snake River, where water and forage were plentiful, and a newborn calf could fatten to two thousand pounds. When the herd became too large, a number of animals were culled. Tribal members lucky to win a lottery would take a few buffalo for themselves.  The rest would be sold to non-members who prized the animals for their meat or their massive heads and horns.

The round-up was a swirl of sights, sounds

and smells. Native men on horses had pushed the buffalo up from the bottomland into a corral, where they trotted nervously back and forth and pawed the dirt with their hooves. Dust hung in the air. Onlookers hollered and cheered. Several men inside the pen waved their arms and shouted. They pressured the buffalo toward the mouth of a narrow chute only a few feet wide. Inside the chute, the buffalo could not turn around. They could move only forward, nose to tail. The noise was deafening. Angry and frightened, the bellowing beasts swung their massive heads and crashed their enormous bodies against the metal bars that confined them.

I moved close to the chute to better see what would happen next. When a buffalo reached the end of the chute, a gate prevented it from escaping into the crowd. The frantic creature also could not push backward because a barrier had been lowered behind it. With the animal isolated, the waiting owner backed his stock trailer to the gate and put out a loading ramp. With the trailer in position, an attendant swung the gate open, and the enraged buffalo barreled out. If everything went as planned, the animal would charge up the ramp into the trailer, which would be slammed shut, and the owner would haul it away.

* * * * *

This happened a number of times, until all the buffalo were gone. I went home in a giddy mood. A piece of history had been enacted before me.

There would be other remarkable moments. One summer day, I drove to the reservation to observe the annual Fort Hall Indian Festival. There was much to see as I wandered around the festival grounds. Hundreds of Indians had come to Fort Hall from reservations and towns around the West. Many families were camped in tipis. Bare-chested boys on horseback galloped past the tipis. Adults and children in traditional finery danced in circles to the metrical thump of drums and wailing chants of men. Teams of men and horses competed in breakneck relay races dubbed the oldest extreme sport in America.

Inside a large tent were two teams of women sitting opposite each other in folding lawn chairs. A blanket was spread out on the ground between them. On the blanket was a sizeable pile of dollar bills.

The women, five or six on each side, were playing a hide-and-seek game, and the winning side would pocket the cash. A noisy throng cheered them on. From what I could tell, a woman on one side of the blanket had concealed in her hands a pair of bones, while her teammates sang, shouted and waved their hands to confuse their opponents who tried to guess where the bones were. I asked someone to explain. The man said if the opposing team guessed correctly they would receive a carved wood stick. If they were wrong, they would give up a stick. The game would continue back and forth until one side acquired all the sticks. Indians have always played hand games, the man said. They are competitions played by adults at social gatherings and festivals. In the old times, winnings might be land or horses, and, sometimes, women. Today, people in hand games play for cash. The games can be intense contests between rivals. Games also teach children fair play and how to be courteous to adversaries.

* * * * *

I would eventually leave Idaho for a job in another state, but not before something else occurred that revealed how little I understood about Native American culture. My wife was a teacher. She was close to a colleague who confided one day that she had a sister in Chicago. She and her husband had adopted a little Indian boy when he was an infant. The boy's mother was Shoshone-Bannock. She placed her child for adoption when he was a few weeks old, possibly with the father's consent. Now the boy was a teenager. He had grown up in a comfortable home, but from an early age he sensed he was different. His adoptive parents had not hidden his heritage from him. For as long as he could remember, the boy knew he was an Indian and his birth parents were members of the Shoshone-Bannock Tribes. He wanted to meet them.

I thought I could help. I rang the Fort Hall Business Council, which put me in touch with the Tribes' Child Support Office. In almost no time, the birth mother's family contacted the boy. And shortly afterward, the boy traveled from Chicago to the reservation to meet them. He was welcomed warmly. For me, the story ends there. I heard nothing else. Did the boy stay with his Indigenous relatives, or did he return to

Chicago and his adoptive parents? Did he find his birth mother? I don't know. But the incident opened for me a window into how Indigenous Tribes viewed adoptions of their children by non-Natives. Over many years, countless numbers of Indian children have been separated from their Tribes to be raised by families with no connection to Native culture. The families usually mean well. They believe they have the child's best interest at heart. But the termination of cultural ties can wound an adopted child. Tribes can be harmed, too. A Tribe is diminished when a boy or girl is adopted. The loss of even one child can weaken a tribe straining to balance its culture and traditions against the outside world. I want to think the reunion of the Shoshone-Bannock boy with his Tribe and his birth mother's family was a severed relationship restored in time.

* * * * *

I moved on from Pocatello but my encounters with Indians continued. One day, I visited Canyon de Chelly National Monument on the Navajo Reservation in Arizona. I could not afford a guided tour of the monument, so I descended a trail by myself from the canyon rim to the bottom, then waded, boots in hand, down an ankle-deep stream to the

Canyon de Chelly National Monument, Arizona.

famous White House cliff ruins. Built at the base of a 600-foot sandstone wall and in an alcove above the canyon floor, the ruins consisted of many mud-and-stone rooms that ancestral Puebloans inhabited until seven hundred years ago, when they suddenly vanished. The ruins were magnificent. I had read accounts of similar ruins tucked away in canyons across the Southwest, but I was not prepared for the emotional impact of seeing the White House ruins for the first time.

Toward evening, I set up my tent in the monument campground. I was not alone. At least a dozen dogs were in the campground, too. I was puzzled. None of the dogs wore collars. They were a mix of forms, colors and ages, as how I imagined dogs looked before men started breeding them. The dogs seemed healthy. None seemed undernourished or diseased. They weren't aggressive toward each other. And they didn't beg. Instead, they ignored me. They were there when I went to sleep. And they were there the next morning when I emerged from my tent.

Dogs seemed to be part of life on other reservations. One November, a friend and I backpacked to Havasu Falls, on the Havasupai Reservation, in the bottom of the Grand Canyon. No roads serve the village of Supai or the famous falls. To reach Supai, visitors must hike into the canyon eight miles on a trail shared by humans and mule trains that bring food and supplies to the village. The trail begins at the end of a two-lane road that crosses sixty miles of the vast Coconino Plateau. We arrived at sunset. Nothing was there, except an empty parking lot and a small dog that suddenly appeared. It didn't seem lost, sick, hungry or unhappy. Randy and I cooked a quick supper, then unrolled our sleeping bags among some boulders. For some reason, the dog took a liking to me. It stayed near, but never approached. When I crawled into my bag to sleep, the dog curled up a few feet away. I feared it would follow me when we started our trek into the canyon the next morning. But it was gone when I awoke. I saw the dog later when we reached Supai. It was with several other dogs.

In my house on a wall is a photograph of two dogs, nose to nose and wagging their tails. Their ears are pricked. One dog is grey with white legs. The other is the color of caramel. Behind them is an adobe kiln. Set in an adobe wall is a window. The dogs are members of a pack of mutts that live at Taos Pueblo in New Mexico, where Indigenous people have dwelled for hundreds of years, apparently with dogs. I have visited Taos Pueblo twice. Part of the pleasure of visiting the pueblo is to see dogs lazing in the sunlight or ambling around the plaza while residents go about their day.

I saw much the same thing at the San Xavier del Bac Mission church on the Tohono O'odham Nation Indian Reservation near Tucson, Arizona. In front of the white stucco church, established in 1700 by Father Eusebio Kino, a Jesuit explorer, several dogs mingled with tourists and Native families, while other dogs stood aloof. One dog caught my attention. She stood at the entrance to the church, twitching her tail. The ancient wooden doors opened inward, and the dog, in a coat of white fur, peered into the dark interior, looking or listening for what or whom I do not know.

An explanation for the curious cross-species relationship between Indians and dogs emerged when my wife and I were driving on the Navajo Reservation a few years ago. The road wound high into the Chuska Mountains in eastern Arizona. Near the crest, I saw through a break in the pine trees a bird's-eye view of the desert floor far below. I stopped the car and began walking to where I thought I could get a better look. Suddenly I noticed a dog coiled on the ground. It did not move. I could not tell if it was alive or dead.

It raised its head as I got closer. It tried to stand. I gasped. The dog was starving. Its dark coat hung against its ribs. I could see the bones of its hips and spine. I scooped her into my arms. She was practically weightless. She didn't resist. I ran to the car where my wife was waiting. We weren't sure what to do, but we were not going to leave the dog. I placed her on top of our camping gear, and we drove away.

The road descended through the mountains for several miles. As I drove, we discussed what we should do. Home was a day's drive in the opposite direction. Should we turn around? Or should we continue our journey with the hope of finding help? We couldn't decide. Maura fed the dog pieces of salami. She was ravenous. Was it safe to feed fatty food to a starving animal? How much food could it tolerate? We didn't know.

After a while we came to a village. I stopped at a gas station. An old Indian man came by while I was filling the gas tank. He said hello, and asked if we were traveling. I told him about finding the dog and asked if there was somebody in the village who sheltered lost animals. No, he said. Just let the dog go. He gestured toward a cluster of houses across the road.

I put the dog on the ground. She walked unsteadily toward the houses. "See, he knows. He's a rez dog," the old man said. "He'll be okay."

I thanked him. We shook hands. I got in my car and drove away. The dog was in the hands of a Native community that cares communally, man or animal, for its own.

Here is a final story. It has nothing to do with dogs, but it reminds me again how little I know about Indigenous Americans or their history with white America. Maura and I were hiking along the Escalante River, a desert stream in southern Utah that flows between soaring walls of pink and white sandstone more than eighty miles to the Colorado River. The river got its name from John Wesley Powell's 1872 survey party. It honors Father Escalante, one of the leaders of the Dominguez-Escalante expedition, which in 1776 attempted to blaze a route between Santa Fe, New Mexico, and the Spanish missions in California. The attempt failed.

The day was sunny, almost hot. I ducked under a rock overhang that gave a bit of shade. I glanced at the underside of the rock. A few inches above my eyes was a pictograph. Many times exploring the desert canyons of the Southwest I have seen rock art painted or pecked into stone surfaces by Indigenous Americans hundreds of years earlier. This symbol was unlike any I had seen. It resembled a double helix. Two strands wound around each other a dozen times, in the same way DNA molecules are represented. The strands were black. The cells formed by the crisscrossing lines were a faded red. The image was old.

Something else caught my eye. Scratched on the rock were these words: "Jessie Cloud Fort Totten, No Dak Nov 28 1936." Did he, like me, chance upon the pictograph, and seeing the work of a fellow native, think to leave his name? I didn't know.

A few days later, I found on the Internet a photograph of a handsome young Indian man. In the photo, he wears a soft newsboy cap. He is kneeling behind a large sheep. His mouth is open, as if he is speaking. His hair is cut short in a manner required by Indian boarding schools of that time. He appears well-fed, which is why many Indian families sent their children to Indian boarding schools, to avoid starvation.

A caption reads, in part, "Jesse Cloud and Sheep . . . Department of the Interior, Office of Indian Affairs, Fort Totten Agency." When the photo was taken isn't clear. The caption shows two sets of dates: 1914-1936, and 1903-1947. There was no other information. Were Jessie and Jesse the same person? Native American Census rolls from the 1930s show the names Jessie and Jesse were often used interchangeably. The rolls show a Jesse Cloud was living in Fort Totten in the 1930s. Jesse, or Jessie, was born in 1915 and was marked a "full blood" Sioux.

Fort Totten was established to enforce the peace and to protect trading routes during the American Indian wars. After it closed in 1890, the fort became a boarding school for Indian children. For a few years in the 1930s, it was also a "preventorium," aimed at protecting Indian children at risk of contracting tuberculosis. The school's academic and vocational programs prepared children for life off the reservation. It also may have had a darker purpose. Many Indian boarding schools endeavored to "save" children from their tribal culture by training them to repudiate their former lives. The first students at Fort Totten were Dakota Sioux children. They were later joined by boys and girls from the Chippewa tribes. Almost certainly, Jesse or Jessie's picture was taken at the school.

I found something else about Jessie. He became a father in 1941, when Aloysius Cloud was born. The mother, Mary Thompson, died during childbirth. Jessie apparently did not raise his son. Aloysius was raised by his grandparents, according to his obituary. He died in 2022 at the age of 80.

I feel uncomfortable when I imagine the life Jessie may have had. It could not have been easy. He found the pictograph only forty-six years after the American frontier officially closed. The pictograph must have touched something in him. He probably grew up hearing stories from tribal elders about the earlier times and the Sioux way of life that was crushed by waves of white settlers who invaded the Great Plains after the Civil War.

And I think of Gilbert Teton, who despite the success he made of his life, surely struggled too. Like Jessie's son, Gilbert apparently was raised without a father. His obituary says Gilbert was brought up by his mother, Rechanta Teton, who gave birth to him at the old Indian hospital at the Fort Hall Indian Agency in 1941. The father is not mentioned. The obituary says Gilbert also was raised by his "cagoo," Lily Cookman Teton, and an aunt, Caroline Teton Racehorse.

Gilbert devoted himself to his tribe. Surely, he too was haunted by the past, which must explain why the "Indian Sunset" song meant so much to him. Even I, a white person, often feel the weight of history. One day a few years ago, the custodian of a native American art gallery on the Navajo Reservation showed me a pair of beaded deerskin moccasins. One of the moccasins was signed by Geronimo, the famous Apache war chief. Geronimo was imprisoned in Alabama when he put his name on the moccasin. He would sometimes sign Apache artifacts as a way for his fellow tribesmen to earn money while in captivity. When I saw the moccasin pair they were priced for sale at $35,000.

* * * * *

A year later I read the novel *The Night Watchman*, for which author Louise Erdrich, a member of the Turtle Mountain Band of Chippewa, received the Pulitzer Prize for fiction in 2021.

Set on an Indian reservation in North Dakota in the 1950s, the book is the story of a community's efforts to resist a plan to terminate federal recognition of several Native American Tribes and seize their land.

The book is based on the life of Erdrich's maternal grandfather, a night watchman, who carried his tribe's fight to Washington, D.C. His name was Patrick Gourneau, and he was tribal chairman of the Turtle Mountain Band during the 1950s. Largely through his efforts, the government's bid to nullify treaties with the Turtle Mountain and other tribes failed.

It's a moving story, made even more poignant to me by unexpected references to the Indian boarding school at Fort Totten. The school is mentioned several times in the book. Erdrich had good reason to mention Fort Totten. Her grandfather went to school there for a period of time.

It's as if Erdrich wrote the book for me. Beyond the references to Fort Totten, it contained another surprise: The surname of one of the characters is Cloud.

It is said that a person is not truly gone if their name is spoken. Jessie Cloud would be pleased if he knew his name is still alive. ■

RON McFARLAND

Three Days in March: Piscatorial Adventures in Sunny Florida

lthough I am on record as a guy who has mixed emotions about fly fishing (see *Professor McFarland in Reel Time: Poems & Prose of an Angler*), someone on the board of the Clearwater Fly Casters, based in eastern Washington and the Idaho panhandle, invited me to give a presentation to their assemblage two years ago last spring. They sweetened the invitation with a hundred-dollar honorarium, free drink at their Dry Fly Hour, and dinner on the house. Per my quondam aversion to casting a fly I shall quote myself: "When I arrived in Idaho about fifty years ago, I swore I would not allow myself to fall prey to the allure and blandishments of fly-fishing enthusiasts. [. . .] I felt the whole business was too precious, a tad too hoity-toity." Also, too pricey. My family devolved from Lowland Scots—parsimonious Presbyterian.

While that book provides abundant evidence of my genesis as a cane-pole bait-fisher more inclined to the bank than to the boat— a blue-collar angler—it also attests to my piscatorial impurity. In short, I evolved from pioneer simplicity to embrace the angling world in all its rich varieties and technical complexities of artificial lures, open face spinning reels, high-speed tournament-level bass boats, and yes, fly rods with a myriad and confusing array of fluffy flies, both wet and dry and possibly some varieties classifiable as "undecided." It's always difficult to account for a fall from one's boyhood ideals, a fall from grace. Members of the Clearwater Fly Casters (CFC), on the other hand, regard my embrace of fly angling not as apostasy but as transcendence.

The monthly CFC meeting opens with a cash bar Dry Fly Hour, proceeds to dinner during which Angling Reports are made table by table, and concludes with a presentation by a guest speaker. Given that I was to be visiting my three siblings in sunny Florida, I knew I'd be expected to come up with something in the way of an angling report for our meeting on the second Wednesday of March, even though our visit would run only a couple days over a week and we had a busy agenda. Alas, I did not have a fly rod at my disposal, so I'd need to rely on my brother Tom's spinning tackle, in this case the rather basic Zebco 404 model. With each cast into the pond (not quite a "lake") behind Tom's place I could imagine my CFC friends wincing in unison as I confessed to the sin of spin casting, but I should note that this degree of perfidy would rank as merely a venial, not a mortal, sin. A tolerable sin as it were, quite forgivable.

With each cast, I promised myself I would think of tenderly my brothers and sisters of the fly shivering that first week of March as they pretended spring was nearly at hand, the icy runoff wasn't really "all that bad," and the murky river tearing at their waders might not offer up rainbows and cuts hungry for a dry pattern, but surely a flashy streamer or two would suffice. I'm occasionally empathetic that way.

On Day #1 I set out with a slice of white bread in search of the wily bream. This constituted a major step down from fishing my brother's pond during past seasons when hot dogs were the bait of choice. Tom explained that bread squeezed into a pea-sized ball (*petit pois*) held better to the hook and attracted no ants when left on top of the tackle box. Having grown up in sunny Florida (an epithet I sprinkled liberally in my email correspondence before flying off at the tail-end of February as snow flurries descended on the Palouse region), I was familiar with that bait but hadn't had recourse to it since my boyhood. On a Boy Scout bike hike, lacking bread, I once landed a small bream on a handline baited with the petal of a wild daisy. Back then the bream weren't as wily as they are nowadays.

On only my second cast, I was awarded with a very respectable bream that would have honored any skillet if I'd been fishing for keeps. But my life as a fly angler has converted me into a catch-and-release kind of guy. Usually. I did not hesitate, however, to have Tom snap a photo for posterity in the form of email attachment to the Clearwater Fly Casters monthly newsletter, *The Tippet*, ably edited by Mr. Fred Muehlbauer. I then landed three more bream in rapid succession, satisfying my lust for piscine action that afternoon. In other parts of this great nation the bluegill or yellow perch abound, but in the fresh waters of sunny Florida the bream (*Abramis brama*) reigns supreme.

Fred promptly responded to my photo congratulating me on my catch and asking for details: when, where, what fly? When was easy enough: March 4, 2023 at about 2:00 p.m. Where was Merritt Island, Florida, but the pond was nameless, so I baptized it with the street where my brother lives: "The locals call it 'Water Oak Pond,' I lied." (Invited speakers at the monthly CFC meetings are awarded a plaque for "Truthful Prevarication" when it comes to relating their "Piscatorial Prowess"; consequently, I am a licensed, certified liar when it comes to angling.) As to the "fly," I noted that I'd employed a concoction known as "White Breadball," Fred appeared to take it all in stride. I'm not sure, but I'm inclined to think he assumes there actually is such a fly, and perhaps he should add a few to his collection.

Certainly, I should point out that I resorted to no high-end dough, no Wonder Bread, no Oroweat, no Franz. No costly multigrain, no dark rye of the sort my wife and I have indulged of late. Georgia not being a Lowland Scot by heritage, the dark Russian rye is altogether her extravagance. Tom provided ordinary OTC Publix white sandwich bread. (Sidebar: When I worked as a bagboy at Publix in 1958, I was told there were 67 of their supermarkets in Florida—today there are 872.)

The next afternoon, Day #2, I aspired to more ambitious piscine quarry: the largemouth bass (*Micropterus salmoides*), to be distinguished from the smallmouth variety (*Micropterus dolomieu*) more common in my neck of the Idaho waters. Tom and I had been observing action on the pond that suggested bass, so for this bigmouth I attached Tom's prized silver Sinking Rapala. On about the third cast I was awarded with a hefty strike. But despite the hit and its apparent size, the bass did not offer much of a battle. Turned out I'd foul-hooked the critter, and what I'd supposed might be a two-pounder came in at more like a pound. At best.

This time Georgia did the honors with her cell phone camera, but to my regret I failed once again to present the bass to its best advantage. (No way I'd blame Georgia for failing to capture that bass in its hugeness.) A worthy Idaho-based literary magazine, *Limberlost Review*, published my essay "Vanishing Points" a couple years ago, in which I detail my lack of success in presenting my catches in such a way as to properly reflect their significant size. Nevertheless, I attached the bass photo to Fred at CFC with only a slight exaggeration as to its bulk, suggesting something in the 2- to 4-pound range. In self-defense here, I would point to the framed certificate cited above, presented to me after my presentation at the May 2022 meeting.

Sadly, only a few casts after the photo-ops (including one of the foul-hooked bass that I did not bother mentioning to Fred) my cast was picked up by a malicious breeze that sent the Rapala sailing into a palm tree where it lodges to this day. The "poetic justice" of this (call it piscatorial irony) was not wasted on me.

Tom had no other appropriate freshwater lures in his tackle box, and we hadn't time to venture out onto the nearby saltwater lagoons or the surf, as I had other sibs to impose upon. But I was not about to leave my brother without a reliable freshwater bass plug, so I purchased a pair of Rapalas that I would try out on Day #3: an X-Rap Xtreme Action Slashbait and a Skitter Pop. To aver that such terms would be regarded as anathema by my fly-angling friends back in icy Idaho would be a gross understatement. Theirs (mine) is the world of Royal Coachman, Wooly Bugger, Caddis, Renegade, Adams, Grasshopper, Stimulator. On my last afternoon in sunny Florida, as the light faded and the wind picked up, I tested these two rather pricey lures, and they behaved just like they sounded they would from their monikers, so I was much impressed. Sadly, the largemouth bass were not. ■

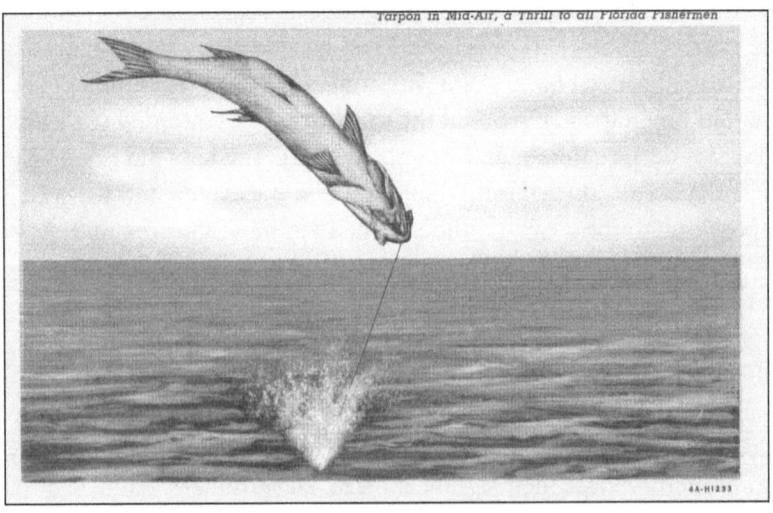

JETT WHITEHEAD

'God Bless the Roots!': Theodore Roethke's Saginaw, Michigan, home

If you are lucky, you have a sibling who helps you along the way. The poet Theodore Huebner Roethke had a younger sister, June, who taught ninth grade English at South Intermediate School in Saginaw, Michigan, and who would help Ted by typing his poems for him at the family home they shared on Gratiot Avenue. Ted couldn't type. I had an older sister, Linda, always smarter than me, who was a student of June Roethke for ninth grade English in 1959 . . . and for me, that's where my Roethke journey all began.

At the time, I was in the fifth grade—paying attention to poetry—and even pretending to write. I didn't have a clue that Ted Roethke was even a poet. The Roethke floral business was my only association with the name. So, you might imagine my surprise when my smart sister came home from school expressing exasperation over her English class assignment—reading the teacher's brother's poetry. How unprofessional I thought! The assignment should be reading real poetry from real poets. *I learn by going where I have to go.*

OAKWOOD

During a recent visit to Oakwood Cemetery in Saginaw, on Gratiot just a few miles west of Roethke's home, finding Ted's grave proved simple. I was last there twenty years ago, and it hasn't moved an inch! What I was really hoping to find was a grave or two of his extended family members—aunts, uncles, and cousins. No luck. As a longtime rare book dealer specializing in poetry, I was researching names from a book inscription by Roethke that appears in a signed copy of his first collection *Open House* (Knopf, 1941). That task is part of a book dealer's job . . . *going where I have to go* to find another clue. I came up short of finding cousins, or anyone other than the immediate family. But here are the tidy headstones of his mother, father, and sister: Helen, Otto, and June. And then the tiny one placed above those three for Ted! The most famous member of the family of four gets the smallest marker. Perhaps understated poetic justice?

The road leading into Oakwood is nothing short of majestic. Tall, stately trees lining the perfectly straight drive. If you've read Roethke's poem "On the Road to Woodlawn" from *Open House*, you can imagine the road to Oakwood likely was the inspiration. I can just see the *powerful black horses* pulling the hearses down this impressive road.

The road into Oakwood Cemetery in Saginaw, Michigan, and Theodore Roethke's gravesite at the cemetery. Photos by Jett Whitehead.

LAW . . . GIVE IT UP!

Upon graduation from Arthur Hill High School in Saginaw, Roethke enrolled at the University of Michigan in Ann Arbor. Four years later, when it was time for graduate school, he followed his family's wishes to prepare for a law career. He stayed in Ann Arbor to attend the School of Literature and Law at U of M. Law studies, however, did not come easy for Roethke. His roommate in law school was his Saginaw friend, Eugene Snow Huff, who knew Ted's real love was poetry. Late one night in their room, while Huff was trying unsuccessfully to help Roethke cram for a law exam, Huff encouraged Ted to *give it up* and pursue his real love of poetry. *I learn by going where I have to go.* Huff continued his law studies and eventually became a Circuit Judge in Saginaw. As a friend of my parents, he occasionally adopted me to be his companion for "father and son" events, and on one such occasion he told me this law school story. Priceless.

PAINTING ROETHKE'S BEDROOM

I'm invited from time to time to participate in programs at the Theodore Roethke Home Museum, and one such occasion was during a huge redecoration project. Funded and organized in part by the generosity of nearby Dow Chemical Company, I was one of two assigned to paint Ted Roethke's bedroom. Honored indeed. The paint color was predetermined to be a very light pale blue and believed to be the original color in Ted's time. *And the sun comes out of a blue cloud over the Tetons.* Ted lived and wrote in this room. It was his haven—his safe place—and he returned to it throughout his life.

> *My secrets cry aloud.*
> *I have no need for tongue.*
> *My heart keeps open house,*
> *My doors are widely swung.*
> *An epic of the eyes*
> *My love, with no disguise.*

BEATRICE O'CONNELL ROETHKE

Roethke's widow, Beatrice, paid a visit to Saginaw in 2011. She stayed as a houseguest in the home of Annie Ransford, who was the founder of the Roethke Home Museum and serving as president of Friends of Theodore Roethke organization at the time. Luck was with me when my wife and I were invited by Annie to be among a handful of people to attend a private dinner party honoring Beatrice and her then-husband, Stephen Lushington. A lovely and cordial cocktail party preceded dinner, with easy conversation between all the guests. Stephen was particularly friendly, animated, and easy to converse with about Roethke, whom he never met. Likewise, though a bit more reserved, Beatrice was open to discussing her earlier life with Ted. When we were seated at the table, Beatrice was immediately across from me, so our conversation continued throughout dinner. As I recall, she and I were the last two remaining when the others began to leave.

> I knew a woman, lovely in her bones
> When small birds sighed, she would sigh back at them.

VISITING POETS

Many poets have passed through the doors of the Roethke Home Museum since it was conceived in 1998. The first to be invited to visit and stay in the home overnight, sleeping in Ted's room, was William Heyen in 2002. Heyen wrote his college thesis on Roethke and was given the honor of being the first poet to sign the quilt that covers Roethke's bed. Another bit of luck for which I am proud is my decades-long friendship with Bill Heyen. We have been houseguests in each other's homes and have talked with each other endlessly about Roethke's life and work. The night after Bill stayed in Roethke's home by himself, he came to spend a night in my home in Bay City. He shared with my wife and me that he felt Roethke's presence through the night. Haunted? Well maybe ... but in a friendly way. Other poets have also shared with me that they believe Roethke has left his presence in the house. Poets Meg Kearney, Robert Fanning, Tess Gallagher, and David Wagoner are among the many who have visited 1805 Gratiot Avenue.

JETT WHITEHEAD

Once I stayed all night.
The light in the morning came slowly over the white
Snow.
There were many kinds of cool
Air.
Then came steam.
Pipe-knock.

ORGANIZED

A popular artifact for visitors at the Roethke Home Museum is an open top file cabinet in Roethke's bedroom. The hanging files have orderly tabs, including: Reading Lists, Letters Writers, Bibliography, Poems Carbon, Yeats' Course, Hopkins' Course, Editors, Greenhouse Poems, Long Poems I, Long Poems II, Long Poems III, Novel Ideas, Essay Ideas, among several other tabs. Each tab is typed, which must have been the job of sister June. Was the organization Ted's idea, or June's?

Where do the roots go?
    Look down under the leaves.
Who put the moss there?
    These stones have been here too long.

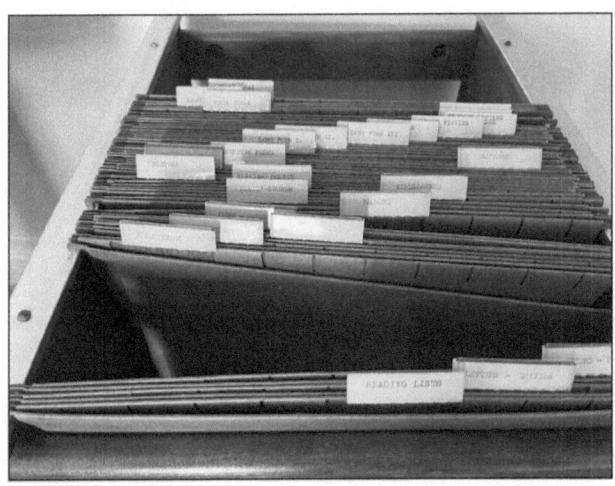

THE FAR FIELD

The title of Roethke's final book, *The Far Field,* is believed to be in reference to the piece of property that is behind the Roethke Home Museum where his family's greenhouses once stood. The area has grown now to be city residential. After the Roethke family sold the former greenhouse land, the piece immediately behind the house was developed and named Roethke Court and divided into several lots for homes. As a personal coincidence, my parents originally purchased the first lot in Roethke Court closest to Roethke's house with the plan of building a home. I was about twelve years old and clueless as to the historical significance of the property. As it turned out, my parents abandoned that plan and sold the property.

> *At the field's end, in the corner missed by the mower,*
> *Where the turf drops off into a grass-hidden culvert,*
> *Haunt of the cat-bird, nesting-place of the field-mouse,*
> *Not too far away from the ever-changing flower-dump . . .*

THE POETRY REMAINS

Theodore Huebner Roethke was born on May 25, 1908, and died on August 1, 1963. Much has been written about his life and work. He was a gifted poet and teacher, at times troubled with mental illness, and often the life of the party. Ted is gone, his work lives on.

The Right Thing

Let others probe the mystery if they can.
Time-harried prisoners of Shall and Will—
The right thing happens to the happy man.

The bird flies out, the bird flies back again;
The hill becomes the valley, and is still;
Let others delve that mystery if they can.

JETT WHITEHEAD

God bless the roots!—Body and soul are one!
The small become the great, the great the small;
The right thing happens to the happy man.

Child of the dark, he can out leap the sun,
His being single, and that being all:
The right thing happens to the happy man.

Or he sits still, a solid figure when
The self-destructive shake the common wall;
Takes to himself what mystery he can,

And, praising change as the slow night comes on,
Wills what he would, surrendering his will
Till mystery is no more: No more he can.
The right thing happens to the happy man. ∎

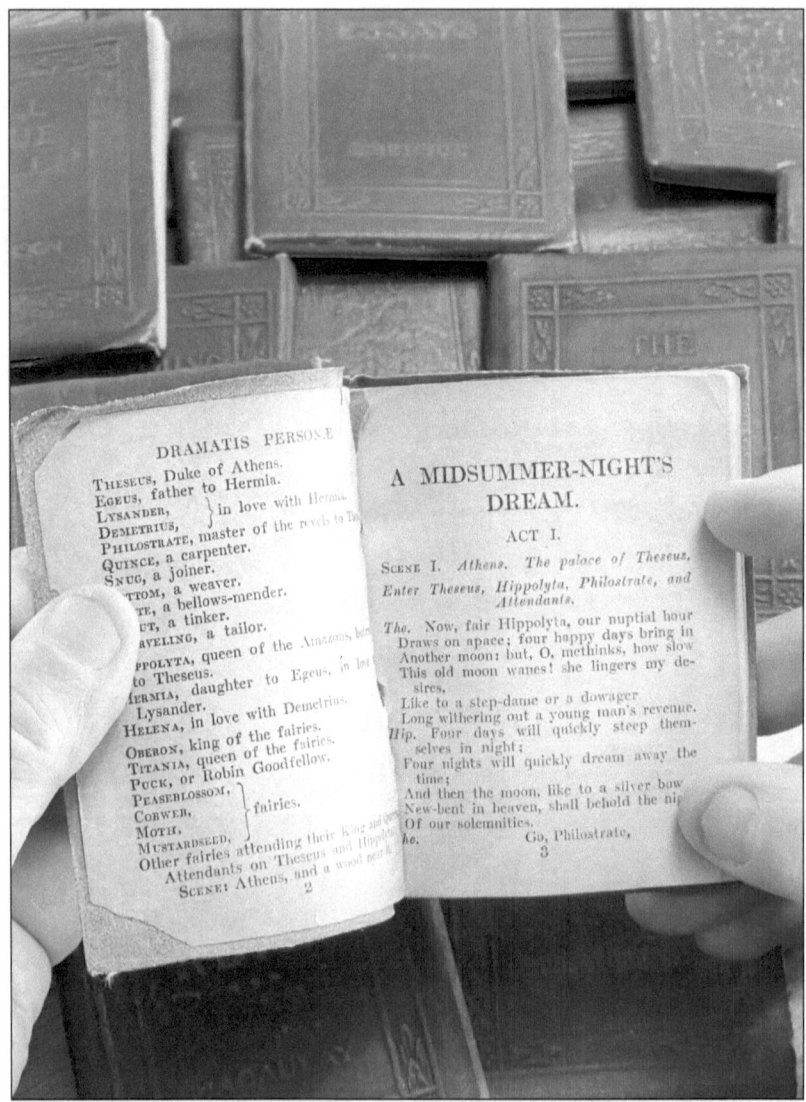

A book from the miniature set of The Complete Works of William Shakespeare, *prinetd by Knickerbocker Leather and Novelty Company, New York, c. 1928.*

DON ZANCANELLA

Becoming a Reader in the West

The Complete Works of Shakespeare

One day in 1928 my my grandfather, an immigrant from Slovenia who made his living in Rock Springs, Wyoming, as a coal miner and delivery truck driver, saw an ad in the *Saturday Evening Post* offering the complete works of William Shakespeare, bound in leather, at the attractive price of $2.98. He filled out the order blank, placed it in an envelope along with a money order, and waited. While he'd never read any of Shakespeare's plays, much less seen one performed, he knew the man was considered a great writer, perhaps the greatest of all time.

Some weeks later a parcel arrived from the Knickerbocker Leather and Novelty Company, New Rochelle, New York. My grandfather had assumed the entire set would come in a single carton, but the size and weight of the package suggested that it contained only one book. Yet what he found when he opened the box were 24 miniature volumes: *Romeo and Juliet. Macbeth. King Lear. As You Like It. The Taming of the Shrew.* The covers were indeed leather, but the books were so diminutive that the accompanying wooden case was less than half the size of a loaf of bread.

It appeared he'd been hoodwinked. Everything about the ad had led him to expect full-sized books. And yet, the print was legible, the paper, although tissue-thin, seemed resistant to tearing, and each volume did in fact contain a complete play. Viewing the set as both a disappointment and a conversation piece, he placed it on top of a chest of drawers where it remained for the next forty years.

As a child I was fascinated by these books and would sometimes ask to examine them. I assumed they'd been shipped to Wyoming all the way from England. It would make no sense for them to come from New Rochelle, a place I knew only as the New York City suburb where Rob and Laura Petrie lived on the *Dick Van Dyke Show*.

The miniature Shakespeare volumes weren't the only books my grandfather purchased through the mail. There was also a six-volume set of Jack London's novels and an eight-volume set of the stories of

THE LIMBERLOST REVIEW

O. Henry. Why London and O. Henry? Maybe because they were among the most popular authors of the day. Or because he'd once again succumbed to a pitch in a magazine ad: "Great tales of adventure in the far north." "A master of the short story who never fails to astonish." I don't recall seeing my grandfather reading these mail-order classics, but I assume he did. Some of them anyway. He wasn't the kind of person who would pay good money for a book, or anything else, merely to display.

What I did see him read was the daily newspaper, the Rock Springs *Rocket-Miner,* as well as a weekly, nationwide newspaper called *Grit*. *Grit* was published in Pennsylvania and sold door-to-door by children and teenagers. During the 1940s, it had a circulation of 500,000.
In the *Archie* comics, Richie Rich's father said he'd gotten his start in business by selling *Grit*. I remember it being a bit like the *Old Farmer's Almanac*—a compendium of human-interest stories, how-to columns, recipes, comics, puzzles, and homespun wisdom. "Ten differences between dogs and cats." "Natural cures for joint pain."

As for the *Rocket-Miner,* it was a fine daily newspaper covering local, state, national, and international events. Even on weekdays it was made up of multiple sections and ran to twenty pages or more. My great uncle supervised the printing of the *Rocket-Miner* and supplied everyone in the family not only with a subscription at a reduced rate but with a useful by-product of the newspaper's production: thick tablets of blank newsprint, 9 inches by 12 inches, off-white in color, dotted with barely visible flecks of wood. Nearly all of my school projects and reports were done using that paper. It had a softer surface than the notebook paper of today and accepted pencil and ballpoint equally well.

My grandfather was fluent in English and Slovenian and he used sheets of that same paper when he helped other Slovenian coalminers write letters to the "Old Country" and then translate the replies. He had a small drop-leaf desk and when I picture him seated at it, I'm reminded of the type of working-class scribe and scholar who appears in stories by Isaac Bashevis Singer.

DON ZANCANELLA

The Year When Stardust Fell

Like my grandfather, my parents obtained books through the mail, although theirs came from "The Literary Guild." This competitor of the Book of the Month Club sent its members a flier every month listing several books from which they could choose. If they didn't mark a choice on the enclosed form and return it, they automatically received the "main selection" for that month. Most of the time my parents took the main selection, either because they didn't get around to choosing something else from the list or because they trusted the Literary Guild's taste. In our living room, three long built-in shelves were filled with these volumes. *Night of Camp David* by Fletcher Knebel, *The Affluent Society* by John Kenneth Galbraith, *A Stillness at Appomattox* by Bruce Catton, *A Song of Sixpence* by A.J. Cronin, *A Thousand Days* by Arthur Schlessinger. Politics and current events, popular social science and history, mainstream fiction. Each month a new book arrived to be unboxed and placed on the shelf. I'm able to be precise about the titles because I can see them in the background of numerous family photos.

We lived in Laramie and my mother took me to the Albany County Public Library often. One of the many libraries built in the early twentieth century with grants from the nineteenth century industrialist Andrew Carnegie, it was a two-story structure made of rust-orange brick. The adult books were in the basement and on the first floor, and the children's room was on the second floor, at the top of a long staircase with a gleaming oak banister. Like most children of the fifties and sixties, I read or had read to me the picture books of the day— Jean de Brunhoff's *Babar*, Ludwig Bemelman's *Madeline*, and, especially, Dr. Seuss. *The Cat in the Hat* and *How the Grinch Stole Christmas* were published in 1957—what a year!—and *One Fish, Two Fish, Red Fish, Blue Fish* and *Green Eggs and Ham* in 1960—again, what a year! I was six years old in 1960 and swam like a fish in the river Suess created.

Laramie, despite the presence of the library and despite being home to a university, had no bookish pretensions. There weren't any bookstores, save for the textbook store on campus which I hardly knew existed. We got only two television networks, CBS and NBC. Two became one or zero during snowstorms when the wind and snow

303

would damage the translator that sent the signal to our rooftop antenna from high on a ridge east of town.

When I was in the fifth grade I began going to the library with a friend who lived next door. Ricky was the same age as me and his mother would drive us there, drop us off while she ran errands, and return an hour or two later. He was my first reading friend. We would each check out three or four books, exchange them when we finished, and discuss them at length. Together, we discovered the series of histories for young readers published as part of Random House's "Landmark Books" series. My favorites included *The Flying Tigers* by John Toland and *To California by Covered Wagon* by George R. Stewart. Toland, Stewart, and many other Landmark authors were well known for their writing for adults. For example, Toland wrote *The Rising Sun: The Decline and Fall of the Japanese Empire, 1936–1945* which won a Pulitzer Prize in 1971, and Stewart wrote *Earth Abides,* a post-apocalyptic science fiction novel published in 1949 which continues to have a cult following. Even Shirley Jackson and Robert Penn Warren wrote for the series.

By sixth grade, Ricky and I moved on to science fiction, prompted by our teacher Mrs. Engen who read us Robert Heinlein's *Tunnel in the Sky* and Raymond F. Jones's *The Year When Stardust Fell*. Tunnel in the Sky was a sort of anti-*Lord of the Flies*, about a group of teenagers who take a field trip to a distant planet but fail to make it home. Rather than descending into savagery, they create a society that functions as well or better than what they left behind on earth. In Jones's novel, the earth passes through the tail of a comet and all metal objects become fused to any other metal they're in contact with. Thus, all forms of transportation freeze up, weapons stop functioning, and factories grind to a halt.

Ricky and I might have continued sharing books and our thoughts about them but one day his father took him antelope hunting in the high desert country west of Laramie and, on a dirt road far from any town, their truck rolled over and Ricky was killed. It was my first intimate experience with death and, while I've since had many friends and acquaintances who were avid readers, never again has there been one with whom I found it so easy to exchange observations and opinions.

DON ZANCANELLA

Mr. Dog

In addition to taking me to the library, my mother bought the occasional Little Golden Book at the grocery store. Two of my favorites were *Mr. Dog* and *Animal Friends*. I was enchanted by these stories of animals trying to find a place for themselves in the wide world, and also by Garth Williams' illustrations. Only as an adult did I discover that both books had been written by the inimitable Margaret Wise Brown, author of *Good Night Moon*.

Mr. Dog is about a dog named Crispin's Crispian who "belonged to himself." When I was five or six or seven, belonging to oneself had an intense appeal. Brown's own Kerry blue terrier was named Crispin's Crispian and the name alone was enough to make the book intriguing. Crispin is Latin for curly haired and there were twin martyred saints named Crispin and Crispian whose feast day is celebrated on October 25. But the name probably came from the famous St. Crispin's day speech before the Battle of Agincourt in Shakespeare's *Henry V*:

> Crispin Crispian shall ne'er go by,
> From this day to the ending of the world,
> But we in it shall be rememberèd;
> We few, we happy few, we band of brothers.

As an adult I would publish a short story in a literary magazine (*The Hopkins Review*) entitled "Mr. Dog," about a young father who discovers the book through reading aloud to his children and then becomes obsessed with Margaret Wise Brown. Here's an excerpt:

> After the girls are asleep, he goes to Wikipedia to find out more about Margaret Wise Brown. The first thing he notices is how attractive she was. The black and white portrait next to the article reminds him of a 1940s movie star—the type known for playing intelligent women, like Joan Fontaine and Deborah Kerr. And she was only forty-two when she died.

> *Now his curiosity is piqued. What was the cause of death? Wikipedia says an embolism, while she was visiting France. Apparently she kicked up her leg in a show of exuberance and a blood clot dislodged and traveled to her heart. She never married but was engaged to a man with the unlikely name of Pebbles Rockefeller. Before that she had a long-term relationship with a woman named Blanche. She had a house in Maine she called "The Only House." She said ideas for books came to her in dreams.*

The grocery store that sold Little Golden Books was also the source of a set of encyclopedias for children, acquired by my mother at the rate of one volume per week until we had the whole set. Called *The Golden Book Encyclopedia*, (it seemed all books for children were golden) there were sixteen in total, each about 100 pages long and profusely illustrated. Volume 1, *Aardvark to Army*; Volume 5, *Daguerreotype to Epiphyte*; Volume 7, *Ghosts to Houseplants*. (An epiphyte is a plant that grows on another plant but is not parasitic. Orchids, for example.) According to Leonard Marcus, "the set sold 60 million copies, making it one of the most commercially successful ventures in modern publishing history." My friend Mark also had a set, but instead of using them as reference books, he read each one cover-to-cover the moment his mother brought it home from the store. This disturbed me. It seemed to violate some sense I had of what the books were for—wasn't "reference" related to "refer," and didn't that suggest you referred to them as necessary and weren't supposed to read them like a novel, straight through. However, the larger problem was that Mark and I tended to compete with one another, and since he was a voracious reader, more energetic and serious about books than me, I thought I ought to be reading *The Golden Book Encyclopedia* straight through but lacked the persistence and attention span to do so.

DON ZANCANELLA

Beat

One of the first adult novels I read was Jack Kerouac's *On the Road*. I don't remember how I came to pick it up but during the 1960s the Signet paperback with the orange and yellow sunset cover was everywhere. It's difficult to overestimate the brilliance of the title: *On the Road*. At age fourteen, I couldn't wait until I was old enough to get in the car and go.

For me, a significant aspect of Kerouac's tale was the role the city of Denver played in it. I'd been to Denver often, it was in my part of the country, not in the East or in California, the two places where everything important seemed to happen. *On the Road* might even have been the first novel I read set in a location I knew firsthand. How appealing to see Denver portrayed as a romantic destination, a frontier town that, in Kerouac's description, also seemed to be drenched in cool. However, I wasn't familiar with the part of Denver Kerouac wrote about the most: Larimar Street, Denver's skid row, the street of bars and flop houses and pawn shops where Sal Paradise meets up with his friend Dean Moriarty:

> I pictured myself in a Denver bar that night . . . there were smokestacks, smoke, railyards, red-brick buildings, and the distant downtown gray-stone buildings, and here I was in Denver. I stumbled along with the most wicked grin of joy in the world, among the old bums and beat cowboys of Larimer Street.

Not long after I read *On the Road*, my mother told me that she and my father had decided to buy me a set of drums. I'd started playing in the jazz band at school and, though they wished I'd chosen a more melodic instrument, not to mention one that was easier to transport, they wanted to encourage my interest in music, an artform they both loved. But if buying books in Laramie wasn't easy, buying a used drum set—given the cost, it had to be used—was impossible. After studying the classified ads in the *Denver Post*, I proposed trying the pawn shops in Denver. Many of them advertised cheap musical instruments. And many of them were on Larimer Street.

A few weeks later, we made the three-hour drive to Denver and found our way downtown. I knew nothing about the mean streets of big cities, but Larimer Street was just as I imagined it, just as Kerouac described it. There were pool halls, there were bars, there were bars that appeared to be strip clubs, and yes, pawn shops, all of them looking as though they'd seen better days. Men huddled in alleys and doorways, some of them with bottles in paper bags and others lounged on corners in groups of two or three. I didn't exactly expect to see Jack and Neal but if they'd crossed the street in front of us I wouldn't have been surprised. My parents, however, found the scene alarming.

"We're not walking around down here," my father said.

My mother scanned the fronts of the buildings. "What was that address again? Are you sure you got it right?"

"Yes. There it is! G.I. Joe's."

My father slowed but didn't stop. "There's no place to park."

"We'll go in," my mother said, "while you drive around the block."

"Are you sure?" His voice sounded uneasy. I could tell he was on the verge of calling off the entire quest.

"Yes," said my mother. "We'll be fine."

So my father stopped the car in the middle of traffic, my mother and I got out and, dodging a car or two, we made our way toward G.I. Joe's. As soon as we entered, I could see it was unlike any store I'd ever been in. It was a jumble, a maze, a riotous emporium. And, incredibly, there was jazz playing, not on a storewide sound system but on a portable phonograph sitting on a shelf near the door. Denver writer Robert Greer, in one of his mystery novels about the bail bondsman CJ Floyd, describes G.I. Joe's like this:

DON ZANCANELLA

The long-established pawnshop shared a white, two-story brick building, erected in 1893, with Lucero's Furniture Store. The second-floor windows of the pawnshop had been bricked over and painted white, giving the building the neo-Gothic look of a mortuary. Harry Steed, a returning World War II veteran, had started the business in the late 1940s, and the shop, along with Pasternack's, a pawnshop next door, had a reputation for selling everything from college scholastic honorary keys to microscopes for medical students.

Moving purposefully into the musty bowels of the store, past glass-topped display cabinets and row after row of shelves chock-full of everything from slide guitars to roller skates, [CJ] had the sense that he was back in the Mekong River Delta, cruising through enemy territory well beyond the safety of his 42nd River Patrol Group's operations base.

After a moment of stunned silence, my mother told an approaching salesman that we had come to see the drum sets advertised in the *Post*. He led us to the back of the store and there it was: a sparkly four-piece Ludwig, with one ride cymbal, a high-hat, and a stool. In the color the Ludwig company called "champagne."

"What do you think?" my mother asked.

I nodded.

"You should try it," said the salesman and handed me a pair of sticks.

I took my seat, adjusted everything, and played a few clumsy riffs.

"How much is it?" my mother asked

"You can have it for one twenty-five."

I looked at my mother and said, "Is that okay?" I'd have preferred turquoise but in a pawn shop you didn't get to choose your color. Besides, the cymbal was engraved with the mark of the Zildjian company, which I knew made the best ones.

"We'll take it," she said, opening her purse, locating her wallet, and placing six twenties and a five into the salesman's outstretched palm. A moment later, he was helping us carry the drums out to the sidewalk where we waited until my father pulled up and double-parked.

"I guess you're in a band," the salesman said as we placed the drums in the trunk. I doubted that what he had in mind was the jazz band of a small high school in Wyoming, so I only nodded and didn't try to explain.

Back in the car and a few blocks away from Larimar Street, my mother looked at my father and said, "That was quite a place."

When I first read *On the Road* in 1968, I was unaware that it had been published in 1957 and that the events described in it had taken place in the late 1940s. Therefore, it was, in a sense, a historical novel and much of the America it described had already disappeared. But Larimar Street, which would later be gentrified and redeveloped out of existence, was still Larimar Street, and GI Joe's Pawn Shop and the sounds of jazz and putting a used drum set in the trunk of a double-parked sedan seemed, at least to a fourteen-year-old from Wyoming, like a moment of humble, street-level beatitude, that thing Kerouac would shorten to beat.

Aunt Joann

Aunt Joann, actually my Italian grandfather's stepsister and so my great aunt, was a forbidding woman who wore high-collared dresses and high button shoes. With a straight spine and severe countenance, she looked as though she could have walked out of an Edith Wharton novel. By the time I knew her, her husband Victor had died and she lived alone in a large house filled with dark furniture and drove a white Lincoln Continental—or didn't drive it, for as she aged, it sat untouched in her garage. Victor had been a sheep rancher and then a banker, so Aunt Joann was quite well off. (The progression from rancher to banker and even to elected office is still fairly common in the West)

Every time we visited my grandparents in Rock Springs, my parents would insist we pay Aunt Joann a visit. I found her frightening and knew that at a certain point she would hold out a glass dish filled with homemade divinity. Although I hated the stuff, studded as it was with nuts and difficult to identify shards of candied fruit, I was not allowed to turn it down. My father made us visit out of a sense of familial obligation, but I could tell he too dreaded going to see Aunt Joann—

not because of the divinity but because he believed she had treated his own father poorly. While she didn't hesitate to call on her stepbrother to drive her places in her Lincoln or do some odd jobs around her house, she didn't seem to consider him fully worthy of her affection and respect.

During our visits, I sat quietly, ate the divinity, and then felt a great rush of relief upon exiting the stuffy atmosphere of the house. But one day Aunt Joann invited me and my older brother to her study, a room only large enough to hold an oak desk and a wall of books.

"I want to show you something," she said, taking down a small volume and holding it with what seemed a certain reverence. "This is a copy of *The Banditti of the Plains*."

According to Aunt Joann, it was one of only a few in existence. Written by journalist A.S. Mercer and published in 1894, *The Banditti of the Plains* was an account of the Johnson County War, an historic conflict between the cattlemen of Wyoming and the state's homesteaders and sheepmen. Fed up with what they considered the encroachment of outsiders on their grazing rights, the cattlemen had, in 1892, sent a private army from Cheyenne to the northeast corner of the state with orders to arrest and even lynch any who refused to allow the cattlemen full sway over the land. The scheme was hatched by the Wyoming Stockgrowers' Association and endorsed by the Governor and the state's senators in Washington. Only when Senator Francis Warren, fearing a genuine bloodbath, changed his mind, were cavalry troops from Fort McKinney ordered to intervene.

Aunt Joann went on to explain that after Mercer published his unsparing account of the affair—the full title was *The Banditti of the Plains* or *The Cattlemen's Invasion of Wyoming in 1892 (The Crowning Infamy of the Ages)*—the Stockgrowers and other powerful Wyoming interests attempted to suppress it. Burning some copies, including, in one instance, an entire wagonload, and stealing others from libraries, they effectively made the book disappear—except, that is, for a few copies, such as the one Aunt Joann was holding in her hands.

Naturally, my brother and I were stunned. I'd never heard about these events, had no idea my aunt could tell such tales, and was astonished to learn that she possessed such a document, one which was apparently rare, dangerous to own, and of real historical significance. I would almost have believed she was speaking from first-hand knowledge except that she was born in 1890 and would have been only two years old when it all happened. But given how well ranchers in Wyoming knew one another, and given her late husband's prominence in that industry, it seemed likely that she had heard the story from someone who did have first-hand knowledge, perhaps even someone who had participated in the war.

After that incident, our visits with Aunt Joann returned to the old pattern and I don't know what became of her copy of the book. But I didn't forget the story and, when I was a little older, I plunged headlong into it. I found that *The Banditti of the Plains* had been republished in 1954 by University of Oklahoma Press so it was available for me to read. I also read Helena Huntington Smith's brilliant account of the Johnson County War, *War on Powder River* (1967). And I discovered that The Johnson County War was the event that inspired Owen Wister to write *The Virginian* (1902), Jack Schaffer to write *Shane* (1949), and Michael Cimino to make the film *Heaven's Gate* (1980), which was such a box office disaster that it bankrupted United Artists—an event Stephen Bach wrote about in his book *The Final Cut*. All of these things inspired me to write an as yet unpublished novel about the Johnson County War, the first chapter of which appeared in the 2024 *Limberlost Review* under the title "A Woman on Horseback."

Through my aunt's story and the books that followed I also discovered the great university presses of the West. If the University of Oklahoma could publish *The Banditti of the Plains* and *War on Powder River,* what other riches awaited me? To name only a few, *Recollections of a Cowpuncher* by E.C. Abbott and Helena Huntington Smith (University of Oklahoma Press), the book that inspired Larry McMurtry to write *Lonesome Dove*; Wright Morris' novels, which are the equal of any American fiction written in the 1950s and 60s (University of Nebraska

Press); and N. Scott Momaday's poetic memoir *The Way to Rainy Mountain* (University of New Mexico Press). These books and others like them helped me understand that while there was nothing wrong with what came in boxes from New Rochelle, there was also literature growing out of the ground on which I stood.■

"Bookmark," linocut by
Riley Sophia Penaluna.

RE-READINGS

Norman Maclean.

JIM HEPWORTH

'And Grace Comes by Art and Art Does Not Come Easy': Norman Maclean and His Critics

"Norman Maclean didn't publish much," reads the headline on Pulitzer Prize winner Kathryn Schulz's "Critic at Large" article in the July 2024 fiction issue of *The New Yorker*, but "What he did [publish] contains everything." [1]

Indeed, Schulz goes on to say, you could read Maclean's entire published oeuvre—"two and a half books" and "a handful of lectures, essays, and sketches, most written or resurrected in the flurry of sudden, late-in-life fame"—in a single day, and "yet," she continues, "it contains almost everything there is to know about what the English language can do." That's why, she says, she continues to read and reread him: "for intellectual and aesthetic resuscitation," especially when, as a writer, she's "stuck on something" she's "trying to write" and has "exhausted all the other options," which, she says, include "ignoring the problem, staring blankly at the problem, moving the problem around to see if it's less annoying in some other location, eating all the chocolate in the house." [2]

If Kathryn Schultz was a literary outlier, of course, we could ignore her, but she is by no means alone in her exceedingly high opinion of Maclean's work. In fact, she joins a chorus of other Pulitzer Prize winners who have sung Maclean's praises (Annie Proulx and Wallace Stegner, to name just two; John McPhee and Richard Ford, to name two more). Maclean's brilliance and critical acclaim as a writer's writer is only seconded by his sales, which, in the case of his first book, *A River Runs through It and Other Stories*, according to his son John, passed the one million copy mark soon after Robert Redford's sensitive film adaptation of the story came out in 1992.[3] That was also the same year Maclean's posthumous *Young Men and Fire* appeared to rave reviews and spent multiple weeks on the *New York Times* non-fiction bestsellers list. Not coincidentally, in the wake of the Redford film's October release, for the week of November 29, 1992, the *New York Times* listed not one but two editions of *River* among its paperback bestsellers: the just-released mass paperback edition published by Pocket Books (#3) and the trade paperback edition published by Chicago (#10).

Given Maclean's stellar reputation as a writer, it seems curious, then—or at least it does to me—that, until now, no single critical or biographical volume has been published on or about Maclean since 1988 when Idaho's Confluence Press brought out *Norman Maclean*, edited by Ron McFarland and Hugh Nichols, as the second volume in its American Authors Series. That's a gap of thirty-six years. Never mind that in the interim dozens of individual critical articles as well as profiles and interviews have popped up in academic and literary journals as well as popular magazines or that Maclean's publisher, University of Chicago Press, tried to monetize their success with Maclean's books by publishing *The Norman Maclean Reader* edited by O. Alan Weltzien. Weltzien's introductory essay is one of the best things ever written about Maclean, but in terms of sales, let's just say they have been respectable but underwhelming. Furthermore, without Weltzien, who was one of only two researchers permitted into the Maclean archives at Chicago prior to their opening in 2013, we might know nothing about Maclean's unfinished *Custer* manuscript or its important place in Maclean's writing career.

Frankly, I don't know what explains the quick burst of Norman Maclean books published in 2024: Rebecca McCarthy's *Norman Maclean: A Life in Letters and Rivers*;[4] George H. Jensen's and Heidi Skurat Harris's *Norman Maclean's A River Runs through It: The Search for Beauty*;[5] and

JIM HEPWORTH

Timothy P. Schilling's *The Writings of Norman Maclean: Seeking Truth amid Tragedy*.[6] Their only recent forerunner was a memoir, *Home Waters: A Chronicle of Family and a River*,[7] published by Maclean's son, John, in 2008.

In her *New Yorker* profile of Maclean, Kathryn Schultz quickly and rightfully dismisses Rebecca McCarthy's biography with a single sentence when she writes that the connection between McCarthy and Maclean "is sometimes illuminating but more often distracting; McCarthy's book dwells too much on their interactions and on his academic career, at the expense of momentum and chronology." McCarthy met Maclean in 1972 while she was still a teenager when she flew to western Montana to visit her brother, John Roberts, "a professional forester with the U.S. Forest Service" in charge of recreation at Seeley Lake, the site of Maclean's cabin. It's her brother's color photograph, a Maclean favorite, that wraps completely around the first paperback edition of *River*. McCarthy entitled the only article she had previously published on Maclean "Norman Maclean and Me,"[8] which would have been a much more accurate title for her book since the emphasis falls on the narcissistic *me* that dominates roughly the first half of her "biography." She also commits numerous factual errors. For example, she confuses oceans when she has smoke from The Big Burn of 1910 making it impossible for ships "five hundred miles off the *Atlantic Coast*" (my emphasis)—to "navigate by the stars at night."[9] And her failures to properly document her sources are numerous.

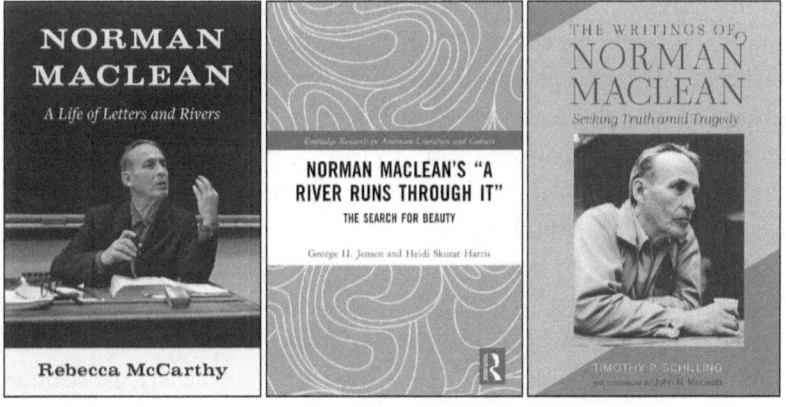

319

Or, equally common, she often provides no evidence for her claims. She simply expects her readers to trust her at her word she says somebody (Norman, Norman's editor, Norman's daughter) told her something but then neglects to document the occasion by telling us when and where the conversation took place. She's also unafraid to operate by salacious hearsay and inuendo: "I heard a story about Norman from his long-ago students, that a young co-ed had hanged herself in Ida Noyes Hall after Norman told her he was married, he was her teacher, and neither could nor would ever become her love interest." [10]

By contrast, the two other books recently published focus far more on Maclean's writing than on his life. When they do examine Maclean's life, they contextualize or illuminate his writing. Both books are scrupulously documented, although their authors take special pains to avoid unnecessary academic jargon and write for a general audience. Still, at $45 for a new copy of Tim Schilling's 155-page paperback and $152 for the 212-page hardcover by Jensen and Harris, it seems obvious their publishers are taking aim almost exclusively at the ever-shrinking academic library market, which is too bad. Both books deserve a much wider general audience of Maclean readers.

Of course, there are plenty of things that illuminate both the life and the writing of Norman Maclean that are found exclusively in *Home Waters*, too, including John Maclean's full account of his Uncle Paul's unsolved murder and his father Norman's near miss with the Pulitzer Prize. John Maclean's stories about his mother, Jessie, and her family, and his grandmother, Clara, illuminate events in the history of his father's first book. He elaborates on characters his father only sketches. Here, too, are stories about his father's favorite fly rod, his father's last fishing trip, and the recovery of the Blackfoot River from the ill-effects of mining, logging, irrigation, and overuse. Although the book also contains plenty of stories and anecdotes of John and his father fishing together with and without the presence of bears, readers might be surprised, as I was, to learn that it was it was not his father, the professional teacher, who taught John Maclean to fly fish but his father's friend, George Croonenberghs, who learned to tie flies from John's grandfather, Rev J.N. Maclean. *Home Waters* is a physically handsome book, with an illustrated interior design reminiscent of the interior design of *River*. The luxurious illustrations in *Home Waters* from original wood engravings by Wesley W. Bates are obviously intended to echo the scratchboard illustrations by R. Williams's in *River*.

Readers of *Home Waters* might be also be interested in such seemingly trivial details that John Maclean relays as how to identify a true first edition of his father's first book or the truth about the submission of his father's manuscript of *River* to Knopf, a story repeated in even more detail by Jensen and Harris, who tell us that the Senior Editor at Knopf, Angus Cameron, actually wanted to publish *A River* but was overruled by Robert Gottleib, the Editor-in-Chief, who described the stories as "well written but unsaleable."[11] John Maclean omits Gottleib's name from his account but nevertheless calls his decision "one of the great misjudgments in history of book publishing."[12] He goes on to say that the "legend" that the book was rejected "because an East Coast publisher complained it 'has trees in it' is often repeated but never happened. The phrase was a casual observation from one of Norman's followers from the East Coast, and it was merely a phrase to explain away the rejections."[13]

In the interest of full disclosure, I should say that I was a pipsqueak contributor to *Home Waters* as well as to the works of Schilling, Jensen, and Harris, but these books are so original, written with such intelligence and so full of fresh ideas and insights resulting from years of research and difficult labor that they are destined to be read and reread well into the foreseeable future. As for their authors, Schilling is an independent scholar who lives and works in the Netherlands but grew up in Washington state and studied English at Princeton and theology in Belgium at the University of Lueven. He received his doctorate in practical theology from the Catholic Theological University in Utrecht where he lives with his wife and two children. George H. Jensen and Heidi Skurat Harris are both closely associated with the Department of Rhetoric and Writing at the University of Arkansas Little Rock, Jensen as a Professor Emeritus and former department chair, Harris as an Associate Professor and Graduate Coordinator. Both have published scholarly books as well as creative non-fiction.

Given his status as professional theologian, it seems only natural that Schilling would bring, as he does, a kind of religious gravitas to Maclean, the self-labeled "religious agnostic," and to the study of Maclean's two major works, *River* and *Fire*, and the existential questions they raise in the minds of readers. In his opening chapter, Schilling begins with an obvious but puzzling question that has probably nagged every close reader of *A River Runs through It* since the story's publication in April of 1976: to what does the pronoun "it" of Maclean's title refer? Whereas the "river" of the title unmistakably points to the Big Blackfoot "and more generally to rivers as sources of material and spiritual sustenance, the 'it'" of the title "is a pronoun without an obvious antecedent."[14] Schilling notes that the question "becomes more urgent when we note its prominent" but equally ambiguous use elsewhere in Maclean's writing: notably, in the opening line of Maclean's other novella, "USFS 1919: The Ranger, the Cook, and a Hole in the Sky," where Maclean writes, "I was young and I thought I was tough and I knew it was beautiful and I was a little bit crazy but hadn't noticed it yet."[15]

"How many times have I read that [sentence]," Schilling asks himself, "and wondered: *What* was beautiful? *Being young and tough? Life? Something else?*"[16] He also notes in passing that Maclean put the word "it" in quotation marks "on four separate pages" of *Young Men and Fire*, but in those cases he provides antecedents for their use. (In an endnote Schilling writes that they refer overtly to "the universe, an inner trial the Smokejumpers must undergo, the fire that eventually kills them, and an illness" that killed Mann Gulch Ranger Robert Jansson).[17] Regardless, Schilling concludes that Maclean clearly wants his readers to wonder what his elusive use of "it" is all about, especially in the title story of his first book. He claims the "the ambiguity" of "It" turns the title "into a puzzle and poem at once."[18]

JIM HEPWORTH

To solve the "puzzle" Schilling points to the paragraph below from one of Maclean's own essays titled "The Woods, Books, and Truant Officers."[19]

> One of my editors admitted to me that he spent two evenings looking through the Bible and Biblical concordances for the source of the title of the book, *A River Runs through It*. But its source, as far as I know, is in such an ordinary farmer's expression as "a creek runs through the north forty," listed to beauty perhaps by the substitution of "river" for "creek" and "it" for "the north forty." The liquid R's that begin and end "river" are to be contrasted to the grunting K's that begin and end "creek"; and the farmer's "north forty" (forty acres being a 16th of a square mile or section of land) is to be contrasted to the substituted "it" which is the "it" of the world to come and the "it" of Shakespeare, as in, "If it be now, 'tis not to come." Also, the farmer's ordinary phrase is without rhythm, made up, except for "forty," of staccato one-syllable words, whereas the two "for "forty," of staccato one-syllable words, whereas the two syllables of "river" turn "A river runs" into running rhythm, the rhythm running over three alliterative R's.

Schilling seizes on "as far as I know" to underscore "the mysteriousness of the artistic process: even artists" he says, "don't fully grasp what gives rise to their art."[20] He notes that Maclean gives us "two explanations for the 'it' of his title: 'It' refers, straight forwardly, to a section of land (possibly that part of Montana in which Maclean was raised) and, more abstractly, to ultimate realities," pointing out that the line from Hamlet Maclean quotes above "refers to the ever-present possibility of death."[21] There, in act 5, scene 2, where *Hamlet* is about to engage Laertes in the fencing matching that ends both their lives, Shakespeare gives Hamlet those immortal words that Shakespeare teachers can often quote from memory: "There is special providence in the fall of a sparrow. If it be now, 'tis not to come; if it be not to come, it will be now; if it be not now yet it will come—the readiness is all."

All his adult life and throughout his essays and interviews, Maclean acknowledged his estrangement from "church religion" while admitting its importance to him. "Messiah?" he says, almost scoffing, to Kay Bonetti in a 1985 interview, "I don't know. . . but I have these feelings that there is design in this strange but brutal universe, but I wouldn't know, darling, how to explain it. I can't make sense out of it, ultimately." [22]

What he could make sense of when he looked back over his life from the lofty perch of his old age, he told Bonetti, were "a few certain kinds of wonderfully composed moments" in which he felt he was "a character" in a story" but was not "shaping the thing," moments Maclean repeatedly refers to throughout his work by borrowing Wordsworth's term, "spots of time." These moments he could and did shape into art as carefully designed stories.

Whether the universe is "something like what [King] Lear hoped it was"— controlled by divinity, harmonious and orderly, benevolent and comprehensible— "or very close to what he feared it was"—chaotic and incomprehensible, godless, pitiless, and cruel— "is still, tragically, the current question" as Maclean notes in his 1952 scholarly essay: "Episode, Scene, Speech, and Word: The Madness of Lear." [23] And, perhaps needless to say, it has always been the "current question" for writers and thinkers across the centuries. In *Young Men and Fire*, Schilling says, Maclean set out not only to "reconstruct the final hours of the smokejumpers, but also to learn something about himself, and to determine 'if there is not some shape, form, design as of artistry in this universe.'" [24]

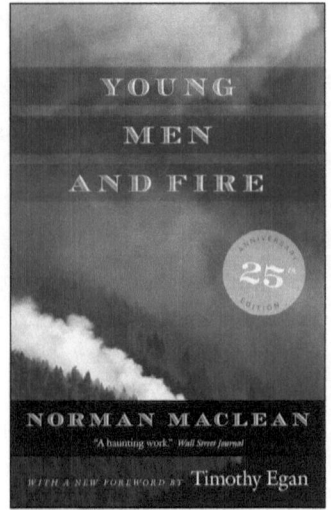

Of course, that Hamlet's "it" should figure so centrally into the title of Maclean's *River*—or Lear's question into the writing of *Fire*—will surprise no one familiar with Maclean's long and legendary teaching career. "He [Shakespeare] must have known more about writing than anybody else ever did," Maclean said to Pete Dexter. "Every year I said to myself, 'You better teach this bastard so you don't forget what great writing is like.' I taught him technically, two whole weeks for the first scene from *Hamlet*. I'd spend the first day on just the first line, 'Who's there?'"[25]

The late Supreme Court Justice John Paul Stevens reportedly told his law school classes that "the best way" he knew "to prepare for the law was to take Shakespeare from Norman Maclean."[26] Clearly, Maclean enjoyed a distinguished career as a teacher, but not quite as distinguished as his critics claim. Without exception his critics and biographer write that he won an unprecedented three Quantrell Awards for Excellence in Undergraduate Teaching at the University of Chicago, beginning in 1932, his first year as an instructor. According to the University of Chicago webpage for the Quantrell Awards,[27] however, the awards were not founded until six years later, in 1938. Maclean may have won a teaching award in 1932, but it was not a Quantrell. He is, nevertheless, like his friend and colleague, Joe Schwab, one of the few to ever win it twice.

Schilling is the first and only one of Maclean's critics to take on a book-length study of both *River* and *Fire*. He is also the first to give us a detailed assessment of Redford's film adaptation. The chapter on Redford primarily examines four issues: (1) how well Redford kept his promises to Maclean and honored the commitments he made regarding Maclean's family, (2) how well the film does "justice to the content and spirit" of the story,[23] (3) how well the film measures up as a work of art "in its own right, and (4) how well it appeals to "a wide audience." Moreover, Schilling is also the first of Maclean's critics to take seriously Maclean's humorous treatment of Isaak Walton and his famous book. "Isaak Walton . . . is not a respectable writer," Rev Maclean tells his two teenage sons in "A River."[29] "He was an Episcopalian and a bait fisherman." "The bastard doesn't even know how to spell complete," a thirteen-year-old Paul Maclean reports back to his brother, "Besides, he has songs to sing to dairymaids. Whoever saw a dairymaid on the Big Blackfoot River?"[30]

As Schilling points out, the "causes for amusement here are multiple. First we have the father's cool dismissal of Walton's writing on nonwriterly grounds: Walton is of the wrong Christian denomination and fishes in the wrong way."[31] Young Paul endorses his father's rejection but "on the grounds of poor spelling and off-topic subject matter." And Paul's implied assertion that Walton sings the songs to the dairymaids shows his misunderstanding of Walton's text. It is, after all, the dairymaids who do the singing. What's more, as Norman the narrator says after he reads the book and reports back to Paul, "Some of those songs are pretty good."[32]

Schilling believes that Maclean intentionally created this humorous allusion to Walton for its entertainment value but more importantly as serious homage to Walton whose book has become something like the *Finnegans Wake* of the angling world: an unread masterpiece. Schilling draws parallels between Walton's fish-eating otter in *The Compleat Angler*[33] and the scene of Neal's "absurd braggadocio in Black Jack's Bar."[34] There, Maclean's readers will recall, Neal regales Old Rawhide with a fabulous story about tracking an otter "all the way to Roger's Pass" where he "mercifully takes the otter's pups into his shirt."[35] Most importantly, Schilling points out that Maclean has adopted Walton's "piscatory ecologue" as a literary form. Without question, Maclean's story lives up to the Schilling definition of the genre as "a theologically rich discourse on the arts of fishing and living."[36]

Unfortunately, Schilling's chapter on Maclean and Walton offers a far more nuanced view than I can summarize here. Suffice it to say that it both teaches and delights as, for example, when Schilling uses historians Lawrence and Angeline Pool to point out that "There was considerable controversy between fishermen in Walton's time as to which was fairer to the fish, fly-fishing or bait-fishing." In fact, fly-fishing was then the more suspect of the two methods. Indeed, seventeenth century fly fishers were charged with being cruel and unfair to the fish for using unnatural means to catch their prey. The Pools quote William Bailey's Bottom Fisher in *The Angler's Instructor*: "I can fly fish as well as you, or any other, but I do not like it; there is something so cowardly about it— it is the worst deception an Angler can make use of."[37] "How amusing, in our time," Schilling writes, "when the slamming of bait fishermen (thanks to Norman Maclean) has become a cliché, to read that fly fishermen were once on the defensive."[38]

Whereas Schilling covers both Maclean's books, lavishing special attention on Maclean's posthumous *Young Men and Fire*, George H. Jensen and Heidi Skurat Harris limit their subject to the single story and single theme of their title: *Norman Maclean's "A River Runs through It": The Search for Beauty*. Their purpose is to "both illuminate Maclean's process of composition and revision and open new ways of viewing the story."[39] They note that "Maclean has arguably had a greater cultural impact than most writers who spend four or five decades writing dozens of books."[40] They call out his special importance to fly fishers and to the history of angling literature. Although reviewers and critics have often commented on the beauty and power of Maclean's prose— "As beautiful as anything in Thoreau or Hemingway" wrote Alfred Kazin—Jensen and Harris are the first to state the complete truth of the matter: that Maclean is "one of the great prose stylists in American literature."[41] Indeed, they go even farther when they write, "He taught some of the great masters of the English language. Then he became one."[42]

It takes genuine courage for any academic critic to make such a bold claim, however much he or she (or they) might suspect it to be true based on the evidence. Most would run in the opposite direction rather than risk their "reputations" by stating such a sweeping generality. Yet Jensen and Harris make another extreme statement that strikes me as daring when they write, "To say that these books [*River* and *Fire*] continue to be read and taught is true enough, but that hardly conveys the deep love—this word is not too strong—many readers feel toward Maclean and his writing."[43] If Jensen and Harris were merely being hyperbolic or metaphorical, their statement would lack the power it has to arrest us, but the formality and emphasis they put on the word *love* assures us they mean the word literally. As someone who has often taught "A River Runs through It," a third statement Jensen and Harris make in their "Conclusion" to their chapter titled "Style and Hidden Art" also affected me. "Most readers of the story," they write, "even those who have never studied poetics, sense that they are reading something beyond ordinary prose, that stylistically something is there [in Maclean's writing] that cannot be adequately explained by calling it rhythmic or poetic or elevated or art."[34]

Most readers of the story, of course, have not been fly fishers, although fly fishers still form part of the story's core audience and were the first to discover it. I've read somewhere that fly fishers read more about their sport than any others do about theirs, including baseball fans, but even if that is true, I'd wager that most fly fishers still have not read the story, although they have seen "The Movie" (as the guides used to call it). And that's because only a small percentage of the world's billions even read books. Indeed, only a small percentage of the world's population ever have. We should remember that for most of human history most people were entirely illiterate. Despite the improvements in literacy rates over the centuries, few of us are truly readers. The late great Ursula K. Le Guin put it this way: "A book won't move your eyes for you the way images on a screen do. It won't move your mind unless you give it your mind, or your heart unless you put your heart in it. It won't do the work for you. To read a story well is to follow it, to act it, to feel it, to become it—everything short of writing it, in fact. Reading is not 'interactive' with a set of rules or options, as games are; reading is actual collaboration with the writer's mind. No wonder not everybody is up to it."[45] Whereas too many academic critics today concern themselves primarily with critical theory and write only for each other, engulfing their wiring in cant and jargon, Jensen and Harris honor common, ordinary readers by giving them enough credit and intelligence to recognize, at least on a subliminal level, that there is something extraordinary about Norman Maclean's prose. But what is this "something"?

Jensen and Harris write, "While sections of 'A River' can certainly be scanned metrically as if they were traditional poetry, Maclean's style does more than this. He uses features of dipodic rhythm and sprung rhythm, he superimposes one rhythm over another, he shifts tempo, he repeats sounds, develops harmonics or tones, and he slowly builds a poetic lexicon with phrases like 'Big Blackfoot River' and 'a four-count rhythm.' Like Gerard Manly Hopkins, he was trying to create a new approach to style."[46] In various interviews, talks, and essays Maclean acknowledges that he consciously pursued such artistry as Jensen and Harris document. In his 1987 Stegner Lecture at Lewiston, Idaho's Lewis-Clark State College, he said, "After all, I do not speak, at least in private, of 'A River Runs through It' as a story about the tragedy of my family—among my friends, I speak of it 'as my love poem to my family.'"[47]

Maclean began to write, by hand, what became the first draft of "A River Runs through It" in the "late spring or early summer" of 1973 just about the time he retired from teaching. He probably started the story in fragments at his Hyde Park apartment before heading for the family cabin in Montana, which he normally did around the middle of June, arriving first in his wife's hometown of Wolf Creek to briefly visit his in-laws before driving on to Seeley Lake. In the process of composing his masterpiece, Maclean produced a total of four handwritten drafts and three typewritten drafts across the span of a little more than two years (Spring 1973 to Fall 1975). "This does not mean," however, as Jensen and Harris point out, that "Maclean only revised 'A River' seven times,"[48] despite any claims Maclean might have made to the contrary. In fact, each of the drafts "shows evidence that Maclean made multiple passes through it—that is, he reread each draft multiple times, making cuts, rewriting sections, and revising phrases."[49] When the handwritten manuscript "became too cluttered with revisions, he recopied it."[50]

While reading Jensen and Harris, it's fascinating, inspiring, and sometimes downright disorienting to witness the story develop from its most primitive state into its most beautiful and refined shape. It's a bit like watching the slow process of a tiny egg hatching and transmogrifying into a hard-shelled nymph and then, after two years of feeding on the bottom, heading to surface where it shucks its exoskeleton and transforms into a speckle-winged Callibaetis mayfly. Here, for example, is how the story originally began:[51]

Fly Fishing

My brother said to me, "He's just as welcome as a dose of gonorrhea."

I said to my brother, "~~He's my brother-in-law.~~" "Go easy on him. He's my brother-in-law."

My brother said, "I won't fish with him."

~~I should have known better than to ask, "Why not?"~~
<I went ahead and asked, "Why not?">

My brother said, "He's from the West Coast and he fishes with worms."

I said, to my brother "Cut it out, Paul. He was born and brought up here in Montana. He just works on the

West Coast. And now he is coming back for a vacation and
he writes and says he wants to fish with us. With you especially."

My brother who was a reporter on **The Helena Independent**, <and was supposed to record facts,> said, "The hell he isn't from the West Coast. **[in margin:]** <insert> **[back to text:]** The fact he was ~~born~~ <born> here in Montana doesn't prove anything. Everybody on the West coast was born in Montana. Either that or Idaho or Utah, or Arizona or New Mexico."

"That's it," he said, "Nobody is born on the West Coast. I think there's a law against it.

I said to my brother, "Cut it out. What about the retired Farmers from North Dakota?"

He said, "All right, all right. And South Dakota, too. But Nobody was ever born on the West Coast. ~~Name me one.~~ Name me one."

Close readers of the story will naturally recognize the scene as a version of the one that unfolds, many pages into the published narrative, between Norman and Paul at ten o'clock in the morning outside The Montana Club in Helena "supposedly on the spot where gold was discovered in Last Chance Gulch."[52] It's funny—or maybe not so funny—what a dramatic difference word choices can make. Imagine what might have happened had Maclean stuck with the title "Fly Fishing." (Or even another of the titles he wrote down as a possibility on his second draft: "Besides the Still Waters.") Some of the dialogue above, of course, survives Maclean's revisions, but he is clearly overwriting and has yet to find his proper emotional tone as the wise old man who begins his story with those now immortal words, "In our family, there was no clear line. . . ."

In short, Jensen and Harris have written a brilliant book that may inspire writers and serious Maclean readers all over the English-speaking world. To help elucidate Maclean's process, they use plenty of illustrations, including a "Flow Chart of Drafts" that provides a timeline alongside each manuscript and typescript phase as well as photos of handwritten and typescript pages. They provide transcriptions of Maclean's handwritten manuscripts using conventional marks that are "fairly standard among bibliographers"[53] and easy to follow (xi). i.e. ~~Cross out,~~ <insert> . . . . Indeed, bibliography and textual studies are the methodologies that ground all their discussions, and, at times, they practice the kind of close reading of texts traditionally practiced at the University of Chicago during Maclean's forty-five years teaching there.

We've already touched on their analysis of Maclean's style, but they also give us rigorous examinations of the way Maclean mixes and blurs multiple genres like fiction and nonfiction, memoir, romance, tragedy, comedy, and mock-tragedy. In Chapter 4 they present us with a thorough discussion of the way Maclean uses variations of time: "Clock time," "Calendar Time," "Historical Time," "Lifespan," "Diurnal Time," "Biblical Time," and "Geological Time."[54] Here below, for example, is how they apply these terms to Maclean famous elegiac ending:[55]

> Now nearly all those I loved and did not understand when I was young are dead, but I still read out to them. [**Life Span**]
> Of course, now I am too old to be much of a fisherman, and now of course I usually fish the big waters alone, although some friends think I shouldn't. [**Lifespan**] Like many fishermen in western Montana where the summer days are almost Arctic in length, I often do not start fishing until the cool of the evening. [**Diurnal Time**] Then in the Arctic half-light of the canyon [**Diurnal Time**], all existence fades to a being with my soul and memories [**Lifespan**] and the sound of the Big Blackfoot River and a four-count rhythm and the hope that a fish will rise. [**Eternity**]
> Eventually, all things merge into one, and a river runs through it. [**Eternity**] The river was cut by the world's great flood and runs over the rocks from the basement of time. [**Geological Time**]
> On some of the rocks are timeless raindrops.[**Geological Time**] Under the rocks are the words, and some of the words are theirs. [**Life Span, Biblical Time, Geological Time, and Eternity**]
> I am haunted by waters. [**Life Span and Eternity**]

These last four paragraphs are supercharged with grace and beauty, but we should remember when we read them that "All good things, trout as well as eternal salvation, come by grace, and grace comes by art, and art does not come easy." To prove as much, Jensen and Harris spend their final chapter telling and showing us the story of "The Evolution" of Maclean's ending. The ending, in fact, may have been one of the first pieces of the story that Maclean wrote.

While Jensen and Harris have done their best "to tell the full story of Maclean's writing process without overwhelming the reader," they admit their attempt has been "difficult to balance" (13).[56] Indeed, despite their success, there's simply no denying that they have written a very academic book, suitable perhaps for English majors, graduate students, and faculty, but not for all undergraduates, especially not a reader like the one that Maclean frequently used to recall. He found her on a visit to the western branch of the University of Minnesota in Morris, South Dakota. Forced by her instructor to describe the plot of a "A River Runs through It," she wrote, "They go fishing, and then they go fishing, and then they get drunk, and then they go fishing again." Her summary delighted Maclean, who commented to his interviewer, Kay Bonetti, "You know, who's to deny that there isn't a great deal of truth in that?"

Jensen and Harris comment that "There is more Shakespeare in 'A River' than a reader might first notice" [57] and they frequently point to examples most of us miss. Maclean's final four paragraphs, however, although they contain no allusions or echoes of the Bard, are positively Shakespearean in their elegance and power. Without seeming to, they invoke the supernatural as surely as *Hamlet* does by invoking the ghost of his father. Without naming "all those" he "loved and did not understand" when he "was young," we know the narrator is referring to his own father and especially to his murdered brother. He is with them and others in the river where the presence of death is always near but where there is also hope for what is to come. And, at least in spirit, they are with him. ■

Endnotes

[1] Katthryn Schultz. *The New Yorker*. July 8 & 15 2024. https://www.newyorker.com/magazine/2024/07/08/norman-maclean-a-life-of-letters-and-rivers-rebecca-mccarthy-book-review

[2] Ibid.

[3] Email from John N. Maclean, July 12, 2024.

[4] Rebecca McCarthy. *Norman Maclean: A Life in Rivers and Letters*. (Seattle: University of Washington Press, 2024. Hereafter, McCarthy.

[5] George H. Jensen and Heidi Skurat Harris. *Norman Maclean's "A River Runs through It": The Search for Beauty."* (New York: Routledge, 2024). Hereafter, Jensen and Harris.

[6] Timothy P. Schilling. *The Writings of Norman Maclean: Searching Truth amid Tragedy*. (Reno: University of Nevada Press). Hereafter Schilling.

[7] John N. Maclean. *Home Waters: A Chronicle of Family and a River*. (New York: Custom House, 2021). Hereafter, *Home Waters*.

[8] McCarthy. "Norman and Me." *The American Scholar*, December 2, 2019. https://theamericanscholar.org/norman-maclean-and-me/

[9] McCarthy, 141.

[10] McCarthy, 70.

[11] Jensen and Harris, 19-20.

[12] *Home Waters*, 192.

[13] Ibid, 192.

[14] Schilling, 3.

[15] Norman Maclean, "USFS 1919: The Ranger, the Cook, and a Hole in the Sky," in *A River Runs through It and Other Stories* (Chicago: University of Chicago Press, 1976), 125. Hereafter, this book is referred to as *A River*.

[16] Schilling, 3.

[17] Schilling, "Notes," 122.

[18] Ibid, 13.

[19] McFarland and Nichols, 83-84.

[20] Schilling, 4.

[21] Ibid, 4.

[22] Kay Bonetti Interview with Norman Maclean in Chicago. American Audio Prose Library, 1985.

[23] This essay is available online at the University of Chicago Press webpage: https://press.uchicago.edu/books/maclean/nmr_lear.html

[24] Schilling, 97.

[25] Pete Dexter's essay first appeared in *Esquire 95* (June 1981), 86, 88-89, 91. It is reprinted in *Norman Maclean*, edited by Ron McFarland and Hugh Nichols, Confluence American Authors Series, (Lewiston: Confluence Press, 1988), 140. Hereafter, McFarland and Nichols.

[26] Dexter in McFarland and Nichols, 146.

[27] A short description of the Qauntrell Awards and a complete list by year of the winners is available online. < https://www.uchicago.edu/who-we-are/global-impact/accolades/llewellyn-john-and-harriet-manchester-quantrell-awards-for-excellence-in-undergraduate-teaching>

[28] Schilling, 47.

[29] *A River*, 5.

[30] Ibid, 5.

[31] Schilling, 16.

[32] *A River,* 5.

33 Izaak Walton, *The Compleat Angler,* or *The Contemplative Man's Recreation* (New York: Modern Library, 2004), 6. The text of this Modern Library paperback edition is from the fifth edition of *The Compleat Angler* as presented in the work compiled by James Russell Lowell in 1889.

34 Schilling, 17.

35 Maclean, *River*, 33.

36 Schilling, 19.

37 Ibid, 18.

38 Ibid, 19.

39 Jensen and Harris, xix.

40 Ibid, xvi.

41 Jensen and Harris, xvi.

42 Ibid, 149.

43 Ibid, xv.

44 Ibid, 149.

45 Ursula K. Le Guin, "Staying Awake: Notes on the Alleged Decline of Reading." *Harper's Magazine*, February 2008. https://harpers.org/archive/2008/02/staying-awake/

46 Jensen and Harris, 149.

47 McFarland and Nichols, 28.

48 Jensen and Harris, 8.

49 Ibid, 8.

50 Ibid, 8.

51 Jensen and Harris, 29.

52 *A River*, 9.

53 Jensen and Harris, xi.

54 Ibid, 71-87.

55 Ibid, 85-86.

56 Ibid, 85.

57 Ibid, 143.

Jimmy Breslin.

MARC C. JOHNSON

Jimmy Breslin: Re-reading the Quintessential New York Columnist

Jimmy Breslin, the quintessential New York newspaper columnist—he was much more than that, but one must begin there—wrote what was arguably his most famous column on November 26, 1963, the day after John Kennedy's funeral and burial at Arlington National Cemetery.

That column—"It's an Honor"—was about one man, an otherwise anonymous World War II veteran named Clifton Pollard who wore overalls to work and just happened to be the guy who dug John Kennedy's grave.

"One of the last to serve John Fitzgerald Kennedy, who was the thirty-fifth president of this country," Breslin wrote, "was a working man who earns $3.01 an hour and said it was an honor to dig the grave." That column was essential Breslin, a writer of extraordinary talent with rare understanding of how the smallest story can illuminate the biggest events. Breslin died in 2017, the last of a now extinct breed of ink-stained wretches who once gave American journalism a gritty, funny, poignant and often sad take on the human condition.

While the column about Pollard, the grave digger, is likely Breslin's most remembered piece it was only one of a thousand efforts that stand as a unique body of American journalistic work. With columns often produced on deadline in a smokey newsroom where every bottom desk drawer held a bottle of something, Breslin was straight off an old school front page, a real-life character at home at the end of any bar. Smoking a cigar.

Re-reading Breslin has been made easy by the release by the Library of America of a collection of the columnist's "essential writings," including much journalism from 1960-2004, but also including two longer form pieces that prove just what a master storyteller Breslin was. The volume, edited by *New York Times* reporter and columnist Dan Berry, is a treasure of the kind of writing that once graced big city dailies, as well as a chronicle of a nation divided by race, class and partisan politics, and torn, as it was for a decade, by a tragic war.

In columns like "The Day I Company Got Killed," a 1965 recounting of a bloody Marine Corps fight, Breslin was among the first to portray the profound tragedy of Vietnam.

"The Marines were hit with shot coming out of the bushes in the sand," he wrote of the battle at Chu Lai that claimed 18 American and countless Vietnamese lives. "They fought with rifles and machine guns. When the Viet Cong were not on the sand anymore, the Marines went into the mud of the paddies after them. The fighting was continuous and the dead were everywhere and now everybody knows that America is in a war."

But Breslin also wrote about baseball—a great book about the hapless 1962 New York Mets—and about bookies, about blue collar workers, mob bosses and big business grifters. He wrote stories about people who rarely get their names in the paper. He could find the human, the comic, the tragic and the uplifting in almost everything. All the while his BS meter was finely tuned. As they say, Jimmy did not suffer fools.

One column not included in the new collection—no criticism since there is so much of his work to choose from—is a piece Breslin wrote in July 1963. Under the headline "Vegas is Endsville to New York Exile," he wrote about the Las Vegas heavyweight title rematch between the champion Sonny Liston and the challenger and former champ Floyd Patterson. Actually, Breslin hardly mentioned the fight beyond calling it "an outrageous disgrace" that ended with Liston knocking Patterson out after a little more than two minutes of the first round.

"Sonny Liston, of course, is not to be blamed," Breslin wrote, "all he tried to do was kill Floyd Patterson," a pithy description that set up the rest of the column that was all about a small-time New York bookmaker who left the big city—under a cloud, as they say—to make a new life in Sin City.

Breslin was clearly more interested in the hijinks of a bookie with a great name, Jasper Martin, than the hijinks of fighters like Sonny and Floyd.

"People were always asking him to leave," Breslin said of Jasper. "One detective division wanted him out of its area. Jasper would leave. Then another division told him to get out. He would leave again. Then, two years ago, they asked him to leave the whole city."

"Jasper went home, got his wife and two daughters and headed for Las Vegas and a bookmaking parlor called the Santa Anita Turf Club, which is where Jasper was found yesterday morning. He was standing behind a counter taking baseball bets from people, and he looked good. He is a dark-haired, blue-eyed guy of 40 who was wearing a thin blue sports shirt and golf slacks."

Jasper went on to recount his life in Vegas, including the casual attire unlike the suits he wore in New York because, as he explained, he had to occasionally serve customers in fancy restaurants. "Out here what you wear doesn't count," Jasper said. "It's a whole new world. The only thing out here that is the same as New York is that everybody goes to a psychiatrist doctor."

One has to wonder how Breslin came to such a story. Well, for starters, he was a hell of a reporter. Breslin had to have known Jasper in New York, and clearly he had known him since we was able to describe in humorous detail Jasper's failed attempts to garner an education at Commerce High School. Breslin knew that Jasper "handled sports, not horses, and he operated out of a saloon, and then a place called Kelly's Deli on Second Avenue, which now is gone."

And he had to have known how to find Jasper for a better story in Las Vegas than a fight that lasted barely 120 seconds.

"See those mountains," Jasper asked of the "big gray and pinkish mountains which come up out of the desert right at the edge" of Las Vegas. "They are just like prison walls as far as I'm concerned. I'm out here doing a bit. When I look at those mountains, you know what I see? I see guard towers. You get me out of New York, it's all jail to me."

Yet even after a particularly awful heavyweight title fight a bookie needs to settle accounts. "Jasper started to thumb through a packet of money," Breslin wrote. "By some good thinking, he did handsomely with the Sonny Liston-Floyd Patterson exhibition Only one bet of $25 was made on a first-round knockout. After paying that off, Jasper swept the board."

That was Jimmy Breslin.

"Breslin was there for all of it," Ross Barken wrote in remembering the columnist. "Born in 1928, he died in early 2017, just long enough to see Trump, one of his many *bêtes noires*, inaugurated as the forty-fifth president of the United States. As hyperreal as that day was for a large swath of America, it must have been especially absurd for Breslin, who grew up several miles south of the Trumps. Whereas young Donald was reared in Jamaica Estates, perhaps the toniest slice of Queens, Breslin spent his youth in working-class Richmond Hill, in the maw of the Depression. He overcame these odds to become one of the most important newspapermen of the last century."

Breslin lived and captured the "rhythm of the city" wrote Harry Siegel, himself a talented columnist. "He was beaten up by a mobster, appeared on *The Tonight Show,* got letters sent to him 'from the sewers of New York' by David Berkowitz (the 'Son of Sam' serial killer whom Breslin later wrote a book about), effectively embedded with the Democrats who worked to bring down Richard Nixon, and starred in a national series of commercials for 'a good-drinking beer' including one somehow lost to the internet with 'Pogo' cartoonist Walt Kelly."

He also ran for New York city council on a ticket with Norman Mailer, who was running for mayor. Their platform: make New York the 51st state. The campaign slogan: "the other guys are the joke."

Much of Breslin's writing is timeless. It reads like a worn cliché, but it's true, as true as Breslin's ability to skewer a pompous pol or takedown a crook, or a failed New York businessman.

Breslin's *How The Good Guys Finally Won: Notes From an Impeachment Summer* is pure gold on the page. The book-length piece recounts the run up to Richard Nixon's near impeachment and ultimate resignation in the summer of 1974. Breslin begins with a moment in a federal courthouse when Nixon aides John Mitchell, H.R. Haldeman, Robert Mardian and John Ehrlichman are found guilty of various crimes related to the break-in at the offices of the Democratic National Committee in the Watergate in Washington, D.C., as well as the subsequent White House inspired coverup.

"I left as Ehrlichman droned on," Breslin wrote. "Outside the building, H.R. Haldeman was standing in the rain in front of television cameras. There is nothing profitable in listening to him. In the end, all convicted criminals are boring."

"I don't want to hear them, or hear much about them again," Breslin said of the Watergate crooks:

> For there are too many decent people, people with honesty and dignity and charm, who were an important part of the summer of 1974 in Washington, the summer in which the nation forced a President to resign from office. And if we are going to talk about the end of Watergate, as we are about to do here, why don't we take a walk away from the convicts and step in the shafts of sunlight provided by some of the people who worked for their country, rather than against it. People who are so much more satisfying to know, and to tell of.

Breslin went on to detail the mostly forgotten men and women, the lawyers, accountants, investigators and politicians—most importantly Tip O'Neill and Peter Rodino—who exposed that entire steamy mess of garbage. Breslin often wrote, as he did with *How the Good Guys Finally Won*, the ignored, unreported story adjacent to the "big" story. His genius resided in observing minute detail and using language that eludes most of us.

His description of July 24, 1974, the day the Supreme Court said Nixon had to turn over his White House tape recordings, is, in one paragraph, a master class in reporting:

> It was strange to be around when it happened, because it was an enormous thing and it had never happened before; but there still was so little to see in Washington in the summer of 1974. White marble sitting in swamp heat. On this day, on the 24th, the news of the Supreme Court decision should have 'rocked' the White House and the nation. It did no such thing. Oh, it wasted Nixon some more. The flesh turned pasty and the eyes hollowed and the flesh under the chin fell through the muscles. He was out in San Clemente when the news of the decision was announced. The story circulated that Nixon had attempted to walk into the ocean and drown himself. The great scene from *A Star is Born*. James Mason going into the ocean while Judy Garland sings. The story was untrue. General Haig, however, apparently did get his hands on Nixon's tranquilizers. The essential Roman Catholic mind: die by the gun if you must, but an overdose of narcotics is sinful; that's for the weirdos.

Regarding weirdos, Breslin had a bead on a certain Queens real estate developer long before that comb-over con man glided down his gilded escalator to give voice to the grievance, fear, hatred and racism that, before Donald Trump, long huddled in the shadows of American life. Trump, as much or more than George Wallace, placed racial resentment at the center of his culture, and our politics.

Trump's reptile-brain genius resides in his ability to dominate—the media, the Republican Party, the national conversation, all of it. Breslin was wise to the con early on, while other New York reporters were bragging about getting a phone call from The Donald.

MARC C. JOHNSON

Consider this column from 1990:

During 1989, when Trump announced he was buying the Eastern Shuttle and about to start a building on the West Side that could be seen from Toledo and would park 9,000 cars, he was on the first page of this paper [Newsday] and others as often as the logo. There were four stories about Trump in one day's issue of the New York Times newspaper. He had the joint from front to back. I remember looking at the paper with the four stories in it and saying to myself, 'Look at this, all these years later and the Times hires a whole room full of guys who are out on the take.' On television that night, all I saw was announcers genuflecting as they mentioned Trump's name. They mentioned it in unrelated conversation, as if Trump were a part of the language. I said, 'What kind of payroll must this guy have?'

But when I started to think about it, I immediately realized I was wrong. Things were even worse. These reporters were doing it for nothing! The scandal in journalism in our time is that ethics have disintegrated to the point where Donald Trump took over news reporters in this city with the art of the return phone call.

Then in his column "Trump: The Master of the Steal" Breslin delivered a Sonny Liston-like knockout.

All Trump has to do is stick to the rules on which he was raised by his father in the County of Queens:
Never use your own money. Steal a good idea and say it's your own. Do anything to get publicity.
Remember that everybody can be bought.

The trouble with Trump's father was that he was a totally naïve man. He had no idea that you could buy the whole news reporting business in New York with a return phone call.

Breslin wrote that 35 years ago.

"A columnist is—or was—out endlessly," Harry Siegel wrote, while remembering a time when everyone read a newspaper, and everyone who could read Jimmy Breslin, "talking to people all over the city and writing every other day or even more frequently, climbing tenement stairs while giving a platform to people who'd otherwise be lost in the crowd.

"Human nature has changed as the technology and the economy have, and the crucial function in civic life that Breslin and others filled is, simply, not being filled now. It's a damn shame."

It is a damn shame. As local and regional newspapers have dwindled or disappeared, with cable TV talking heads bloviating as informed "analysts," and while American civic life from the bowling alley to the library to a school board meeting has become meaner, less forgiving, more judgmental and less decent, the unifying voice of a guy willing to climb the tenement stairs has all but disappeared.

No Walter Cronkite gathers us around a national hearth to share a big event. No Jimmy Breslin or Pete Hamill or, hell, even ol' Andy Rooney speaks truth to the multitudes fixated on their devices.

Breslin wasn't perfect. He had his moments of old white guy insensitivity— even racism—but he was a profoundly gifted observer of this big, diverse and it seems, increasingly ungovernable country. Read him. Enjoy the prose. And mourn what has been lost when there is no longer a place for his kind.■

ADAM M. SOWARDS

Gossamer Possibilities: Re-reading Ivan Doig's Winter Brothers *in a New Season*

I won't pretend I come to this assignment dispassionately: Ivan Doig is my favorite writer. I own all his books. I've read them all, except for his final one, *Last Bus to Wisdom* (2015), because I have not been able to bring myself to do so, knowing that I will never again have the chance to read a Doig book fresh.

Yet re-reading *Winter Brothers: A Season at the Edge of America* (1980) tells me I can still experience Doig with open eyes. I last read it more than twenty years ago, the baby I had then when I was a freshly minted Ph.D. now is a doctoral student herself. Perspectives change as calendars pile up year upon year.

Winter Brothers is few fans' favorite Doig book, I'm sure. It was only his second. His trade became novelist, and *Winter Brothers* was nonfiction, one of only three nonfiction efforts and the only one not fully a memoir. What's more, *Winter Brothers* is an odd book, which is not to say it is a bad book or a confusing one, just unusual.

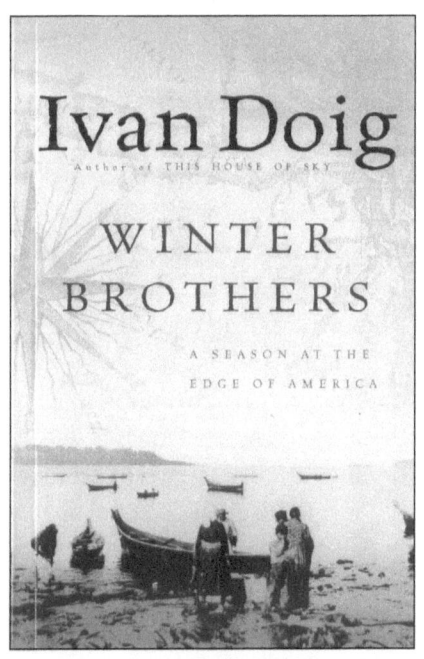

It is Doig's account of a winter reading James G. Swan's diaries, spanning 1859 to 1900. In *Winter Brothers*, Doig braided biography of Swan with excerpts of the diaries and memoir of his own seasonal quest. "A journal of a journal," he called it. This makes my re-reading of it a journal of a journal of a journal, I suppose.

Revisiting *Winter Brothers* resonates for me now, because I'm living through a season of change myself. Doig had gone to graduate school in history and decided the classroom wasn't for him; he would write instead. I, too, went to graduate school in history, and I, too, decided to write — although I spent 25 years in classrooms first. I'm drifting out of those spaces now, blinking at the brightness, a couple years into this new season. Also like Doig, I moved from two decades in the dry interior West to the seawater coast of the Salish Sea. Sinking into *Winter Brothers* again is something of a homecoming in geography, an inspiration in subject, and an aspiration in style. Here was a historian-writer bouncing between present and past, words the medium of time travel on this western edge. While rereading and remembering, I stayed alert to capture something tangible in the fleeting whirlpool of time and prose that I might learn from.

Encountering Ivan Doig

In the autumn of my junior year of college, I spent some time in the bookstore. On a shelf I found Ivan Doig's *This House of Sky: Landscapes of a Western Mind* (1978). So many intriguing words shaped that title I found it irresistible. In the time since, I gathered his books, most in hardcover because I could not wait for paperback editions. More than one bear his signature. I'm sad when each book comes to an end, because saying goodbye to Doig's characters and settings and stories is like moving away from home.

I learned in graduate school that Doig had earned a Ph.D. in history. I discovered an article he wrote in a scholarly journal I have also published in. During one of my own dissertation research trips to Suzzallo Library at the University of Washington, I tracked down that Doig dissertation—about an important man in Northwest history, just like mine would be. I slid that bound dissertation off a low shelf for just a moment to help connect me to Doig, the closest I ever expected to be.

Although I lingered for decades among such shelves, Doig ventured out. Between 1978 and 2015, he published 16 books. Only a couple of them take place in contemporary times, meaning he put his historical training to work to ensure details pointed true north. He set nearly all of them in his native Montana, a place he moved away from in 1957 but never truly left. *Winter Brothers*—nonfiction and set in Washington—stands apart, almost insular.

ADAM M. SOWARDS

Swan and Doig (and Me)

The main subject of *Winter Brothers* is Swan, a nineteenth-century man who spent most of his long, unusual life on Washington's Olympic Peninsula, trying to understand local tribes, hoping to attract the railroad, performing various government jobs—"white grooves of routine" in Doig's apt phrasing—and writing all the time: books, letters, articles, and, most of all, diaries. Those diaries, some two and a half million words, a substantial "wake of ink" as Doig put it, constituted a record of daily life in Washington Territory from the 1850s until Swan's death in 1900.

As the book's title notes, Doig felt a kinship, much of that rooted in a westering quest both author and subject embodied. Intangible factors also matched them. This means that on many occasions when Doig characterized Swan, he also characterized himself, such as when he said Swan was "as steadily curious as a question mark" with a "fetish for fact," qualities any scribbler must possess, cultivate, and guard.

Doig had discovered Swan earlier, likely in graduate school. Instinctively, Doig knew he wanted to spend more time with this man Swan, "oyster entrepreneur, schoolteacher, railroad speculator, amateur ethnologist, lawyer, judge, homesteader, linguist, ship's outfitter, explorer, customs collector, author, small town bureaucrat, artist, clerk." Perhaps Swan's character made him inherently interesting and attractive to Doig's curiosity. Perhaps Doig knew a good story lurked in those diaries. Perhaps the siren song of the Northwest Coast proved too captivating.

But a greater awakening worked in Doig. He had become "more aware that I dwell in a community of time as well as of people" and wanted to know more about this "mysterious citizenship, how far it goes, where it touches." Swan would be his navigator and guide.

If time connected Doig to Swan, the West served as the medium. "More and more it seems to me that the *westernness* of my existence in this land is some consequence having to do with that community of time, one of the terms of my particular citizenship in it," he wrote in *Winter Brothers'* opening pages. Had Swan resided those same years in Chicago or Chattanooga, Doig would have sailed past him like a captain who realizes the bay is too shallow for a good anchorage.

"Markings, streaks and whorls of the West and the past are left in some of us," Doig wrote. The words resonate because the western past has been my territory, too. When I first read *Winter Brothers*, I was a graduate student studying the West and recognizing, like Doig, that the West was distinctive, that I was a "westerner" tied deeply to those who had come before me. *Winter Brothers* tracks Doig's own preoccupation with the West, or Wests, a constant hum in the background.

The Place of the West(s)

Born in Massachusetts, Swan left for California in 1850, wandered north to Shoalwater (now Willapa) Bay in Washington Territory, before nosing even further north where he bounced between the northwest and northeast tips of the Olympic Peninsula starting in 1859. There, even when canoeing from one end to the other across the top of the peninsula, Swan found a home. "Finding the place to invest his life meant, as it has to me, finding a West," wrote Doig, speaking for all three of us. He continued, noting that he recognized from Swan's writing and his own "that there are and always have been many Wests, personal as well as geographical." Differences abound in the West and within the West, establishing distinct subregions, subcultures, and experiences: "Perhaps that is what the many Wests are, common in their stubborn separatenesses: each West a kind of cabin, insistent that it is no other sort of dwelling whatsoever."

Western historians coming of age in the wake of *Winter Brothers* in the 1980s and 1990s spilled much ink on whether the West was a place or a process, a region or a frontier. In other words, did the West's natural extremes or federal presence or distinct racial composition make it unique? Or, was the process of confrontation, conflict, and colonization something that replicated itself across a continent?

Then, I was a partisan of place, a believer in distinctiveness. And if I'm honest, I favored the West as best, an adherence I shared with Doig, who quoted from his own journals: "The west of America draws some of us not because it is the newest region of the country but because it is the oldest, in the sense that the landscape here—the fundament, nature's shape of things—more resembles the original continent than does the city-nation of the Eastern Seaboard or the agricultural factory of the Midwest." I might have said the same.

ADAM M. SOWARDS

On the page with these words of Doig, I found my bookmark from my last reading of *Winter Brothers*. A simple index card, an artifact of my mind from two decades past. My jottings were brief, meant as discussion starters, not even ten points of emphasis. But offset in a place of prominence, I had written: WESTS of Book (Doig & Swan). We all were interrogating why the West placed a hold on us. Again and again, Doig wrestled with this West, these Wests, as he grasped toward understanding Swan, seeming to believe if he understood the place he could finally comprehend Swan, a man whose voluminous writings included abundant daily details and little introspection. Doig's search for Swan's anchor is his own struggle to explain himself. That I marked those "West" passages suggests I hungered for this grounding, too.

Reconsidering

When I read *Winter Brothers* first, as a nascent historian of the Pacific Northwest and an unabashed fan of Doig, I found it a volume that illustrated a region in the throes of transformation. *Winter Brothers* shone a light primarily on that past world, along with furnishing a happy dose of Doig prose. What stands out now are other qualities—and silences.

A couple generations of scholarship have cycled since 1980, and today, consequences of colonialism feel more important than the muted attention Doig gave them. He did deliver a Swan passage, channeling William Blake's "Proverbs of Hell," about what he witnessed among the Makah: "We have indeed caused the plowshare of civilization to pass over the graves of their ancestors and open to the light the remains of ancient lodge fires." A surprising metaphor from Swan, who tracked more often with matter-of-factness. But little analysis or commentary from him, or from Doig, spilled forth.

After two decades of reservation living, the Makah, in Doig's assessment, were "not quite citizens of either their ancestral world or the new white world, but of some shifting ground between." It is the sort of comment that I encountered frequently in graduate school in the 1990s during obsessions with so-called middle grounds but that today reads as simplistic. Given the growing sophistication of Indigenous Studies and the increasing political power of Tribes in the contemporary West, I find it hard to imagine Doig rewriting *Winter Brothers* today and not attending more to these sorts of themes. Swan's curiosity might be recast as surveillance, his collecting as theft.

Besides riding these waves of change in scholarship and politics since publication and my first reading, my sense of where *Winter Brothers* fits in Doig's body of work has also shifted. When I read it first, I knew Doig as the established author already of more than half a dozen books; I had published none and was steeped only in scholarly creations. Today, I see more clearly Doig as a writer starting out, a career and identity still forming; now, after unmooring myself from the academy, I am sensitive to the ways Doig may have been adrift and seeking both safe harbor and new ports. He may have been 39 during the winter sojourn that produced *Winter Brothers*, but Doig was still figuring out what he was doing, who he was, whether his writing success would last. It must have been exhilarating and exhausting.

Consider a very minor scene a third of the way through the book. Doig read Swan's diary entry of his 42nd birthday while visiting Cape Flattery, that far corner tip of the continental United States. Doig was triangulating the actual place, Swan's words, and himself. "Some men and women are never part of the time they were born into and walk the streets or highways of their generations as strangers."

These words, Doig mused, are ones he might have written about Swan. Instead, his wife Carol read them to him, "hunched in the phone booth at Clallam Bay." The words described Doig and appeared in the *New York Times Book Review* for *This House of Sky*. A poignant moment between the couple, sharing a triumph and recognition that any writer craves—especially at the start when the risks of a writing career weigh heaviest.

I also draw on firsthand information to read *into* Doig's state of mind when creating *Winter Brothers*.

Doig and wife Carol.

ADAM M. SOWARDS

A job took me temporarily to Shoreline Community College where I eventually learned Ivan's wife Carol had taught for decades. In a hallway conversation, I revealed to a colleague my admiration of Doig's books. I've considered teaching *Winter Brothers*, I said. My colleague said he'd happily arrange an introduction. And that's how Ivan Doig walked into my classroom to discuss with my students his quirky book, *Winter Brothers*.

Doig met me at my classroom, no time to visit before or after. *I have to finish the damn book,* he told me on the phone. (That book turned out to be *Prairie Nocturne* [2003], one of his loveliest.) I sat off to the side, allowing students to have unmediated access. My admiration and excitement and joy charged the classroom atmosphere. I felt like a teenaged fan meeting a rockstar.

I asked Doig how he came to write *Winter Brothers*, to tell the story behind the book. *Winter Brothers,* Doig said to my class, *is not easy to describe, as you now know.* He reminisced about trying to sell the book. A memoir like *This House of Sky* is uncomplicated to characterize, and it had succeeded beyond any reasonable debut author's expectations, including a National Book Award nomination. But second books are hard, and what Doig had in mind with *Winter Brothers* took no clear course. Getting a publisher to understand the book's unique blend of biography-excerpts-journal with an unusual nineteenth-century character at the center was not easy.

Still distracted by his mere presence, I let his story's details float over me. Today, though, this moment looms larger, a hint of unsettledness rises to the surface. That effort to get a publisher to understand his vision must have filled his winter pairing with Swan with uncertainty. His career's success was by no means assured or even likely with one book under his belt, even a well-regarded one. His career worked out.

As did *Winter Brothers*. This time the *Times*'s review assessed: "Sometimes the exercise is forced; sometimes it pushes Mr. Doig into overwriting. But the occasional patches of dullness or lushness should deter no one from devouring this gorgeous tribute to a man and a region unjustly neglected heretofore. The reader has the pleasure of encountering two contrasting styles and two angles of view, both infused

with the fresh air and spirit of the Northwest." It remains,
too, a "gorgeous tribute" to the writer, who I never saw again.

The Elliptical Past

Winter Brothers exemplifies how history shades our world. Doig saw his surroundings as he did because of that "mysterious citizenship" he felt with the past, the one he nurtured through his winter communion with Swan. Once recognized, it is hard to avoid tacking between the depths of the past and surface of the present. Realizing that we dwell in time is perhaps the historian's special way of seeing the world, a way of navigating society's shoals.

Our world is in constant conversation between then and now. This can be difficult because the past is gapped in incompleteness. It is elliptical. Doig says this after one of Swan's diary entries drifts off in the middle of relating a Haida story, the teller having grown tired and left Swan without the denouement.

So it is with all history. We only have scraps, scraps we weave into stories, stories we believe to be coherent and true. But even those are incomplete, elliptical. "I've heard it offered that a period is simply the shorthand for the dots of an ellipsis," Doig wrote. "That a story never does end, only can pause." I take this to mean, partly, that time is not fully recoverable and that our efforts to make meaning of it will remain endless because of that. Writing about history, then, will continually evolve, reflecting the concerns of authors and their contexts. Just as the same reader can encounter the same words at different times and come to different conclusions given their shifting preoccupations. And just as a writer can encounter the same place and find endless curiosities to explore.

"So much of Swan I still do not know, even after studying him through the fifteen thousand days and two and a half million words of his diaries," Doig wrote on Day 88 of his 90 days of winter. He wondered about Swan's thoughts and why he wrote of some things and not others. "Or why, like me, he chose to invest his life at this edge of America over all other—although I think it has most to do in both our cases with a preference for gossamer possibilities, such as words, rather than hard and fast obligations, such as terms of employment."

Closing *Winter Brothers* twenty-some years after teaching it, looking out at the one corner of Puget Sound I can glimpse from my home on almost the exact latitude of Cape Flattery, I see those gossamer possibilities more clearly than ever, and finally, I open *Last Bus to Wisdom*. ∎

Poet John Clare, 1793-1864.

KURT CASWELL

Meeting with a Sudden Shower: John Clare's "Journey out of Essex"

> There is something to be learned from a rainstorm. When meeting with a sudden shower, you try not to get wet and run quickly along the road. But doing such things as passing under the eaves of houses, you still get wet. When you are resolved from the beginning, you will not be perplexed, though you will still get the same soaking. This understanding extends to everything.
>
> —Tsunetomo, Yamamoto, *Hagakure*

Years ago when I fell in love with the English Romantics and their American inheritors, I set John Clare aside as a psychologically broken figure, merely aspirational to the ideals I associated with Byron, Keats, Shelley, and Wordsworth: an obsession with freedom and freedom of expression, a love for the natural world and for the natural passions of the body, and a rejection of the technological revolution unfolding in the 19th century. But then I discovered Clare's "Journey out of Essex," a rambling account (you would not really call it an essay) of his four-day walk home from Dr. Matthew Allen's asylum at High Beech in the Epping Forest northeast of London where he had been living for four years. What so captivated me in Clare's astonishing story, and so gave me access to his poems, is not about Romanticism, but about his expression of fortitude that I had previously found in Tsunetomo's *Hagakure*, which may be paraphrased like this: no matter what you do to escape hardship, hardship finds you anyway. So, if you are resolved from the beginning to complete your task, you can endure most any hardship without being perplexed. I found Tsunetomo's assertion hopeful and inspiring, and now here was John Clare putting it into action.

The incident in "Journey out of Essex" that brought Clare and Tsunetomor together for me comes on July 21, 1841, when Clare walks into a public house known as The Plough and escapes a heavy rainstorm.

355

Clare does not go into The Plough to escape the rain, but rather to buy a half pint of beer with a penny thrown to him by a man on horseback who mistakes him for a poor haymaker. Why in that moment the penny came to him, and how in that moment a public house appeared on the road, and both just when a storm rode in and doused the countryside, seems like a thing from a fiction. It all fit too perfectly together. Clare writes only lightly of the incident in his accounting, "I called for a half pint and drank it and got a rest and escaped a very heavy shower in the bargain by having a shelter till it was over," he writes. The incident is all the more worthy of attention as receiving the penny from the man on horseback was a singular event. Clare tried to repeat his good fortune by later begging a penny from two drovers, but, he writes, they "were very saucey so I begged no more of any body meet who I would pass."

    Reading "Journey out of Essex," it is easy to overlook Clare's meeting with a sudden shower, and I would have overlooked it too, but for its buoyancy in an otherwise sad tale colored with hardship, suffering, and delusion. This brief respite inside The Plough strikes me as conditional to understanding John Clare, not as a victim of his own psychological deterioration, but as a man piloted by will and purpose. While Clare does note that he escaped the heavy shower, it seems to have mattered little to him that he did. He does not mark the moment as special, a stroke of good luck. Rather, he simply marks what happened.

    When John Clare walked out of the asylum that day, he left its protection and comfort and routine for a rogue world where he met with of all kinds of weathers, hunger, thirst, sleep deprivation, the unkindness of strangers, and the attrition due the body from walking miles and miles on a broken road in poor shoes, sometimes at night, and with little rest. Clare walked ninety miles in four days—a highly respectable physical accomplishment. And perhaps more respectable still is his commitment, his resolve to complete the walk and arrive home, which carried him through ease and good fortune as well as hardship and suffering, as if one were no different from the other. He accepted both as they came upon him without disturbance or deterrence to his purpose.

* * * * *

Clare organizes "Journey out of Essex" by dates and places to track his progress, but its temporal orderliness vanishes as day and night become nearly indistinguishable to him. He shambles footsore for much of his passage in a nearly hallucinogenic state. It is worth noting that when a writer sits down to his work, he is managing two selves: the person who is writing (himself) and the person he is writing about (a past self). So here are two John Clares: the John Clare who made the journey out of Essex, and the John Clare who wrote the story of his journey out of Essex. It is not possible to know if night and day became indistinguishable to Clare while he was walking, or if it became so only as he was writing, if from the safety of his writing desk, he simply put the journey back together in his mind that way. It is clear, however, that both John Clares remain unshakeable in their purpose, in the drive to complete the walk and arrive home.

The asylum where Clare had been living was modeled on the same standards as a nearby asylum operated by York Quakers (no bars on windows and doors, heated rooms, good food, plenty of fresh air, and meaningful activity, like working in an adjoining garden). Still, Clare had come to regard his life there as intolerable, a kind of hell. Upon reaching his home in Northborough, he wrote a letter to Dr. Allen explaining that as good as the conditions were at the asylum, the "keepers" treated him like a prisoner, and not "likeing to quarrel [he] put up with it till [he] was weary of the place altogether so [he] heard the voice of freedom and started."

Clare's decision to go is astonishing, really. What made him think that he could? What drives any dreamer to action? What, in 1933 at the age of 18, made Patrick Leigh Fermor think he could walk from London to Constantinople? What, in 1863, made Tolstoy think he could write a novel so long and with so many characters that hardly anyone can read it? What, in 1783, made the Montgolfier brothers think they could ascend into the heavens in a balloon? Clare's decision to go is an act of innovation and creativity, even courage, the courage necessary to imagine a path outside the boundaries set up against him, and then to execute what he had imagined.

"Journey out of Essex" begins on July 18, 1841, a Sunday, three days before his escape, with Clare expressing that he "Felt very melancholy."

As an emetic, he "went a walk on the forest in the afternoon" where he "fell in with some gipseys." One of the gypsies offers to help him escape from the "mad house" with the promise of fifty pounds. Clare walks into the forest again to make his escape, but the gypsy is now reluctant to help. He goes a third time, but the gypsies all have quit the camp and moved on, leaving nothing but a couple of hats on the ground, one of which Clare takes with him.

Clare waits another full day before walking out of the asylum, and makes a curious note, which reads in entirety: "July 19—Monday—Did nothing." For Clare to bother writing such a note indicates, I think, that the nothing he did must have been filled with a lot of something. Perhaps he spent the day considering his course of action. Perhaps he asked himself if life in the asylum was really so bad. Perhaps he asked himself if life back home would fulfill him after living in such routine confinement. While an escape to freedom sounds better than life in an asylum, by leaving, Clare would give up daily access to resources, security, and routine, all of which can be of some value to a poet. In fact, as it turned out, Clare was highly productive while living at Dr. Allen's asylum at High Beech, and later too when he was recommitted, this time at Northampton General Lunatic Asylum, where he lived for the rest of his life. To report doing nothing on that day, in fact, indicates a position of some privilege, only possible for nobles, the monied, the leisure class, people who Clare neither identified with or in whose company he was much welcomed. Clare spent much of his adult life scraping together a living as a laborer, so it is a wonder, really, for Clare to do nothing on a Monday and have the luxury to report that nothing is what he did.

The next day, July 20, John Clare quits the asylum and walks home. His decision to go must have been grounded in two fundamental aspects of his psychology. First, he possessed a genuine love for living unbound, for the personal freedom to wander and muse, for the autonomy and choice and privilege of time and space, all conducive to writing poems. And second, home was the landscape of his imagination, the place from which his poems were born. Near the end of his life at Northampton, Clare often expressed his desire to return home. He remarked, "I have lived too long," and "I want to go home." Tragically, he never did.
In 1864, John Clare died at Northhampton after a series of strokes.

KURT CASWELL

Clare characterizes his escape as a kind of military campaign. With "only honest courage and myself in my army," he writes, "I led the way and my troops soon followed." What I admire about this entry is that Clare writes of his courage not as leading him, but rather he leads his courage. He goes, and his courage follows, by which I understand him to mean that courage is the state you find yourself in only after taking the action for which courage is required. Most of us search for courage as a resource necessary for taking action, but Clare instructs us that it works the other way around. For Clare to understand this, whether conscious of his understanding or no, is an achievement far beyond the ordinary, and worthy of attention.

On the first day of his escape, out the Great York Road, Clare walks all the way to Stevenage by nightfall. He notes that his "legs were nearly knocked up" and he "began to stagger." With some effort, he climbs into some clover bales in a hay shed to sleep, where he has a "very uneasy dream." He dreams that his first wife, Mary, is asleep by his side and someone takes her away, which startles him awake. He hears a voice speak Mary's name, but finds no one about. He then lies down again, this time "with [his] head towards the north to show [himself] the steering point in the morning." I love this little detail, that in the darkness upon waking, Clare is aware of his confusion and instability, and knows he must somehow accommodate his physical and mental attrition.

Clare's dream is all the more unsettling when squared with the fact that his first and current wife is not Mary, but Martha "Patty" Turner, formerly a church milkmaid, to whom he had been married for twenty-one years. Mary Joyce, the woman he dreams about, is the daughter of a successful farmer with whom Clare had fallen in love as a schoolboy. Mary's father forbid the match, and according to Jonathan Bate in his comprehensive book, *John Clare: A Biography*, Clare acknowledges in his autobiographical writings that she is above his station, yet he hopes one day to "renew the acquaintance and disclose the smothered passion." Lying asleep in the hay that night dreaming of Mary would be the only possible renewal, for by this time Mary had been dead for three years, having burned to death when her clothes caught fire in a brew house.

Clare wakes from that dream with his head pointed to the north and notes the date: July 21, the same day he meets with that sudden shower while inside The Plough. It is the last date he records in "Journey out of Essex" until he is home again on July 24. His temperament continues to be that of a captain leading a special military operation, which perhaps urges him forward, "[when I awoke] Daylight was looking in on every side and fearing my garrison might be taken by storm and myself be made prisoner I left my lodging by the way I got in." Soon Clare is inside The Plough escaping the rain, and upon setting out on the road again, he tumbles into a confused and bewildering series of encounters and hardships, none of which, astonishingly, much dissuades him from his purpose.

    Clare passes through several villages, the names of which he cannot remember, sits in the shade of a great tree and wishes for breakfast, "but wishes was no hearty meal so I got up as hungry as I sat down," he writes. He walks all day as his shoes come apart, and fill with pebbles from the road. His feet are increasingly bruised and sore and he can barely walk. He trudges on. Nearing nightfall, a country fellow advises him that he may find a shed and some dry straw near a public house called The Ram onward along the road. He lies down between a shed and some trees, but a cold wind blows in and he cannot sleep so he gets up and walks on in darkness envying the warm light from house windows. "The inside tennants lots very comfortable," he writes, "and my outside lot very uncomfortable and wretched," and "the road was very lonely and dark." At a fork in the road he is suddenly unsure if he is going the right way. "I went on mile after mile," he writes, "almost convinced I was going the same way I came" and "doubt and hopelessness made me so feeble that I was scarcely able to walk yet I could not sit down or give up but shuffled along till I saw a lamp shining as bright as the moon" at a tollgate. The man at the tollgate affirms Clare is indeed headed in the right direction, which helps him to regain some of his strength and vanish his doubt. He walks on until he reaches an isolated house near some woods. He notes that the inhabitants inside are already asleep, so he crawls up onto their front porch like a stray animal and sleeps until morning.

    It's a common phenomenon for walkers that the route going out seems longer than the same route coming back, and the trail you manage in three hours on a fair day takes you five hours in darkness and foul weather. Storms and night and fatigue make roads longer, all three of which were part of Clare's journey. Unfamiliarity, too, can lengthen a road, for when you know it by its character and landmarks, by its turns and straightaways, by its difficulties and simplicities, you feel more at home and so more at ease. Clare enjoys none of these benefits. He walks in a bewilderment of unknowing, and yet, so committed is he to his purpose, he does not turn back.

Along with an unassuming sense of wonder and joy got from the pageantry of the natural world, John Clare had long prized the freedom to wander and explore. It's not that he was often in search of something in particular, but that he desired to be out there in it, exposed, unlatched, the self so stripped bare and reduced as to be made elemental, whenever and wherever he pleased. Long before Clare went to live in the asylum, he wrote poems that serve as a testament to this desire to break free from boundaries wherever he found them.

In his poem, "Sunday Walks" Clare writes, "As on a sunday morning at his ease/he takes his rambles just as fancys please" (3-4). It is fair to understand the character in this poem, "he," as Clare himself, striking out on a day of leisure for a walk to wherever chance would take him. And this word, "rambles," is a suitable expression of the kind of freedom

Silver Birches, Epping Forest No. 684

usually reserved for the leisure class, who have the resources to spend a day as their "fancys please." For Clare, there could be no better day than a day of rambling and following one's fancys, an experience which might end up the subject of a poem. Rambling, whether met with ease or hardship, is far superior to being caged or confined, even if only by foul weather. Out on such a walk, the poet has space and time to muse, as the mind unites with the body's movement to find an expression of itself and a way to be in the world. In fact, movement itself allowed Clare to focus his poetic sensibilities on the diminutive, even what might be perceived as static in the landscape, and amplify it in his poems. In such a state of freedom, the poet need not be a deep thinker so much as an observer and reveler in nature's beauty and bounty, silence and sound, and also in its cruelty and indifference. Clare writes:

> He pores wi wonder on the mighty change
> Which suns and showers perform and thinks it strange
> And tho no philosophic reasoning draws
> His musing marvels home to natures cause" (47-50)

Nature does not require the poet's reason or understanding, Clare asserts. Instead, musing leads to a recognition of "natures cause," meaning derived from the recognition that nature is impervious to human wishing and striving. It is itself, only. And that, Clare tells us, is more than enough. The poet may arrive at such a marvel only through the agency of a walk without boundaries or limitations. In another walking poem, "The Mores," Clare expresses a similar freedom while out on a country walk:

> Unbounded freedom ruled the wandering scene
> Nor fence or ownership crept in between
> To hide the prospect of the following eye
> Its only bondage was the circling sky (7-10)

Clare's use of the word "ruled" suggests the possibility of a dictatorial landowner who might interrupt the poet and experience. In this poem, however, the land is without a landowner, so the word "ruled" points to a landscape ruled by itself only. The word also offers the connotation of measurement. The land is measured by its condition, which in this poem is without bounds, but for the "circling sky."

Yet, in the poem, the land does not remain unfenced, and such freedom falls behind into the province of Clare's boyhood imagination. Certainly, the boy who wanders over private property is less a threat to the landowner than a man who is bound by the law:

> Now this sweet vision of my boyish hours
> Free as spring clouds and wild as summer flowers
> Is faded all—a hope that blossomed free
> And hath been once no more shall ever be
> Inclosure came and trampled on the grave
> Of labours rights and left the poor a slave (15-20)

Clearly, Clare regards wealthy landowners who fence and gate once free and open lands as de facto slavers. The poor are not able to buy land of their own, and as the wealthy take ownership of parcel after parcel, John Clare, and most of the rest of us, have no place to go. Later in the poem, Clare characterizes such landowners as having "little minds" who imprison "men and flocks." The result is, the poet tells us, that "where man claims earth glows no more divine" (68).

All considerations and recollections from those hours of freedom while wandering out on the land, the poet makes orderly on the page while confined in his study. The poet is compelled to make order from an experience dependent on no order at all. The poem itself is a kind of fencing, its structure and musicality, even as its meaning is central to breaking free from that same confinement. The words expressing unbidden freedom through the silences broken only by the sweet sounds of the natural world are as important as the things themselves. The poet's poem, like the landowner's fence, offers another opportunity to experience freedom by setting it alongside freedom's fragility and impermanence.

In Clare's "Sonnet: 'I dreaded walking where there was no path,'" he writes, "Yet everything about where I had gone/Appeared so beautiful I ventured on" and "But having nought I never feel alone/And cannot use another's as my own" (5-6, 13-14). It is the very nature of walking where there is no path that Clare feels a heightened sense of beauty and adventure. It is precisely the condition of confinement that builds in

Clare a desire for freedom, and in breaking out of that confinement he "never feel[s] alone." While it seems a superior condition to live a life of unbridle freedom, the poet needs something to push against to make his art, and for Clare, it is confinement, confinement that gives birth to both the urgency to break free and the urgency to write poems.

On the morning of July 22 (though he does not report the date), Clare wakes refreshed, and blesses his two wives and the queen of England. Of course, he has but one wife, a delusion which tips him into a day clouded in fantasy. He starts out, and as he wanders on, he is increasingly plagued by confusion and disorientation. At one point he naps in a ditch and wakes soaking wet. He struggles on in his cold wet clothes, and stops again for a rest on the ground. "I then got up and pushed onward," he writes, "seeing little to notice for the road very often looked as stupid as myself and I was very often half asleep as I went." Here in the narrative, Clare mentions that it is the third day since leaving Essex (July 23), and in a daze of hunger and confusion, he eats the grass growing along the roadside and proclaims it tastes "something like bread." I imagine Clare pulling up grass with his hands and stuffing it into his mouth, or bending to the earth to pull grass with his teeth like a cow. It is an image that for me evokes pity and sadness. Yet, Clare seems to be rather happy with his ingenuity. "I was hungry and eat heartily till I was satisfied," he writes, "and in fact the meal seemed to do me good." Perhaps he is pleased with the exchange he is making: eating grass is a kind of payment for his freedom. Having run out of matches, he now takes to chewing his remaining pipe tobacco, and then eventually swallows it, which acting as a stimulant, quells his hunger further. "I was never hungry afterwards," he writes. What need a man of food, he seems to say, when he may live free on grass and tobacco?

Clare's several resting places during his four day walk on the road out of Essex—a shed full of clover, the front porch of a stranger's home, a patch of grass on which he feeds, the various flint heaps where he sits to get off his aching feet, and certainly The Plough, where he escaped the rain—are as much a part of his walk as the walk itself. All travelers depend on the network of roads and pathways over which others have traveled before. And all travelers depend on suitable places to rest, places other travelers have rested before them, and in Clare's case, places where few travelers would dare to rest. In retrospect, we might think of Clare's journey out of Essex as a series of resting places to which he walks, and in those places events unfold worthy of his remembrance. It is not the road solely that matters, but the interstitial, the interruption, the wayside.

Upon nearing home, Clare realizes he is no longer walking among strangers, but now walking among people he knows. Near Peterborough, he writes, "I felt myself in homes way and went on rather more cheerfull though I forced to rest oftener then usual." A man and woman in a cart call out as they come by, and Clare discovers "they were neighbors from Helpstone where [he] used to live." He explains that he is "knocked up" and hungry and thirsty, so they pitch in and give him fivepence. Clare enters another public house and buys two half pints of ale to go with his bread and cheese. While the food and drink refresh him, his feet are in a frightful condition, and the rest only makes this more clear to him. "My feet was more crippled then ever and I could scarcely make a walk of it over the stones," he writes.

He walks on, rests for a bit on a stone heap, reaches a town called Werrington and is headed onward when a cart approaches carrying Clare's wife, Patty, a man and a boy. Patty apparently had been informed that her husband was out on the road headed home, and comes to fetch him, but Clare doesn't recognize her. He thinks she is a stranger "either drunk or mad," but is then informed the woman is his wife. Believing the fantasy that Mary was his first wife, he calls Patty his "second wife," and upon arriving home, searches for Mary, who is dead. Clare refuses to believe she is dead, and exclaims, "So here I am homeless at home." For me, these are the saddest words Clare writes in "Journey out of Essex." To be so driven to reach the refuge of home, and then to arrive finding no refuge at all. He quickly rallies to his situation, and then proclaims, "I can be happy any where."

At this point in the narrative, Clare returns to tracking his journey by date, "July 24, 1841," and makes a brief entry that serves as an Afterword. "Returned home out of Essex and found no Mary," he writes, and then she "was once the dearest of all—and how can I forget." He includes no final mark of punctuation. No question mark to open a door to possibility: "and how can I forget?" No period to reassure himself: "and how can I forget." No exclamation point to express his exaltation: "and how can I forget!" Nothing at all here at the end. The narrative just trails out into a laconic absence, white space on the page, for it seems that Clare has indeed forgotten.

Despite the fractured nature of "Journey out of Essex," John Clare is not a puzzle of scattered pieces that must be put back together. Even in his broken state during his escape out of Essex, and once home again upon his rest, he is whole already, and whole in both degrees. It is the body that makes the words, and daily fitness and exercise is essential to an artist's productivity and longevity. So it is the body we must care for, else the mind is a surface only. What Clare knew, even in the fog of his failing mind, was that to be outside in nature, to be bare and exposed to the elements, to be steaming along under the body's power, to be free, was fundamental to his art.

In my imagining of John Clare on his foot journey out of Essex, he is a lone figure in the landscape, and in places, great trees overhang the road revealing him in shadow. Mornings bring a mist about him that settles and dampens his clothes and hair. Any passerby would find little to note, just another walker moving from one place to another, but inside the man is a fountainhead of thought and memory and feeling overflowing, desire and love for the words and the world and the world made by words. The rain comes in on him, but he does not notice so much as he notes it, another subject to be absorbed by his art. He embraces fortune and hardship as companions to his desire to be free, to free himself from all confinement, even the confinement of his poetic spirit by his body. His singleness of purpose, his decision to go and to go on, his embrace in that sudden shower are worthy of our admiration. At least they are worthy of mine. For John Clare, the journey out of Essex was a portal to freedom. With an open road out ahead and the will to walk it, what need he of any mark of punctuation at all, period ■

Works Cited and Consulted

Bate, Jonathan. *John Clare: A Biography*. Farrar, Straus and Giroux, 2003.

Clare, John. *John Clare: Major Works*. Edited by Eric Robinson and David Powell. Oxford University Press, 2008.

Coverley, Merlin. *The Art of Wandering: The Writer as Walker*. Old Castle Books, 2012.

Houghton-Walker, Sarah. "Life Stories: The Coroner's Report on the Death of Mary Joyce." *John Clare Society Journal* 37, 2018.

Jarvis, Robin. *Romantic Writing and Pedestrian Travel*. MacMillian Press, 1997.

Keats, John. *Selected Poems and Letters*. Edited by Douglas Bush. Houghton Mifflin Company, 1959.

Yamamoto, Tsunetomo. *Hagakure*. Translated by Alexander Bennett. Tuttle Publishing, 2014.

John Clare was photographed shortly before his death in 1864.

Sir Thomas Wyatt, 1503-1542.

BARON WORMSER

Haunted: On Re-reading a Poem by Sir Thomas Wyatt

When I used to visit schools and talk to young people about poetry, I used to say that I was "h and o," which meant haunted and obsessed. I joked about this and told them they might rather become a nurse or accountant rather than a poet. Giving me the skeptical eye, they agreed. Since I was typically only in that classroom for an hour or so, a visitor from some form of Mars, I had no need to conform to any notions of anything. I wasn't, however, exaggerating. Not at all. That's how the endeavor has been for me and, indeed, I have a hard time understanding those who go through this world and aren't haunted by the sheer fact of being here and the knowledge that a day will come when they won't be here.

Poems very much haunt me, too. Again, that seems understandable since they are spirit presences rather than little corpses waiting to be explicated or theorized about. During my one not particularly happy year of graduate school I encountered a poem that has haunted me since then—over fifty years. In one of the texts the poem is untitled but accompanied by a parenthetical remark at the head of the poem: "[The lover showeth how he is forsaken of such as he sometime enjoyed.]" This situation has happened more than once, but for me was made immemorial by Sir Thomas Wyatt sometime in the 1530s.

Here is the text in the original, late-medieval English as Wyatt wrote it. (I have put the modernized version at the end of this essay as an addendum.):

> They fle from me that sometyme did me seke
>   With naked fote stalking in my chambre.
> I have sene theim gentill tame and meke
>   That nowe are wyld and do not remembre
> That sometyme they put theimself in daunger
>   To take bred at my hand; and now they raunge
> Besely seking with a continuell chaunge.

> Thancked be fortune, it hath ben othrewise
> > Twenty tymes better; but ons in speciall,
> In thin arraye after a pleasaunt gyse,
> > When her lose gowne from her shoulders did fall,
> And she me caught in her armes long and small;
> > Therewithall swetely did me kysse,
> And softely saide, *dere hert, howe like you this?*
>
> It was no dreme: I lay brode waking.
> But all is torned thorough my gentilnes
> > Into a straunge fasshion of forsaking;
> And I have leve to goo of her goodenes,
> > And she also to use new fangilnes.
> But syns that I so kyndely ame served,
> > I would fain knowe what she hath deserved.

    When reading lyric poetry from any century, we can get so numbed by the word "love" that we can forget sex as a fact, poetic and otherwise. Wyatt, who translated some of Petrarch's sonnets ("she that me learneth to love and suffer"), did not forget. Indeed, he was haunted—what seemed a vision was real. He touches, thus, on the very source of poetry, that sense of how each moment of life is imaginative, how much we are constantly making up, how much experience is mixed up in fancy, desire, longing, and sheer confusion, how much the mind dilutes and rearranges everything and yet—a kiss can be a kiss. The physical will have its say and more than its say.

    Wyatt was taken to task as a poet for being less than strictly metrical. Where the accents fall can be equivocal, not within the pentameter schema, as in "When her lose gowne from her shoulders did fall" or "It was no dreme: I lay brode waking." Some of this can be traced to the shift that English was going through, among other things, in making the final "e" silent but some of this is Wyatt's voice. That voice, for me, is part of the fascination of this poem, how it could have been written yesterday, how the reader feels Wyatt speaking to himself and to the reader, how thoroughly Wyatt is embedded in the drama of the poem. The telling is low-key, a man musing, but the passion that underlies the events is unmistakable: "howe like you this?" Wyatt is wonderfully alert to the shifts that passion can encompass, including its loss. We see him trying to figure out what happened. He doesn't know and in that sense, again, he is at a source of poetry: what we don't know provokes us. We wonder; we would "fain knowe."

Once the women were "gentill tame and meke." We almost see them as deer, yet they were "stalking," an equivocal word. The stalker moves furtively, yet the stalker typically is after some creature. The women are thus both—at "daunger" to consort with him yet also willful in their coming to his room. They have changed, a change that is "continuell." He cannot keep up with them. He thought he had them in his sights as they took "bred at my hand." That was then, this is now: an old story. So is they "do not remember." Human feeling will not stay still; attraction will not stay still; situations will not stay still. Poems can approximate, if not capture, such movements. Alertness is all, yet our alertness will have its limits.

Wyatt's thankfulness recommends itself: "it hath ben othrewise / Twenty tymes better." How wonderful that number is! We feel it—a whole lot better. To show us how much better he shows us a moment of revelatory intimacy. That moment is rich in words that are common yet here Wyatt touches their depths: the sweetness of a kiss, the softness of a voice, the term of endearment. Meanwhile, he remains alert to the grasping aspect, all that is in that word "caught." He doesn't pin the word "love" on the scene. No need for that. Bodies are bodies: "Thancked be fortune." Love often wants monuments that attest to some dimension of the experience. Wyatt refuses that stance or he may not have been interested in it in the first place. After all, he isn't running the show. The women are.

Lovers are always making attestations and in that regard Wyatt follows a tradition: "It was no dreme: I lay brode waking," which is to say, "I was very much awake, wonderfully awake, deliciously awake." Surely one starting point for a poem lies in our being truly awake— no sleepwalking, no rote, no platitude that downgrades experience. After this avowal we come to the turn, the perhaps inevitable "but." His language registers the complexity of the experience. He is implicated in his "gentilness," qualities of mannerliness, breeding, comportment, even a certain softness. The "forsaking" is "straunge." One wants to say, "Isn't it always that way? We try to understand but we can't quite get there. We want the good moments to stay but they vanish. Other intimacies beckon. Or situations simply change. He has to let go of her "goodenes," another rich word that can signify both high and low directions. And she is, well, newfangled. How bracing to find that word in the 1530s. New mores, new styles, new fashions, new assertions. Wyatt touches on both definitions of this Middle English word, that is the "often needlessly novel" and the "fond of novelty." The women will do it the way they do it. They may be "fond;" he may feel that "needlessly."

He ends up with a touché of sorts. He has had some memorable times; he also has been treated "kyndely" in the senses of kind and in kind. It takes one to know one. "I would fain knowe what she hath deserved." What is all this to her? Surely one of the great questions that leads to others. Is there a balance between the man's experience and the woman's? Is there a scintilla of justice in such affairs? Or not? One feels a wry shrug in his words. He's not complaining. Far from it. He's merely considering something that deserves consideration. No need to make too much of it but no need to dismiss it either. The changes are real.

Poets tend to be fond of the notion of "voice," but it's very hard to pin down. It has to do with the literal breath that goes into speaking a poem and how that breath is felt in the words and lines on the page. It has to do as much with pauses as it does with momentum. It has to do with the human presence as it occurs within a limited period of time, both a lifetime and the time of a poem, age bearing down on the poem and the poem holding tenaciously to its brevity. For me Wyatt's droll openness embodies voice, how he is willing to show different sides of the experience and how he refuses to simplify or disavow the experience. Things happen to us and we participate in that happening. We are actors and, indeed, in its quiet, sexy way, Wyatt's poem is stagy. Women appear and women leave; he is in his "chambre." We can hear the footsteps. Little wonder I am haunted five hundred or so years later by that "naked fote" and that "ons in speciall." The subtleties, intensities, and uncertainties of intimacy are all present.

BARON WORMSER

The modernized text that follows is taken from the Poetry Foundation Website and mirrors, for instance, the version in *Poetry of the English Renaissance 1509 – 1660*, edited by Hebel and Hudson. Something is lost in the modernization, particularly in regard to sound, but the genius of the poem still shines through. Over the course of my career as a poet, I have sought a blend of artifice and naturalness, a beckoning ideal that has kept me writing. Wyatt nailed it.

>They flee from me that sometime did me seek,
>With naked foot, stalking in my chamber.
>I have seen them gentle, tame, and meek,
>That now are wild and do not remember
>That sometime they put themself in danger
>To take bread at my hand; and now they range,
>Busily seeking with a continual change.
>
>Thanked be fortune it hath been otherwise,
>Twenty times better; but once in special,
>In thin array after a pleasant guise,
>When her loose gown from her shoulders did fall,
>And she me caught in her arms long and small;
>Therewithall sweetly did me kiss
>And softly said, "Dear heart, how like you this?"
>
>It was no dream: I lay broad waking.
>But all is turned thorough my gentleness,
>Into a strange fashion of forsaking;
>And I have leave to go of her goodness,
>And she also, to use newfangleness.
>But since that I so kindly am served,
>I would fain know what she hath deserved. ∎

John Clellon Holmes at home in Old Saybrook, Connecticut, June 1977, the summer before The Bowling Green Poems *appeared. Photo by Rosemary Ardinger.*

DAVID L. KUEBECK

Finding Redemption in Ohio: A Re-reading of John Clellon Holmes's The Bowling Green Poems

John Clellon Holmes, an unemployed novelist, spent March 12, 1975, in a pensive mood. It was his forty-ninth birthday. Apart from the typical glooms accompanying the annual turns of middle age, Holmes was anxiously awaiting an answer from Bowling Green State University in Ohio regarding the position of Visiting Writer in Fiction for the spring quarter. The job, with its $3,000 salary, was an opportunity he could ill-afford to lose.

At the vanguard of the Beat Generation movement of the early 1950s, Holmes had been much in demand at that time, publishing articles tracing the origins and philosophy of the Beats; authoring *Go* (1952), recognized as the first Beat novel; which he followed with *The Horn* (1958), a lyric meditation on black jazz musicians, "the indigenous American artist(s)." Holmes viewed himself as an observer on the periphery of the Beat group, allowing him a measure of objectivity when exploring the activities of his brethren. A serious writer, his aim was to build a major literary reputation.

Always on the edge of penury, a pattern played out in Holmes's financial life, a familiar sequence in which he received a large advance from a publisher, enabling him to rescue his wife, Shirley, from a low-paying job. Shirley was the consistent breadwinner, working a series

of office jobs to supplement Holmes's sporadic income. When Holmes received an advance it bought them a few blissful months, but inevitably grounded when the funds ran dry, sending Shirley back to undistinguished work. Naturally, resentment arose, as Shirley was not only the primary breadwinner, but also expected by her husband to perform the domestic duties of cook, laundress, and housekeeper. No matter their financial struggles, no matter his lack of publication, Holmes was unable to conceive of himself as anything but a novelist.

The death of his close friend Jack Kerouac in 1969 coincided with an extended ebbing for Holmes. Though he labored on several novels after 1964's *Get Home Free,* none were accepted for publication. By the spring of 1975 his last book contract was eight years previous, for 1967's essay collection *Nothing More to Declare.* His writing work since that time constituted freelancing for magazines—as Holmes termed it "hustling my ass for wherewithal." He'd found a reliable market with *Playboy* where editor Robie Macauley had transformed the men's magazine into a distinguished showcase of serious literature, Holmes contributing six essays between January 1968 and February 1973. Eventually that vein tapped out. With the arrival of spring 1975, Holmes had not published any commercial work in over two years. When Shirley, who had been suffering difficulties with her eyes, received a diagnosis of glaucoma, the disabling condition left her unable to work, and the couple's finances dire. Fortunately for Holmes, Bowling Green offered him the job.

Bowling Green needed Holmes as much as he needed them. Philip F. O'Connor, director of the school's graduate Creative Writing program, had reached out to him about the opening. Holmes taught at the university twice before on a visiting basis, so was acquainted with O'Connor and the modes of the writing workshop. O'Connor, however, had lost control of the workshop's cohort, contacting Holmes in an act of surrender. He was fed-up with the group, who Holmes later described as "obstreperous and brilliant." The dynamics of the workshop were contentious, with testosterone fueling condescension of the female students' work. Dismissive comments from several male students like "This piece is so pedestrian it walks," and "I didn't finish reading this story because the *Times* crossword was more interesting," had served to create an atmosphere that was blatantly sexist. A rumor spread among the women that Carolyn Forché, a dazzling talent who went on to receive the Yale Younger Poets prize, discovered the ashes of her unread poems in her department mailbox, burned by a male student. Holmes had his work cut out for him.

He arrived in Bowling Green having taught elsewhere sporadically. Throughout his itinerant career Holmes had enjoyed short visiting stints at the Iowa Writer's Workshop, the University of Arkansas, and Brown University, where he taught creative writing and contemporary literature courses. He took his teaching responsibilities seriously, reading up to thirty books in preparation, scrawling reams of notes for his seminar lectures. Holmes worked hard to compensate for a lack of formal education. Widely read and possessing a formidable intellect, Holmes was an autodidact who never graduated high school. He briefly attended Columbia University on the GI Bill, but did not obtain a degree. Holmes's work ethic served to blunt the intimidation he felt within academic environs.

Aware of the contentiousness teeming at Bowling Green, Holmes deftly handled the issue of predation within the workshop. At the first opportunity for a female student's work to be analyzed—the vocal minority of men chomping at the bit for a chance to disparage— Holmes gelded them: "Only the women will speak tonight," he told the workshop's participants. The men would remain silent. The solution was simple enough, but effective, as the women in the workshop found their voices, tentatively at first but gradually with more assurance. An experience they had come to dread was reclaimed, as Holmes made clear the obnoxious comments that had previously reigned were no longer acceptable. "After that, it was easier in the workshop," remembered Karen Loeb, a creative writing student. "Everyone respected him." These sentiments were echoed by Susan Neville, another student in the workshop. "John was much smarter, older, dressed in suits, wiser, and he was kind. He changed the culture and dynamics of the program. John stood up for our work."

Holmes was a careful and sensitive reader of his students' writing. In an interview with the campus newspaper he outlined his philosophy: "I take a student's work and analyze it, tear it to pieces. There is no one way to write, but I try to help a student see how his work can be improved." He offered warmth and encouragement to the talented young writers, as evidenced by a letter to Loeb: "You're a young woman in whom I believe, for whatever that's worth. I like your qualities of observation, your honesty, your intent to find the human truth in the things you write about . . . You're moving along, and I have few doubts about your future." Holmes took great pains to provide constructive comments on student projects, as the ultimate aim for each was to have a portfolio of publishable quality at the program's completion.

The culture of the writer's workshop saw students and faculty socializing after hours. It was not uncommon for faculty members to attend gatherings at the apartments of students where gallons of Pisano wine flowed freely. Holmes attended, bringing with him canned martinis and canned daiquiris. His drinking habits caused concern for his welfare. "John was a prodigious drinker," recalled one student. "He had to have alcohol in huge amounts in order to survive, but we never saw him drunk." Though Holmes did not identify as an alcoholic, the strain of writing led to a dependence on scotch and cigarettes. "What you want at the end of a writing session is not more consciousness—you want less," he once said. "The stress of writing—and the stress of the world, and particularly the stress of a long day of making sentences and moving the thing forward—when you've finished you're exhausted. You're intellectually worn-out from being so deep down in human motivations and character, that what you want is a return to yourself. Alcohol promises that for a very brief period. And beyond that it promises oblivion."

At his home in Old Saybrook, Connecticut, many evenings ended in drunken quarrels with Shirley. Years of resentment over money were compounded by sexual conventions tossed aside at Holmes's behest. In the mid-sixties, Holmes documented the sexual latitudes he took in his unexpurgated journals. In his quest for the truth, seeking to pinpoint something in his basic nature, Holmes recorded in excruciating detail his sexual self-destruction—dallying with neighbors, swapping with couple friends, taking a phenomenological view of his liaisons and promiscuity. These peccadillos, in character conjuring the bourgeois ribaldry depicted in John Updike's *Couples*, threatened to destroy his marriage. In his journals, Holmes revealed how the cumulative corrosive effect caused Shirley to withdraw emotionally and physically from her husband. "We are like strangers in the flesh," Holmes lamented at one point.

Shirley remained in Connecticut during Holmes's stint at Bowling Green. Lonely, suffering from one of his numerous periods of "terminal writer's block," Holmes settled into a rented house, his dismal mood finding its embodiment in the uninspiring Ohio landscape. It was here in April and May of 1975 that he started work on a group of poems that would be deemed by one critic as "the strongest sequence he has had published to date."

Holmes had written poems at the outset of his career, finding success with publication in *Poetry* and other major journals. However, he had given up poetry to pursue the novel, which he considered the more serious and lucrative avenue for a writer; additionally, Holmes deplored the hints of emptiness and falsehood he detected in his poetic voice. Though serious about his work, Holmes's misgivings in taking up poetry again are evident in this excerpt from a letter to Karen Loeb: "While teaching fiction, I find I can't write it well, so I usually fool with poems on these gigs." Holmes was intentionally downplaying the work—he was a novelist after all, "fooling" with poems—the casual quip belying insecurity at his new endeavor.

The result was *The Bowling Green Poems* (1977), a nine-poem sequence which can be read as a Lawrencian exploration of consciousness. Holmes was a great admirer of D.H. Lawrence, who he deemed

The Bowling Green Poems

JOHN CLELLON HOLMES

"The protean artist and thinker of this century . . . a writer who pioneered territories of consciousness the rest of us are only now starting to glimpse, much less map." Holmes believed that most important twentieth-century literature furthered the "great venture in consciousness," as the revelations of experience brought about breakthroughs to unimagined freedoms. To further these aims in the poetic sequence, Holmes employed the imagist-objectivist techniques of William Carlos Williams, whose influence he rediscovered while at Bowling Green. Williams's mantra "Say it, no ideas but in things!" found its expression through the direct perception of objects.

The early poems in the sequence locate the "gypsy scrivener" uninspired "waiting to be used" in Ohio after his "failure of precaution & exchequer." Holmes perceives a "landscape inhospitable/to visions" with its "pickle factories in an old bog," "dark loam ready for tomatoes—/mud on asphalt/where the tractors cross—." He is marooned in rural environs, formerly the alluvial Great Black Swamp, flat and dull, where Holmes questions "Can one persist without architecture?"

> God knows
>   the maples will enleaf again,
>   the sentience of wrens among them,
>   and consciousness relent.

Holmes invokes an entreaty for inspiration; the artist is dying on the vine, frustrated by his lot in life and finding himself in a dark hour, hostage for want of funds from his college job, in a land that will not sustain him. Aware of spring's as-yet-obscured emergence, he follows with another dose of grim reality:

> God put this place underwater
> then some boring asshole
>   went and drained it
>   to build a filling station.

In this place, Holmes makes clear, he will be unable to find beauty or redemption, only the cold solidities of everyday existence. Holmes goes on to ruminate over dead friends Walker Evans and Jack Kerouac:

DAVID L. KUEBECK

"Here, in the mud, eating sausages at dawn,/I ransack memory
in history's name."

>Now smokes and booze have thrust the body,
>>like a spike, into the tireless mind,
>and hope, a spinning tire, into the mud.

"Now those certainties have all the charm/of boyhood's notes
to God/returned to sender—/A calico cat foraging a doom of garbage
cans." Holmes's laments are those of "a tired and a baffled man," as
he phrased it in his introduction, and it is uncertain if this man can
see his way through.

Throughout his time in Bowling Green, Holmes exchanged a series
of letters with Shirley back in Connecticut. Heartened by her tone,
and missing her terribly, he spirited away, traveling to New England
for a weekend together. Their physical intimacy, which had been so
compromised by Holmes's behavior in the sixties, was restored. Holmes
and Shirley's reconnection buoyed him: "And if there can be love again/
between such wearied people" there can be "return of the old sensual
fevers/resting the expended parts of us,/So life's got savor now—/
there's grace in it."

>For if there can be flesh-love again
>>between bodies so self-haunted—
>>hand-colloquies in hotel-beds,
>>words become tongues—
>in time there could be all the rest,
>memory proven tougher than despair,
>>an end of soldiering-through.

>I kissed you in the marriage-places,
>>grounded again,
>there's nothing more to lose.
>>The old Zen canniness occurred—
>mountains were mountains once again.

THE LIMBERLOST REVIEW

The "tired . . . baffled" "gypsy scrivener" has found his redemption. Holmes can face the reality of his teaching job with the optimism that "an end of soldiering-through" is in sight. This he cements with a familiar Zen koan, hinting that, if not a satori, the artist has at the very least experienced a step forward. He is back on stable footing. The optimistic tone of *Weekend Away* carries through the remainder of the sequence, whose strongest poem is its denouement.

In September 1975 after his departure from Bowling Green, Holmes wrote to student Karen Loeb:

> I wrote a series of poems while I was in Bowling Green, and the day your letter came I was revising the last one in the series, in which you figure. It mentions walking up your street on Memorial Day, and encountering you (in shorts & halter) on your way to the mailbox. Do you remember? Anyway, I've got you in there, because you looked brown and summery, and you have a cute navel, and I passed up having coffee with you in your nice, cool apartment so that I could continue a train of thought I was pursuing, and later regretted it. It's one of those odd, glancing poems, and it doesn't quite mesh yet . . .

That poem did, in fact, mesh in the final editing, as it is the most fully-realized exploration of consciousness within the sequence. The inventory of maladies plaguing Holmes—the crises of money and troubled marriage; the dispirit of the uninspiring college town; the lean years mired in failed projects; the elegies for dead friends—all have been exorcised. What remains is the purity of the present moment, the direct perception of Holmes's surroundings leading, in the tradition of Rousseau's *Solitary Walker*, to reverie:

> Women move air across their chests,
> iced glasses bead porch railings,
> a fat man wheezes on a mower-cord,
> anarchic urges lurk behind the jalousies—
>   a *King's Row* vision of midsummer lassitude.

DAVID L. KUEBECK

The tree-lined streets of "commodious houses" transport Holmes to his childhood; he meanders slowly down Prospect Street, at its junction with Ridge Street coming across, by happenstance, his student Karen. Holmes is "astonished to discover/the porches of my past/are peopled by imagination," these lines recalling William Carlos Williams's 1917 poem *Good Night*, in which the author discovers "It is memory playing the clown." Holmes's encounter with Loeb forces him back to reality, the image of his youth to fade, "contracting like an offed-TV." She invites him for coffee. Holmes writes "I'd like her to feel easy, I want her to smile./But make excuses and walk on, wanting instead"

> Ann Sheridan skinny in the ice-house,
> bike-pumps blowing up the world of glum,
> rebellion born of too much love to give.

He clings to this image from the 1942 film *King's Row* (Holmes had a lifelong love of film), the familiar grounds of imagination proving a safe space for the man so beleaguered in the sequence's earlier poems. The sound of "a clattering" beer can brings Holmes to, interrupting his reverie, and introduces regret at his failure to take-up Karen on her invitation, "at least for the time it takes/for fancy to resume its archaeology." Holmes ends the poem with a pure perception, lost in sensation. Back in his hermit quarters, he takes a sip of iced tea:

> a flash of bliss irradiates me,
>   and I dissolve to sweetness,
>   I become a taste,
>   and consciousness
>   relents.

This final stanza recalls Williams once again, who documented rummaging in his icebox, the taste of eating plums "delicious/so sweet/and so cold" in his poem "This Is Just to Say." Holmes dissolving in succor, "become a taste," arouses a spectral implication, the disappearance of self entirely, transcending substance and corporeality, atomized and obliviated, to become the purity of sensation itself. Wiser now, the artist is aware of the Zen inherent in the everyday act of drinking iced tea. Holmes's sequence has come full circle, returning to an earlier refrain, originally posed as an appeal, this time closing with the affirmation that consciousness, indeed, "relents." This final Keatsian line ("Oh for a life of sensations rather than thoughts!") is a muted echo of earlier Beat declarations, reaching for ecstatic heights, a fitting end to Holmes's sequence. *The Bowling Green Poems* was praised by one critic for Holmes's "highly individual tone" with "lyrical flickers."

Holmes the "self-silenced poet" found in poetry's heightened expression the method to convey the break-up of the "logjam in his spirit." Though Holmes's teaching in Bowling Green amounted to one academic quarter in 1975, his time there provides an important autobiographical document. "The act of writing . . . preserves indelibly the moment when a truth broke through," Holmes asserted. "To write about your own life is to transfer it forever from memory to fact." Assessing himself from a reduced vantage, dispirited, Holmes refused to wallow in self-pity. If Bowling Green represents the low tide of Holmes's life and career, it provided a catalyst for rebound, as favorable breezes filled his sails shortly after. In August 1975 he joined the faculty of the University of Arkansas on a permanent basis, the tenure-track position heralding the end of financial difficulties. Given Shirley's health challenges, Holmes admitted to the necessity that he was now solely responsible for providing a stable income. Shirley joined him in Fayetteville, setting up a home there; they summered in Old Saybrook.

Holmes enjoyed teaching the Arkansas students he humorously described as "ranging from astounding (bad) to astounding (good)." He stayed in touch with many of the writers he encountered in Bowling Green, corresponding with Karen Loeb; hosting Phil O'Connor as a visiting writer in Arkansas; seeing Tony Ardizzone and Dara Wier at professional association board meetings; and adding Carolyn Forché as a colleague on the MFA staff in Fayetteville. Though he worked on two more novels, the manuscripts were never completed to publishable form. Holmes's first novel, *Go*, was re-released in a new hardcover edition with a new introduction by Holmes in 1976 after being years out of print.

In addition to *The Bowling Green Poems*, Holmes continued to pursue poetry, publishing two more collections in his lifetime; he published five more collections of essays before his death at 62 in 1988. ■

DAVID L. KUEBECK

Author's endnote: *This piece is the result of a 20-year interest in the life and work of John Clellon Holmes, having first stumbled across his faculty dossier in the University Archives at Bowling Green State University while employed there as an undergraduate reference assistant. I am deeply indebted to Rick Ardinger, Karen Loeb, and Susan Neville who provided invaluable assistance in my research; and must acknowledge the works produced by Ardinger; Ann and Samuel Charters; and Jaap van der Bent which laid the foundation for future Holmes studies. The present study may be inadequate in many ways in its attempts to capture a deeply human, intelligent, thoughtful, and compelling man, but as Holmes himself wrote "the filial respect a younger writer feels for an older ought to be acknowledged, because such insignificant acts may be all that remains of the old communions . . . " I hope that this work provides biographical context which better informs the understanding of* The Bowling Green Poems, *and that it honors the struggle of the artist to persevere.*

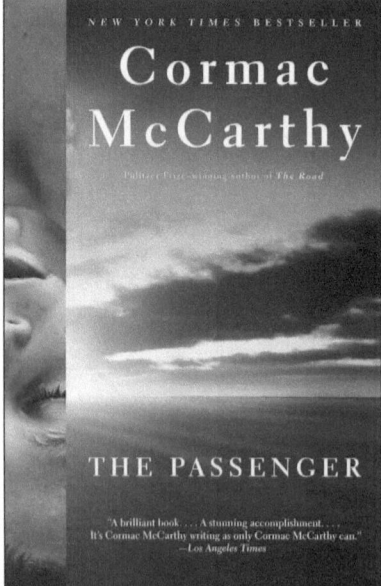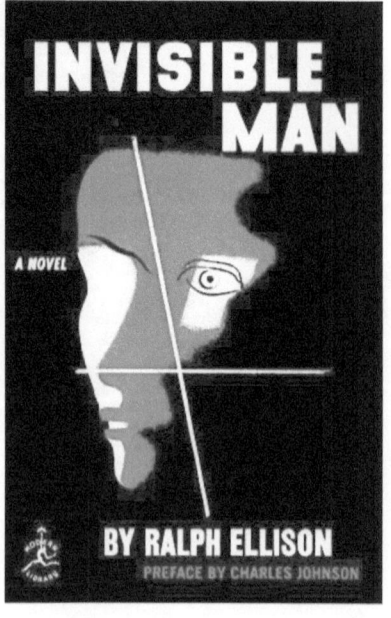

ALAN MINSKOFF

Listening: The Pleasures of Fiction on Audiobooks

I have been listening to audiobooks for decades. When my now mid-thirties children went to school at Boise, Idaho's Hidden Springs—45 minutes from our home on Boise's Loggers Creek—we listened to E.B. White on the way up and I switched to Isabel Allende or John Irving or Philip Roth on the way down. For a long time, my library card served one grand purpose to pull brown plastic boxes of books on tape off the shelves and insert spinning words onto my car's playback machine.

Happily and not, those days and technologies are gone. Now as a longtime reviewer for *AudioFile Magazine* and a member of their podcast team (on *Behind the Mic* recommending titles one week a month) audiobooks arrive as either down- or up-loadable. I consider myself very fortunate to have a gig where I can take advantage of twin mobilities: my commute from Boise to Caldwell for my teaching at the College of Idaho and walking my flat-coated retrievers on the greenbelt by the Boise River and around my southeast Boise neighborhood. For their part the dogs seem to know from my gait—my ignoring their behaviors or a literary contact high—that these walks are to be savored. While there are no official records, I believe that *Cutting for Stone* by Abraham Verghese and Dickens' *Nicholas Nickleby* hold the titles for lengthiest dog walk-and-listens.

I am an audiobook omnivore both as a reviewer and consumer. *AudioFile* supplies me with lots of listens on food, wine, journalism, the environment as well as memoirs, histories, biographies—you name it. But my listener's heart and reader's soul love nothing so much as fiction. And over the decades I've reviewed Chekov and Saki, Gish Jen and Tony Doerr, George Orwell and John Banville, Teju Coles and Jason Mott, Annie Ernaux and Olga Tokarczuk, Larissa Fasthorse and Tommy Orange. It's a long list.

And I am convinced that some fiction is not just worth listening to but the audiobook version is an improvement with a great narrator or cast. Take the dark cowboy of American fiction, the recently passed Cormac McCarthy novels like *The Road* and *The Passenger* with their minimalistic punctuation and the latter's freaks benefit from a voice and interpreter. The narrators clarify the voices through tone and cadence—the kind of things you hear in your head. They perform and inform.

In McCarthy's *The Passenger*, the character Alicia Western hears voices, sees the apparitions that may only be in her head. They are vaudevillians, kibitzers, entertainers whose purpose is to cajole and interact with the suicidal mathematician—to keep her alive. By contrast her brother (once a physicist, now a deep-sea diver) is the other protagonist and he behaves as every bit the McCarthy man's man and he sounds just so. Other characters, whose voices range from a New Orleans fop to a waterfront tough, come alive in their performances. Here is what I said in my review of the audiobook and I am sticking to it:

> Candidly, some works of fiction—those in which tone, literary style, and sound matter—work very well (maybe better) as audiobooks. The protagonists of this audiobook are superbly portrayed by MacLeod Andrews and Julia Whelan. They are gifted mimics and switch off in this braided tale of loss, hopeless love, and social collapse. Both plumb the depths of the wounded brother and sister Bobby and Alicia Western, who are lost souls in this excursion into the dark, soul-depleting demimonde of Cormac McCarthy. Whelan and MacLeod put authentic voices to the dual protagonists' thoughts and conversations that make the characters materialize—those who are human, anyway.

Without a doubt McCarthy is worth reading, and I am not arguing against the pleasures of the page. But some works of dialogue-rich fiction are better when given new life by the interpretation of the sounds on the page. Take three disparate examples.

Actor Joe Morton's tour de force performance of Ralph Ellison's classic Invisible Man. His intonation is mesmerizing and his reading illuminates the crisis of identity that this epoch-making novel (originally published in 1952) detailed. Here is the essence of my review:

ALAN MINSKOFF

This iconic novel, which won the 1953 National Book Award, is widely thought of as one of the most important of the twentieth century. Morton rises to every occasion. Whether he's evoking the famous race riot scene or the harrowing episode at the paint factory—all is made real and memorable.

Morton simply inhabits Ellison's unnamed protagonist, and the result is spellbinding. He treats the angsty narrator as a man who happens to be black, therefore unseen, as constantly engaged in observation and seeking identity. His character is in an existential rather than merely a racial crisis.

This decade has been a halcyon moment for fiction on audiobook. In the lonely category of great self-narrated audiobooks, Abraham Varghese's deft and eloquent narration of *The Covenant of Water* was the exception that proves the rule: Audiobooks are overwhelmingly better performed by professional narrators, voice actors who bring nuance, color, gradations of tone to the works and experiences. Verghese navigated the varied south Indian accents expertly and was as flawless with the speakers' class distinctions. Of course, as a doctor himself, his knowledge of medical terminology helped.

Here an author is a rarity, a gifted performer. Writers give readings but an audiobook is different. It is a performance, a show. Readers like Edoardo Ballerini bring their own artistic renditions to the work.

Fiction performed by full casts have a theatricality that rises them above a typical reading or listening experience. They become life-like characters, close your eyes and you can see them, their dress, affect and personality. The full cast captures the various voices, states of mind and idiosyncrasies of multiple characters. Two recent examples will suffice. Indulge me for one more review (okay bits of two):

> The ensemble performance of Jennifer Egan's *The Candy House* is exceptional. Michael Boatman captures the interior life of the enigmatic Bix Boughton, a social media genius who invents the world-altering technology "Own Your Unconscious," Alex Allwine delivers a haunting automaton-like second-person narration of the chapter titled "Lulu the

Spy, 2032," Tyra Lynne Barr emulates the chirpy sound of 13-year-old Molly in "The Perimeter After-Molly," and Dan Bittner supplies sharply insightful tone as Ames, whose life story ends this imaginative tour de force.

And the recent and highly praised second novel, *Wandering Stars*, from Tommy Orange has a stellar cast and includes a show-stopping performance: Charley Flyte's reading of Victoria Bear Shield's dramatic monologue to her unborn daughter is a grand piece—a haunting performance with an expressive tone and intimate voice.

What makes fiction so enjoyable on audiobook? Part of the answer is the audiobook experience itself—take Dickens with you on a walk, drive to the mountains or the sea with a thought-provoking contemporary like Teju Cole or have the most fun holiday with Larissa Fasthorse's *Thanksgiving Play* or discover a fine debut writer like Dawnie Walton, whose *The Final Revival of Opal and Ned* is another consummate example of a shining full cast. For me it is the echo of the spoken word, the slow deliberate listening process that can catapult the audience to unexplored places and give voice to characters who open the imagination. And you can introduce your kids to *The Trumpet of the Swan* while driving through Montana or Mark Twain when approaching the Mississippi.

Listening does what we all need in these hyperactive times—it slows down the process and lets the language sink in. In these days of ear worms and eye candy, a great audiobook performance is aural champagne. For me few experiences of literature equal the good company of a great storyteller or fabulist on the page but especially in my ears. ∎

ALAN MINSKOFF

Recommendations

Rules of Civility, by Amor Towles, captures New York in the late thirties through the wit and candid voice of heroine Kate Kontent, read splendidly by Rebecca Lowman.

The Candy House by Jennifer Egan (see above) read by a full cast. Egan spins the world of social media and the result is a mesmerizing audiobook.

Night of the Living Rez by Morgan Talty. Darrell Dennis narrates these 12 interconnected short stories with calculated restraint, empathy, and a sure sense of the author's voice.

Cloud Cuckoo Land by Anthony Doerr, the Boise-based Pulitzer Prize winner. Marin Ireland and Simon Jones sparkle as they narrate this immersive time-traveling novel.

The Final Revival of Opal and Ned by Dawnie Walton. A fine cast does a first-rate performance of this rock and roll themed first novel.

The Golden Compass by Philip Pullman. Behind the Mic host Jo Reed called this "a miracle of an audiobook" read by a full cast (young adult).

Charlotte's Web by E.B. White read by a full cast including Meryl Streep, January LaVoy and Macleod Andrews (children).

The Penguin Book of the Modern American Short Story, a fine collection including classic stories by Susan Sontag, Louise Erdrich, and George Saunders read by a full cast that includes Cassandra Campbell and Scott Brick.

The Thanksgiving Play by Larissa FastHorse, read by Ellis Greer, Josh Stamberg, mark Jude Sullivan and Liza Weil From L.A. Theatre Works is a laugh-out-loud satire of woke culture.

Nicholas Nickleby by Charles Dickens, read by the inimitable Rupert Degas immerses the reader in the language and world of 19th century England.

Wandering Stars by Tommy Orange. This follow-up to Orange's *There There* has a splendid cast including Charlie Flyte, Shaun Taylor-Corbett, Alma Cuervo among other fine performers.

The Angel of Rome and Other Stories by Jess Walter. Edoardo Ballerini and Julia Whelan narrate these empathic, witty, and finely wrought short stories.

Demon Copperhead by Barbara Kingsolver, read by Charlie Thurston. My colleague at the College of Idaho Diane Raptosh recommended this Pulitzer Prize winner read with a true down county Virginia accent.

Wyndham Lewis.

TED DYER

Wyndham Lewis: Lighting the Fuse
Re-reading the Work of a Modernist Warrior

> We are not only the last men of an epoch . . . We are the first men of a future that has not materialized. We belong to a great age that has not yet come off.
>
> —Wyndham Lewis, 1937

Editor's note: *When Wyndham Lewis penned the tag, "Men of 1914," for the four emerging talents of international modernism—Lewis, Ezra Pound, T. S. Eliot, and James Joyce, with himself as the first among equals—alert segments of the English arts community agreed. After all, Lewis was arguably the first to promote modernism as an avant-garde critique of a newly mechanized society, the first to publish a modernist prose, and the first modernist artist to gain public notoriety. Today, however, he is largely unknown—his paintings lost, his novels out of print until the 1980s, and his reputation badly tarnished. What happened to him begins below with an account of an exasperated Lewis in London, 1910.*

atching the English press vilify the avant-garde wave surging across Europe during the 20th Century's second decade, Percy Wyndham Lewis, a seemingly self-created young man, writhed in frustration.

His reason: fronting England's very first exposure to the avant-garde was, alas, Roger Fry, a Bloomsbury art critic and Francophile who had just scandalized an insular London public with an art-exhibition series that featured paintings by Cezanne, Matisse, Seurat, Van Gogh, Gauguin and Picasso.

Several others also felt this series' seismic impact. Marveling at the English public's "paroxysms of rage and laughter," Virginia Woolf, another leading Bloomsburyite, promptly announced that in 1910 "human character [had] changed."

393

Lewis, by contrast, feared that a newspaper freak-out in which artistic experimentalism was condemned and continental painters slandered could only damage prospects for England's own native painters.

Worse still, this entire messy affair could only distract English society from its vital need to transform itself, something, according to Lewis, that only authentic, homegrown art movements could accomplish.

To no-one in particular, then, Lewis proclaimed his intention to "manufacture fresh eyes for people, and fresh souls to go with those eyes." He also sought to elevate art to higher levels of abstraction and to expand its scope to include the irrational.

But most importantly, Lewis sought to initiate an unsparing avant-garde critique of his entire 20th Century moment: its media, art, politics, architecture, and especially its emerging machine-based technologies.

Himself an emerging fiction writer and cutting-edge painter—in fact, the first English Abstractionist and eventually its leading modernist—Lewis had worked briefly as an interior designer for Fry but thought him a stodgy antiquarian posing as an avant-garde impresario. Convinced that such fakers had to be called out, Lewis rashly broke with Fry and the entire Bloomsbury lot in a flurry of public denunciation.

Lewis filled this alleged leadership void with a new and properly radical art movement called Vorticism, and, with his good friend Ezra Pound, launched a magazine to proclaim its ascendancy: *Blast: The Review of the Great English Vortex*. Unlike any other publication with its provocative poster-like typography and layout, *Blast* offered blistering polemics and critiques of current avant-garde activity throughout Europe. *Blast* also offered tongue-in-cheek entertainments to draw in the upper classes and the culturally aware. It parodied avant-garde rituals, such as the ping-pong match of manifesto and counter-manifesto, and offered a section called Blasts and Blesses, to proclaim in banner-headline typography the events and cultural trends that its editors and contributors championed and/or disdained.

TED DYER

Among the new writers introduced, of course, was Lewis himself, who penned essays and manifestos, and announced his literary arrival with a startling and completely unstageable stage play. Viewing himself mainly as a polemicist and painter, Lewis wrote *The Enemy of the Stars* in large part to model a cinema-inspired, genre-bending avant-garde prose style for a new but lagging generation of English writers. (His short-story sequence, which is the subject of this essay, reached its final form years later.)

This play had no precedent. *Enemy* was not a play, strictly speaking, but a description of a play being shown, far in the future, to the elite of Posterity. It was also an uncanny precursor to Beckett's *Waiting for Godot*, and the sole manifestation in English drama of German Expressionism, an art movement that Lewis' cultural antennae instantly dialed onto. (Unlike his developing English-speaking modernist peers, who were Frenchified to the core, Lewis came to write his fable-like fiction in seemingly derivative forms, such as the picaresque tale or the detective story, and drew inspiration from Russia and Germany rather than Western Europe—with Dostoyevsky being his primary influence.)

Says Lewis scholar Andrzej Gasionrek:

> *Enemy of the Stars* enacts the conflict between the lone artist-figure [Arghol] seeking to maintain an unsullied identity by conceiving it in unitary terms as self-grounding; the idea that it may emerge out of and depend on intersubjective relations [coming to term with Hanp, his psychic double or *doppelgänger*] is rejected in favor of a myth of self-creation or a desire to return to a Platonic transcendent origin. Contact with others is depicted as degrading, since it places the self in jeopardy by allowing these

395

others to destroy its isolated 'purity' or to
batten on it parasitically.

This Vorticist moment, with Lewis' groundbreaking avant-garde play at its forefront, signaled the emergence of a unique literary career that still commands our serious attention today, despite its many controversies, especially those of the 1930s.

Lewis, in short, emerged in early 1914 to become a great many things: a novelist of astonishing range, a critic of art, literature and film, a poet and dramatist, a philosopher, a political theorist, an active journalist of many types, a contributor to and editor of art and literary journals including three of his own, a travel writer, a memoirist, a writer of radio plays—he was an all-purpose broadcast and media pioneer—and finally a critic of culture in the current post-modern sense of that term, a genre that Lewis arguably invented.

Stated another way, Lewis, throughout his career, internalized simultaneously rather than sequentially each of Soren Kierkegaard's three developmental stages of human consciousness: the aesthetic, the ethical and the religious.

This career began with his brief stint as the editor of *Blast*, his first and arguably most famous project. To find appropriately avant-garde contributors, Lewis solicited copy from a few up-and-comers who were, at that time, largely unknown. Lewis met T.S. Eliot in Pound's little triangular sitting room in Kensington in 1915. Eliot had only recently met Pound there himself, when Pound had proudly shown him Lewis' drawings created to illustrate Lewis' favorite Shakespeare play, *Timon of Athens*.

Portrait of T.S. Eliot by Lewis.

Pound feared that Lewis wouldn't take to the prim and clerical Eliot—called "the undertaker" by a leading Bloomsbury salon hostess—but these two hit it off splendidly. In fact, Lewis felt a powerful *doppelgänger* connection: he loved to play Marlow to Eliot's Shakespeare. Moreover, all three men became lifelong comrades, despite the challenge of staying friends with Lewis.

Lewis promptly blue-pencilled one of the poems Pound offered to the first *Blast*, and for the second and final issue—*Blast* was another casualty of World War I—he also rejected Eliot's "The Triumph of Bullshit" and the "Ballad of Big Louise," saying that censors would object to "words ending in -uck, -unt and -ugger," despite declaring Eliot's poems to be "excellent bits of scholarly ribaldry."

But included in the final 1915 issue were two of Eliot's poems, "Preludes" and "Rhapsody of a Windy Night." Luckily, editor Lewis was able to put forth a second volume because he was still in London, trying to secure a British officer's commission as an artilleryman. Also, he needed to finish his first novel and recover from a debilitating bout of gonorrhea. Hoping the latter would simply disappear resulted in a septicemia infection that rendered him bedridden, thus delaying his entrance into uniform until 1916—and quite possibly saving his life.

At this point, Pound's intervention for Lewis proved decisive. He secured Lewis £50 for the serial rights to *Tarr*, Lewis' novelistic debut, from *The Egoist*, a famous literary magazine, which, at Pound's instigation, had just concluded its serialization of James Joyce's *Portrait of the Artist as a Young Man*—thus branding these two as the very first modernist novels.

While helping Lewis get his affairs in order, Pound also found people willing to store his paintings. He even sold several to Modernist arts-patron John Quinn and had him organize a second Vorticist painting exhibition in America. He also had Quinn find an American publisher for *Tarr*.

Before finally reaching the front at Ypres, Belgium, for the third battle of Passchendaele, a grateful Lewis offered a salute of tribute to Pound and the other leading *Blast* contributors, coining the phrase "Men of 1914" to define the core quartet—adding Joyce at Pound's insistence—who constituted the vanguard of a new literary movement, a quartet that critic and scholar Hugh Kenner eventually called the four titans of modernism.

Even today their collective contribution is not fully appreciated. The quartet's most outspoken were Lewis, who wanted a revolution, and Pound, who wanted a renaissance: hence their personal bond. Eliot, meanwhile, tactically navigated rather than rejected a Bloomsbury-dominated literary scene that Joyce, an Irishman, largely ignored.

But all four shared much in common. Each wanted an end to what then passed for literature in middlebrow Edwardian England: pedestrian realism, feeble impressionism, and the absurd cults of boy-scout wholesomeness, outdoor manliness, and ethereal feminine purity. This required, in turn, purging Edwardian literary language of its prettified subject matter and ornamental diction, its devotion to a moldy and largely Romantic tradition, and its endless kowtowing to a sentimental reading public. Their solution: inaugurate a new classicism. Even if human nature had not changed, the need to apprehend it anew certainly had.

Drawing of James Joyce by Lewis.

Thus emboldened, these new moderns, as Eliot said of Joyce, "killed the whole of the Nineteenth Century," and Eliot, furthermore, was particularly clear about whose new language held the most promise. No matter how much he admired Joyce and his mythic method and respected Pound's poetry and later his forceful editing of *The Wasteland*, Eliot saved his most fulsome, and often extravagant, praise for Lewis.

At that first meeting, Eliot found Lewis to be a brilliant and amusing conversationalist with a sharp critical intelligence and powerful visual imagination. "The most fascinating personality of our time," said Eliot, in a review of *Tarr*. He then added, famously: in "Mr. Lewis we recognize the thought of the modern and the energy of the caveman."

In the coming years, he became Lewis' staunch defender and ultimately considered him superior to Joyce as a prose stylist. Eliot later declared that Lewis was "without, qualification a man of genius. . . [and] the greatest prose master of my generation—perhaps the only one to have invented a new style."

When *Blast* appeared in June of 1914, however, Lewis promptly garnered a different kind of recognition: he became a media darling, both famous and infamous, both for publishing a shocking new literary magazine and for importing into England the new abstractionist Continental painting trends—organizing, as he later quipped, "the Cubist invasion of England without the loss of a single cube."

Lewis cultivated a combative, Byronic persona: he was mad, bad and dangerous to know. He relished intellectual combat. Dark, grim-jawed, and frequently silent and saturnine, his slender, 6-foot form shrouded in a heavy overcoat, scarf, and black sombrero, Lewis sold himself as the forbidding mystery man of the arts.

He also enjoyed romantic liaisons with many of the titled women and female art patrons with whom he dined and worked. Even Prime Minister H. H. Asquith came calling. A cultured man who wanted the low-down on modern painting, Asquith hoped to make sure that Lewis' "stunt" of importing international art movements did not also include the import of revolutionary politics.

But perhaps the best way to grasp the tone of this heady and evanescent moment is to reflect upon Lewis' brief association with Frida Strindberg, the Swedish playwright's second wife, and her London nightclub, The Cave of the Golden Calf.

Among many amusing anecdotes, Lewis biographer Jeffery Meyers tells this one:

> After bolting from Fry's interior design company, Lewis promptly launched one of his own, called The Rebel Arts Centre, which claimed a few prominent commissions during its brief and financially troubled existence.
>
> Strindberg, a beautiful and emotionally unstable woman with strong opinions and appetites, hired Lewis to decorate The Cave, which was London's first ultra-modern arty nightclub, and the place to be for London's prewar intelligentsia.

Featuring a Viennese chef, a corps of dutiful Austrian
waiters and a peppy orchestra led by a gesticulating gypsy
fiddler, the Cave subjected its guests, all decked out in the
finest evening wear, to various questionable experiments
in avant-garde theatre and performance art.
Young girls were introduced to rich, older men,
who treated them to the latest dances and the finest food
and wine.
Rebecca West recalled seeing Katherine Mansfield
perform at The Cave in an oriental cabaret review dressed
in full Chinese costume, her black hair appropriately coiffed;
Osbert Sitwell, at this same time, reported The Cave to
be "a Vorticist garden of gesticulating figures, dancing and
talking, while the rhythm of primitive forms of ragtime
throbbed through the wide room."
Frida had originally contracted to pay Lewis £60 for
paintings, wall screens, and a huge drop-curtain painted
the color of raw meat, which, still damp, stuck to the stage
on opening night.
As their relationship deteriorated, Frida refused
to pay, so Lewis seized £60 directly from the club's till;
furious, Frida, wrote him a nasty letter just before the war
proclaiming him a charlatan as she vanished to America with
all of his paintings.

Such, then, were the antics of the celebrity avant-garde and their upscale friends in that time; newspapers and gossip mongers couldn't get enough of Lewis and his beau monde. In terms of fame and notoriety, this was the zenith of Lewis' career, but the very brief cultural whirl initiated by the great lark that was *Blast* soon disappeared into the calamity that we now call the First World War.

Kenner, in his magisterial study of modernism, *The Pound Era*, said the death of Vorticism in its cradle caused Pound to suffer "long-term psychic damage . . . ." Kenner also memorialized a cultural movement—"Genius might turn up at any moment"—that was obliterated just as it began to take shape.

Vorticism's erasure also transformed Lewis' pre-1914 celebrity world into a purgatorial nightmare that gave birth, twenty-five years later, to a second and even more devastating world war.

Like many European avant-garde artists of 1914, who were cosmopolitan yet fiercely nationalistic, Lewis raced to join the conflagration. The only member of the titan four to see active service, Wyndham Lewis enlisted as soon as he got healthy and—just in case had secured some kind of literary legacy with a completed first novel. As he toiled at his typewriter, the war's first five months claimed one third of a million French lives.

Painting of Ezra Pound by Wyndham Lewis.

* * * * *

Lewis enlisted as a British artillery officer largely because of his family's tradition of war-service established by two of his paternal uncles and his American father, Charles Edward Lewis, who boasted in print of a dashing career in the American Civil War.

Despite quitting West Point due to deteriorating eyesight, the elder Lewis enlisted promptly as a Union private when war erupted and was immediately promoted.

As a cavalry officer at the second battle of Manassas in 1862, he led a 15-man charge to capture an unoccupied enemy earthwork, and then, without orders, galloped to attack a second, during which he suffered a gunshot wound to his left groin.

Following a long convalescence, Lewis returned to active duty only to be captured in the Battle of the Wilderness in May,1864. Following a protracted and peril-filled escape after six months of confinement in several Confederate prisons, he reached the safety of Union lines. Upon leaving the army, Lewis received a Brevet promotion to Captain signed by Abraham Lincoln. He was now an official war hero.

By this time also his groin injury had apparently healed, for Lewis was treated for primary syphilis in April,1865.

Next, he became a traveling salesman for a brother's wine business in Montreal but soon quit in favor of the gentlemanly pursuits of memoir writing, horse breeding, and traveling between America, Canada and England, where the 33-year-old, mutton-chopped war veteran found a bride:16-year-old Anne Prickett, plucked from her mother's London boarding house.

Their first-born died within hours of its birth; their second, a boy, born in Nova Scotia in 1882, was named after a flamboyant mercenary soldier, Percy Wyndham, who Lewis had met after this man's arrival from Europe to serve as a Union colonel. (Our infant modernist came to despise his first name as effeminate, apparently never learning of its swashbuckling origins.)

Anne and the infant Percy lived alone for extended periods while Lewis travelled, ostensibly to sell wine, and her letters during this period speak of loneliness, fear for her infant's health, and financial distress. Then came a horrific discovery: her husband had set up a completely separate household with another woman.

Our initial couple argued, separated, and split permanently when Anne refused Lewis' demand for a divorce. Charles responded by bigamously remarrying at least once and fathering at least two more children.

As Anne's child support shriveled, she turned to another of Charles' successful-in-business brothers, George, a coal-mine owner and operator, whom Charles had sponged off of for years. George graciously came to Anne's rescue only to die suddenly. Thereafter Anne started a barely profitable laundry business and lived day-to-day as a single mother taking in other people's wash.

Young Wyndham proved to be a lackluster and troublesome student, but once his considerable artistic and intellectual gifts became apparent, Anne—who had artistic skills herself—sent him to the prestigious and expensive Slade School of Fine Art in London, where teachers recognized and rewarded his talent before expelling him for insubordination and truancy. After "graduation," Lewis left England to languish in Europe's most infamous bohemian hot spots without a degree, realistic plans, or any marketable skills. As a burgeoning artist, he felt free to write home incessantly to ask for money. Somehow Anne always provided.

But ultimately it was not money but a towering self-confidence that proved to be Anne's greatest gift to her son, the result of years of unceasing devotion, sacrifice, and a sustaining, lifelong intimacy. As Freud taught us, "A man who has been the indisputable favorite of his mother keeps for life the feeling of a conqueror."

But when his hopes for a relationship with his flamboyant but absent father died, Lewis came to resent "the old rip," seeing him as an occasional source of funds but mostly as a morose and solitary recluse who became "eccentric almost to the point of madness."

To sell himself to the world as a self-created genius and leader, Lewis repurposed his early family strife to forge an adult self that was an idealized projection of both his talented parents.

But Lewis could never shake his father's psychic imprint, mimicking his reckless bravado and—in a perverse gesture of one-upmanship—surpassing him as an abuser of women. Underpinning all this was his mother's legacy, which forged a rock-solid emotional core that gave Lewis his energy, confidence and unrelenting drive.

So imagine his anguish upon returning home intact from the western front only to watch helplessly as the Spanish influenza—killer of millions in the war's aftermath—extinguished his one true life partner: Anne Lewis. Her son always blamed the war for her death. Afterwards he tried, sort of, to remake himself.

After fathering but not supporting four (five?) children with two live-in mistresses and one deceived girlfriend, Lewis set up a household following his mother's death with a woman 18 years his junior who eventually became his wife and survived him to promote his posthumous reputation. She was as loyal and totally devoted as his mother had been. Her birth- and marriage-certificate name was Gladys Hoskins, but for him she gave herself a new middle name that her husband was to use daily: Anne.

* * * * *

Lewis' fiction-writing career began not with the murky Shakespeare-inspired sonnets he wrote in art school, where he was known as "the poet," but with the short stories spontaneously produced during the first of several painting excursions.

Starting in 1907, Lewis travelled to the peasant worlds of Spain and Brittany, which was a peninsula-shaped French province on the Atlantic, where Gaugin and Monet had painted in the 1880s, as did Picasso in the 1920s. Two world wars destroyed European peasant culture utterly, but it flourished during Lewis' youth, and it transformed his creative life, just as Tahiti's native culture did for Gaugin. (Experiencing a similar transformation was Lewis' literary contemporary, playwright John Synge, who floundered aimlessly in Paris before discovering the peasant folklore and antiquities of the western islands of his native Ireland, and, thus inspired, wrote *The Playboy of the Western World* and other world-famous dramas.)

"What I started to do in Brittany I have been developing ever since," said Lewis in his memoirs. He continues:

> I was painting a blind [Breton] beggar. The "short story" was the crystallization *of what I had to keep out of my consciousness while painting.* Otherwise the painting would have been a bad painting. A lot of discarded matter began collecting in the back . . . of my consciousness. As I squeezed out everything that smacked of literature from my vision of the beggar, it collected in the back of my mind. It imposed itself upon me as a complimentary creation . . . .
>
> The characters I chose to create . . . were all primitive creatures, immersed in life, as such as birds, or big, obsessed, sun-drunk insects.

No amount of Rousseauist, noble-savage nonsense could explain these Breton and Spanish peasants, whose energies and various states of psychological turbulence proved to be identical with those of the "peasants" Lewis found in Paris' many outdoor cafes. Nor were these primitives fundamentally different from the average Englishman who—fresh from a brutal Darwinian downgrade in Victorian times—now toiled for substandard wages in a newly mechanized London that was rapidly shedding its horse-and-buggy past.

Each titan-four modernist embraced some vision of the primitive; for Lewis the painter, this crystallized into what he came to call "The Tyro," a kind of primordial human archetype. Eventually Lewis created an art journal of that same name, as well as a series of Tyro paintings. These paintings, including two self-portraits, featured gangly and massive beast-like humans who smile with teeth that resemble piano keys and bubble over with primal energies. In Freudian terms, a Tyro is an Id-and-Ego creature who lacks a Superego.

This primitivism was also the inspiration for the anti-humanistic characters that populate much of Lewis' fictional world: puppets, bobbins, squeak-dolls, and shells. Shocked readers and critics who view this vision as some kind of moral defect—F.R. Leavis, for example, dismissed Lewis as both "brutal and boring"—fail to grasp, first of all, that all his writing was informed by a fully internalized grasp of world literature.

Lewis' depiction of his Breton peasants is of a piece with the humors-theory dramas of Ben Jonson, the ruling-passion characterizations of poet Alexander Pope, the picaresque novels of Tobias Smollett, and the hobby-horsical, satirical-psychological comedy of novelist Laurence Sterne.

Secondly, these primitives were the means by which Lewis measured his own contemporary scene. Although they may lack the detached self-consciousness of urbanites, his primitives are not offered as pastoral alternatives to bourgeoise alienation; in fact, they depict a more stark and closer-to-the bone example of it.

And finally and most importantly, Lewis instinctively grasped how his Breton peasants were the perfect lens through which to depict the new primitivism descending upon a post-war Europe. Besides killing *10 million*, The Great War produced 20 million wounded. These physically and mentally shattered veterans, who were inundating Europe's street corners, alleyways, parks, and transport stations, became the models for Lewis' many limbless and mind-warped fictional characters. A shattered human body is frightening to behold, as is mental illness, especially when both are palpable daily presences.

In addition, these same post-war reverberations shook Lewis personally, leaving him distressed and obsessed—especially by a new post-war media world of print, radio and film that served as a conduit for new political ideologies that both complicated artistic creation and amplified economic and social strife.

To address this new post-war world, Lewis ambitiously repurposed himself in the 1920s as a political theorist and philosopher with *The Art of Being Ruled* (1926), and *Time and Western Man* (1927). He also tried, unsuccessfully, to launch a modernist painting movement in England.

Next he created a new literary genre—later called theological science fiction by renowned Post-modernist and Marxist literary critic Frederic Jameson—with *The Childermass* (1928). The first of what eventually became a trilogy, this novel featured two English casualties of The Great War who posthumously navigate a Dantesque, purgatorial afterlife while awaiting admission into something called The Magnetic City, a sort of Gnostic New Jerusalem.

Jameson praised himself for overlooking Lewis' alleged "deep misogyny and violent anti-communism" to trumpet Lewis' "explosive and window-breaking" sentence production and visionary power.

Whatever their value, Lewis' immersion in these demanding works removed him from literature's world stage at the very moment in 1922 when Eliot and Joyce broke into the Western cultural mainstream with *The Wasteland* and *Ulysses*.

Lewis' friends, moreover, were left wondering why he had abandoned what he was good at. Lewis defensively proclaimed his non-fiction to be cultural criticism, something designed to create a cultural space for all artists, and his novels to be a kind of Gnostic dream vision. But his many detractors thought otherwise, including Pound, who dismissed Lewis' entire post-war transformation as futile, especially since Lewis in *Time and Western Man* had harshly criticized both Pound ("a revolutionary simpleton") and Joyce's *Ulysses* ("a record diarrhea"). Thundered Mr. Make-It-New: (1) leave these tedious political and philosophical tomes to the academics, (2) stop hassling your (now ex-) friends, (3) and start producing some fresh art.

Lewis responded with his famous buzz-off letter, demanding that Pound stop directing his artistic life. Joyce, meanwhile, blindsided by the personal attack, later struck back in *Finnegans Wake* and never forgave, while Pound, who shared Lewis' commitment to cultural renewal, shrugged off the assault. Also, Pound was later reassured somewhat when Lewis turned his pre-*Blast* peasant pieces into a full-on Modernist short-story sequence, one that remains largely unknown to this day and is almost never represented in short-story anthologies: *The Wild Body* (1927).

* * * * *

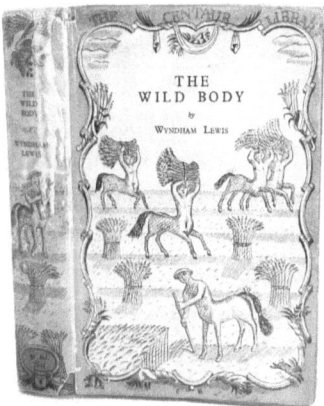

The Wild Body begins with a first-person narrator who jumps out at us from the opening story, "A Soldier of Humor." He is to be our host and impresario on an unsettling, anthropological peasant journey through Spain and Brittany. Boasting the strange, double-barreled name of Kell-Orr (Teller of Stories), our narrator presents himself in radically Cartesian and third-person terms as a new archetypal kind of human, a Tyro, which is a skin sack (i.e., a "wild body") containing a jumble of scattered psychic impulses.

> I have large strong teeth which I gnash and flash when I laugh . . . . I know much more about myself than people generally do. For instance I am aware that I am a barbarian… My body is large, white and savage. But all the fierceness has become transformed into laughter . . . . This forked, strange-scented, blond-skinned gut-bag, with its two bright rolling marbles with which it sees, bull's-eyes full of mockery and madness, is my stalking horse. I sit somewhere in its midst, operating it with detachment.

Kell-Orr is on a mission as a "soldier of humor" to catalog the absurdities of this human menagerie in order to create and promote a philosophy of Neitzschean laughter. He seeks to "overcome" this primordial world by co-opting for himself the natural forces that successful wild bodies apparently have harnessed, and by distancing himself from those that struggle.

"Everywhere where formerly I would fly at throats, I now howl with laughter," he says. "That is me.... I am never serious about anything."

Kell-Orr also intrudes upon the actions he records, sometimes installing himself in the midst of the mayhem to more effectively gauge the psychic toll. Glib and overbearing, our narrator laughs when "his" characters double-down on their psychological obsessions in a vain attempt to maintain predictable lives. This very strategy, however, proves to be Kell-Orr's own obsession: he attempts to mimic the Demiurge, this world's creator, with a will-to-power strategy that he believes will exempt him from suffering.

Other *Wild Body* characters suffer similar delusions: Valdimore, in "A Solider of Humor" believes himself to be American despite being native to France; Ludo, the blind beggar in "The Death of Ankou," believes himself to be hounded by a primitive death god; and Cornac and his wife, leaders of a troupe of itinerant acrobats in a story of that same name, find themselves trapped in their perpetual loathing of their own unruly audiences.

The most vivid character in the collection, however, is the innkeeper Bestre, a premier Tyro and a true grotesque, who, in his own eponymous story, discovers how to revenge himself upon the bourgeoise types who descend upon Brittany by the trainload to gawk at the locals. Perpetually irritated, Bestre, responds by glaring back at them through the windows of their rented villas. Kell-Orr describes how the Bestre glare could create a shocking contrast to the typical countryside view:

> ... his brown arms were for the moment genitals, snakes in one massive twist beneath his mamillary slabs, gently riding on a pancreatic swell, each hair on his oil-bearing skin contributing its message of porcine affront.

With these Tyro stories from *The Wild Body*, in short, Lewis announced to the world his updated version of the shock of the new. For Lewis fans and lovers of late modernism, this depiction of human motivation and creativity is cutting edge stuff, but how, exactly, was the average reader to respond?

Imagine the plight of an English reader of that day, who, accustomed to Virginia Woolf, suddenly confronts a Lewisian inferno that incinerates all values and grand narratives—including the stock modernist trope of finding a nugget of authenticity within the human psyche. (Lewis says there is no "within.")

To make matters worse, these stories seem to wage war on the short story form itself, a revered and popular tradition inherited from the 19th Century French and Russian masters. Lyrical like poems and defined by mood rather than plot, this tradition offers readers a portrayal of the submerged lives of characters as they navigate the pains of personal growth and muffled tragedy.

Other short-fiction modernists flourished in this mode—Joyce, Hemingway, Mansfield, Woolf, and Lawrence—so why not Lewis? Because this entire sense of character—a mere pastiche of Romantic sentiments, really— is yet another casualty of The Great War to be flung aside with a bark of delight.

Lewis therefore replaces all such inner blossoms with inflamed rhetoric, callously portrayed characters, mansplaining narrators, a fizzed-up sense difference or otherness, plot-based storytelling, and, most difficult of all, an outside-in, hard-shelled narrative that deflects our moral involvement as readers. My stories, Lewis seems to say, should all be warning-stamped: no epiphanies allowed.

So here, at last, we arrive at Lewis' formula for a new classicism: swap out 19th Century "narcissism" for traditional storytelling, such as that found in the epic literature of antiquity, Greek myth and tragedy, medieval allegory, the Bible, fairy tales, much of English renaissance drama, and, in our time, pop-culture forms, such as westerns, romance novels and science fiction.

Rooted in the ancient world, this brand of parable-like storytelling does not create order out of chaos, it challenges order with chaos, placing under siege all human social and psychological structures. Traditional story, in other words, features characters stunned into senselessness by the overwhelming demands of an Absolute that is completely Other; or, stated more simply, in narrative terms, these stories are finished before they start.

Readers in this genre do not bother to ask why Yahweh subjected Job to such terrible trials, or why Snow White's stepmother was so evil, or why the Greek gods inflicted such a ghastly fate upon Oedipus. Nor do they bother hoping that Romeo and Juliet or Bonnie and Clyde—same difference—can somehow escape their doom.

Readers would be mistaken, however, to interpret Lewis' use of traditional narrative in *The Wild Body* as a gesture of despair; rather it becomes the staging platform for a shaman-like reboot of the creative mind.

Bestre's glare, for example, is the glare of a painter apprehending the living model before him; his face, framed by a customer's window, is exactly that of the artist's picture in its final frame. The rude adolescent who bursts into jeering laughter when itinerant acrobats clash with their unruly customers turns out to be a "poet" who has just experienced "an unaccountable awakening." And after outwitting a Frenchman who believes himself to be an American, Kell-Orr "roll[s] about on his pillow... howling like an exultant wolf" to celebrate his success as a satirist.

In short, these timeless breakout moments resemble a Buddhist awakening or a road-to-Damascus zap.

Says Lewis scholar Paul Edwards:

> By re-presenting and projecting our world into a new, quasi-platonic model, the artist reveals the potential inherent in our actual world. His imagination projects into a larger air: a realm of imagined possibility rather than one whose perfection mocks man's enterprise.

Standard human consciousness, in other words, consists of a made-up narrative past, a gauzy projection called the future, and—thank the gods, Art—plus, of course, all the prescribed routines, both ideological and psychological, of regular, daily life.

Zen practitioners call this Everyday Mind; Lewis' plural term is traditionally theological: Inferior Religions.

In *The Wild Body*, therefore, our former artillery officer provides the perfect tool for blasting away all Inferior Religions—satire—which, in turn, clears the pathway to that spark of divinity which is our sole paradigm for human exploration: the artistic self.

* * * * *

Lewis' remaining years as an artist, were, alas, both troubled and anti-climactic.

The low and dishonest 1930s saw his literary reputation damaged by poverty, feuds, an ill-considered book on Hitler, and serious medical problems, including four abdominal surgeries and a pituitary-gland brain tumor that ultimately took his eyesight.

Furthermore, Lewis confronted in 1939 his deepest and most debilitating fear: a second world war.

Something broke in Lewis when he grasped this inevitability while composing his Spanish civil war novel, *Revenge for Love* (1937), his most accessible and popular work. His characters were still puppets, but Lewis now gave them a tragic dignity and an inner life as well.

Following that second war, Lewis finalized *Self-Condemned* (1954), a novel about a shell named Rene Harding, an egotistical academic who, for reasons of "integrity," abandons his prestigious Oxbridge post for Canada, where he degenerates into a morose and solitary recluse, eccentric almost to the point of madness. Harding's subjugated wife then commits suicide Anna-Karenina style by throwing herself before a train. Earlier in the novel, Harding's mother had asked him, "You are not by any chance a fool, my son?"

Eliot called it "a book of almost unbearable spiritual agony." Pound thought it deserved The Nobel Prize.

Lewis went totally blind in 1951 and thus retired as a painter and an art critic but still finished his theo-sci-fi trilogy and *Self-Condemned*. To compose these, he painstakingly employed a ruler to orient his large and loopy long-hand sentences before dropping his pages to the carpet for Anna to type up.

Before he died in 1957 Lewis received an honorary literature degree, got his trilogy adapted for BBC radio, and even had a send-off art exhibit. In his final years, Lewis also inspired the development of Marshall McLuhan, a fellow Catholic Canadian literary scholar and emerging cultural critic.

McLuhan's famous slogan, the medium is the message, the first post-modernist concept to go mainstream, resulted directly from Lewis' influence. A young McLuhan protege, Hugh Kenner, took notice. Eliot remained close in those final years as well. After Lewis' death, he continued to support his former friend generously, both financially and editorially.

Certainly, Lewis chose a very difficult life. He could have crafted a career of international renown, and paraded about—as he once quipped about Eliot—"disguised as Westminster Abby;" should have focused more effectively on his major art and literary works instead of cranking out 50 books and 360 essays to keep the wolf from the door; and, of course, should have made a decent effort as a husband and father.

But Lewis, always a member of the devil's party, did none of these things. He never abandoned his commitment to the avant-garde, never converted to Catholicism, and always fought ferociously for the art he championed no matter the cost.

"What's the use of being an island," he once asked, "if you're not a *volcanic* island." ∎

GROVE KOGER

Becoming a Whole Man: Re-reading Richard McKenna's The Sand Pebbles

The opening sentence is both simple and masterful: "'Hello, ship,' Jake Holman said under his breath."

The ship is the USS *San Pablo*, the novel is *The Sand Pebbles*, and its author is Richard McKenna, who was born in Mountain Home, Idaho, in 1913. His only substantial work published in his lifetime, *The Sand Pebbles* was serialized in the *Saturday Evening Post*, won the 1963 Harper Novel Prize, and was made into a film in 1966 with Steve McQueen.

Some six decades later, the movie remains relatively well-known, but the man and, I suspect, the novel—and, I'm quite sure, the strange situation that the novel deals with—have faded from memory.

You can pick up the basics about McKenna and his novel online, but thanks to Dennis L. Noble, whose study *The Sailor's Homer* was published by the Naval Institute Press in 2015, we know quite a bit more. Subtitled, a bit too helpfully, *The Life and Times of Richard McKenna, Author of The Sand Pebbles*, it's the only full-length work devoted to the writer.

As Noble makes clear, the future novelist endured a hardscrabble youth in the little Idaho community of Mountain Home, particularly after his father deserted the family in 1927. However, McKenna persevered, discovering the local public library and the wealth of information and excitement it offered. By the time he graduated in 1930, he had worked on the school's newspaper and its yearbook, and had received honors in Spanish, English, and debate.

McKenna's achievements won him a year's scholarship at the College of Idaho in Caldwell, but he was unable to pay the $50 necessary for the following year.

Richard McKenna, 1913-1964.

However, he doesn't seem to have regretted the loss of what might have been a well-paid professional career. As he wrote much later, "The problem was much more starkly elemental. How to escape the iron pinch of enforced idleness and poverty and the terrible sense of personal unworth they generated."

The year was 1931, the country was in the grip of the Great Depression, choices were few, and so McKenna did what many young men did in those years: he enlisted. He signed his papers in Boise, was sent to the Naval Recruiting Station in Salt Lake City, Utah, and after a period of apparently unrewarding service, was assigned to the USS *Gold Star* in 1933.

The *Gold Star* was classified as a general auxiliary ship, and it was aboard it that McKenna acquired the rating of machinist's mate. What's more, the assignment introduced him to the cultures of the northwestern Pacific and the Far East: the island of Guam, the Philippines, Japan, and coastal China. Always curious, McKenna found the places fascinating, and the experiences changed his life forever. Noble calls the young man's years aboard the ship "seminal," adding that while on board, McKenna "developed a great love of machinery and of people who shared his respect for machinery, and he honed his skills as an enlisted man in the engineering force." McKenna was also addicted to reading, and remembered that the Cavite Navy Yard in the Philippines, for instance, had (in Noble's words) the "best library for sailors he ever saw in the Far East." He especially enjoyed the geckoes that nested among the library's unread books, "running around the ceiling eating flies and mosquitoes and making musical chirps."

Considering the possibilities open to him in 1937, McKenna reenlisted—with the request that he be assigned to what was known as the China Station. It was a choice that led him to serving on two American gunboats on the Yangtze River, the USS *Tulsa* and the USS *Asheville*. The period gave him, in Noble's formulation, a chance to see "the best slice of old China," and provided him the material for *The Sand Pebbles*. McKenna himself wrote that such ships "became distinctly different culturally from 'stateside ships.'" Afterward, he remained in the Navy, serving during World War II and the Korean War, and retired—"swallowed the anchor," his fellow sailors called it— in 1953, in what was apparently a dishearteningly perfunctory sendoff.

"Looking back, I can see that I was in a very unstable, neurotic condition when I left the Navy," McKenna later wrote. Following the advice of an officer he had befriended, he enrolled at the University of North Carolina at Chapel Hill, majoring in English but tackling several other subjects, including science. (He wanted to write science fiction and eventually published several excellent stories in the genre.) McKenna graduated *summa cum laude* and made Phi Beta Kappa, but rather than entering graduate school, he chose a literary path—a decision that led in time to *The Sand Pebbles*. Along the way, he also made the acquaintance of librarian Eva Mae Grice, and the two married in 1956.

But to get back to the China Station: I can't help stressing that we're talking about *American* gunboats deep in the interior of *China*. It's a strikingly strange situation—the reality, which McKenna experienced, as well as the fictional depiction, which he placed a decade earlier. At one point in the novel, a teacher at the China Light Mission, Shirley Eckert, remarks to Holman, "Think of a Japanese gunboat at St. Louis, in defiance of our wishes." But the real comparison these days, of course, would be a *Chinese* gunboat at St. Louis. In case you wonder why China seems to resent Western Europe and the United States so much, *The Sand Pebbles* provides a clear reason.

Wisely enough, McKenna doesn't go out of his way to provide the historical background to the period in which *The Sand Pebbles* is set, but I think one is necessary for today's readers. Basically, the decades of the late nineteenth and early twentieth centuries were those of the "unequal treaties," legal agreements that had been forced upon a fragmented and weakened China by the United States, Russia, Japan, and several European countries, including the United Kingdom. The treaties and the onerous trading concessions that they legalized, along with the stationing of foreign army and navy forces in China, contributed to the rise of Chinese nationalism during the 1920s and ultimately the triumph of the Chinese Communist Party.

McKenna apparently had little trouble recreating the period in which *The Sand Pebbles* is set. "It was not too hard for me to recreate those times from a Naval viewpoint," he wrote later. "I had only to extrapolate the attitudes and behavior of the men I knew a few years backward into a scene which had not changed much physically." McKenna's fictional gunboat, the USS *San Pablo* (or *Sand Pebble*, as everyone calls it) is an aging vessel captured in the Philippines during the Spanish-American War of 1898 and put to work on the shallow, southern tributaries of the Yangtze. Chinese workers have insinuated themselves into the ship's workings and everyday life, running the engine, shaving the men (the "Sand Pebbles"), washing their laundry, and cooking their food. And of course they manage to extract payment for every task. The sailors themselves have gotten lazy and resent any move that might rock their boat.

Jake Holman, whom we met in the novel's first line, is a Motor Machinist Mate First Class, a man in love with machinery but on poor terms with his fellow sailors. It's the latter situation that has forced him from one ship to another, and presumably his period of service aboard the *San Pablo* will also be short. But Holman comes to realize that his attitudes have held him back: "He had long known that his dislike of military crap was like a private disease, which no one else could understand. Other guys hated it and said so, but it did not curdle the inside of their bones."

However, Holman learns how to deal with the recurring situation:

> An old help he had once used came back to him. They could command you what you had to do, he thought, but they could not command you how you had to feel about it, although they tried. So you did things their way and you felt about them your own way, and you did not let them know how you felt. That way you kept the two things separate and you could stand it.

The Sand Pebbles dramatizes, in plain and seemingly artless prose, Holman's uncertain steps toward wholeness. He eventually becomes a valued member of the crew, carousing ashore with his fellow crewmen and learning to appreciate them. He succeeds in teaching one of the more perceptive Chinese workers how the gunboat's engines work. He sympathizes with another crewman who has fallen in love with a Chinese woman he hopes (in vain) to marry and finds *himself* falling in love with the teacher and fantasizing about living at the Mission.

McKenna shows how individuals can cohere into something more than themselves—and how they can lose that coherence. With equal care but a bit less clarity, he describes how Holman manages to repair a persistent but complicated malfunction in the aging ship's drive shaft. Groups and machines, it seems, have much in common: In order to function properly, the parts must work together.

Complications arise when Holman, beset with emotions he scarcely understands, actually decides to desert. He seeks the help of "Banger" Knox, a sailor from a British ship. But once they're ashore, the two see a pig lying on its back on a wheelbarrow in a market. In order to keep the pig under control, its owner has *threaded cords through its eyelids and tied them to the sides of the barrow.* "The pig was smart enough to know that if he moved he would tear off his eyelids. He did not move. His little red eyes hunted back and forth, back and forth." Holman is appalled, but urges Knox to move on: "Let it go. It's how they do it here." But Knox cuts the pig loose instead, and a melee ensues. The two men manage to get back to their ships, but repercussions of the act spread. Chinese agitators accuse Knox and Holman of murdering a farmer, Holman's fellow crew members turn against him, and the ship's captain threatens him with a court-martial. At the same time, larger forces are also at work: Chinese anger at the foreigners among them is growing throughout the country. The *San Pablo* itself is attacked, and the men and women at the China Light Mission are in danger.

McKenna had originally intended to give *The Sand Pebbles* a happy ending, but the literary agent who had taken him on, along with an editor at Harper & Brothers, talked him out of it. So, McKenna gave it a violent and distinctly downbeat one instead.

The Sand Pebbles was a critical and popular success, and McKenna began work on a semi-autobiographical novel set in Guam and Japan, *The Sons of Martha*. Before he could complete it, however, he died in his sleep at age 51 in November of 1964.

* * * * *

I can't resist adding one intriguing fact that Noble mentions in passing: Despite all his years of service in the Navy, McKenna never learned to swim. ∎

Near the Postcard Beautiful

Gino Sky

JOHN HOOPES

Re-reading Gino Sky's Near the Postcard Beautiful: *An Epistolary Appreciation*

Dear Gino: I've been thinking and talking to myself about your collection of stories *Near the Postcard Beautiful* [Floating Ink Books, 1993] until I'm feeling like I should be making that conversation to you. And though these thoughts are meant for you, I hope they may also be read by other old fans of yours or by readers who've not yet discovered you. Your stories take me back to a time and place of personal discovery and eruptive cultural change.

I don't know if I told you that I left Idaho early in 1964 in a snowstorm and arrived the next day in San Francisco's Union Square, where it was 72 degrees. I took off my shirt to lay out in the sun, basking in the hardly believable change of weather. Sixty years later I look back on that moment and realize what a perfect metaphor that climate disparity was for the whole cultural transformation that was occurring in America at that moment, which I had first sensed reading Jack Kerouac's *On the Road* a few years earlier, committing me, without a second thought, to that new Beat dynamic and which several years later influenced my getting to San Francisco. Even so, neither I nor anyone else realized that the greater part of that thunderous transformation was still to come, simmering to life right there in the sunshine of Union Square that February afternoon, completing the great cultural leap between that Beat world of the fifties and the emerging hippy revolution of the sixties.

Memories of reading Kerouac for the first time inevitably are part of that recollection, even as—perhaps not by coincidence—I've recently re-read your 16 stories in *Near the Postcard Beautiful*, and it dawns on me how you and Kerouac, using your own life stories to fuel your fiction, complement each other and make that accounting complete in a way I hadn't seen at the time we'd both lived it.

I will forever be grateful for what *On the Road* did for me in 1958, celebrating the unmasking and demolition of the rigid conventions of the fifties, which Kerouac often calls "the Doldrums," and, as memory serves, rightly so. Dean Moriarty (Neal Cassady) is a wrecking ball to all that, not just to those conventions, but to almost everything he chases down.

But when I tried reading that iconic book again 40 years later, the moods and attitudes of the characters, the glorification of Dean as an "angelic" idol, energized by alcohol and amphetamine, the macho misogyny, the frenzy just to be going to another Dean-centric kicks party, just didn't work for me. Though Dean Moriarity's passions are superhuman and his empathy penetrates everything and everyone to the core, all that he so voraciously absorbs lives and dies only within him. Any empathy rarely, if ever, arouses real compassion in Dean.

There is a refreshing difference in Kerouac's *The Dharma Bums*. The first necessary chaos and destruction of the fifties ethos in *Road* has settled into attempts at re-ordering the mess into something still hip but which also resembles reasonable, peaceful, compassionate life again, but without the rigidity and anemia of the fifties. There's only a brief, silent cameo by bad boy Neal Cassady. Kerouac's new hero in this novel is the very respectable Japhy Rhyder (Gary Snyder), anthropologist, sinologist, poet, mountain climber extraordinaire, a kind, compassionate man, an adept Buddhist who instructs Kerouac (humbly renamed Ray Smith) in the rudiments of Zen. There's no more mad, incessant chasing back and forth cross-country. Kerouac's story portrays a new, prophetic locus: the Bay Area, San Francisco. In his life at that time, Kerouac embraced this new order, though for him it's still murky. Kerouac's Ray Smith embraces Rhyder's life view and spiritual practices, but he often gets tongue-tied comprehending and explaining the vast, mysterious Zen Buddhism. He sees himself quickly become a bodhisattva, ever ready with his teaching.

In his real life at the time of publication (1958), Kerouac is an unrepentant drunk. He goes so far as to develop a doctrine he derives from a Buddhist story he's heard that makes drunkenness an accepted aspect of enlightenment. Nonetheless, Kerouac gave us shoulders to stand on for a better perspective on what complete liberation might look like. We were also lucky to be blessed with the cultural shock-transformative medicinal of lysergic acid.

I find it natural to compare your *Near the Postcard Beautiful* stories to Kerouac's novels *On the Road* and *The Dharma Bums*. From Kerouac's novels we derived our conception of the Beat vision, and how that evolved into the sixties revolution we lived through.

The best-known celebrations of the psychedelic revolution we experienced mostly focused on Ken Kesey and the Merry Pranksters. Tom Wolfe's *Electric Kool-Aid Acid Test*, for example, has, for me, no satisfying ending, and I don't believe it is true to the best of what that revolution produced. To locate, read, and experience an alternative, the seeker must go to your *Near the Postcard Beautiful* stories, written a couple decades after these earlier accounts, in order to see other possibilities inspired by these Beat and psychedelic experiences.

Of course, your *Postcard* stories about "you" and your character Drift (in the stories "The Lady" and "Ghost Seed") are a world apart from Sal Paradise and Dean Moriarity, as personalities and as consciousnesses. And it's not just you and Drift and your 1960s adventures in Haight-Ashbury that are so essential to your stories, but all the before-and-after that you record in your other *Postcard* stories about growing up as both witness and participant to all that led up to Haight and what came after.

To me, one of the finest moments in *Postcard* is the short, eloquent chapter "Primed to Go" [originally published in *The Limberlost Review,* 1984] in which you first sense the new, greater revolution about to thunder in. It should go down as one of your finest poems, disguised though it be as a prose story-sketch. I'll remind you of the opening lines: "It was in the early sixties. A fatness around the middle of boxer-shorts America was beginning to be stripped." This poem goes on like that for several pages. It is a swift, clear, lean voice from nowhere we've expected. Something new, vital, vibrant is on the way. Hold on to your seat.

My own memories of that time are still vivid, living on Ashbury Street, just off the bus from Pocatello, wide-eyed witnessing this sudden cultural revolution exploding all around me: Timothy Leary telling us all to "Turn on, tune in, drop out," hearing that clarion call, accepted and acted upon by virtually everyone there. And hearing a new music, old rock 'n' roll constants of boy-and-girl romance suddenly transformed into tremendously dynamic psychedelic anthems that further inflamed the almost universal excitement that I, the can-hardly-believe-what-I'm-seeing/hearing kid from Idaho, witnessed more and more every morning as I walked up and down Haight Street, astonished, agog.

My belief systems had been radically reoriented by *On the Road*. But my experience in the Haight was something else, something much bigger, more profound. What I saw conspicuously was that my Beat heroes, the poets, seemed enchanted by it too. When the God of the new music, Bob Dylan, came to town the *San Francisco Chronicle* printed photos of the Beat poets of North Beach hanging out with him, wrote daily articles of their time together. I idolized Dylan too and went to his concert at Masonic Auditorium one memorable December night in 1965. In the entire front row were seated all those same Beat poets. All of us had the cosmic good fortune to witness that night as a dramatic, dynamic moment that still ranks as one of the most memorable of my life. It was after an intermission that had terminated Dylan's solo, acoustic, folksong set, he came out with Robbie Robertson and The Band and they rocketed off with an all-electric "Tombstone Blues," electrifying the audience, causing an explosion of joy in the auditorium like none of us I'm sure had ever witnessed. At least half the audience shot up out of their seats, leaped into the aisles and began screaming their joy and—not exactly dancing—but letting their bodies spontaneously, wildly, whirl and gyrate, jumping up and down, expressing an ecstatic joy with more exuberance than seemed possible. I was stunned and speechless: the world had just turned upside down, the Earth's poles had reversed.

I bumped into one of those Beat poets two nights later, Michael McClure, whom I'd met recently, and he talked incessantly about Dylan, obviously in awe, said how Dylan had given him an autoharp and suggested he learn to accompany himself as he recited, and sing his poems, not just read them. He'd begun practicing that. That same month in a little club on Divisadero I'd gone to see a group called The Great Society, featuring Grace Slick (before she joined Jefferson Airplane). In between sets Allen Ginsberg and partner Peter Orlovsky circulated, greeting and shaking hands with almost every one of those young

JOHN HOOPES

people in the audience, many of whom I was sure had never heard of either poet. It became clear to me that what was going on here, and with McClure and the other Beat poets too, was not that the elders were giving their blessing and offering mentorship to the new, upstart generation, but that these elders were there to lay hands on that new lightning bolt of primal energy they could see was being generated through and into these jubilant newly-reborns, to absorb it, become empowered by it themselves, anxious not to be left behind.

For reasons I can't remember, Gino, I'd lost track of you around then. Only much later did you tell me how you'd moved into an apartment on Downey Street in the upper Haight, continued to publish your literary magazine *Wild Dog* (*Ghost Seed* in your stories) and how so many of those Beat poets were coming by your apartment, sucking up more of that vital new energy from you and "Drift," two of the newest revolution.

Comparing Kerouac's novels to your *Postcard* stories, I just see that you're showing something completely different—a new cultural leap—with a fresh, compassionate, and refreshing sense of humor, a respect and reverence for women that is also monumentally missing from Kerouac's Dean Moriarity, expanding way beyond old macho 1949 norms, something that I don't believe our Beat heroes considered. You also are often on the road, but this time it feels natural, organic, it always feels like you're running free, not driven by amphetamine and restlessness. There's purpose, that whatever you experience makes you bigger.

Your stories in *Near the Postcard Beautiful* about childhood, witnessing the dysfunctional marriage of your parents, is as grim and ugly as anything Kerouac or Neal Cassady had to live with. Your salvation, however, was a sister who in your story "The Dixie Sun" adored and protected you, and two glorious grandparents in stories like "Wine Man and Glue Boy," "The Kid," "Coyote Ugly," "Oliver Sudden" and the title story who deserve the appropriate hall of fame. We might recognize that your full-bodied depiction of them in this book is that hall of fame. These two are as independent and apparently contrary as any two people can be; but they are also deeply in love, fully tolerant of each other's eccentricities and criticisms. They are a perfectly matched, complimentary set of opposites, yin and yang, wholly deserving of all the love and admiration you have for both of them.

For me, your stories of your teenage years, especially the bits with your wonderful grandparents in southern Utah establish and illustrate the essence of who you are as a person, so that all the fun and adventure you have as a 1960s adult is a natural carryover from that and not a contrived personae. Your first hunting trip: at last you're one of the Real Man hunters, so you think, going out for your first kill, earning your first real stripe of manhood. Your rifle shot that kills a deer is efficient and easy; but staring into the eyes of the dying deer is something profoundly different. That shock and the and compassion it arouses instantly gives birth to a vow never to kill or harm another creature, demands a reverence for the mountains that is shelter for all these innocent creatures—a transformation that will permanently remove you from that macho culture and make you already a charter member of the psychedelic generation that will not awaken till years in the future, which you will announce when the time comes with your story "Primed to Go."

Much as I was delighted identifying with your activities in the sixties, I thought the best and most powerful pieces were the early stories, how and why you admired and learned from grandparents, sister and the rest of the family—the nonconforming and the conforming both; and it seemed like all of it tended to refine and encourage the fine sense of humor you were probably born with, which is one of your trademarks.

Then your post-Haight-Ashbury stories in *Postcard* reveal how "you" matured by all that sixties experience, coming to a true peace and spiritual accomplishment that I don't pick up in our Beat heroes in their maturities. Note the deaths of a groundless Neal Cassady (Dean Moriarity) and lonely, bitter Kerouac (Sal Paradise), both dead in their forties in 1968 and 1969 respectively by poisonous excesses. For me the sad irony here is that the transformative revolution Kerouac did so much to bring about for us did not actually succeed in transforming him.

Some of your stories are really classics—like your grandfather's quest in the title story for his Indian origins, bringing back that Shoshone story of the longest and most adventuresome penis on record.

JOHN HOOPES

I partic-ularly enjoyed your so-conservative grandmother's acceptance of his recounting and her whimsical commentary, and obvious love of and admiration for him, despite—even because of—his eccentricities.

Your stories about the 1950s testing of atomic bombs in the Nevada desert a hundred miles from your grandparents' house explore a theme mentioned briefly several times. They haunted me as I progressed through these stories. Then you make it the vivid dynamic that it truly is when in the story "Coyote Ugly" Grandpa at last takes you on a long hike to a mountaintop so you may witness that hell-inspired explosion all those hundred miles away. And yes, Grandpa hates it, verifying it's the ultimate coyote ugly. Had Grandpa been born two generations later he would probably be out on the streets demonstrating. But he can still do what is possible for him then on that mountaintop by dropping his pants and mooning the blasphemy as he dances his defiance. More inspirational behavior for you to grow with.

Another example of your separation from the macho male bias that, to me, seems like Kerouac's natural bent—nonchalantly accepting all that Dean's women put up with, for example—is your "Christmas Story." Aunt Eve is plagued with just such a womanizer husband, but her response is finally to lock him out and banish him for good, as all the family celebrates on Christmas Eve. You significantly call her "revolutionary" and rejoice in "her emancipation."

Your spiritual evolution feels honest. You declare your religious preferences: "I believe in them all." And you express it in action without a spiritual cliché when you isolate yourself in the Tetons for a ten-day fast. Day by day you observe your emotional ups and downs, doubts, fears and joys, and we come to understand what the spiritual essence of you has come to be after all these years and experiences, reflected and communicated during that fast without cant, swagger, glorification, or any conventional fifties expressions of religiosity. Here's a freed spirit.

A comic masterpiece in *Postcard* is your story "The DNA Poetry Fandango," so delicately understated that throughout I could hardly tell when I'm reading factual reporting or when I'd been seduced into believing a most preposterous of tall tales. I refrain from revealing too much detail here because this is a piece that readers should read to appreciate fully all the nuances of comedy that abound within it. The premise is that you have come to Salt Lake City to read your poetry at a festival. Not much of a drinker, you nonetheless desire to have a drink or two as part of the celebration. Though you're no longer a church-goer, your allegiance to your Mormon affiliation requires you to go to the Temple and the Church Ancestral Alcohol Control Board to get a permit to allow you to possess some definite amount of booze for this one occasion. You're interrogated at length by the Controller and both the questions and the answers are the source of all the fun. And it is great fun. The most significant beauty for me of this narrative is that the arch-conservative Controller is in perfect position to be the butt of endless jokes and sarcasms; your psychedelically evolved awareness makes you the perfect foil to deliver a hundred of these devastating responses and asides that he won't even see coming. By a miracle of storytelling, without losing an iota of potential comedy, none of that snide kind of commentary takes place. You always communicate to him with respect and compassion; it's to me remarkable restraint. And after I finished reading all your stories, I recall that same thing is true of all the characters you create—everybody gets to walk out of their scene with their dignity intact. Everybody. In any new, revolutionary-affirmed, compassionate world, who could ask for more than that?

To me, the most stunning, however, of the 16 stories in *Near the Postcard Beautiful*, is "The Round Church," as mystical, spiritual and profound as anything could be. A shamanic friend of the family, an Indian named Sundance, comes to heal Aunt Sarah, who has terminal cancer. Her doctors have no more solutions. That healing is narrated by a teenager (you?), who's so fascinated and underfoot that Sundance makes him his associate. Your recounting is deadly serious and clinically observant as I watch the medicine man perform a long series of intricate maneuvers and manipulations to drive the devil out of Aunt Sarah's body. New readers will be hypnotized by the magic and mystery of it. As far beyond the ordinary as possible, the ritual is haunting, scary even, and utterly convincing. And as I read along, how can I not believe dear Aunt Sarah will be healed? Sundance will be able after it's over to show the still squirming devil-tumor he's managed to explode out of her body.

All this shamanic magic was no doubt added to the catalog of spiritualities you'll believe in.

Most of the stories in the book are certainly autobiographical. But for all the book's collected "reminiscences" of childhood, you relate very little about your mother. What there is is mostly sympathy for how she suffered from your wandering father, and because of which you and sister Dixie were sent by Greyhound bus to spend your summers in the shelter, love and wise graciousness of your grandparents in southern Utah.

You end *Postcard* with one of your finest stories, "The Fruitcake," a story about you and your mother and a fitting conclusion to the book. In the story, you've come back from Stinson Beach after a long absence to see her in Pocatello, Idaho, for one reason: to document and sanctify her most special fruitcake recipe. Her fruitcake has been savored and celebrated for decades, but only she possesses the recipe, and only in her memory. By helping make the fruitcakes you record the recipe for posterity.

The story expresses so empathetically the often-tense relationship between you and your religiously conservative mother, and at the same time you render the aura of love that binds you two together so beautifully. She is 83 years old in the story, and there's an unspoken feeling this could be one of the last times you'll ever share with her. The story is fueled by the edgy repartee between the two of you while making the fruitcake, neither of you backing off an iota from the different belief systems you each have been insisting upon all your lives. As quick-witted as you both are, neither ever gets the advantage or the last word. It's like a tennis match between two all-stars. Yet at the same time you are there together, teasing each other in and out of those frictions, the humor continually building, however much you're trying not to show it. Your repartee as you two mix and cook is a delightful, pungent blend of sweet and sour, a deeply felt tribute to your mother, and at the same time, as you illustrate throughout your stories another affectionate homage to the female spirit.

No wonder when you read "The Fruitcake" at your mother's funeral just a few years ago that your wife Barb overheard someone ask, "Is it all right to laugh in a funeral?"

Near the Postcard Beautiful, as a record of the amazing cultural revolution we both lived through, is more satisfying for me than Kerouac. Thank you for all the fun you have telling your stories, delivering the sharp criticism and snappy wit that is always so true and, by the grace of the Cowboy Buddha, always gentle and compassionate. As much as I like your novels *Appaloosa Rising* and *Coyote Silk* and all your Cowboy Buddha Hotel mythos, *Postcard* is your book I like best. ■

Out of Sight *magazine editorial board meeting,*
San Francisco (1966), editor Gino Sky in a mask.

There are no maintained trails to this lake in the Sawtooth Mountains, just an off-trail scramble beside waterfalls lined with alpine flowers and white granite. Photograph by Glenn Oakley.

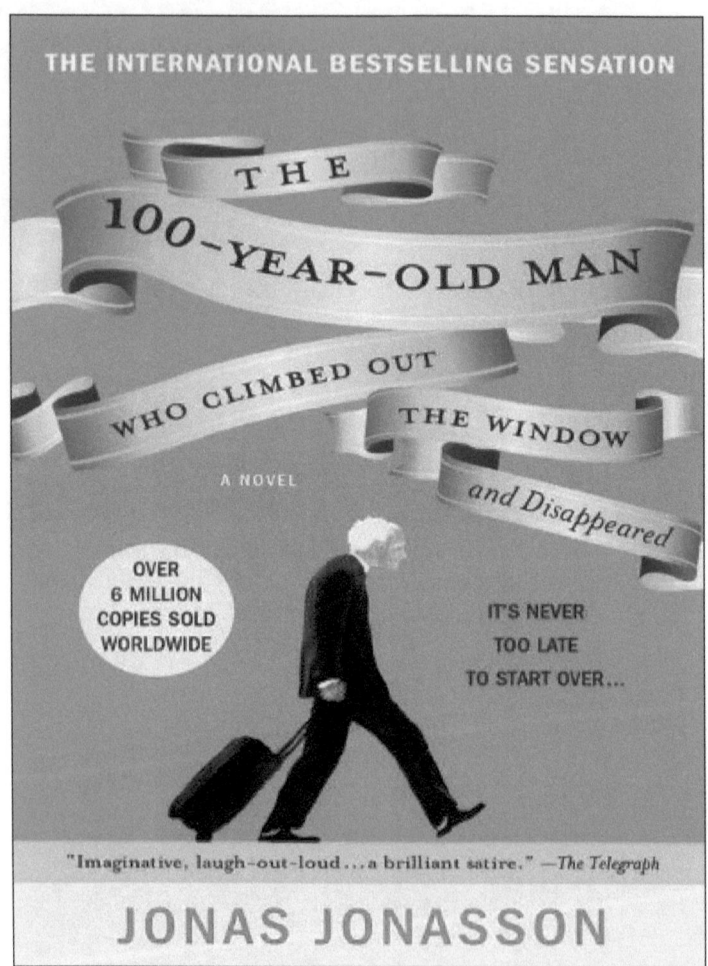

GARY SOTO

*Books as Drinking Buddies: Re-reading
Jonas Jonasson, Nick Hornby, Francois Boucher,
Amanda Gorman, T.S. Eliot, and then some*

I'm not a book reviewer but an "influencer," a word that recently parted the wiry hairs around my ears and entered my gray matter. I get it now: influencers are people who would like us to think how they think. Podcast is another word—you are expected to listen to people who are not in the room you're in, but faraway, like Idaho or Montana. Podcasts involve headsets and electronics, I think, and time zones, I also think. For this sort of activity, no license from the FCC is needed to talk stupid.

Jonas Jonasson's *The 100-Year-Old Man Who Climbed Out the Window and Disappeared*

Let me take up your time by highlighting a book that involves, in part, time—or the lack of it. The book is *The 100-Year-Old Man Who Climbed Out the Window and Disappeared* by Jonas Jonasson. May I influence you? May I take up some of your time?

First, the book doesn't need me. This 2012 bestseller was first published in Sweden and then, with cheerful clamor, traveled worldwide on hearsay. The book sold 11 million copies, which allowed the author to purchase a nice home on the island of Gollard, Sweden. I next happily report that the book has been translated into every major language. But hold your Christian horses, readers. Isn't every language a major language if you're speaking it?

This book features our eccentric hero Allan Karlson, who's in a state-run nursing home, a birthday boy who refuses a party among other residences befuddled by age. However, Karlson will not have any of it—stubborn, so stubborn, and sober to boot: the head nurse keeps confiscating his bottles of vodka. Without a proper drink, life is grim, nearly impossible, a pitiful existence. But he's wily and cagey, with a verifiable history of bravery we quickly learn. Because he's locked away in the nursing home, he masterminds an escape by slipping out a window, smashing a few precious flowers in the flower bed in the process. He looks about. Go left, go right? he wonders. He then gazes down at his feet: he's wearing a pair of "pee slippers." Like, what? Did you read that correctly? "Pee slippers?" It's true that men his age— or in their seventies and upward—can't pee farther than their slippers when they're standing at the bowl. In youth, most teens can pee the length of a football field—hyperbole here.

Forgive this influencer, as I'm not Hugh Kener or Harold Bloom or an assistant professor at an Ivy League university. The literary significance of pee slippers is small, so why bring it up? I'll drop it for good. I continue: Karlson is of sound mind and not done with life. True, he is a hundred on the day of his escape and putters about with a bent back. He's old, certifiably old. No washcloth has yet been patented that would erase wrinkles from his Nordic face. Yet, he's alive, not dead like his amigo, Henning Algotson, a friend in his adult years, a friend who made a career-changing decision by dying at age 39. Is his friend Algotson important in this escapade? Not really. But if you escape from a window of a nursing home, travel down a lane and, within a hundred yards, find yourself in a churchyard cemetery where your friend is buried, then, yes, maybe it is worthy of comment. Still, like the pee slippers, I'm done with Henning Algotson. Perhaps it's time for me to ramp up my critical thoughts about this 384-page novel.

It's totally good.

But is this a novel about aches and pains? Memory loss? Hair loss? The worm of an old man's sexual organ that was once the snake of desire? Not in the least. It's an adventure, which is established on page five when Karlson, already on the run, purchases a bus ticket that departs (he looks up at the station's clock) in three minutes, the exact amount of time it would have taken him to blow out a hundred candles on his cake back at the nursing home. And the reader will recognize the dramatic tension when a gangster (they got them in Sweden too) asks our hero to guard his roller-bag suitcase while he goes and takes a "dump," the author's word, not mine. Our hero blinks at the suitcase, blinks and considers the moment as *his* bus honks its horn for latecomers to giddy-up and get their asses on board. He rises from a bench, takes the roller-bag suitcase, and boards the bus, which pulls away from the curb before the gangster emerges from the john, zipping up.

GARY SOTO

Young Bad Guy with a suitcase, Young Bad Guy without a suitcase. Young Bad Guy, steaming mad, utters: "You're a dead man, you old bastard. Once I've found you."

This threat occurs on page nine, a threat that is justifiable. I mean, come on, what has the world come to when you can't trust an old geezer?

A few pages later Young Bad Guy kidnaps a bus driver and his bus and tracks down Karlson (in a rural town of no importance), where an hour earlier our hero, still trudging in his pee slippers, encountered a loner named Julius Jonasson. And how deep is this new character's loneliness? He hasn't spoken to a soul in several years, that is, until Karlson, in desperation, asks for help while shivering in the cold. It's near sunset, I believe, and surely in Sweden a man's nuts have a habit of crawling into his body for warmth. There's a remedy, though, when one is shivering from the cold. Vodka. Jonasson and Karlson become friends after a proper drink, then lifelong buds after six shots. This takes place in a yellow building, where Julius Jonsson bunks down with rats big as muskrats, rats that in my world live by chewing on insulation and electrical wires in the wall—a burnt rat is something to see at least once in your life.

But unbeknownst to them, Young Bad Guy locates Karlson, who unwisely maneuvered the roller-bag suitcase over gravel, leaving tracks to follow. Young Bad Guy giggles to himself; he's found the old bastard, the author's word, not mine. Young Bad Guy boldly enters the building while Karlson is taking a leak in a closet-like toilet just off the kitchen. Karlson stalls for a second when he hears a commotion. He zips up and returns to the kitchen, where he discovers Young Bad Guy twisting Julius's ears. Brave Karlson will not have any of that. He looks about for a suitable weapon. His choices: a crowbar, a wooden plank, insect spray or rat poison He decides on the plank. Raising it like a crucifix, he brings it down against the forehead of Young Bad Guy, who falls and clips his gourd on the edge of a kitchen table.

No blood, no visible wound. Do stars rotate inside his thick head? It's anyone's guess.

The unconscious villain is heaved like a sack of potatoes into the freezer, where elk meat is stored, possibly along with the antlers that huge Swedes use as toothpicks. He groggily wakes up a few minutes later and bangs on the door. Karlson and Jonasson wave off the human noise and the threats muffled by the freezer's noisy motor. They sit down to dessert, then more drinks, lots of drinks I imagine, because they forget about Young Bad Guy. The next morning, Jonsson opens the freezer to fetch a slab of bacon—oops, his bad. The young man, hugging himself, wears a coat of frost. He's dead as the bacon, dead as the elk.

In chapter four, titled "1905-1929," we glimpse the backstory of Karlson's life, which began on May 2, 1905, he is the son a radical woman who marched in May Day parades and hollered to the heavens for an eight-hour workday. His father, in turn, was open minded and believed, for instance, in contraceptives, and dutifully handed over to his wife his weekly wages as a railroad worker. The chapter provides lovely details and comforting moments. I should enlarge upon them, but as an influencer I recognize the attention span of my followers. So, let's return to the present—2005, the year of our narrative—and Julius Jonasson licking the spoon he had used for supper. He pries open the suitcase. Holy shit! A treasure! In its confines are bundles of 500-crown notes, to the tune of 37 million. Neither of the men whistle at that sum. Me, I would have sung like a bird!

Mucho dinero!

There's never a dull moment in the novel. You like elephants? They're there, as are Chairman Mao, President Truman, Stalin, Kim Il-sung, Einstein, Einstein's brother, landlocked dictators, a Russian Czar, mysterious lovelies, rivers that sweep away all guilt, a platoon or two of the French Foreign Legion, along with seemingly inflated tales that involve the Spanish Civil War and the Manhattan Project—all with our benign hero padding about in boots, clogs, dress shoes, loafers, and pee slippers. We love our man. He's an indestructible anti-hero worth rooting for, a clever type who went to war and came back from war. For one week, down with French novels! For two weeks, down with Chekov and Dostoevsky! Tonight, I might throw my chops into a plate of herring, with proper drinks of course. I'll eat by candlelight and, once finished, permit my kitten to lick my fingers. I'm a happy clam. And, finally, out of courtesy to Swedish men, I'm fully aware that you don't use elk antlers as toothpicks. But, *ay, chihuahua*, can you guys drink yourselves beautifully senseless.

GARY SOTO

Songbook *by Nick Hornby*

There's no rest for influencers. We recognize our duty to humanity. We're busy herding our followers toward viewpoints that will make them ponder life until the next paycheck. This brings me to Hornby's favorite bands and songs—songs hummed, I imagine, as he cobbled together this delightfully readable book. He confesses somewhere in the initial pages that he doesn't listen to either classical or jazz giants. I'm surprised at the exclusion by Hornby, the lauded British novelist, an Academy Award nominee for screenplays, a commercially successful writer with the freedom to call his own shots during the day. I shrug at his apparent indifference. I could listen for hours to "The Flower Duet" from *Lakmé* or Dave Brubeck, with a proper drink in my paw. Bach? I could sit still for twenty minutes. Pharaoh Sanders? Fifteen minutes of screeching sax should do it.

    I skim this book, with interest, with a glass of red, and scour the names of rock groups that I missed in my own musical upbringing. Let's see, what do we have here . . . there is a group called the Blockheads. Funny, I thought they were the twins that lived next door to us—the blockheads who did a little time in juvie, a longer time in a prison, and finally an even longer sentence in a cemetery outside of Fresno. But Hornby thinks highly of the group, and because I think highly of Hornby, I make a mental note to check out the Blockheads. What about a band called Suicide and their song called "Frankie Teardrop"? Hornby describes it as "ten-and-half minutes of genuinely terrifying industrial noise, a sort of aural equivalent of *Eraserhead*."

    Gee, that sounds like a danceable tune, if your partner was an inflatable doll. Spooky.

In the comfort of my living room, I scratch the top of my skull, where black hair once waved with genius, then flew away when, during a Sunday drive, I rolled down the window of my Buick Century. I scratch my dome, sip my wine, and blink at the water stain on the ceiling—now, what is that water stain telling me? Sometimes it looks like an elephant, other times like an early microwave oven—my mind, a gray mush, is wandering.

Think, Gary, I tell myself. Get a grip!

I scan the table of contents of this 2002 publication. I wince, I become confused. I don't know of any of this music. Who's Nelly Furtado, Mark Mulcahy, Royksopp, The Avalanches, Soulwax, The Bible, The Chemical Brothers, Ron Sexsmith, O. V. Wright, or Badly Drawn Boy? Patti Smith—oh, I know her. Here Hornby speaks to the almighty heavens about her ditty "Pissing in the River." This underpaid influencer wonders whether Smith waded into the river or let it roll down her slender legs as she stood on a sandy bank.

Music gives us pleasure, gives us an opportunity to be somewhere else and, perhaps, someone else. For a few minutes in 1975, I wanted to be Bruce Springsteen, a rocker with immense talent and bouncy stage presence. I also wanted to be Paul McCartney in 1965, and then, after a costume change, Little Richard, the King *and* Queen of Rock and Roll. After the night ended and the fans dispersed, I could return to my regular junior high status, a nobody.

In *Songbook,* Hornby praises the expected figures, like The Beatles, Rod Stewart, Arthea Franklin, and The Supremes, who all recorded catchy tunes. He's a spendthrift with his generosity—he likes lots of music. There are references to Sonny Boy Williamson, Jackson Browne, Smokey Robinson, the brother who did "Let's Get It On," Rufus Wainright,and durable Willie Nelson. There is a small moment when he cites a CD called *Reggae for Kids*. Got to start them young, kids grooving in a park, their faces stained with candy.

I'm an influencer, yet, like our readers, a human with heart, lungs, and a digestive tract. I raise my head toward the ceiling. I blink, I wipe my tired eyes, sigh at the meaning of it all. Jesus, the water stain now resembles a baby hippo. No, a robot that egghead teens in India might create as a classroom project during a wind-howling monsoon.

GARY SOTO

I consider my glass of wine and pour some more.

Van Morrison? He's the rocker of all geriatric rockers. Hornby says of *It's Too Late to Stop Now,* "the most enjoyable album, unarguably, so don't even think about arguing" and proposes that a song from the album could be used as the movie credits roll. Now that's high praise—got to locate Van Morrison's music on YouTube, play him loud, with hearing aids in, my equally deaf cat in my lap.

And I haven't listened to a lot of the groups and solo acts referenced in *Songbook*. Hornby sometimes becomes opinionated, even angry, when the public applauds the inane. He puts his foot down on the sordid 1980 punk rockers. Witty him, he invents a few names of these bands. He would never listen to rockers with names like Thuggy, Breakskull and PusShit. Girl singers with coiffured hairdos? No. And no to rockers with blood coming out their nostrils. Hornby likes what he likes. Joni Mitchell, for instance, he doesn't quite trust—or at least the album called *Blue*. Maybe it's a guy thing, maybe not. I admit that I never followed Mitchell's music.

I stopped my musical journey in the early about the time I could afford Santana's *Abraxas*—great album, the pride of Chicanos. What? Did you hear right? Yes, this influencer did not dip his toes in music beyond 1975. I followed some artists, like Fleetwood Mac, and in the 1980s was head-bobbing to George Clinton's "Atomic Dog," plus a song or two by mumbling Bob Dylan. And for a few seconds in the early 1980s, I had a major crush on Blondie—I just loved her teeth. Everyone one of her top-ten songs was dedicated to me.

But since my personality was starched into place by the late 1960s, I remained musically stuck in that period—or in the period that preceded the Beatles and Stones and Motown. Examples, please, and keep it short. OK, readers, I will keep it short. I name Nancy Sinatra in and out of go-go boots—and Bobbie Gentry with her false eyelashes in place. I loved the Ronettes, Harry Belafonte, Dusty Springfield, Lou Rawls, and hip-shaking Lulu singing "Shout!" The theme song to "Bonanza"? It's right up there.

But my favorite, the one song that did it to me—and about the time the blockhead neighborhood kids first bunked down in juvie. I gulp here, I bring my eyes back to the water stain on the ceiling. To me it resembles my cat's pawprints and has me puzzled. How in the world did our furry gentleman manage to walk on the ceiling?

OK, I'm stalling, but I'm ready to fess up. I, influencer to an audience in several western states, including Idaho and Montana, admit that my favorite song from the 1960s is "Sukiyaki" by Kyu Sakamoto.

A period of silence is due here. Go ahead and scratch your own depleted scalp, adjust your bra strap if you must. Get up and go to the fridge for another Pabst Blue Ribbon.

I repeat, "Sukiyaki" by Kyu Sakamoto.

More silence, with added eye blinking. Has the mush called my brain finally drained into my digestive tract? Should I hurry to the toilet?

Let me explain. "Sukiyaki," called "Ue o Muite Aruko" ("I Look Up When I Walk"), was a massive tsunami of a hit in Japan, with millions of red vinyl copies sold in 1961. The hit song next traveled to Australia and England, and finally in 1963 to the United States. It became a sensation in the Japanese American community in my hometown of Fresno, a song embraced because of its message—walk with your head up, though, if you know your nation's history, the Japanese Americans (along with the confused Peruvian Japanese who were arrested during World War II for no reason and ferried over to our country) were put into concentration camps—Roosevelt signed off on Executive Order 9066 and over 110,000 were rounded up. This song evoked pride. It deepened this group of hard-working and loyal citizens. For me, the song was mysterious and foreign, with a lilt of promise in Sakamoto's voice. It's a catchy melody—sung in Japanese—that encourages the people of Japan to keep their head up and believe in the future. Promoted by a disc jockey named

Sam Schwan, "Sukiyaki" played on our local radio station KYNO every hour in the summer of 1963. This was a favorite of my late father-in-law, Sadao Oda, WWII veteran of the 442, a Nisei cotton and grape farmer, sports fan to the hapless San Francisco Giants, carrier of a small transistor radio in his shirt pocket.

I didn't know Sadao Oda back then. I was across town, a city boy, and most likely in a neighbor's tree eating butt-faced plums that summer. But no matter the place, when "Sukiyaki" came on, say on the radio of a passing car, I grew very, very still and listened, as if it was calling me, a song that said in indecipherable language, "I'm over here, over here, Gary."

That would be my future wife, Carolyn Sadako Oda who, in the summer of 1963, was picking Thompson grapes. She was a true farm worker earning coins for school clothes for the fall.

Hornby's *Songbook* could be a boilerplate for your own musical reprise. Look in your attic, rummage your closets, and, if lucky, hug the record albums, cassettes and CDs of your teen years. I encourage you to travel back in time when you were first in love, then out of love, and back in love. Scribble your own list of favorites, sing them, mumble them, tap the beat on the arm rest of your La-Z-Boy recliner. At our age, we've got to keep the music going. Dead, we'll have nothing to sing about.

20,000 Years of Fashion (Expanded Edition) by Francois Boucher

This influencer was on night duty when I asked my wife of five decades, "Do you think I should join a think tank?" I sipped my beer, ran a tongue over the froth on my upper lip. I had in mind the Brookings Institute, the Council of Foreign Affairs, the Carnegie Endowment for International Peace, maybe the MacArthur people, possibly the Guggenheim people, organizations where male thinkers wore suits and leather shoes, their throats fashionably adorned with either English or Italian ties. The women thinkers? They would resemble Margaret Thatcher or Hillary Clinton in pantsuits. The fountain pens for both sexes, oh, let's see . . . gold-tipped Mont Blancs.

THE LIMBERLOST REVIEW

My wife was seated in a chair reupholstered by a Hungarian master, a centerpiece in our mid-century living room. In her lap was the hefty tome titled *20,000 Years of Fashion*. She turned a page, not bothering to respond to the noise that had come out of my mouth. I brought my St Pauli's Girl beer up like a chalice, flirted with the buxom lass on the label, glugged more of the brew, and peered down at my attire. I was dressed in mismatched pajamas. The slippers on my feet resembled dustmops. Sleep was not far off.

When I repeated my question, she still didn't bother to raise her head and look in my direction. Finally, at my third calling from across the living room, she sighed in frustration and directed her eyes at me—what? I had interrupted her revelry of fashions and textiles, the linen worn by the Twelve Tribes of Israel, jewelry cast by Babylonians, heavy cloaks from Armenia, Irish lace, Dutch clogs, Mexican beadwork, Scottish kilts, headdresses from Nigeria, the stone-ground dyes of Northern Africa, the early Roman sandal, stone age Switzerland's weavings, woolen textiles with broad and narrow stripes found in the salt mines in Austria . . .

I had destroyed her concentration. Still, her face brightened, like a flower, and she allowed herself to remember my question about think tank thingy. She blinked at me. Her smile became a chuckle that would have had known no end, except her phone rang. She jumped from the chair and left in a hurry. A girlfriend on the phone. She had no interest in my drunken ambition.

My status improved. I moved from the couch to the cushy chair that since its arrival she has claimed as her own. I lifted that massive book into my lap. I remembered the book. My wife and I had once looked at it in bed ages ago, when we were young and vital, a time when if I brought up a think tank thingy my wife would have been full of enthusiasm for my secret ambition to go beyond my calling as regional poet with an MFA. Ah, young love.

I opened the book and scanned the pages, beginning with sixteenth century Italy when Turkish turbans were all the rage, provided you had a monkey on a leash to accompany you from one glorious room to another. I thumbed through the pages until, like a time machine, I arrived at the beginning, when Adam wore a fig leaf to hide his six-incher. Here's how one of its zillion paragraphs sounds like:

> If one admits that clothing has to do with covering one's body, and costume with the choice of a particular of garment for a particular use, is it then permissible to deduce that clothing depends primarily on such physical conditions as climate and health, and on textile manufacture, whereas costume reflects social factors such as religious beliefs, magic, aesthetics, personal status, the wish to be distinguished from or to emulate one's fellow, and so on?

My first reaction to this long sentence? I was glad that there were pictures in this erudite study on costumes and fashion. To read block after block of such information would have made me search for a bottle of No-Doze in the medicine cabinet. Second, after another swig of beer, I scolded myself at my snickering appraisal. Boucher's intellect was on display and deserved patience if not respect—old dude, I hold myself, she worked on this book for years! I was secretly jealous of her. She had an appreciative soul for all things of beauty and could in one clear sentence explain herself. I sometimes write paragraphs, and no one can grasp what I'm talking about.

I understood Boucher's duty. She was going to start from the very beginning, that reference to a fig leaf that hid Adam's tool, for instance, and end with the 1980s couture fashions of Thierry Mugler. That's a lot of history here, history for the serious minded who know a thing or two about textiles and haute couture. To me, this is a book that was meant to be viewed, not read, like a picture gallery in which the art-goer leans toward the painting on the wall, looks and looks, and then goes to the next artwork on the wall. Boucher backs up the text with illustrations and photographs, maps and graphs, plus lots of explanations if you follow the text. This I learned: we humans never grow tired of adorning ourselves, making ourselves fresh, flirting with extremes, showing off, separating ourselves class-wise from one group or another, confusing the public by going beyond our biologically assigned gender roles. Early on we liked what clothes brought to the body: warmth *and* beauty. I imagine a caveman returning from the big hunt, a huge lion over his shoulder, and his wife greeting him, saying something like "Zakcruoff Kiihal Mo Mo Zow," which, roughly translated from a lost language from the Mongolian steppes, means, "Dear, what do you think of my new necklace?" The necklace would have been the teeth of a saber-tooth tiger.

There's much in this book to stitch into your memory: the Paleolithic period (600,000 to 160,000 BC), think nakedness and fur; the Mesolithic period (8000 to 3000 BC), think fur *and* animal hides; the Neolithic period, 3000 to 1000 BC), think animal hides and early weaving; Bronze age (2100 to 1000 BC), think early use of wool along with woven and decorated garments; the Iron age (1000 to 50 BC), think woven and very complicated garments, including the two-piece swimsuit worn by adolescent girls who dipped their toes into the Tigress River. And I noticed this right away: men and women dressed to the nines when making offerings to the Gods. They didn't dress sloppily, say in the jeans and sweatshirts of their time. The statuettes of the late Minoan period presented important figures in fabulous skirts and tunics. Religious festivals and galas in palaces—again, the costumes were elegant and obviously for the wealthy and those in position. And wait, I just read this! Around 1750 BC, men and woman wore loin cloths and then, almost overnight, the loin cloth for women stretched into skirts, very short skirts apparently, the flirty little things.

This is 20,000 thousand years of fashion and begins when Fred Flintstone roamed the earth. And did we learn from our ancestors? Doesn't appear so. Stand in front of a mirror, poets and writers, you too retired professors with shirt buttons in the wrong holes. Gads, you'll think in that momentary reflection, am I wearing my faded university sweatshirt? Is this the L.L Bean plaid shirt I bought in the 1990s, when I was married to my first wife? These Birkenstocks that belong in a landfill! This single-rock brooch from the county fair! This baseball cap hailing a team that hasn't won a ring since Jimmy Carter was in the oval office.

GARY SOTO

20,000 Years of Fashion is not a rarity in our house. We have three bookshelves dedicated to similar titles. My wife is a high-level clothes designer, with a limited customer base, namely me. After all, I must be prepared, well dressed, if, indeed, our landline rings and the voice on the other end is the executive director of an East Coast think tank.

Climbing the Hill by Amanda Gorman

Good grief.

Selected Poems by T. S. Eliot

A novelist once quipped after reading "The Waste Land," *Beautifully written but I don't believe a word of it.* This made me chuckle, the tide of G & T sloshing against my tumbler. I rattled the ice, peered into the drink, and then instructed myself to reread this poem that I hadn't considered in thirty years, a poem that begins with "April is the cruelest month" and ends with (no joke) "Datta. Dayadhvam. Damyata. / Shantih   Shantih   Shantih."

A late Estonian poet friend—best man in our wedding, in fact—spoke like that when he had one too many. He would drink heavily, usually in his backyard, sometimes in my backyard, and then lay on the grass. Face down, he would slur in Estonian lines that sounded like "Datta, Dayadhavam . . . rosebud, rosebud."

And Eliot's poetry, with the use of ancient languages to illustrate his smartness, reminded me of a caption in a movie whose title I don't recall. But the caption, delivered in a seriously mature tone, was "Truth is like poetry . . . and you know everyone hates poetry." That got the audience howling. After that, we just sat in the dark, unmoved by a so-so movie.

"The Waste Land" is no fun at all. Maybe the novelist has a point. And why is Eliot's anger directed at April? Because of tax season?

443

THE LIMBERLOST REVIEW

The pollen count from flowering fruit trees? Weeds muscling skyward in the cracks in the driveway? His pant legs wet from gray waves rolling onto the shore? I'm sure a professor in every state of our nation, including Puerto Rico and Guam, has an answer to my question. But this influencer doesn't know any of them.

On that day when I revisited "The Waste Land," I drank my drink and got another. I didn't find April cruel at all; after all, The San Francisco Giants were inching up in the standings. So, I sipped my refreshed G & T. I reflected, like a mirror. I was born in the glorious month of April, the 12th if my readers want to know—plug that date in your gray matter and remember I'm on friendly terms with Dom Pérignon Rosé P2. A case of that good stuff would make me happy. My street address is listed on the internet.

The next day this influencer got to work. I thought and thought, sober minded, with my cat twitching his whiskers at me. Does literature influence behavior? I asked myself. I would do a little research. For a day—just one day—I decided to become a full-fledged drag. Get grumpy! I hollered to my inner self, be like T.S. Eliot. If I shared a long face with the world, I might make an impression on it. The word on the street would then spread, and the word, once monolingual and suddenly polylingual, would reach universities and institutions, maybe the MacArthur people. Yes, the MacArthur Foundation! I could see it, a big truck backing up into my driveway to deliver $250,000 dollars in twenties. I liked that image. I could get the money and a certificate of honor, some declarative gibberish about my genius. I would glance at it for a few seconds and then store in my garage. To that end, I dressed in black and drank my morning coffee black. Black leather shoes and black knee-length wool coat. My eyeshadow? Black. I could chew Blackjack chewing gum. I also instructed the remaining black hairs on my scalp to do just that—think black. My cat, all black except for his white paws, led the way by prancing from the room.

I put joy aside and left my house full of self-pity, with a pouting face even. A secret only for the ears and eyes of small press readers: I'm a writer of regional importance, a dot among larger dots on the throat-cutting literary landscape. As such, I am occasionally considered for literary prizes, which have eluded me decade after decade. One major prize—won't mention it here because maybe it's still to come—was awarded to another Hispanic poet of slim literary talent but with an ego hefty as a wet burrito. He lives in Fresno, doesn't live in Fresno. He's sort of a slam poet, then he's not a slam poet. He's overweight, then so fricking overweight he can't fit in a car. He teaches and attends faculty meetings, and I don't have to.

I dressed nicely and went outside, admiring my recently bought handsewn moccasins from Yuketen. I forced myself to alter my mood and display my dark mind on the streets. A sad violin played a sonata in the heart of this influencer—no, I corrected myself, a whole orchestra of lament and sadness! I took my dark disposition onto the street, where I often come upon quirky subjects worth sharing with my wife, a clothes designer, and now with you, readers. A story for TikTok? If so, let me tell you that this story is not fiction but a truthful encounter.

I was walking near the Rose Garden in Berkeley when I heard a muffler pop from an old Volkswagen Bug. When I turned, I saw a ratty VW convertible Bug tooling up the street. I wasn't happy with that ugly noise. I wanted nothing to disturb my mood. I was busy in my self-pity, the color of ash, which had filled me with unhappy thoughts—why was that Hispanic poet chosen over me, I sniveled. But when the car slowed at the stop sign, I noticed a German Shepard in the passenger seat wearing a red kerchief around his neck, with his head tilted back and . . . eating an apple. Yes! A dog juggling an apple in his chops, a miraculous moment showcasing superb doggie talent. How he managed without his paws I'll never understand.

My heart leapt, the ash inside me blew away! I saw that the driver was munching on an apple as well. It was a Sunday, with a blue sky and a few clouds, and these buddies—man and man's best friend—were off on a carefree drive.

I turned my attention back to the German Shepherd. His eyes met mine, minds coming together on a public street. Then, when the driver started up again, the car chugged slightly, sending the apple tumbling from the dog's mouth. It rolled into the gutter, this apple with all the DNA of joy; the dog looked at me briefly, with what I can only describe as a smile. (I'll have to ask our daughter, a veterinarian, whether dogs smile). I hurried over to the apple, toed it with my black leather shoe, saw teeth marks and dog slobber. It was the best thing I was going to see all day. I looked up as the VW bug turned the corner with its muffler popping.

    I spit out my black chewing gum. I became a frisky pooch, wagging a tail and dancing on my hind legs. I moved the apple up from one of my least favorite fruits to my most favorite. I couldn't wait to get home, bare my teeth, and chomp into a crisp Fuji apple. For a goofy moment I wondered whether I could lie on the couch and eat this fruit without the aid of my hands.

    Sometimes when I'm in a somber mood, I remember that dog and his apple, which in a way he shared with me by letting it roll into the gutter. I was awarded a prize called joy, and Eliot, great poet, author of "The Waste Land" and the even more depressing "J. Alfred Prufrock," got the Nobel Prize in Literature. *Hijole,* the truck that backed into his driveway must have been enormous. ■

"VW Memories," photo collage by Betty Rodgers.

"Bad Hand," linocut by Riley Sophia Penaluna.

FROM THE ARCHIVE

Painting of Bruce Embree by his uncle Phil Behymer.

REMEMBERING BRUCE EMBREE

Thirty years ago, 1995, we letterpress printed the second two chapbooks we published by poet Bruce Embree, of Inkom, Idaho, a spot on the map south of the railroad town of Pocatello. Given this three-decade anniversary, we thought we should feature a couple of Bruce's poems here in "From the Archive." His first chapbook, *No Wild Dog Howled*, was the first chapbook we ever letterpress printed in 1987 after winching a century-old Chandler & Price platen press and type cases into our garage a year earlier. We still miss Bruce's presence in this world.

Rosemary and I landed at Idaho State University in Pocatello in the summer of 1977 for a teaching assistantship and grad school and by the following spring were helping organize poetry readings in a little beer/wine bar on Main Street called The Bistro, renamed The Dead Horse Saloon for the few years it lasted. Student poor, we drank beer by the pitcher in what became the bohemian hangout for local writers and artists. Just a block away from the railroad yards—so close the building shook when the cars coupled—the Bistro had a long shuffle-board, a jukebox, and a piano—no TVs—and we spent many nights listening to some great pianists. One tune I'll never forget, perhaps because we requested it often, was "Here's that Rainy Day," a melancholy 1950s jazz standard played in the Bistro by a pianist named Merlin, a retired military band musician from Alaska, who said he played at one of JFK's inauguration parties. How he landed in Pocatello as we all did, I have no idea. The beautiful way he played and could bring the entire bar to pin-drop quiet I'll compare in my memory to the quiet that came over the place when Bruce Embree got up to read his poems.

No Wild Dog Howled *by Bruce Embree, the first chapbook letterpress-printed by Limberlost Press in 1987 after an apprenticeship with Barb and Tom Rea of Dooryard Press, Story, Wyoming.*

Bruce worked as an oiler for the train engines, and he'd often show up after his shift to read in his oil-stained coveralls, his hands smudging the poems he read, cigarette between his fingers. Many of his poems then were about working at the railroad, the other guys he worked with, the idiot rules and bosses, the bulls who chased off riders from some far-off place. He got married, and he and his wife had a baby girl named Hannah. He lost his job when he was busted for growing pot and then his poems told stories about simply surviving by cutting and delivering firewood in a worn-out old truck in desperate need of new brakes. He typed up and photocopied collections of his poems that he pinched into those cardstock theme-paper covers sold in stationery stores with titles written in magic marker like *Now that the Past Is Gone* (1976-77), *A Feeling I Go Blind Trying to Keep* (1978-79), *Scum* (1982-87), *No Time* (1987-91), and he'd peddle them at readings.

His poems, born of an unmasked honesty about a life of hard-scrabble poverty, mental instability, alcohol and cigarettes, run-ins with the law, and a stark, raw perspective on existence, and often buoyant with a dark wry humor, stunned those of us who were there to hear him read.

After we pulled the press and typecases into our garage and needed a first chapbook to handset and press into existence, we asked Bruce for a manuscript. He sent many poems, and we selected a collection of 16 we thought held together as a representative sampling of the work he did up to that time. In 1995, we letterpressed *Beneath the Chickenshit Mormon Sun*. In October of 1996, he took his own life.

Beneath the Chickenshit Mormon Sun, *poems by Bruce Embree, letterpress-printed by Limberlost Press (1995).* All Mine, *a compilation of Embree's work published by Blue Scarab Press in 2003.*

REMEMBERING BRUCE EMBREE

In 2003, our poet friend Harald Wyndham, publisher of Blue Scarab press in Pocatello, published a 175-page compilation of Bruce's work along with several essays about Bruce written by his friends under the title *All Mine: New and Selected Poems*. Before Harald died, he asked us to take his leftover inventory of the book, a large box too heavy for one to carry. It deserves to be released into the world. Here are two of Bruce's poems from the two chapbooks we published in 1987 and 1995 respectively.

—*Rick Ardinger*

* * * * *

Stick Together

    I was drunk when we met
but she let me stay anyway

    Close to five years
and we're still together
in spite of
drunk driving tickets
snow up to the top wire
screaming chainsaws and buried trucks
rejected stories
middle age
jobs that come and go
ships that never come in

    She snores at night
and I never cut my toenails
Our roof leaks
cars are all junkers
Chickens eat the dogfood
dog gets the eggs
and we just got busted
for growing pot

Days, years go by
sometimes looks
like everything is shot in the ass
Yes, but we're made for each other
We stick together
like Vibram soles and dogshit.

* * * * *

American Hero

Jeany and I went out to dinner last night
the food was good
We overheard a man who had really been up against it
and had somehow come out to the good
"The ball was almost completely covered in sand
but I played a wedge and came out
six feet from the pin"
He slouched back in his chair like the old vet
recalling the Jap machine gun he took out

Was splitting firewood this morning
when Brigham the pup got run over
He just looked at me with his busted jaw
eyes already going funny
The vet will call
If he don't come out of shock

The mad old Ayatollah
sends kids up against mines and tanks

The silent millions die
cutting timber, digging ditches in Siberia

REMEMBERING BRUCE EMBREE

    You can drive along the freeway in El Paso
look across the river to shacktown
where kids die for lack of water
in the hundred degree sun

    These kind of bad movies
have no end
list goes on and on
But don't you think there is something magnificent
uniquely American
yes in a man standing alone
against it all
with his sand wedge? ■

"Shroud" by Rod Burks. Graphite and oil paint on wood panel.

THE LAST WORD

That Fellow's Razor

Entities ought not to be multiplied
except by necessity

If it ain't broke don't fix it

If you don't want her don't whistle

Be careful what you ask for,
Lest it be granted.

Gary Snyder

 LIMBERLOST PRESS 1993

GARY SNYDER

That Fellow's Razor

Editor's Note: *We thought we'd end this 2025 edition of* The Limberlost Review *with another gem from our Limberlost Press archive, a broadside we letterpress printed in 1993 by Gary Snyder, "That Fellow's Razor." Given the current drift of the U.S. toward totalitarianism, we thought that bookending this edition with Clifford Burke's "Kakistocracy" and ending with Gary Snyder's "be careful" warning would be most appropriate. Hold onto your hats, friends.* ■

Gary Snyder, photo by Kurt Lorenz.

Bison use their massive heads to plow through deep snow in search of grasses, but ribs are showing after a long winter. Photograph by Glenn Oakley.

CONTRIBUTORS

LIMBERLOST LETTERPRESS

www.limberlostpress.com

CONTRIBUTORS

SHERMAN ALEXIE has published 26 books including his recent memoir *You Don't Have to Say You Love Me* (Little, Brown). He has won the PEN/Faulkner Award for Fiction, the PEN/Malamud Award for Short Fiction, a PEN/Hemingway Citation for Best First Fiction, and the National Book Award for Young People's Literature. Born a Spokane/Coeur d'Alene Indian, Alexie grew up in Wellpinit, Washington, on the Spokane Indian Reservation. He's been an urban Indian since 1994 and lives in Seattle with his family. *A Memory of Elephants,* a letterpress-printed, limited edition chapbook of his poems, was published in the summer of 2020 by Limberlost Press.

DAN ARMSTRONG is a novelist and publisher of *Mad City Press,* an online magazine focusing on the environment and sustainable agriculture out of Eugene, Oregon. He has published thirteen novels and a collection of short stories through *Mad City.* His latest, *Quicksand,* published in 2022. He's served as the archivist for the Southern Willamette Valley Bean and Grain Project, on the board of directors for the Lane County Farmers' Market, and as a member of the Lane County Food Policy Council. He won the *Wayne Morris Now Award* for community service in 2010 for his work as a farm advocate.

TIM BARNES taught in the English Department at Portland Community College for 25 years, where he was the chair of the creative writing department and advisor on the literary magazine *Alchemy.* He is the author of several poetry collections, most recently *Definitions for a Lost Language.* He co-edited *Wood Works: The Life and Writings of Charles Erskine Scott Wood* and he has edited *Friends of William Stafford: A Journal and Newsletter for Poets and Poetry* since 2011.

PAUL BEEBE is a retired journalist. He worked for newspapers in Idaho, Pennsylvania, Colorado, and Utah. He lives in Salt Lake City, close to the entrance to Big Cottonwood Canyon, at the interface of the Rocky Mountains and the Great Basin, and a short drive to the Colorado Plateau. He holds degrees in English literature and agriculture, a strange mixture that for him has formed a bridge between the ordinary and the All.

WENDELL BERRY is the author of more than 40 books of fiction, poetry, and essays, including the novels *Memory of Old Jack* and *Jabber Crow,* the much revered and most relevant *The Unsettling of America* and *Citizenship Papers*, and so much more.

FLORENCE K. BLANCHARD lives and writes from her home in Bellevue, Idaho. When she was 10 years old, she distributed a neighborhood newspaper written in long hand and hasn't stopped writing. She has an ancient BA in English. In 2011 she received a writer's residency at Ragdale from the Idaho Commission for the Arts and her work has been published in local newspapers and magazines. She is the founder and range manager of the Free Range Poetry Society, a "disorganization" supporting poets and poetry near Sun Valley, Idaho. She recently self-published a chapbook, *Passing Through Idaho*, featuring a triptych of poems inspired by 35 years of participation in the annual Pocatello Literary Festival.

CLIFFORD BURKE is a life and work partner with Virginia Mudd at Desert Rose Press in northern New Mexico. ***Editor's note:*** *He is also a renowned letterpress printer-teacher extraordinaire of the small press literary renaissance and author of the literary letterpress Bible* Printing Poetry: A Workbook of Typographic Reification *(1980).*

ROD BURKS graduated from the University of Wisconsin-Madison in 1979 with a degree in Art Education. He taught in Kalispell, Montana, for one year, then accepted a position with the Herrett Center at the College of Southern Idaho as an Exhibits Curator. Eventually he joined the family Agriculture and Construction Equipment business in Twin Falls and Caldwell, where he's worked for the past thirty-seven years. After a 40-year lull and encouraged by friendships with numerous artists from the James Castle House Residency Program, he began painting again in 2019.

BOB BUSHNELL was raised in Wilder, Idaho, and attended the University of Idaho, Stanford University, and the University of Washington School of Law. He returned to Boise in 1972 to practice law before becoming a fsull-time businessman and a single parent, nourished by a membership in the Boise Great Books Club for four decades. He now devotes his time to reading, writing, and cultivating old and new friendships.

BONNIE JO CAMPBELL is the bestselling author of *Mothers, Tell Your Daughters, Once Upon a River,* and *American Salvage,* among other works of fiction. She is a National Book Award finalist, a Guggenheim Fellow, and winner of the 2019 Mark Twain Award. W.W. Norton published her new novel, *The Waters,* in January of 2024. She is six foot tall and rides a donkey.

KURT CASWELL was born in Fairbanks, Alaska, and grew up in the Cascade Range in Oregon. He has worked as a teacher in Hokkaido, Japan; on the Navajo Reservation; and at schools inArizona, California, and Wyoming. Currently, he is professor of creative writing and literature in the Honors College at Texas Tech University in Lubbock, Texas. He's published several nonfiction works, including *Laika's Window: The Legacy of a Soviet Space Dog, Getting to Grey Owl: Journeys on Four Continents, In the Sun's House: My Year Teaching on the Navajo Reservation,*

and *Inside Passage,* which won the 2008 River Teeth Literary Nonfiction Book Prize. His latest is *Iceland Summer: Travels along the Ring Road* (Trinity University Press, 2023).

BRYAN CHERNICK has been working in the environmental field for over 35 years as a Response Manager on U.S. EPA Superfund projects all over the U.S., including Alaska, Hawaii, and the Pacific Territories. Though he works long hours managing such projects, he always finds time to explore with his film camera in his time off, taking black and white, later developing his own film in his darkroom at home. He holds a degree in geology from Washington State University and lives in Bothel, Washington, near

Seattle. His photo of the "Rez Dogs" (p. 274) was taken during an asbestos cleanup project in Navajo, New Mexico using a Leica camera and film that expired in 1963.

MICHAEL DALEY, born and raised in Dorchester, Massachusetts, is the author of seven collections of poetry, several chapbooks, a novel, a book of essays and two translations. His work has been supported by Artist Trust, Seattle Arts Commission, Fessenden Foundation, Fulbright, National Endowment for the Humanities, Massachusetts Cultural Council, Skagit River Poetry Foundation, and Washington State Arts Commission. A retired high school English teacher, he and his wife live near Deception Pass in Anacortes, Washington. "The Restorers" will be included in *Ground Work*, forthcoming from Ravenna Press, Edmonds, Washington.

TED DYER received his MA in English from Washington State University and taught 20 years as a composition instructor for the College of Southern Idaho extension service in Blaine County, Idaho. He also taught literature and jazz history for several years for the Idaho State University Department of Continuing Education. He also worked extensively as a speaker on Ernest Hemingway and Ezra Pound for the Idaho Humanities Council, which has been a moveable feast in its own way.

BRUCE EMBREE is the author of *No Wild Dog Howled* and *Beneath the Chickenshit Mormon Sun* (Limberlost Press, 1987 and 1995, respectively), and *All Mine: New and Selected Poems* (Blue Scarab Press, 2003), plus several self-published collections from the 1970s-80s. He died in 1996.

REBECCA EVANS is a memoirist, poet, essayist and instructor of frequent writing and empowerment workshops. An adjunct instructor at Boise State University, she teaches teens in the juvenile system. She's also the co-host of *Writer to Writer* on Radio Boise. She is disabled, a Veteran, a Jew, a mother, a worrier, and more. She's earned two MFAs from the University of Nevada, Reno. Her memoir-in-verse, *Tangled by Blood*, is available from Moon Tide Press. Read more at **www.rebeccaevanswriter.com**.

JEFF FEREDAY is a retired water rights lawyer who grew up in Boise, Idaho, went east to college, worked summers as a smokejumper ("Best job I ever had!"), then became executive director of the Idaho Conservation League in that organization's formative years. In 1977, he entered law school in Portland, Oregon. Upon graduation, he went east again for his first job as a lawyer with the Department of the Interior. After his stint in D.C., Jeff worked in the areas of

water rights, public lands, and environmental law with a Denver firm. In 1985, he returned to Idaho to join the Boise law firm of Givens Pursley LLP. He retired in 2016. He and his wife Kay Hummel have two grown sons, Wyatt and Charlie.

JUDITH FREEMAN is the author of a short story collection and several novels, including *The Chinchilla Farm* and *Red Water,* as well as a biography of Raymond Chandler, *The Long Embrace,* and her memoir, *The Latter Days*. Her fifth novel, *MacArthur Park* (Pantheon, New York) was published in the spring of 2022. The recipient of a John Simon Guggenheim Fellowship in fiction, she was also awarded an Erle Stanley Gardner Fellowship from the Harry Ransom Center, and the Western Heritage Award for her novel *Set for Life*. Her essays and reviews have appeared in *The New York Times, The Chicago Tribune, The Los Angeles Times, The Washington Post,* and *The Los Angeles Review of Books*, among other publications. She lives on the Camas Prairie near Fairfield, Idaho, with her husband, artist-photographer Anthony Hernandez.

MARK GIBBONS grew up in a small Milwaukee Railroad town in western Montana and married his high school sweetheart. They have two children. Mark was introduced to poetry by writer James Welch in a 1970 high school workshop. He's been writing ever since. He has many collections of poems to date, most recently a chapbook from Bottlecap Press, *Cross Country* (2024) and a full-length collection, *Sister Buffalo* (2024) from FootHills Publishing. He's taught poetry workshops in Missoula and across the state for the last 30 years and edited the *Montana Poets Series for FootHills* and three books of poetry for *Drumlummon Institute*. Mark served as Montana's Poet Laureate 2021-2023 where he conducted and archived 60 interviews with poets reading their own work.

GARY GILDNER's collection of personal essays, *How I Married Michele*, is out from BkMk Press. *Calling from the Scaffold*, his ninth collection of poems, was published by University of Pittsburgh Press in 2022. *The Capital of Kansas City* (BkMk, 2016) is his fifth and most recent book of stories. He has given readings at the Library of Congress, Shakespeare & Company in Paris, the 92nd St. Y and Manhattan Theater Club in New York, and on the ferry crossing Lake Michigan. He lives outside Tucson.

SALLY GREEN has been a resident of Waldron Island, in the San Juan Islands off the coast of Washington, since 1982. With her husband Sam she edits the award-winning Brooding Heron Press and Bindery. She has been the recipient of an Artist Trust GAP grant and a Stanley W. Lindberg Editor's Award for excellence. Her latest collection of poems is *Full Immersion* (Expedition Press, 2014).

SAMUEL GREEN's most recent collection of poems is *Disturbing the Light* (Carnegie Mellon University Press, 2020). With his wife Sally, he has been co-editor of the award-winning Brooding Heron Press on Waldron Island, Washington, since 1982. He has been a visiting professor at multiple colleges and universities, and he has taught as a visiting Poet-in-the-Schools for nearly 50 years. In 2008 he was selected as the first Poet Laureate of Washington State. Honors include an NEA Fellowship in Poetry, an Artist Trust Fellowship in Literature, a Washington State Book Award in Poetry, and an Honorary Doctorate from Seattle University. From 1966-1970 he was in the U.S. Coast Guard, with service in Vietnam.

SHAUN T. GRIFFIN is the co-founder and development director of the Community Chest, a rural social justice agency serving northwestern Nevada since 1991. Southern Utah University Press released his *Anthem for a Burnished Land*, a memoir, in 2016. *This Is What the Desert Surrenders: New and Selected Poems* came out from Black Rock Press in 2012, and Limberlost Press released his letterpressed chapbook of poems *Driving the Tender Desert Home* in 2014. His most recent books include a collection of essays, *Because the Light Will Not Forgive Me* (University of Nevada Press in 2019), and *The Monastery of Stars* (poems, Kelsay Books 2020). He lives in Virginia City, Nevada, in the shadow of the former home of novelist Walter Van Tilburg Clark.

EDWARD HARKNESS is the author of four full-length poetry collections, *Saying the Necessary, Beautiful Passing Lives, The Law of the Unforeseen*, and most recently, *Avalanche: A Survival Guide* (2023). Of it, novelist David Long wrote, "No poet I know moves so nimbly between the cadences of formal poetry and the quirky, often hilarious, rhythms of actual speech . . . or devotes himself so lovingly to family—past, present and future. Put simply: Edward Harkness has become an indispensable poet." Harkness' *Creek Water: New & Selected Poems*, is slated for publication in summer, 2025. He lives with his life-mate, Linda, in Shoreline, Washington.

JIM HEPWORTH lives at the junction of two great trout rivers, the Clearwater and the Snake, in Lewiston, Idaho. In 1989, as editor/publisher of Confluence Press, he published the first book on Norman Maclean in the short-lived Confluence American Authors Series. The book was edited by Ron McFarland and Hugh Nichols and titled simply *Norman Maclean*. It has since become a standard reference book for Maclean scholars.

JOHN HOOPES lived in San Francisco for decades, until he migrated to Lake Chapala, Jalisco, Mexico, seven years there renewing his life; thereafter re-settling in Sacramento with his wife to raise their four grandchildren. He'd written by then three historical novels of San Francisco's origins; three novels of his Mexico experience, one narrative nonfiction of his parents' depression-era traveling the U.S. selling magazine subscriptions; a fantasy novel of human-transformed-to-dolphin; plus several hundred pages of narrative poetry, his fondest obsession.

JAY JOHNSON is a lawyer and writer working in Moscow, Idaho. After college, he lived in Oregon, Colorado, Washington, and California before settling in Idaho in 1995. He repaired automobiles and logged for twenty-five years prior to law school. Most of his law practice is criminal defense, generally for indigent clients. His fiction has appeared recently in *The Limberlost Review* and *Talking River Review*.

MARC C. JOHNSON is a fellow at the Mansfield Center at the University of Montana and the author of three books on American political history, including, most recently, *Mansfield and Dirksen: Bipartisan Giants of the Senate*, published by the University of Oklahoma Press in 2023. His award-winning biography of Montana Senator Burton K. Wheeler—*Political Hell-Raiser*—was recently released in paperback. Johnson served as press secretary and chief of staff to Idaho four-term governor Cecil D. Andrus. He lives on the north coast of Oregon.

KATHERINE JONES worked at the the *Idaho Statesman* for 31 years as photojournalist and writer, winning numerous awards for her work, including Idaho Press Club's Photographer of the Year and Reporter of the Year. She wrote a column called "Heart of the Treasure Valley" for more than a decade. She is now retired, traveling, and training her camera on the world in new ways. Her personal work has often been with (and influenced by) a plastic, medium-format film camera, called a Holga, because of its square images, intentional vignetting and unique aesthetic.

TERESA JORDAN is an artist and author inspired by animals and the natural world. Her books include the memoir *Riding the White Horse Home* and *The Year of Living Virtuously, Weekends Off*, a series of non-righteous meditations on virtue and vice. During the pandemic she undertook "My Year of Birds," painting a bird each day for a year. Teresa and her husband, folklorist and musician Hal Cannon, recently moved from the Utah desert to Portland, Oregon, where Teresa works as a Buddhist hospital chaplain (**www.TeresaJordan.com**).

GREG KEELER is the author of two memoirs, *Waltzing with the Captain: Remembering Richard Brautigan* (Limberlost Press) and *Trash Fish: A Life* (Counterpoint Press), and eight collections of poetry, including, most recently, *The Bluebird Run* (Elk River Books). He writes, paints, fishes, and composes irreverent songs in Bozeman, Montana, where he taught in the English Department of Montana State University for 30 years.

GROVE KOGER is the author of *When the Going Was Good: A Guide to the 99 Best Narratives of Travel, Exploration, and Adventure;* Assistant Editor of *Deus Loci: The Lawrence Durrell Journal;* and former Assistant Editor of *Art Patron* magazine. Recently he's published fiction in *Roi Fainéant* and *Danse Macabre* and nonfiction in *Amsterdam Quarterly* and *History Magazine*. He blogs about travel and related subjects at **worldenoughblog.wordpress.com/author/gkoger/**.

MARGARET KOGER is a Lascaux Poetry Prize finalist living near the river in Boise, Idaho. She taught English at Boise's Borah High for many years and served as a Poet-in-the-Schools. Her work has appeared in numerous journals, including *The Amsterdam Quarterly*, the *Writers in the Attic* series, *Red Rock Review, Collective Unrest, Burning House, Tiny Seed, The Chaffey Review, Forbidden Peak, Déraciné, Ponder Savant,* and *Gravitas*.

TED KOOSER's most recent collection of poems is *Raft* from Copper Canyon Press (2024). He is a former U.S. Poet Laureate and Pulitzer Prize winner who lives in eastern Nebraska. In addition to poetry, he has published a memoir of his mother's family, a book about the area where he lives, two books on writing, and six illustrated children's books, plus a number of chapbooks and special editions. His weekly newspaper column, "American Life in Poetry," sponsored by the Poetry Foundation, had, at the time he retired from the editorship, four and a half million readers worldwide.

DAVID L. KUEBECK is Director of Budgets and Technology at University Libraries, Bowling Green State University. His poetry has appeared in *Big Scream*. A native of Bowling Green, Ohio, Kuebeck lives there with his wife and three children.

HOWARD LEVY is the author of two books of poetry, *A Day this Lit* (2000) and *Spooky Action at a Distance* (2014), both from CavanKerry Press. He has just finished a new manuscript, *Place Free of Names*, that imagines Antarctica in the 14th century, before any human has known of its existence. He was on the faculty at The Frost Place Festival of Poetry for many years and taught both at The Metropolitan Museum of Art and The Museum of Modern Art in New York City. He lives and works in Amagansett, New York.

RAE LEWIS (photo from 1978), a writer and artist in Kanarraville, Utah, is at work on a memoir of her life and career during an amazing time in magazine journalism of the 1970s and 1980s and her marriage to New Journalism pioneer and *Rolling Stone* writer/editor Grover Lewis (1934-1995).

RON McFARLAND retired from the University of Idaho English department in 2018 after "47 years of blithe self-indulgence." He's the author of 20 books and served as Idaho's first State Writer-in-Residence (1984-1985). Current projects include a collection of poems tentatively titled *A Variable Sense of Things* and a book-length study of the poetry & prose of Chicano writer Gary Soto. His most recent book is a biography of Colonel Edward J. Steptoe (1815-1865), *Edward J. Steptoe and the Indian Wars* (2016).

CHARLOTTE MEARS received her MFA in writing from the University of Arkansas, where she studied with John Clellon Holmes, James Whitehead, and Miller Williams. She has taught writing and literature in eight colleges and universities, received ten awards for her poetry, and published two books of poems, *Sweet Air* (2013) and *Winds of New York* (2014). As often as she can be, Mears is in New Orleans at the Maple Leaf reading series, the longest-running poetry reading series in the South. She currently lives in Madison, Mississippi.

ALAN MINSKOFF moved to Boise, Idaho, from New York in 1972. He lives in Boise and teaches journalism at the College of Idaho. The author of *Idaho Wine Country* and *The Idaho Traveler* (both from Caxton Press), he's also published two chapbooks of poetry from Limberlost Press, *Blue Ink Runs Out on a Partly Cloudy Day* and *Point Blank*. His essays have appeared in *Harper's*, the anthology *Where the Morning Light's Still Blue*, and elsewhere. He reviews audiobooks for *AudioFile Magazine* and can be heard one week a month on its "Behind the Mic" podcast.

GLENN OAKLEY is a Boise-based photographer and filmmaker specializing in outdoor projects. His work synthesizes the aesthetics and lighting of landscape photography with the story-telling impact of photojournalism. A three-time winner of the Banff Mountain Photo Competition, he has shot feature stories for *Smithsonian, Sunset, Outside, Life and Time*, as well as advertising shoots for Sierra, LL Bean, Yakima, Giant Bikes and Dagger. A former contributing editor to *High Country News*, he has written and photographed several books, including *Frommer's Bed & Breakfast Guides to New England, Wolf!* and *The San Luis Valley: Sand Dunes & Sandhill Cranes*. His work with NBCNews.com on the multimedia project *In Plain Sight* garnered a Peabody Award. His film *The Falconer* was an official selection for the Wild & Scenic Film Festival.

BARBARA OLIC-HAMILTON—originally from a suburb of Chicago where city lights bleached the night sky—moved to the dark skies of rural Idaho in 1976 and then to Boise in 1980. After a long career as a secondary English teacher, she worked as an adjunct instructor at Boise State University and a part-time bookseller. She has spent 17 years in the same book club and 38 years in the same writing group. Recent publications include essays in *BookWomen* and *The Limberlost Review* (2022), and poetry in *Ireland: You Can't Miss It* and *Moon: Writers in the Attic* (2022).

BRIAN OLSON is a fourth generation Idahoan, born and raised on a small farm in Southern Idaho. He is a firefighter by trade, poet and avid river runner. His primary joy in life is finding the loneliest spots in the Idaho backcountry with his wife, two sons and dog.

RILEY SOPHIA PENALUNA currently resides in Corvallis, Oregon, though her queer heart belongs to the Salish Sea and the North Cascades. Her bona fides are few, but she has dabbled as a theatre artist and graphic designer, among other creative pursuits. These days she is mainly occupied with making linocut prints of weird little guys at her wobbly kitchen table and posting them to Instagram as @studio.rsp.

TOM REA is the author of *Bone Wars: The Excavation and Celebrity of Andrew Carnegie's Dinosaur* (University of Pittsburgh Press, 2001), winner of the Western Writers of America Spur Award for contemporary nonfiction, *Devil's Gate: Owning the Land, Owning the Story* (University of Oklahoma Press, 2006), *The Hole in the Wall Ranch: A History* (Pronghorn Press, 2010) and two chapbooks of poetry, *Man In a Rowboat* (Copper Canyon, 1977) and *Smith,* (Dooryard Press, 1985.) With his wife Barbara he founded Dooryard Press in 1979, in Story, Wyoming, and for eight years they published beautifully letterpress-printed books by such poets as Alberto Rios, Sam Hazo, Edward Harkness, Richard Hugo, and many others. Later he worked for a dozen years as a reporter and editor on the *Casper Star-Tribune,* Wyoming's largest newspaper, and since 2010 has edited WyoHistory.org, a state-history website published by the Wyoming State Historical Society. He lives with his family in Casper.

BETTY RODGERS began exploring the world through a lens at a young age, influenced by her father who was a photographer for the Air Force during World War II. She remembers the allure of the red lightbulb in the temporary dark room he would set up in the family bathroom. Betty's images now live in homes, offices, and publications around the country. In 2010, she added documentary filmmaking to her repertoire by partnering with her husband, Ken, to create two award-winning films: *Bravo! Common Men, Uncommon Valor,* and then more recently, *I Married the War.* Both inspiring films have received accolades for bringing to light the individual human cost of war.

KEN RODGERS is a writer, poet and documentary filmmaker who lives in Vail, Arizona. Both a Pushcart Prize nominee and a Best American Short Stories nominee, Ken's stories, poems and essays have appeared in fine journals. His published books include a collection of short stories, *The Gods of Angkor Wat* (BK Publications), and two collections of poems, *Trench Dining* (Running Wolf Press) and *Passenger Pigeons* (Jaxon Press.) Along with his wife Betty, Ken co-directed and co-produced *Bravo! Common Men, Uncommon Valor*, a feature-length documentary film about Ken's company of Marines at the Siege of Khe Sanh in 1968. Betty and Ken's latest documentary, *I Married the War*, is about caregivers to combat veterans. Ken blogs fairly regularly at **KennethRodgers.com**.

EDWARD SANDERS is a poet, inventive musician, pubisher, and longtime member of "The Fugs" folk/rock band. Born in 1939, he has produced dozens of books of poems, CDs, a novel, and several works of nonfiction, including the American Book Award winner *Thirsting for Peace in a Raging Century: Selected Poems 1961–1985* (1987). Author of the manifesto *Investigative Poetry* (1976), he has composed several biographies in verse, including *Chekhov* (1995) and *The Poetry and Life of Allen Ginsberg* (2000). In 1998 he began work on *America, A History in Verse*, a multi-volume history in poetry. Student of Greek, participant exorcisor during the 1967 March on the Pentagon, editor/publisher of *Fuck You: A Magazine of the Arts* ("published from a secret location on the Lower East Side"), editor of the online *Woodstock Journal*, husband of Miriam R. Sanders for a half-century, Ed carries on poetically and politically, bridging the Beat generation to the Hippie generation, to a contemporary insistence that poetry matters and will change the world.

GARY SHORT's fourth book of poems, *The Stars That Fell*, is forthcoming from the University of Nevada Press. His second volume, *Flying Over Sonny Liston*, received the Western States Book Award. Among his honors are a fellowship from the NEA, a Pushcart Prize, a Stegner Fellowship at Stanford, a fellowship at the Fine Arts Work Center in Provincetown, and several residencies at MacDowell and the Virginia Center for the Arts. He divides his time between the night and the day in Panahachel, Guatemala.

GINO SKY is the author of the novels *Appaloosa Rising* (Doubleday, 1980) and *Coyote Silk* (North Atlantic Books, 1987), the story collection *Near the Postcard Beautiful* (Floating Ink Books, 1994), and a dozen collections of poetry, including *Wild Dog Days* (Limberlost Press, 2015). He was an editor of the legendary 1960s literary magazine *Wild Dog* that began in Pocatello, Idaho, and moved on to Salt Lake City, and then to the Haight-Ashbury district of San Francisco prior to the 1967 Summer of Love, publishing many of the great poets of the day He and his wife Barbara Jensen currently live in Salt Lake City. An interview with Gino appears in the 2020 edition of *The Limberlost Review*.

ANNICK SMITH is a writer and filmmaker whose work focuses on the literature and history of the Northern Rockies. Her books include the memoir *Homestead*, the Montana anthology *The Last Best Place*, which she edited with William Kittredge, and *The Big Bluestem*, about Oklahoma's tallgrass prairies. Her articles, essays, and stories have appeared in *Audubon, Outside, National Geographic Traveler,* the *New York Times*, and *Story* and have been widely anthologized. She was executive producer of
the film *Heartland*, a co-producer of *A River Runs through It*, and producer of the public television series *The Real People*, about Native Americas in the Inland Northwest. Smith is a founding board member of the Sundance Film Institute and founder of Hellgate Writers, a literary center in Missoula. She has lived in western Montana since 1964.

GARY SNYDER Gary Snyder is the author of 16 collections of poetry and prose. Since 1970 he has lived in the watershed of the South Yuba River in the foothills of the Sierra Nevada. Winner of the Pulitzer Prize in 1975 and a finalist for the National Book Award in 1992, he has been awarded the Bollingen Poetry Prize and the Robert Kirsch Lifetime Achievement Award. In 1996, Limberlost Press letterpress printed in a limited edition *Three on Community*, essays by Gary Snyder, Wendell Berry, and Carole Koda.

GARY SOTO is the author of dozens of books of poetry, memoir, novels and more, as well as dozens more books for adolescent and younger readers that deal with the stories of growing up in Mexican American communities. In his many works, Soto recreates the world of the barrio, the urban, Spanish-speaking neighborhood where he was raised, evoking the harsh forces that often shape life for Chicanos, including racism, poverty, and crime.
He's a recipient of the American Book Award and numerous other awards, including Guggenheim and NEA Fellowships. Limberlost Press will publish his humorous Books as Drinking Buddies in 2025.

ADAM M. SOWARDS retired from the history department at the University of Idaho in 2022. Now, he makes his home in the Skagit Valley of Western Washington where he continues to write and report on topics connected to the environment, democracy, and the U.S. West. He is an award-winning historian and author or editor of several books, most recently *Making America's Public Lands: The Contested History of Conservation on Federal Lands* (Rowman & Littlefield, 2022), as well as numerous
academic articles and book chapters. His essays have appeared widely, including in *South Dakota Review, Talking River Review,* and *Wild Roof Journal*. You can find his work and learn more at **https://adamsowards.net**.

BRAD TEARE was raised in Kansas and later moved to Idaho, where he built a log cabin near Moscow Mountain in northern Idaho. After studying illustration, he pursued a successful career in New York City as a woodcut artist, creating book covers for renowned titles. Teare attended residencies at Maynard Dixon's Mount Carmel and Trinchera Ranch in Colorado. His work has been exhibited at the Salmagundi Club, The Forbes Galleries, and Quest for the West at the Eiteljorg Museum. In 2021, he won an award from the American Impressionist Society. His art has been featured in *American Artist, Southwest Art, Western Art and Architecture, International Artist, Western Art Collector*, and *Gulf Connoisseur* (Dubai).

GARY THOMPSON studied with Richard Hugo, Madeline DeFrees, and Bill Kittredge at the University of Montana during the early 1970s. He taught in the creative writing program at CSU, Chico for nearly thirty years, all the while playing second base for The Pests, Chico's storied softball team. He has published six collections of poetry, and the most recent, *Broken by Water: Salish Sea Years,* was a finalist for the 2022 Washington State Book Award in Poetry. He and his wife Linda still live on San Juan Island, though they no longer putter about the Salish Sea aboard their old trawler, *Keats*.

GEORGIA TIFFANY's poems have appeared in such publications as *Calyx, Antigonish Review, South Carolina Review, Threepenny Review,* and the anthology *Poets of the American West*. Her limited-edition chapbook *Cut from the Score* was published by Night Owl Press. Her new book *Body Be Sound* was released by Encircle Publications in November of 2023. A native of Spokane, Washington, she now lives in Moscow, Idaho.

RANDY VAN DYCK's work has been published in many books and magazines, including *SouthWest Art, Acrylic Artist, American Art Collector, Artist's Magazine,* and *International Artist*. His artwork also has been accepted in numerous juried shows, receiving several awards. He was the 2019 recipient of the Boise Mayor's Award for Excellence in the Arts. Three paintings were accepted into the prestigious Leigh Yawkey Woodson Museum's *Birds in Art* show in 2020, 2021, and 2023.

O. ALAN WELTZIEN, longtime English professor at the University of Montana Western (Dillon), retired from teaching in 2020. He has published dozens of articles and nine books, including three poetry collections and a memoir, *A Father and an Island* (2008). He's also the author of a biography of neglected Montana novelist Thomas Savage with the University of Nevada Press.

JETT W. WHITEHEAD is a full-time rare books seller, dealing exclusively in modern poetry, from his homebase in Bay City, Michigan. While in graduate school at Central Michigan University he founded Wheatfield Press and served as editor of its journal *Poetry of the Wheatfield*. His poems have appeared in *The Antigonish Review, Small Pond, The AB Bookman's Weekly*, among many others. He was born in Theodore Roethke's hometown of Saginaw, Michigan.

MITCH WIELAND is the author of the novels *Willy Slater's Lane* and *God's Dogs* (Southern Methodist University Press, 1996 and 2009 respectively). *Willy Slater's Lane* received starred reviews in *Publisher's Weekly* and *Booklist* and was optioned for a film. Named "Idaho Book of the Year," *God's Dogs* was featured in the annual *Best of the West* prize anthology, and was a finalist for the John Gardner Fiction Book Award. Wieland's third novel, *The Ghosts of Okuma*, will be published in 2026. His stories have appeared in *The Missouri Review, The Southern Review, The Kenyon Review, The Yale Review, The Sewanee Review*, and the anthology *Hello, I Love You*, among other publications. "The Last Days of Ferrell Swan" in this edition of *The Limberlost Review* features the main character from *God's Dogs*.

JOE WILKINS is the author of the novels *The Entire Sky* and *Fall Back Down When I Die*, both of which have garnered wide critical acclaim. His latest collection of poetry is *Pastoral, 1994* (River River Books, 2025). He lives with his family in the foothills of the Coast Range of Oregon.

BARON WORMSER is the author most recently of *Some Months in 1968: A Novel* (Woodhall Press) and *The History Hotel: Poems* (CavanKerry Press). His memoir, *The Road Washes Out in Spring: A Poet's Memoir of Living Off the Grid,* has been reissued by Brandeis University Press. His essays have appeared frequently in *Vox Populi*.

JANET WORMSER is a self-taught painter who has been painting for decades and has exhibited in Maine, Vermont, and elsewhere. She says her painting is "tied up with my spiritual journey, which is about my effort to be present to my life from moment to moment. This applies to my relationship with paint, particularly watercolor because it is not easy to control . . . I encourage the paint to spread, wander, and pool by soaking and/or spraying the paper." More of her work can be seen at **www.janetwormser.com.**

ROBERT WRIGLEY is a Distinguished Professor Emeritus at the University of Idaho, recipient of numerous awards, including the Kingsley Tufts Poetry Award, the San Francisco Poetry Center Award, and the Pacific Northwest Book Award, and the author of a dozen full-length collections of poetry. His most recent collection is *The True Account of Myself as a Bird* (Penguin Books, 2022).

DON ZANCANELLA has won the John S. Simmons/Iowa Short Fiction Award and an O. Henry Prize. One of his stories was cited as a distinguished story of the year in the 2019 *Best American Short Stories*, and he has published widely in literary magazines. His books include *Western Electric* (University of Iowa Press), a collection of stories set mostly in Wyoming; *Concord* (Serving House Books), a novel about Henry David Thoreau, Sophia Peabody Hawthorne, and Margaret Fuller; and *A Storm in the Stars* (Delphinium/Harper Collins), a novel about the lives of Mary Shelley and Percy Bysshe Shelley and the writing of *Frankenstein*. He was born in Laramie, Wyoming, and has lived in Virginia, Colorado, Missouri, and New Mexico, where he taught at the University of New Mexico. He now lives in Boise, Idaho, with his wife and their rescue dogs.

LIMBERLOST LETTERPRESS

www.limberlostpress.com

FROM LIMBERLOST PRESS

Wild Dog Days
By Gino Sky

In this long poem, published in honor of the poet's 75th year, the indefatigable **Gino Sky**, author of the novel *Appaloosa Rising: The Legend of the Cowboy Buddha* (Doubleday, 1980), reflects on history, memory, and the power of poetry in bringing an end to the Vietnam War.

Publishing a 1960s underground literary magazine called *Wild Dog* that the FBI took notice of, Sky tells a story of all that swirled around the magazine during an eruptive time in America. First published by the poet Ed Dorn in Pocatello in 1963, *Wild Dog* was handed off to Sky who moved it to Salt Lake City and then to San Francisco's Haight-Ashbury District right at the moment of the counter-cultural revolution. Sky exuberantly chronicles the time, the place, and the peace movement with hallucinogenic clarity.

Illustrated with photos of some of the poets who helped hand-crank the small press literary movement, *Wild Dog Days* is dedicated to "every man, every woman, every kid, every dog who marched for peace and stopped the war."

Gino Sky has published two novels, a collection of stories, and a dozen books of poetry (including *Hallelujah 2 Groundhogs & 16 Valentines*, also available from Limberlost Press). *Appaloosa Rising* and his novel *Coyote Silk* (North Atlantic Books, 1987) have been translated and published in Korea. He and his wife Barb Jensen live in Salt Lake City.

Letterpress printed in a limited edition of 400 copies.
$15 (Plus $5 postage) Idaho orders please add 6% state sales tax.
Purchase this and other books at: www.limberlostpress.com

FROM LIMBERLOST PRESS

Gone in October
Last Reflections on Jack Kerouac

By John Clellon Holmes

"He has awed me with his talents, enraged me with his stubbornness, educated me in my craft, hurt me through indifference, dogged my imagination, upset most of my notions, and generally enlarged me as a writer more than anyone else I know."
—*John Clellon Holmes,
from "The Great Rememberer"*

On the July 4th weekend of 1948, John Clellon Holmes (1926-1988) met Jack Kerouac (1922-1969) in New York City for the first time, and the two became lifelong friends. As young, ambitious novelists, Holmes saw Kerouac as a mentor and comrade in a literary movement eventually known as the Beat Generation. They shared New England roots and the same birthday. They were characters in each other's novels, and they fed each other encouragement through letters and get-togethers at Holmes's home in Old Saybrook, Connecticut, until Kerouac's untimely death at 47, on October 21, 1969.

Originally published in a very limited edition by Limberlost Press in 1985, Holmes's essays/memoirs here reflect on Kerouac's burning innovation as a writer, on their New England heritage, on attending his funeral with poets AllenGinsberg and Gregory Corso, and on the 1982 Naropa Institute celebration of the 25th anniversary of the publication of Kerouac's novel *On the Road*, a gathering which Holmes saw as a last hurrah with other movers and shakers of the Beat movement.

This new edition of *Gone in October*, newly designed and illustrated with more photographs, comprises a deeply heart-felt remembrance of literary friendship and personal loss, reprinted in commemoration of the 2022 Jack Kerouac centennial.

$17.95 (Plus $5 postage) Idaho orders please add 6% state sales tax.
Purchase this and other books at: www.limberlostpress.com

FROM LIMBERLOST PRESS

Waltzing with the Captain: Remembering Richard Brautigan

By Greg Keeler

Teaching English at Montana State University, Greg Keeler met *Trout Fishing in America* author Richard Brautigan in 1978 and opened a wildly memorable chapter in his own life. Having secluded himself on a 40-acre ranch in Paradise Valley, Montana, in the mid-1970s, Brautigan needed a friend with whom to talk and carouse. Attracted like a moth to the flame, Keeler became that friend and confidant, driver and clumsy co-conspirator in a number of escapades on the trout streams and rivers, at bars and cafes, and along the back roads of Montana. Together they waltzed through many late nights, until Brautigan took his own life in Bolinas, California, in 1984.

    Two decades after Brautigan's death, Greg Keeler recalls those times with haunting clarity. Illustrated with photographs and the author's cartoon-like drawings at the head of every chapter, *Waltzing with the Captain* is darkly funny and poignant in its revealing portrait of an important contemporary American writer, and in its candid story of an often-tested and bumbling friendship between two poets.

    Keeler taught English literature and Creative Writing at Montana State University for 30 years. A prolific painter and musician, he's written several musicals and published a dozen books of poetry, including *American Falls* (Confluence Press, 1987), *Epiphany at Goofy's Gas* (Clark City Press, 1991), and *Almost Happy* (Limberlost Press, 2015). He's recorded more than a dozen CDs of his satiric and flat-out funny collections of songs and poems, including *Live from Nowhere* (Troutball Productions). Winner of a number of awards for teaching and writing, he was awarded the Governor's Award for Outstanding Achievement in the Humanities from the Montana Committee for the Humanities in 2001.

Quality paperback original first edition. 168 pages.
$20 (Plus $5 postage) Idaho orders please add 6% state sales tax.
Purchase this and other books at: www.limberlostpress.com

FROM LIMBERLOST PRESS

A Memory of Elephants

A Chapbook of Poems
By Sherman Alexie

A Memory of Elephants is a deeply reflective, introspective, and confessional collection of poems that explore the mysteries of a mental disorder, regret for things left unsaid to parents before their passing, tribal identity, raising sons in the urban world, the power of love, questions to God.

Printed on Mohawk Superfine paper and folded and sewn by hand into Stonehenge wrappers with illustrations by Erin Ann Jensen.

A Spokane/Coeur d'Alene Indian, Sherman Alexie grew up in Wellpinit, Washington, on the Spokane Indian Reservation. He has been an urban Indian since 1994 and lives in Seattle with his family. He is a poet, short story writer, novelist, and performer, and he has won the PEN/Faulkner Award for Fiction, the PEN/Malamud Award for Short Fiction, a PEN/Hemingway Citation for Best First Fiction, and the National Book Award for Young People's Literature.

He's published 26 books, including his recently released memoir, *You Don't Have to Say You Love Me*, and young adult novel, *The Absolutely True Diary of a Part-Time Indian* (all from Little, Brown Books); *What I've Stolen, What I've Earned*, a book of poetry, from Hanging Loose Press; and *Blasphemy: New and Selected Stories*, from Grove Press. Limberlost Press published letterpress-printed limited editions of his poetry chapbooks *Dangerous Astronomy*, *The Man Who Loves Salmon*, and *Water Flowing Home*. *Smoke Signals*, the movie he wrote and co-produced, won the Audience Award and Filmmakers Trophy at the 1998 Sundance Film Festival.

Letterpress printed in a limited edition of only 500 copies during the COVID-19 summer of 2020 on Mohawk Superfine paper and folded and sewn by hand into Rising Stonehenge wrappers. $55 for signed copies. (Plus $5 postage) Idaho orders please add 6% state sales tax. Purchase this and other books at: www.limberlostpress.com

FROM LIMBERLOST PRESS

John Thomsen & Friends: Songs from Loafer's Glory

AUDIO CD

In commemoration of his 80th year, Limberlost Press released a CD by longtime Idaho folk musician John Thomsen, of Idaho City, featuring an impressive list of musicians from the region backing up their musical mentor, friend, and collaborator.

John Thomsen & Friends: Songs from Loafer's Glory features an array of favorites by Hank Williams, Hank Snow, Roger Miller, Tex Ritter, Sean McCarthy, and others, as well as a couple of Thomsen originals. Despite decades of making music at folk festivals, weddings, birthdays, political events, plays, dances, funerals, and backyard barbecues, *Songs from Loafer's Glory* is Thomsen's first CD.

Recorded by Sam Aarons of Idaho City Sound over several daylong sessions, the long overdue recording offers a sampling of Thomsen's musical versatility. The CD, which includes a colorful booklet of photos and tributes by admirers, features Thomsen's own "Idaho Spud," a bitingly satirical song-story about nuclear waste, the Atomic Energy Commission, and raising kids on "nuclear taters."

Limberlost Press publisher Rick Ardinger likens the recording to the work of Smithsonian folk music preservationist Alan Lomax, who saved from obscurity so much American folk music during the 20th century.

"Johnny has set the bar for being an authentic folk treasure. I am very fortunate to have had so many great times with 'the Golden Voice of the Boise Basin.'"
—*Dave Daley, fiddle player and longtime More's Creek String Band collaborator*

"I have never failed to be impressed by his repertoire and his abilities on guitar, concertina, and Dobro. He was, and is, the complete folklorist and musician. His wit and sense of humor are unmatched."
—*Jake Hoffman, veteran musician, and lap steel guitar artist*

"Johnny is a walking library of songs. He knows so many verses and choruses and the stories that go with them that he has to keep his interest by rewriting some with words most clever and slightly scandalous . . . I've been honored to play along, harmonizing on the fly."
—*Beth Wilson, Idaho City folk musician and collaborator*

**$12 (Plus $5 postage) Idaho orders please add 6% state sales tax.
Purchase this and other books at: www.limberlostpress.com**

FROM LIMBERLOST PRESS

This Morning's Joy
By Ed Sanders

Here is a collection of anti-war poems that also offers elegies to friends (Allen Ginsberg, Robert Creeley, Harry Smith, Charles Olson), and reflects on memories of revolutionary times and the joys of carrying on despite "war-mongering sleaze" of governments.

Born in 1939, Ed Sanders is a poet, inventive musician, publisher, and founding member of "The Fugs" rock and roll band. Student of Greek, participant exorcisor during the 1967 March on the Pentagon, founder of the Investigative Poetry movement, editor/publisher of *Fuck You* magazine ("published from a secret location on the Lower East Side"), editor of the online *Woodstock Journal*, husband of Miriam R. Sanders for more than a half-century, he carries on poetically and politically, bridging the Beat generation to the Hippie generation,  to a contemporary insistence that poetry matters and will change the world.

**350 copies letterpress printed and sewn by hand into paper covers.
$20 (Plus $5 postage) Idaho orders please add 6% state sales tax.
Purchase this and other books at: www.limberlostpress.com**

FROM LIMBERLOST PRESS

Collect all six revival editions of *The Limberlost Review*

More than 2,000 pages of poetry, fiction, essays, memoirs, re-readings, interviews and artwork by highly-regarded writers and artists from the Mountain West

Order your copies of *The Limberlost Review* at:
www.limberlostpress.com

CALL FOR SUBMISSIONS 2025

The Limberlost Review
A Literary Journal of the Mountain West

DEADLINE FOR NEXT EDITION (2026)
OCTOBER 1, 2025

As a literary annual, **The Limberlost Review** is an anthology of work to read and re-read throughout the year. We recommend that new contributors read a previous edition or two to get a sense of what we like and have featured.

We have a special interest in personal essays, stories of memorable moments, experiences, people, mentor writers, and writer/artist friends.

We have a very special interest in **"Re-readings"** of books that have had a personal impact and why certain writers are worth rediscovery, worthy of wider readership.

What's in store for the 2026 Edition so far . . .
Jeff Fox on Wendell Berry's *The Memory of Old Jack*
Ted Dyer on literary critic Irving Howe
Donald W. Watts on poet Richard Brautigan
Vince Hannity on poet Seamus Heaney

Queries Welcome.

Word documents as attachments accepted:
editors@limberlostpress.com

LIMBERLOST LETTERPRESS

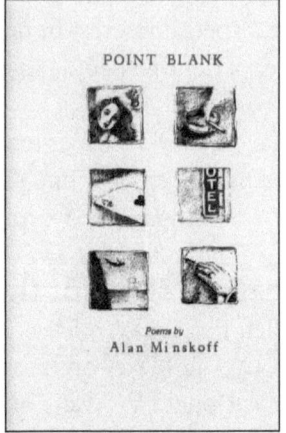

www.limberlostpress.com

COLPOHON

The Limberlost Review body copy is ITC BERKELEY OLD STYLE, based on Frederic W. Goudy's 1938 typeface. It was originally titled "University of California Old Style," which Goudy designed for exclusive use at the University of California Press at Berkeley. After Goudy's death in 1958, the typeface was re-released by Monotype as "Californian." In 1983, ITC redesigned it as "ITC Berkeley Old Style."

The Limberlost Review header font is TRAJAN PRO, designed for Adobe by Carol Twombly in 1989. The design is based on inscribed Roman capital letters such as those on the Trajan Column. Because the Romans didn't use lower-case letters, Twombly designed this as an all-caps typeface.

The Limberlost Review is designed and typeset by Meggan Laxalt Mackey of Studio M Publications & Design in Boise, Idaho, in collaboration with Rick and Rosemary Ardinger of Limberlost Press.

Since its inception, *The Limberlost Review* has celebrated the spirit of excellence in writing, artwork, book design, and typography.

LIMBERLOST PRESS

www.ingramcontent.com/pod-product-compliance
Lightning Source LLC
LaVergne TN
LVHW042045070526
838201LV00077B/809